MY NEIGHBOR'S SECRET

USA Today and International Bestselling Author

Lauren Rowe

Copyright © 2024 by Lauren Rowe

All rights reserved.

No part of this book may be reproduced in any form or by any electronic or mechanical means, including information storage and retrieval systems, without written permission from the author, except for the use of brief quotations in a book review.

Published by SoCoRo Publishing

Illustrated Couple by - Staci Hart

Cover design Shannon Passmore of **Shanoff Designs**

BOOKS BY LAUREN ROWE

Meet Me At Captain's Series of Standalone Romantic comedies

Who's Your Daddy

Textual Relations

My Neighbor's Secret

The Secret Note: A Spicy Standalone Novella with HEA

The Morgan Brothers (a series of related standalones):

Hero

Captain

Ball Peen Hammer

Mister Bodyguard

ROCKSTAR

Dive into Lauren's universe of interconnected trilogies and duets, all books available individually and as a bundle, in any order.

A full suggested reading order can be found here!

The Club Trilogy (to be read in order)

The Club: Obsession

The Club: Reclamation

The Club: Redemption

The Club: Culmination (A Full-Length Epilogue Book)

The Josh and Kat Trilogy (to be read in order)

Infatuation

Revelation

Consummation

The Reed Rivers Trilogy (to be read in order)

Bad Liar

Beautiful Liar

Beloved Liar

The Hate Love Duet

Falling Out Of Hate With You

Falling Into Love With You

Interconnected Standalones within the same universe:

Hacker in Love

Smitten

Swoon

Misadventures Standalones (unrelated standalones not within the above universe):

Misadventures on the Night Shift

Misadventures of a College Girl

Misadventures on the Rebound

Standalone Psychological Thriller/Dark Comedy

Countdown to Killing Kurtis

1

CHARLOTTE

did it.

I've finally arrived in my new, temporary hometown of Seattle after three long days of driving by myself. As soon as I can get myself a new job that returns me to my old life, and also figure out a way to unload the pricey condo I never should have bought, I'll be out of here. But for now, I'm thrilled to get to live in the same city as my lifelong bestie again, if only for a few months.

Buzzing with excitement, I burst through the front door of Captain's, Tessa's downtown bar, and immediately scan the place looking for her. Captain's is a popular hot spot, so it'll surely be packed later; but at this time in the afternoon, it's easy to spot Tessa Morgan—Tessa Rodriguez, when growing up with me—standing near the bar. She's chatting with one of her employees and looking equal parts Argentinian assassin, badass businesswoman, and pregnant supermodel.

I take two bounding steps into the trendy space before planting my feet like a gymnast sticking a landing and shriek, "Let's get this party started, Crazy Girl!"

Tessa's dark eyes abruptly shift to me, and the moment

she beholds my beaming, ecstatic face, she whoops, throws her arms up, and bounds gleefully toward me, her adorable baby bump leading the way.

As Tessa makes her way toward me, I launch enthusiastically into the silly dance moves we choreographed together as tweens at a birthday sleepover. Later that year, we performed the routine at our sixth-grade talent show, much to the mortification of both sets of our older brothers, and we've been performing the dance, ever since.

Despite being in her place of business, Tessa stops short before reaching me and enthusiastically mirrors my gyrating, flailing movements without missing a beat. Although Tessa, unlike me, is making our ridiculous choreography look graceful and sexy, while I look like a clown on cocaine who's been shot out of a cannon. But that's per usual. Tessa's always been the effortlessly elegant, mysterious brunette of our duo, while I've always been the comedic relief—a high-energy redhead who telegraphs every emotion on her expressive face and who'll do basically anything for a laugh.

Midway through our routine, we both dissolve into laughter, meet in the middle, and fall into a warm embrace. "Welcome to Seattle, Nut Job," Tessa whispers into my hair.

"I'm so excited to be here with you, Crazy Girl. I've missed you." Even though I won't be here long, I know whatever time spent here will be exactly what my bedraggled, paranoid, sleep-deprived soul needs. God, I've missed this woman. When I got laid off from my job as a flight attendant last month and lost the perk of free flights, I could no longer hop a free flight to visit Tessa and her family on a whim. Such a bummer. Due to that specific loss of benefits, and the loss of my job and income in general, and also combined with the heightened anxiety I've caused myself by doing that idiotic, stupid thing the day before my layoff, and this has been the most stressful, isolating, and nerve-wracking period of my entire life.

"Are you feeling any better?" I ask, touching Tessa's blooming belly. She's been feeling acute morning sickness with this, her third pregnancy.

Tessa nods. "Now that I'm in my second trimester, I'm sure I'll feel much better soon. That's how it went with Zach and Claire, so I'm hoping this one follows suit. How are *you* feeling?"

She's referring to my lay off and the lack of progress I've been making with my job search. Tessa doesn't know about the *other* major stress I've been under—the one I caused myself by making that colossally stupid mistake, and I'm hoping to keep it that way. If I tell Tessa about the mess I've made, she'll try to fix it for me. Because that's what she does. And there's no way I'm going to drag anyone I love into this particular mess of mine, especially not someone I love as much as Tessa.

"I'm feeling a lot better," I lie. "Now that I'm finally here with you."

"How long do you think you'll stay?"

"However long it takes to get a new job and/or fix up the condo enough to sell it for a profit or rent it out at a rate that makes sense with my mortgage payment. I'm guessing no longer than a couple months."

Tessa pouts. She's tried to get me to move from our hometown of LA to her new city many times over the past six years. But like I keep telling her, the rainy, gloomy weather in Seattle isn't my jam. Not to live in, anyway. I love pulling out a fashionable raincoat when visiting Paris or London. Bad weather is glamorous when traveling. But in my real life, give me all the Southern California sunshine, please.

"Have you gotten any interviews yet?" Tessa asks. She knows I've been submitting applications right and left.

"Nope. Nothing yet."

"Hang in there. I'm sure your dream job is right around the corner."

God, I hope she's right. As excited as I am to spend some quality time with Tessa and her family, I can't wait to get back to my old life and put this entire chapter of my life behind me.

"Have you eaten yet?" Tessa asks. "If not, let's have lunch."

"Awesome. I woke up crazy-early to drive the last leg and didn't stop to eat. I didn't even stop to pee, so I'd better get to a bathroom or we're going to need a mop."

Tessa chuckles. "I'll grab us a table."

I gallop toward the restrooms, while Tessa heads in the other direction toward the table area. When I emerge a few minutes later, Tessa's sitting at a table in the back. As I walk toward her, I look around nervously for a certain someone I'd rather not run into today. To be clear, I don't want to run into Brody the Bouncer ever again, but if I *must*, I don't want it to be when I'm sleep-deprived, makeup-less, and dressed in sweats. If ever I see that ghosting motherfucker again, I want to be looking fine-as-fuck and fuck-you-fierce.

Why, oh, why did I drunkenly send Brody that stupid text a few weeks ago telling him I'd been laid off and was coming to live in Seattle for a few months? By then, he'd already ghosted me, quite effectively, so why'd I think he'd care about me coming to his city? I swear, if that moron thinks I bought my condo to temporarily live near *him*, rather than my lifelong best friend, I'll die of humiliation.

"Crisis averted," I say, as I slide into a chair across from Tessa. "I made it to the toilet, like a big girl."

Tessa snickers. "There's no need to look around the place like a bank robber casing a joint, babe. Hans is working tonight. Not Brody."

"Thank God."

"No, thank *me*. I made the schedule, in anticipation of your arrival today."

I laugh. "Thank *you*."

"You're welcome."

Tessa knows all about my regrettable, short-lived fling with Brody, one of the bouncers at Captain's. I met Brody when I flew in for Tessa's thirty-third birthday bash several months ago, and then came back to see him three consecutive weekends thereafter. Why'd I do that? Because I was bored and Brody was available, and I'm a sucker for highly mediocre sex, I guess. Because that's all it ever was with Brody, unfortunately. Talk about a snoozefest.

When I got laid off and couldn't fly for free anymore, Brody immediately went dark on me, confirming he'd only ever been in it for the easy, mediocre sex, too.

Tessa holds up a laminated menu card. "Do you need to look at this or do you want your usual?"

"My usual would be great. Thank you." Tessa always generously supplies me with unlimited food and drinks for free when I come into her bar, and I'm always grateful for it. Especially now, though, when I'm unemployed, dead-ass broke, and questioning all my life choices.

As Tessa flags down a server, I let my gaze drift around the bar until it lands on a pair of stunning blue eyes trained directly on me. The owner of the blue eyeballs is a handsome, fit dude sitting at the bar. Light brown hair. Athletic frame. When our gazes meet, he maintains eye contact, so I do the same. Mostly, because I'm fascinated by the intensity of his stare. It's like the man is memorizing my face for a portrait he's planning to paint later on. His intensity would be kind of creepy, actually, if only he didn't look so damned harmless and wholesome. The man looks like a former Disney channel star. A model in a toothpaste commercial. *Or, no, a former boy bander*. The one who went solo after the boy band took off.

How long ago was he in this boy band? Frankly, it could be anywhere from five to fifteen years. He could be anywhere from twenty to thirty with a face that boyishly handsome. Which means he's the antithesis of my type. Yes, he's fit and handsome and cute. Also, his eyes are objectively gorgeous. But I like my men to be more rugged than that. Preferably, much uglier, too.

Aw, fuck.

I've maintained eye contact for a beat too long. I know this because Mr. Blue Eyes Boy Bander is now flashing me a wide, brilliant smile that, not surprisingly, reveals white, straight teeth.

I look away from his dazzling smile and return to Tessa, but she's busy chatting with a server.

When our server walks away, Tessa smiles at me and says, "So, when can you get into the condo?"

"Tomorrow. I can pick up the keys any time after two."

She squeals. "Can I come with you? I'm dying to see it."

"Absolutely. I'd love your expert opinion on what needs to be done to flip it as quickly and cheaply as possible." Tessa and her husband, Ryan, have been investing in real estate for a few years now, including fixing up rental properties, so she's the perfect person to tag along. I don't know why I didn't invite her to come with me in the first place. Chalk it up to my frazzled state as of late. I'm truly not myself right now.

"So, tell me the latest about your job search," Tessa says. "Maybe I can help."

Tessa has already offered me a serving job at Captain's, but I told her I'm taking a much-needed break from serving drinks to the general public for a while. And that's partly true. But even more than that, I think I should lay low and work from home while fixing up the condo. Better safe than sorry.

We chat and catch up, and soon, our food arrives, courtesy of a server who sticks around to ask her boss a question about the schedule. While Tessa chats with her employee, my eyes drift to the guy at the bar again, out of sheer curiosity. Is he still staring at me?

Nope.

Since I locked eyes with him earlier, Mr. Blue Eyes has been joined at the bar by a well-dressed older man—a stylish man with well-groomed silver hair and a perfectly tailored suit. Is that handsome silver fox the boy bander's boss? Friend? Father? I snicker to myself. His *daddy*? Ha. If those two swing that way, they'd make an insanely hot couple, honestly.

Fuck.

While I'm still contemplating the dynamics possibly at play over there, the boy bander abruptly shifts his gaze from his silver-haired companion to *me*. And thanks to those mesmerizing blue eyes of his, I can't immediately look away.

Like before, he's encouraged by our eye contact. His face breaks into a flirtatious, beaming smile—one that's even more enthusiastic than the last one. This smile is so unrestrained, in fact, I feel the need to shake my head, subtly, to let him know he's misread me. I love looking into the dazzling blue eyes of Tessa's beloved husky, Rudy, as well, but that doesn't mean I want to *fuck* my bestie's dog, now does it?

The guy at the bar stops smiling and matches my scowl. Actually, no, he ups the ante: right before looking away, he shoots me a glare that quite effectively says, "I get it. You're not interested. No need to be fucking *rude* about it."

I chuckle to myself as he looks away. That non-verbal "fuck you" he flashed me was unexpected, given his generally wholesome vibe. Color me impressed. If I hadn't sworn-off men for my short stay in Seattle, that little kiss-off *might* have inspired me to reel him back in, despite him not being my usual type. Why'd he get so bent out of shape, for fuck's sake? He's an extremely attractive dude. I'm sure he'll have zero problems landing the next woman he flirts with at a bar. You can't win 'em all, dude. Not even when you're as boy-band-handsome as you.

"Who are you looking at?" Tessa asks, causing me to jerk my attention back to her. She's smirking at me. Flashing me a knowing look.

"Nobody."

She doesn't buy it.

As I whisper-shout, "Don't look!" Tessa twists around, all the way, and looks toward the bar. As she does so, to my absolute mortification, my new enemy at the bar smirks wickedly at me. This time, his smile isn't flirtatious. Nope. His smug face this time says, "You told your friend about me, huh? That's a weird thing for you to do, if you're truly not interested, don't you think?"

I roll my eyes, feeling thoroughly annoyed with this arrogant man. Given his conventional handsomeness, I'm sure he's used to women falling at his feet. Hence, the reason I'm sworn off his type. Ten times out of ten, give me a guy who thinks I'm out of his league, a guy who thinks he's *lucky* to get with me, over a guy like him who surely thinks he's got his pick in every room he enters.

Tessa returns to me, leans forward, and whispers, "Which one are you flirting with—the older one in the fancy suit or the hottie with the pretty blue eyes?"

"Neither. The younger dude has been flirting with *me*, so I flashed him a bitchy look that said, *"Not a chance, boy bander."* And now, he's moved swiftly along to phase two of our brief courtship: despising me for being the first woman in this history of his gilded life to reject him."

Tessa chuckles. "Boy bander?"

"Doesn't he look like he's five years out from being the lead singer in an off-brand boy band?"

Laughing, Tessa peeks again. "Ten years, at the very least."

She returns to me, snickering. "But he'd definitely be 'The Hot One' in the band."

"He definitely went solo after their second album."

She laughs. "Oh, one hundred percent. And the rest of the guys *hated* him for it."

"They've been trying to get him to do a reunion tour, but he won't do it."

"Selfish bastard."

We both laugh.

"Why is it a bad thing he looks like a former boy bander, when your teenage walls were covered in *NSYNC posters?"

I snort. "If you think, at *thirty-two*, my type is the same as when I was twelve, you're sorely mistaken, my friend."

"Well, all grown up, obviously."

I roll my eyes. "Either way, it's a moot point because the guy at the bar is now my mortal enemy."

"Based on what?"

"The glaring and scowling we've been doing since I had the audacity not to smile back at him."

Tessa giggles. "Hey, don't knock hate-sex till you've tried it, babe."

Oh, Tessa. My bestie loves to think of herself as an expert in the sport of hate-fucking, but the reality is she's only engaged in it with one person, ever: her now-husband, Mr. Tattooed Hottie himself, Ryan Morgan. Also, Ryan didn't even hate Tessa at the time of their hate-fuckery, unbeknownst to Tessa. That man always knew she was The One. But whatever. I'd never deprive my bestie of her sexy fantasies, especially her all-time favorite one, where she spent a week in paradise indulging her wildest, hate-sex fantasies with the man she wound up marrying.

"You keep saying you're not interested in dating anyone seriously while you're here," Tessa says, her dark eyebrow raised. "So why not have some fun with a gorgeous former boy bander you'd never date. That's one way to chase your blues away, if only fleetingly. Live a little."

Tessa's so freaking cute, I want to pinch her chiseled cheeks. Growing up, I was the one urging *Tessa* to have some fun. To live a little. Oh, how the tables have turned. "I'm gonna be way too busy with the condo and my job search—and, hopefully, a side gig, too, to bother with a fuck buddy." It's all true. The other true thing I'm not saying out loud, however, is that, if I were going to waste time with a fuck buddy, I wouldn't pick one as classically handsome as the boy bander at the bar.

I've never told Tessa or anyone else this secret, but I've discovered, after years of trying, I can't have an orgasm with a guy who's too conventionally hot. It's weird, I know, but I'm now convinced it's not a fluke.

When I sleep with a guy who's objectively more attractive than me, like Mr. Blue Eyes over there, I can't relax enough to fully let go and get there. I'm too self-conscious about my body—worried I'm not measuring up to all the conventionally hot women he's banged before me. I've got high self-esteem in most areas, even with my clothes off; but put me naked in a bed with a man who's too hot, and my self-esteem flies right out the window.

On the other hand, however, when I'm banging what I'd call an "ugly-hot man," I feel like a naked goddess. When I see myself through the eyes of a guy like that, I feel *glorious*. And the result is sex that's *fire*. Well, usually. Not always. Brody wasn't much to look at and I couldn't get there with him, even once. But Brody excluded, ugly-hot guys *normally* work extra hard to please, I've found, and the end result is that I come easily and intensely. As a matter of fact, with the right kind of ugly-hot guy, I almost always turn into a box of firecrackers that's been left near a burning fireplace: *pop, pop, poppity, pop!*

"Welcome to Seattle, Nut Job!" A booming male voice say,

yanking me from my thoughts. It's Ryan "Captain" Morgan, Tessa's gorgeous, tattooed husband, descending upon our table with a huge, toothy grin on his chiseled face. After hugging me and kissing his beloved wife, Ryan pulls up a chair. "I can't stay long, ladies. I have to go to the airport. I just wanted to welcome Char to Seattle and find out if the condo is worse or better than hoped."

"I don't know yet. I'm picking up the keys tomorrow."

"And I'm going with her," Tessa says proudly.

"Send pics," Ryan says. "It feels like that game show with the mystery doors. Did you pick the door with a pile of money . . . or a pile of dogshit?"

Tessa swats her husband's broad shoulder. "Don't stress her out. She's nervous enough."

"Bah. Char knows I'm just teasing her. No matter what shape it's in, she'll be fine. The place is right near campus. You can't lose in a location like that."

Yes, you can, when part of your down payment wasn't yours to spend, and now you need to pay it back more quickly than the place could possibly appreciate.

Ryan continues, "That is, unless you open the door tomorrow and find the former owner dead and fused to his couch. The value might take a hit, in that instance."

"Ryan Morgan, *stop*," Tessa says. This time, she bats her husband's muscled arm. "Char's been losing sleep. Don't torture her."

"It's okay," I say. "One of the few things I know about the place is that the former owner—one Lloyd Graham—didn't die on the premises." I also know the man died without an heir, according to the auction write-up—hence, the online auction. After a frenzied bidding war, I "won" the place, sight unseen and in "as is" condition. I did get to see a floorplan diagram in the description. Also, some photos of a similar unit on the fourth floor in the same building. I've also been assured there's no major structural damage, so at least I know what-ever fixes or renovations are needed won't be too complicated or time-consuming. Cosmetic, mostly. But beyond all that, I know nothing else.

The truth is I bought the place on a wing and a prayer, while panicking about the stupid, colossal mistake I'd made. I thought buying the place would help my situation; unfortu-nately, though, I found out shortly after my purchase I'd only made things worse. And now, here I am, coming off a month of sleepless nights and looking over my shoulder, bound and determined to set things right in time. "Why are you headed to the airport?" I ask Ryan, trying to change the subject. "A work trip or something fun?"

"Well, work *is* fun to me," he says. "But it's both. I'm going to LA to check out a possible new location for Captain's, and while I'm there, I'm having dinner with the LA Branch of the family." Ryan and Tessa have been expanding their successful bar in various locations along the West Coast for several years now, and they've been killing it.

"Has Maddy had her baby yet?" I ask. It's hard for me to keep track of all four of Ryan's siblings and their partners and kids, but I'm pretty sure the woman married to Ryan's actor-brother, Keane, is at the bitter end of her pregnancy. Tessa threw her sister-in-law a fabulous baby shower several months ago, and since I've hung out with Ryan's various family members at multiple parties thrown at Ryan and Tessa's house, the mommy-to-be kindly included me on the guest list.

"Maddy's due to pop in a week or so," Tessa says. "The whole Seattle Branch is going to fly down there once the baby comes. That reminds me. Would you be willing to house- and dog-sit for us when we go? I'm sorry to ask, but everyone who normally watches Rudy for us will be going to LA, too."

"Of course. I'd love to stay with Rudy the Cutie Patootie. By then, I'm sure I'll relish the chance to stay in a clean and orderly home, after all the work I'll be doing on the condo."

"It might be a full week."

"Call me and I'll come running for however long you need. I'm unemployed, remember? I've got nowhere else I need to be."

Tessa touches Ryan's forearm. "Char hasn't had any luck in her job search yet, babe. While she's looking for a flight attendant gig, she's hoping to find something part-time she can do from home to make ends meet. Got any ideas?"

Ryan twists his perfect lips, considering the question. "Not off the top, but I'll make some calls on my drive to the airport."

Tessa and I both thank him, and Ryan says he's happy to help.

"I'd better go, ladies," he says, looking at his watch. He kisses his wife goodbye and pats me on the head—something he's been doing to me since meeting me—his way of emphasizing my shortness; and then, the handsome man strides across the large space like he owns the place—which he does, of course, along with his wife and some exceedingly wealthy business partners.

Just when I'm about to look away from Ryan's retreating frame, the front door of the bar opens, and none other than Brody the Bouncer walks into the bar. *Fuck my life.*

I can't let that ghost see me sitting here looking like a haggard hot mess! Even worse, I can't let him think, even for a second, that I chose Seattle as my temporary new city because I'm hoping to rekindle things with *him*. Ha! Whatever it takes, I'm going to make it clear I've already moved on from our meaningless fling and mediocre sex. In fact, I'm going to make sure Brody thinks I haven't given him another thought since sending him that regrettable, stupid text.

2

AUGGIE

"Thanks," I mumble to the bartender, when he slides a second draft beer in front of me. I shouldn't have ordered it; I've got to study for an upcoming exam when I get back home. But Dad is ridiculously late for the mysterious "drinks" he wanted to have with me, in the middle of a workday, and I'm feeling anxious. Dad couldn't have asked me here simply to spend quality time with his second son. That's not a thing for Alexander Vaughn. Even during my childhood, when my parents were still married and supposedly happy, Mom was essentially a single parent to my brother and me, thanks to all the travel Dad "had" to do to build his budding empire.

Sure, Dad swooped in to watch Max's water polo matches and my swim meets. And he always looked the part in family portraits and Christmas cards. But I can't remember a single time my father ever wanted to simply talk to me in order to get to know me as a person. That was especially true during the time I had to go to speech therapy as a kid to overcome a stutter. I think, in his mind, that old stammer somehow made me defective. An embarrassment. It certainly doesn't help that, nowadays, my stutter comes back, now and again, if only subtly, when I'm nervous or stressed.

My phone buzzes with a text from Dad:

On my way. Work meeting went long.

God, I hope I'm only being paranoid and Dad didn't ask me here to give me some bad news in person. But what else could it be? Dad would never schedule an in-person conversation when a text or phone call would do. Especially with me. I'm far from his favorite person, so sitting down and having a beer with me isn't how he'd ever choose to spend his valuable time, if something wasn't up. Frankly, considering the man pays my tuition, I'd have thought he'd want me to get every bang for his buck by attending every possible class, rather than ditching an important one to come here to have drinks with him for no apparent reason.

If I had to guess I think Dad's going to tell me he's cutting my brother and me out of his will. I bet when he asked his lawyer to change his will to exclude his now-ex-wife, Ashley, he got the bright idea to exclude Max and me, too. Max doesn't speak to him at all anymore, and my communications with him mostly revolve around his tuition payments. I've tried to talk to him about more than that, of course, but he doesn't seem interested. Without Max or Grandpa around to serve as a translator for the two of us—a bridge, if you will— it's become harder and harder for us to find common ground.

Movement at the front door of the bar interrupts my wandering thoughts. But it's not Dad bursting into the bar; it's a curvy sprite of a redhead who looks like she's come to Captain's to claim winnings on a Powerball lottery ticket. As she bounds into the bar, I can't help chuckling at her enthusiasm. She's adorable. Exuberant. Effervescent, I'd even say. The kind of person who lights up every room she graces with her presence, including this one.

She reminds me of my first love, Kelly Gessler, actually—the vivacious, freckled redhead who stole my heart at age fourteen at summer camp in June, and then did me the honor of touching my hard dick for the first time as a parting gift in August. Both in terms of her physical looks and general vibe, that redhead is a dead ringer for Kelly.

Hold up. Does this adorable redhead *remind* me of Kelly Gessler . . . or is she *actually* Kelly, all grown up? She looks to be around my age, so she could be the genuine article. Granted, Kelly's family moved to Massachusetts after our magical summer together, and I never saw or heard from her after that, much to my teenage heartache. But it's not far-fetched to think Kelly might have moved back to Seattle as an adult, the same way I did to attend vet school.

With a whoop, the exuberant redhead plants both feet at once, like she's leaping to safety in a game of "The Floor is Lava." After sticking her landing, she throws up her arms, wiggles her hips, and shouts, "Let's get this party started, Crazy Girl!" *And that's it.* I'm now convinced she's Kelly Gessler because that's exactly the sort of funny, exuberant thing Kelly would have said back in the day. Either way, though, even if this firecracker isn't Kelly, she's definitely got my undivided attention.

A female whoop erupts to my left, and the next thing I know, a pregnant brunette has joined the redhead in some bizarre choreography that makes the entire bar, not only me, laugh and applaud. The show doesn't last nearly long enough, if you ask me. In short order, the two women are hugging and chatting.

I sip my beer and look at the front door, hoping Dad will

appear. When he doesn't, I return my attention to the two women. They've left their prior spot now. The redhead is heading one way, perhaps toward the bathrooms, while the brunette grabs a table.

I scroll on my phone for a bit. Sip my beer. Try to stuff down the anxiety I'm feeling about this mysterious meeting. When I finally look up, the redhead is now sitting across from the brunette in the corner—and lucky me, she's chosen the chair facing me.

Man, she's pretty. Charismatic, too. She seems to be an animated conversationalist. Oh, man, when she belly laughs with her friend, she's drop-dead gorgeous.

Shit. She's caught me staring at her. Normally, I'd look away so I don't come off like a creep. But she's not looking away, so I don't either. *Holy fuck. Is she maintaining eye contact with me because she recognizes me from our summer together fifteen years ago?*

I'm much taller now, and I've got some facial hair. Also, I've filled out quite a bit since age fourteen, thankfully. But in terms of my facial structure, I look basically the same as I did back then. As a matter of fact, I had a girlfriend a few years ago who easily picked me out of my *kindergarten* class photo, so I think it's reasonable to think a person who's good with faces would be able to draw a straight line from the teenage version of me to the thirty-year-old version sitting here now.

Figuring there's no time like the present to figure out if this woman recognizes me or not, I muster the courage to smile broadly at her. And, unfortunately, she quickly looks away.

"Hello, Augustus," my father says. He pats my back awkwardly, settles onto the stool next to me, and orders his usual expensive Scotch, as well as another beer for me, even though mine is half-full and I've just said no thank you to his offer.

"So, what's up?" I ask. I figure we might as well get straight to whatever shitty thing he came to say so I can get back home and study.

Dad doesn't take the bait. Rather than cutting to the chase, he tells me about some big deal he's been working on—the thing that delayed him. And since I don't give a shit about that, as Dad talks, I let my gaze drift to the redhead again. When my eyes find her, she's deep in conversation with her friend, which makes it easy for me to study her pretty features again, undetected.

"Here you go," the bartender says, sliding our drinks in front of us. He's interrupted Dad's monologue about work, so I use the break as an opening to nudge our conversation along.

"That all sounds great, Dad. What else is new?"

"Well, I've got a new girlfriend," Dad says brightly. "Cara. She's in PR." And off he goes, telling me about yet another thing I don't care about. The ink is barely dry on his recent divorce from Ashley, but he's not a man who likes being alone. Even when he's got a wife, he's usually got at least one secret girlfriend in the wings, too. He's always denied that's how he rolls. When he's married, he pretends to be the perfect husband until he's found out. But I've seen how the sausage is made, unfortunately, thanks to my big brother. I was thirteen when Max discovered indisputable evidence of our father cheating on our mother, and it's my firm belief a cheating leopard never changes his spots.

I absent-mindedly draw a little sad-face in the condensation on my new beer glass and ask, "Is your girlfriend older or younger than me?" As of yet, Alexander Vaughn has drawn a line at thirty and never dipped below it, in terms of the women he dates. But I've always felt like it's only a matter of time before he winds up dating or even marrying a twenty-something.

"She's exactly your age, actually," Dad says. "Twenty-nine."

I roll my eyes. "I'm thirty. I had a birthday last month."

"Oh, yeah. I meant, give or take."

I sip my new beer, since it's colder than my other one, and wait for Dad to tell me what the fuck I'm doing here. But he doesn't. He's now telling me the rather boring story of how he met his latest girlfriend.

As Dad talks, I glance at the redhead. And this time, to my thrill, she's already looking straight at me. Okay, whether she's Kelly or not, I'm feeling a full-bodied attraction to this woman. Reflexively, I smile again, this time even bigger and wider than the last time, but she not only doesn't return my smile, she shakes head and *scowls* at me. Apparently, she wants to make it clear she's not into me, even though she was the one looking at me first this time.

I match her scowl to let her know I've received her rejection, loud and clear, and quickly look away like I couldn't care less. But it's not true, because now I'm wondering, *Well, shit. What if she's Kelly Gessler and finding out I'm Auggie Vaughn would turn that scowl into a smile?* I totally get her not being interested in some random creep in a bar—fair enough. Men can be total trash. Just look at the man to my left. But if she's Kelly, maybe she'd have a different reaction to me, if she knew my identity. Maybe, if she's Kelly, she'd like catching up with a blast from her past.

"And what's new with you, Augustus?" Dad asks, jerking my attention back to him. *Well, that's weird.* Normally, my father doesn't ask that question. Once it became clear I plan to help abandoned and abused animals at shelters and rescues after graduation, rather than joining a practice that caters to rich suburbanites and their designer dogs—which therefore means I'll probably never make the kind of money my father equates with human value—Dad lost all interest in my schooling.

"Nothing much," I say. "I've been going to school. Studying. Oh, I moved into Grandma's condo six weeks ago. Did you hear about that?"

"Sorry to hear she passed. She was a good woman."

My grandmother, my mom's mom, fucking *hated* my father. But I manage to say, "She was the best," before taking another sip of my beer. "Oh, I do have some exciting school-related news. I've got a second interview for a really coveted summer internship tomorrow morning. It's at this renowned animal hospital where—"

"Is it a paid internship?"

I shift on my stool. "No, but if I get it, knock on wood, all hours worked this summer will count toward class credits in the fall, which ultimately will save you money, because tuition is based on the amount of units—"

"That's actually a perfect segue," Dad says. "I've got some news I wanted to deliver to you in person, son. About your tuition."

Fucking hell. I knew Dad asked me here to deliver some bad news. But I never in a million years thought it'd have something to do with my tuition. At Grandpa's final birthday party last year, Dad repeated his prior promise to pay all four years of tuition, as long as I continued covering my living expenses, which I've done. The veterinary program is four years, and I'm only just now about to finish up my second year. So, what could he possibly have to say about my tuition *now*?

Dad calmly sets down his Scotch. "You're on your own, kid."

I wait for him to explain further. When he doesn't, I ask, "What does that mean? What percentage of tuition will I need to cover myself and starting when?"

"All of it, starting now." He's dropped his bomb like he's

talking about the weather, rather than delivering a deathblow to me. With a shrug, he adds, "I've gotten you halfway there. Now, it's up to you to get yourself the rest of the way."

I can't believe my ears. If I'd known Dad was going to ditch his promise halfway through my schooling, I surely would have made some different choices. I might have worked construction this past summer to save money, the same way I did during my undergrad summers, rather than volunteering at that animal shelter for free. I might have applied for student loans, none of which are available to me now. Or perhaps I would have skipped vet school completely, opting instead to remain in my vet tech job. But what are my options now that I'm halfway through and stuck?

"Dad, please," I choke out. "The invoice for fall semester is due *tomorrow*, and it's too late for me to apply for financial aid. If I don't secure my spot, I'll get dropped from the program."

"Don't be dramatic. I'm sure there's a grace period."

I take a deep breath. "Yeah, it's two weeks. But I won't have the money in two weeks, any more than I've got it now. Dad, please, you promised in front of Grandpa you'd—"

"My priorities have changed. There are no guarantees in life, Augustus. Borrow the money from your mother or brother, if you must. Negotiate a payment plan with the school and then work double the hours at that data entry job of yours to make the payments. You've got other options here, so don't look at me like I've drowned your favorite puppy."

I stare at my beer, trying to corral my racing thoughts. There might be some validity to his suggestion about negotiating a payment plan. I make a panicked mental note to check that out. But nothing else he's suggested is even remotely possible. My mother and brother have already done enough for me. They're letting me live in Grandma's condo rent-free, since her place is only two blocks from campus.

And that data entry job Dad mentioned? It doesn't exist.

That's what I called the side hustle I've been doing to cover living expenses when Grandpa, Dad's father, asked me at his final birthday party how I've been paying my bills during school. And I haven't even been doing that side hustle lately! Not since moving into Grandma's place. And even if I were still doing it, it was never the kind of moneymaker for me that would offer any kind of a solution here. Not even close. I force myself to look Dad in the eyes. "What happened to make you go back on your promise?"

"It's more like *who* happened. *Cara.* She's got some big dreams and I've decided to make 'em come true for her." Dad shrugs. "It just so happens the money Cara needs is basically the same amount as your tuition."

"Figures," I mumble.

"I'm actually doing you a favor here, Augustus. This will force you to be self-sufficient, as every man should be."

I'm shaking as rage boils up inside me. Before taking the plunge and going to vet school, I was completely self-sufficient, motherfucker. I took a job as a vet tech after college graduation that paid all my bills, if only barely. When I got admitted to veterinary school, which isn't easy to do, by the way, it was a huge decision for me, whether to go or not. Should I take on student loans? If so, would I ever be able to pay them off, considering the kind of veterinary practice I dream of having?

Ultimately, it was the unexpected promise Dad made me, right in front of his fucking father, that made the decision for me. At the time, it felt like the answer to my prayers. Like Dad's Redemption Arc. Why the fuck didn't I listen to Max back then when he told me Dad couldn't be trusted, ever? *He warned me.* But I was so fucking excited to make my lifelong dreams come true, I convinced myself Dad had changed. "Look," I told Max, "I know Dad's a scumbag as a general matter; but I choose to believe redemption is possible for anyone. I believe in second chances." I was an idiot.

"Hey there!" a female voice whisper-shouts. *It's the redhead.* She's here . . . and, fuck my life, she's speaking to *Dad*. With a bat of her eyelashes, she says, "I'm wondering if you'd do me a *huge* favor. This guy I dated briefly, who then had the *audacity* to ghost me, just walked in and I'd love to have some smoking-hot man candy on my arm when he sees me."

Dad laughs. "As you should."

"What can I say, I'm a petty bitch. You're the hottest man in the bar, so I'm hoping you'll agree to play the part of my man candy?"

The hits just keep on coming. This pretty redhead who looks *my* age thinks my fifty-something-year-old *father* would make a hotter fake boyfriend than me?

"I'd be honored to help you," Dad says gallantly. "Come here, beautiful. Let's make this believable." He pulls her to him, and the next thing I know, they're whispering intimately, their faces mere inches apart, like they fucked each other's brains out right before coming to Captain's.

I look away from the spectacle in disgust with perfect timing to catch a burly, tattooed dude with a crooked nose walking by with that brunette from earlier. As he walks by, the dude's dark eyes are locked on Dad and the redhead.

"*Charlotte?*"

Welp, thank goodness for small mercies. At least, she's not Kelly Gessler.

The redhead—*Charlotte*—deigns to look from my father to the burly dude. "Oh, hey, Brody." She motions to Dad. "This is George, my fiancé. Georgie, this is Brody. He works here."

Dad smiles. "Nice to meet you, Brody."

The guy stalks away without replying and heads into a back office with the brunette. And that's it. Dad's performance is done.

"Where are you going?" Dad says, as the redhead pulls away. He pats the empty stool to his other side. "Let me buy you a drink. I'm Alexander, by the way. And this is my son—"

"Who's leaving." Not only is she *not* Kelly Gessler, she thinks my father is hotter than me? I can't get out of here fast enough. Without another word, I stride toward the front door like my hair's on fire. Fuck my father and his promises. Whatever it takes, I'm going to graduate in two years and make all my dreams come true. I don't know *how* I'm going to do that, in this moment, but I will. And anyone who doesn't believe that, anyone who doesn't believe in *me*—whether they're my asshole father or some random redhead in a bar who thinks my father is hotter than me—can get the fuck out of my way. *Or better yet, they can stay, kneel before me, and suck my big, fat cock.*

3

CHARLOTTE

"I'm gonna get you!"

I'm playing cars with my beloved godson, Zach, five years old, on his bedroom floor, while Tessa bathes Zach's little sister, Claire, down the hall. The family's husky, Rudy, is here, too. I think his tail is a gas pump in our game, but I'm not sure. It might give our little metal cars magical powers. The only thing I know for sure is that my red car is supposed to chase Zach's yellow one. *Over and over again.*

I'm spending the night at Tessa's gorgeous, sprawling house tonight and feeling the most relaxed I've been in weeks. Even though I love Ryan like a brother and thoroughly enjoy his company, it's been lovely to hang out with Tessa and the kids while he's away on business. In fact, tonight's been a perfect balm for my exhausted, paranoid soul.

"You'll never catch me!" Zachary shouts. He's trying to sound like a badass, I think, but there's nothing that adorable kid can do to his tiny, squeaky voice to make it sound anything but darling.

"Darn you!" I shout, after Zachary's eluded me, yet again.

"I play cars!" a high-pitched voice shouts. It's two-year-old Claire, careening into her big brother's bedroom in her jammies, as her mommy strides behind on a FaceTime call.

Claire plops herself into my lap, like it's the most natural thing in the world to do, and repeats her command. Only this time, she adds the words I live to hear: "I play cars, too, *Auntie Char Char!" Oh, my heart.*

"That's great news, babe," Tessa says on her call. She takes a seat on Zach's twin bed, as Ryan on their call says, "The space is a homerun." As he proceeds to elaborate, I lean down and smell Claire's towel-dried hair like a junkie getting a fix. I freaking *love* the smell of freshly shampooed toddler hair. It's crack to me.

I didn't always want kids. For a long time, I was pretty sure kids weren't in my future. But then Zach came along and made my heart ache and yearn in a whole new way. And if that wasn't enough to make my biological clock start ticking for good, Claire came along almost three years later to perform that service. For a while, I thought Carlo might be the father of my future babies. But man, when I found out what he truly does for a living, that plan was immediately scrapped, along with the relationship itself.

"You can hold a car while Auntie Char Char chases me," Zach says, his tone brimming with the authority of an older sibling. I should know: I've got two older brothers who always used to boss me around, just like that.

Not surprisingly , Claire protests, and I have to jump in and play referee, at which point, Zach begrudgingly hands his little sister the blue car she wants.

"Okay, keep me posted," Tessa says on her call with Ryan. "Are the kids still awake?"

"They're right here, playing cars with Auntie Charlotte and Rudy." Tessa holds up her phone to our happy group on the floor, and both kids call out their happy hellos to their doting daddy, while I shoot Ryan a wave and a smile.

As Ryan chats with his enthusiastic kiddos, Tessa gets up and hands me the phone to make it easier for everyone to converse—and, suddenly, I'm the meat in an adorable kid-sandwich, as the kids smash themselves against me to fit their faces onto the screen.

"All that sounds amazing, guys," Ryan says to his kids, after they've told him about their day. "Can I get a goodnight kiss? It's your bedtime, I think." When the kids lean into the camera, Ryan does the same on his end; and when all good-nights and I love you's have been administered, and Tessa has started herding her kiddos off to bed, Ryan says to me, "Hang on, Crazy Girl. I have some good news for you."

"I'm Nut Job. I'll go into the other room." The kids are talking so loudly with Tessa, I don't need to explain my change of venue. I bound into the living room with Rudy at my heels and plop onto the couch. "Much better. What's up?"

Ryan grins. "I made some calls on my way to the airport, and you've got a job interview tomorrow morning."

"Oh my gosh. Thank you!"

Ryan explains that his old boss at the brokerage firm where he used to work is looking for a part-time, remote personal assistant. He tells me the hourly wage, and I whoop with glee. "Fair warning, though," he says, "the reason he pays so well is he keeps churning through assistants. They keep quitting on him."

"Why?"

"He's super demanding and meticulous. He's not a creep at all, or I wouldn't set you up with him. But he's got some peculiar tendencies, for sure."

"That's fine with me, especially at that hourly rate. After serving drunk and nervous passengers for twelve years, I've seen it all. My skin is thicker than a rhino's at this point."

Ryan chuckles. "I figured you wouldn't mind working for a

weirdo for a few months. You only need the job while you're fixing up the condo, right?"

"Or I get a flight attendant job. But yeah, once I'm done with the condo, I'm definitely heading back to sunny LA."

"Okay, don't tell him that. Make him think you're imagining working for him for ten years."

"Got it."

"Nobody ever lasts long with him, so I don't feel bad about you leaving the job after a few months."

"If I get it."

"The odds are high. He's already got a bunch of interviews lined up tomorrow, but I talked him into squeezing you in, first thing at eight o'clock—a full hour before his first scheduled interview. He hates wasting time, so if you impress him, I'm positive he'll offer you the job on the spot and cancel everyone else."

"Holy crap, Ryan. Seriously? This is amazing. Do you have any tips for how I might knock his socks off tomorrow?"

As I'm asking the question, Tessa sits down next to me on the couch, so Ryan and I quickly get her up to speed. Tessa questions me working for a demanding prick, even part-time and temporarily, but I quickly convince her I'll be fine.

"Okay, I've got some important tips for you, Char," Ryan says. "Wear all white to the interview tomorrow and make sure whatever you're wearing is meticulously ironed. If you're dressed in crisp, spotless white, Jerry will think you're detail-oriented and meticulous across the board. He'll eat that shit up."

I frown. "Most of my clothes are in storage in LA, along with my furniture. I only brought one small suitcase of clothes with me to Seattle, and I didn't pack anything white."

Tessa waves at the air. "No worries, babe. I've got the perfect thing for you—a sleek, white jumpsuit romper thing that's super flattering. I'll hem the bottoms for you tonight, and you'll look like a million bucks tomorrow."

I snort. "You'd better take in the chest area, too, or else I'm going to need to stuff my bra." Besides being quite a bit taller than me, Tessa's also got the world's most jaw-dropping hourglass figure, when she's not cooking a baby. Despite those differences in our body types, however, I think Tessa's outfit could easily be altered to fit me, well enough.

"Okay, hot tip number two," Ryan continues. "Bring Jerry his favorite specialty coffee tomorrow, and make sure it's still piping hot when you set it down in front of him—on a coaster, for fuck's sake. *On a coaster.*" He says he finagled Jerry's usual coffee order from a buddy's assistant at the brokerage firm, on the down low. Also, that there's a coffee place only a block away from Jerry's office, so I'll be able to park, get the coffee, and then walk to my appointment, coffee in hand.

"Will do," I say. "Anything else?"

"Hot tip number three," Ryan says. "Arrive at Jerry's door, with the piping hot coffee, exactly five minutes early for your interview. If you're on time with Jerry, then you're late."

"I'll be there at 7:50, to be safe."

"Nope. 7:55 on the nose, or else his coffee won't be piping hot when he calls you into his office at 7:56."

I chuckle. "I'll get to the coffee place a full half-hour early and sit around till it's the precise time to order and walk up the street."

"Now you're getting it. Perfect. Now, when you sit down for the interview . . ." Ryan details several more things he wants me to do. So, I pull out my phone and take meticulous notes. Finally, Ryan wraps up his tutorial with, "If you do everything I've told you, you'll walk away with a job tomorrow."

"Fingers crossed." I don't want to tell Ryan and Tessa this, but I'm down to my last hundred-fifty bucks in my bank account. I've still got some room on my credit cards, in case of a dire emergency, but I'm already in so much debt, I'd rather not take on more.

"Thank you so much, Ryan. I can't thank you enough."

"No thanks necessary," Ryan replies. "You're family, Charlotte."

A lump rises in my throat. On top of everything else, I've been missing my father terribly. It's been two years since he passed, but it never gets easier. Ryan and Tessa can't take Dad's place, of course. Nobody can. But Ryan's and Tessa's kindness makes me feel supported and loved in a way I really need right now.

"Thank you. That means a lot," I choke out.

Ryan's features soften. "You're not alone, okay? You're never alone."

Well, shit. I'm crying now. I've needed to feel exactly this kind of support lately, after the mess I've made of my life. I inhale deeply, trying to control my emotions, and feel a wave of genuine optimism rise up inside me. "Thank you so much. To both of you. Thanks to you, I can already tell, without a doubt, tomorrow is going to be my lucky day."

4
CHARLOTTE

I look at the clock on my car's dashboard and shudder.

Thanks to a massive accident on the freeway this morning, I'm now officially running late for my interview, even though I left Tessa's house ridiculously early this morning—early enough, I thought, to get to the coffee place and chill for at least a half-hour before grabbing the weirdo's coffee order with perfect timing to arrive at his office at precisely 7:55. But now, thanks to this traffic, I might not have time to grab the guy a coffee at all. I suppose it will depend on the parking situation when I get there.

Okay, I'm finally on surface streets now, and traffic isn't as bad over here. I glance at the clock on my dashboard again and groan. I'm cutting it close. Please, parking gods, be good to me when I get to my destination.

I see the guy's building! And there's the coffee place down the street, exactly like Ryan said. Now, where's that parking garage that should be right across the street?

No.

A sign at its entrance says it's completely full and only monthly parkers are allowed in with a pass. Fuck! Practically hyperventilating with stress, I drive past the structure and anxiously scour the packed curb, searching for an open spot. I pass an animal hospital, a bank, a nail salon, all the while getting farther and farther away from my destination.

It's okay, Charlotte. Calm down. You've still got a solid six minutes until all hope is lost of arriving at the interview with the guy's coffee order in hand. *You can do this.*

I drive slowly around the block, keeping an eagle eye out for street parking . . . and suddenly, I'm right back where I started and no closer to parking my car.

I check the clock. Say a prayer. And slow down to an even slower crawl. God help me, if someone pulls away from the curb right *behind* me, rather than in front of me, and someone else quickly grabs the newly vacated spot, I'll never forgive myself.

There's a line of cars in the near distance. They're stopped about fifty feet ahead of me at a red light. If a spot doesn't magically appear between here and the last car in that line, I'll get stuck at the back for who-knows-how-long until the light changes.

I slow down even more, hoping and praying for a miracle. And, suddenly, I get one. Am I a witch? *A magical unicorn?* At the very least, I'm The Parking God's favorite, because a black minivan parked only about twenty feet ahead of me has suddenly pulled away from the curb, leaving a perfect stretch of curb vacant for *me*. It's a Christmas miracle in April!

Like a woman possessed, I gun my little car and whip my front bumper into the spot to claim it as mine. When that light up ahead turns green and that line of cars moves through it, I'll have room to maneuver and parallel-park into the spot. I'm horrible at doing that, so I'll need a wide berth to make it happen. But for now, I'm relieved to have marked this strip of curb as *mine*.

A car horn blares loudly, making me jolt, and a quick scan

of my surroundings reveals the angry sound came from the SUV immediately ahead of me—the last car waiting in that long line for the red light to turn green.

"What the heck?" I murmur, raising my hand to the honking car.

The driver raises *both* hands at me, so I shoot the gesture back at him. I don't know what he's all riled up about. I'm obviously planning to straighten out my car after he moves through the light. Only a maniac would leave their car's ass hanging out and blocking traffic. Give me some credit, dude. But even if I were planning to leave my car askew like this, it's none of his concern.

The guy honks again, but thankfully, it's just as the distant light is turning green, which means he'll be gone and out of my hair, soon enough.

Oh no.

The asshole in the SUV isn't driving away, even though the line of cars is moving along now. No, he's bursting out of his car and marching toward me with palpable fury. Oh, no. *He's the boy bander from Captain's!* Well, shit. I guess I'm not The Parking God's favorite, after all.

When the guy reaches my car window, he bends down to make eye contact. My window is closed, but I can clearly make out the words "What the fuck?" hurtling from his mouth. With an angry scowl, he raps his knuckles on my car window and motions for me to roll it down. But I'm never one to willingly subject myself to an angry man, if I can help it. And that's especially true now, when I'm in the biggest hurry of my life. Also, when the angry man in question already hates me, thanks to our run-in at the bar yesterday. Although . . . I've turned many an irate passenger into a purring kitten, so maybe it's worth a try to see if I can calm him down and make him quickly go away and let me park my freaking car.

I plaster my best flight-attendant smile onto my face and

crack my window an inch. "What a small world!" I say brightly through the small gap. "We met at Captain's yesterday, remember?"

"Yeah, you're the one who practically made out with my 'smoking-hot' asshole of a father."

Crap. "You're actually way hotter than him. The only reason I asked your father to help me, instead of you, is—"

"I don't give a shit, Charlotte. All I care about is you moving your car, so I can make it on time to an important interview. If you wouldn't mind . . ." He gestures for me to skedaddle.

I'm surprised he remembered my name from yesterday. Honestly, I don't remember his, if I heard it at all. "I've actually got an important interview, too. And I grabbed this spot, fair and square, so . . ." I shoot his "skedaddle" gesture right back at him.

The boy bander looks incredulous. "Didn't you see me waiting on the minivan to pull away? I was sitting right there."

"I saw you waiting in a line of cars for the light up ahead to change."

"I was waiting for this spot! For five full minutes, I watched the driver get into her minivan, and check her phone, and put on some lipstick, before *finally* pulling away."

"You were in *front* of the minivan, at the back of the line of cars."

"So I could parallel park after she pulled away!" he shouts. "I was behind her, at first."

I smirk. "Listen, if you're going to lie, then at least do it well. I drove past here not three minutes ago, and you were nowhere to be found. Not in front or behind. *Nowhere.*" I make the "skedaddle" motion again. "Now, please, do the right thing and move your car, because I'm late for a very important job interview, and I'll be damned if I'm gonna let a petty little man who can't handle being rejected by a woman at a bar mess things up for me." He's actually quite tall. Much taller than I realized at the bar. But in my experience, all men despise being called "little" in any context, so "little" is what I'm calling him now.

He turns pale. In a strained voice, he says, "Please, please, tell me you're not interviewing at the animal hospital."

"Thankfully, no, if that's where you're going."

"Thank god."

"The feeling's mutual, I assure you." I glance at the clock on my dashboard and anxiety rockets through me. "Move your car, *please*. I need to go now, or I'm going to be late."

The boy bander crosses his arms over his chest and shakes his head. "Maybe I wasn't there for a full five minutes. Maybe it only felt that long. But I was one-hundred-percent waiting there, patiently, for at least two minutes. When you came along and stole the spot like an asshole, I'd only just moved forward to get into position to parallel park after the minivan drove away."

"Maybe take a look in the mirror before calling someone an asshole, *asshole*. I'm not the one getting petty revenge because I got rejected at a fucking bar for the first time in my life."

He scoffs. "*Revenge?* I didn't even know you were the driver of this car until I walked up to your window!"

A car horn blares. And then another. We're blocking the road, and drivers have to wait for gaps in oncoming traffic to get around us.

"Even if you were waiting for the spot, which I don't believe is true," I sniff, "then possession is nine-tenths of the law. And *I'm the one* in possession of this spot."

"That's a myth. My brother's a lawyer, and he told me—"

"I don't care what your brother told you!" I shriek, sounding unhinged, even to myself. But I can't help it. I'm on the verge of a nervous breakdown here. With each passing second, I can feel that perfect job slipping away. God help me, if this former-Disney-star-toothpaste-model-aged-out-boy-bander makes me miss out on this perfect opportunity to make some much-needed money, I'll make him rue the day. Through gritted teeth, I say, "Move your car and be the bigger man. Wouldn't that feel good, to know you've helped me get the perfect job?"

He scoffs. "Sorry, this is one time being gorgeous won't get you what you want, Charlotte."

Well, that was flattering. I mean, it would be, if I didn't know he was only saying it to butter me up and get the spot. "Nice try," I spit out. "But flattery will get you nowhere." I look at my watch and jolt in frustration. I've reached a fork in the road here. *I'm out of time.* Should I leave my car here, as is, and risk getting a parking ticket that I'd surely be able to pay off if I get the job? If I leave now, I'd still be able to sprint to the coffee place, like a bat out of hell, and make my job interview with the weirdo's coffee in hand. I might be two or three minutes early, rather than five, like Ryan advised, but all things considered, I think that's the best path forward.

I take a deep breath, swing my car door open, and march out of my diagonally parked car with my head held high, and the man I've come to despise jumps back to accommodate me, his piercing, blue eyes wide.

"What are you doing?" he gasps out.

I slam my car door. "Going to my job interview." Without further explanation, I march away. But after a couple steps, I can't resist throwing over my shoulder, "I hope you're late for your interview and you tank it when you get there."

"Yeah, back at you," he calls out. "Chin up, though, if your interviewer is an old, skeevy guy without an ounce of charac-ter, all you have to do is call him 'smoking hot' and 'man candy,' and I'm sure the job will be yours."

"Fuck you," I shout, raising both arms to double-flip him

off, right before swinging open the door to the coffee place and waltzing inside.

———

Thankfully, the line inside the coffee place is short. Bonus points, the barista who serves me is a sweetheart who puts a rush on my order when I tell her the situation. As she makes the drink, I race to the bathroom to pee and check my hair and makeup—and, lucky me, by the time I'm exiting the restroom, the barista is calling my name with perfect timing.

I wouldn't have believed it possible, but I'm now on course to make it to my interview at 7:58, coffee in hand, provided I sprint to the guy's office at full speed now. I'm talking I've got to *haul ass.* Yes, I'll be there three minutes later than Ryan recommended, but it's also two minutes *early* for the interview, so all things considered, I'm pretty impressed with myself.

"You're an angel on earth!" I shout to the barista as I sprint toward the front door of the coffee place. Once outside, I run like the wind up the sidewalk toward the guy's office building a block away . . .

Crash.

The coffee cup goes flying. My body goes tilting. And, suddenly, I'm thudding onto my ass on the hard sidewalk. I look up in shock from my landing spot and discover I've collided with *him.* The boy bander. The asshole. My *nemesis.* I look down at my chest and discover—oh, shit—the front of my white outfit is now splattered with dark, brown coffee. *I look like a dairy cow.* The kind in cartoons that are always white with black splotches.

"Are you okay?" the asshole gasps out. "Oh my god. I'm so sorry. Are you hurt? Did the coffee burn you?"

In a heartbeat, my shock gives way to fury. "You did that on purpose!"

"W-what? *No*. I was running because I'm late for my interview, and—"

"You ran straight into me!"

"Not on purpose, though. I was high-tailing it because I'm super late."

I'm stuffing down tears now. "It was a blind corner, and you ran around it without slowing down?"

He runs his hand through his light-brown hair. "Yeah, I-I had to park several b-blocks away, so I was running at top speed. I-I should have been more careful. Are you hurt?"

I look down at my splattered chest again, hoping it's not as bad as I'd initially surmised, but it is. Oh, fuck. My brain suddenly registers cold wetness against my ass cheeks. On top of everything else, I think I'm sitting in a mud puddle left over from last night's rain. Fucking Seattle.

"I'm not physically hurt, I don't think," I mutter. "But in all other ways, I'm totally fucked."

The guy reaches for me, apparently trying to help me up, but I bat his hand away and shout, "Don't you dare touch me!"

"You seriously think I did this to you on p-purpose?" he says. "It was a blind corner. You said so yourself."

"You followed me here? I asked your daddy to help me, instead of you, and now you're hell-bent on making me pay for that unthinkable crime?"

"Are you insane? I was already sitting there when you drove up, remember? I couldn't p-possibly have followed you here."

I pinch the bridge of my nose and murmur, "Please, stop talking." I take a moment to breathe in and out, so I won't burst into tears in front of this asshole, and when I'm in full control of myself, I get up and twist around to try to peek at my ass. "Is my butt covered in mud?"

"Does it matter? I think the coffee on your chest has already ruined the outfit."

I hang my head. He's right.

What would be the point in heading to that interview now, when I'm late, coffee-less, and my formerly crisp, white outfit now looks like a series of Rorschach ink blots?

The boy bander looks anxious. He glances at his phone and exhales. "Um, so . . . If you're not hurt, then why don't you give me your Venmo, and I'll send you money for dry cleaning. Or a new outfit, maybe. Whatever." He looks at his phone again. "I-I really have to go." His blue eyes are begging me to accept his solution and set him free. Clearly, he's freaking out about his interview. In fact, he looks on the cusp of physically combusting. *And I like it.* Good. Let him suffer. If this little run-in of ours is going to cost *me* the perfect job, then it's only fair for him to suffer the same fate.

I shift all my weight to one leg and wince, morphing into a pained human flamingo. "Shit. My knee really hurts," I choke out, laying it on thick. "Can you help me to the coffee place, so I can sit down and get some ice for it?"

His chest heaves. His face contorts. Clearly, the man feels conflicted. Frazzled. He looks at his phone again and visibly shudders. But in the end, he exhales, steps forward, and offers me his arm. "Of course. I'm so sorry, Charlotte."

As I take his arm, I say, "You're gonna have to pay for more than a new outfit, you know. You also owe me for lost wages. I just lost out on the perfect job because of you. And then there's going to be my medical expenses. Pain and suffering."

"Are you fucking kidding me?" He stops walking, poised to say more, but before he does, a loud clacking noise followed by a loud beeping sound behind us attracts our mutual attention. Oh, fuck. *My car.* A guy in a mechanic's uniform is in the process of preparing it for towing, and he's almost finished!

"Wait! No!" I scream. I drop the boy bander's arm and

sprint at full speed toward my elevated car, flailing my arms. "Stop! Wait! I'm here! *Please!*"

I'm too late. By the time I get over there, the job is done. The driver has secured my car for towing, and he's walking back to his truck's driver's side door.

"Please, sir! Wait!" I shout, as I come to a stop at my back bumper. "This is mine. I was only gone for a few minutes. Can you please take it down?"

"Can't do that."

"I'll pay the fine right now. I've got a credit card." I begin frantically rummaging into my purse, but it's no use. He's shaking his head.

"You were blocking traffic," he says flatly. "That's an automatic tow."

"I'll pay the fine. Do you accept credit cards?"

He ignores the question and tells me where I can get it out of impound.

"*Impound?*" I shriek. "How much will that cost me?"

"Three hundred, if you get it today."

"*Three hundred dollars?* Sir, I can't afford that. I'm here for a job interview. I'm broke. Please, sir, I'm begging you."

He shrugs. "Action, meet consequences, lady."

I'm trembling. Sick to my stomach. He's right, of course. I did this to myself. I let my anger at the boy bander cloud my judgment. *Why'd I do that?* Normally, I'm grace under pressure, thanks to years of training and dealing with irate, drunk, and/or anxious passengers. I've been trained to remain on a burning aircraft and help everyone else out first. And yet, I let some petty asshole with piercing, blue eyes get under my skin? *Why, why, why?* Ever since I made that colossal, stupid, paranoia-inducing mistake, I've turned into someone else. Someone I don't recognize. Obviously, karma knows what I did, and she's arrived to have her way with me now.

Behind me on the sidewalk, the asshole snickers and says, "Your knee seems to have healed in record time. *It's a miracle!*"

I turn around, seething with anger. Yes, I'm an idiot. But my crimes are more of the bumbling variety. Whereas, this guy? He's mean. Petty. Thin-skinned and vengeful. Which is why, as of this moment, I officially hate his fucking guts.

"You called the tow truck on me!" I scream. "You got your fragile ego bruised by a woman at a bar who *dared* to be the first, ever, not to flirt back with you, and you couldn't handle it!"

He's aghast. Or at least, he's pretending to be. "You're so off the mark, it's insane." He takes a deep breath and runs a hand through his hair. "This was a simple case of actions meeting consequences, like the tow truck guy said. You're the one who left your car half in the road, not me. Y-you did that. Not me. So, own it."

I run my palm down my face. I feel like I'm being swept down a river without a life vest. I feel adrift in my life. Out of control. Not to mention, sleep deprived, paranoid, and scared shitless. If I could rewind the clock, I would; but since that's not possible, I was hoping this job would help me get myself back on track.

"Also," he says, "I wasn't flirting with you at Captain's, so I therefore didn't feel rejected when you didn't smile back at me. I was staring at you because I thought you were someone I used to know as a teenager. So, don't flatter yourself and think I've somehow engineered fucking *revenge* against you for rejecting me." He scoffs. "That's utterly ridiculous. Frankly, the fact that you think I've engineered some kind of vengeance plot against you for not flirting with me in a fucking bar tells me everything I need to know about your overblown ego and twisted sense of importance in this world."

Well, damn. That stings a bit, I must admit. Before I've figured out what to say to that, however, the tow truck's engine roars to life. And then, off it goes, with my car hanging off its back.

As I watch my car being driven away to the tune of three hundred bucks I don't have, I feel like I'm falling into a deep, dark hole. If it turns out the condo needs more than a fresh coat of paint, I'll need to go into even more debt on my credit cards. And then what? Will I be able to flip the place for a profit in time to meet that deadline? If not, will I have to go on the run? I can't imagine doing that, since I can't go a single day without talking to Tessa. What would be the point of going on the run, if I'm living a miserable life without access to the people I love the most? What if Zach and Claire don't remember their Auntie Charlotte by the time it's safe for me to come out of hiding, if ever?

The boy bander slow-claps. "Wow, in addition to artfully faking knee injuries, you're also brilliant at producing fake tears on command, too. Bravo, Charlotte."

I wipe my wet cheeks and scowl. "Stop using my name. I didn't tell it to *you*; I told it to your smoking-hot father—who, by the way, is a million times hotter than *you*." I turn and march down the sidewalk to parts unknown. I know my retort wasn't a clever one. Also, it wasn't true. I only asked the silver fox to be my fake boyfriend, rather than his fit, hunky, dreamboat of a son, because I knew an older, rich guy would get under Brody's skin far more than a young, fit, squeaky-clean, boy-bander type. Brody constantly says, "eat the rich!", so who better to needle him with than an older dude with a flashy watch and a designer suit? Not to mention, thanks to the exchange of scowls I'd already had with the boy bander, I didn't think he'd agree to help me, anyway.

"Wow, look at that knee go!" the asshole calls after me. "It's a miracle, I tell ya. *Praise Jesus.*"

"Go fuck yourself!" I call back.

He laughs. "Oh, I will. First thing, when I get back home.

And when I do it, rest assured, *Charlotte*, I'll be thinking about *you*. Specifically, the look on your face when you saw your car hooked up to the tow truck!"

I don't have a witty comeback for that one, so I continue marching up the sidewalk without looking back. When I turn a corner and know for certain my sworn enemy can't see or hear me, however, I let my tears flow.

After a few blocks, I come upon a small neighborhood park, so I flop onto a bench and sob. When I feel able to speak, I pull out my phone and call Tessa.

"How'd it go?" Tessa asks brightly. "Did he hire you on the spot?"

"I blew it, Tessa. I fucked up."

"Oh no. What happened?"

My chin trembles as I press my phone against my ear. "Will you come get me, T? Please?" I know I sound like a kindergartner with separation anxiety calling her mommy, but I can't help it. I'm lost, at my lowest, and I need my bestie. The only good thing I've got going for me right now is my friendship with this amazing woman and the fact that I'll never have to see that petty, vindictive, tow-truck-calling boy bander, ever again.

"I've got your location," Tessa says, instantly flipping into fixer mode. "I'm coming now."

"I fucked up, T," I murmur, sniffling. "I really, really fucked up."

"Anything is fixable. It's gonna be okay."

"Thank you, Tessa. I'm sorry."

"I'm coming now. Hang in there, love. I'm coming right now."

5

AUGGIE

"Yeah, no worries, Mom. I'm sure I'll find another internship. If not, I'll get a job as a barista or something this summer. It'll be fine." I'm honestly not confident it'll be fine, but I don't want my mother worrying about me.

I'm heading down the long hallway toward my unit at the end, and I'm somehow acting much calmer than I actually feel during this phone call. In truth, after losing out on that coveted internship this morning, thanks to the craziness that happened with Charlotte, I don't have high hopes I'll find something else. At least, nothing as amazing as the internship that slipped through my fingers this morning. Apparently, busy veterinarians interrupting their day for internship interviews aren't impressed by candidates who arrive twenty minutes late for no good reason and appear frazzled and out of sorts once they finally show up. *Go figure.*

I decide to change the subject. Mom and her fiancé, Henry, are sitting in an Uber, as we speak, on their way to the airport for a long visit with my brother, Max, and his family in California, so I ask, "Do you need me to pick you up from the airport when you get back in two weeks?"

"No, we'll grab an Uber on that end, too. If you're going to take a break from studying, then it should be for something fun or relaxing."

That's my mother for you. She's the best. The thing she doesn't realize, however, is that I might not need to study by the time she gets back from her trip. Not if I can't pay that invoice by the time the grace period expires.

"I'm gonna go now, Mom," I say, stopping in front of my door. "I'm home. Say hi to Max and Marnie and the kids for me. Tell them Uncle Auggie wishes he were there."

"I will, my love. Chin up about the internship. You'll get something even better."

We say our goodbyes, and I enter my place, where I'm immediately greeted by my grandmother's shaggy, three-legged terrier mutt, Lucky—her beloved companion for the last several years of her life. After Grandma rescued Lucky from death row at the pound, he repaid her by worshipping the ground she walked on. But now that Grandma is gone, Lucky's transferred all his loyalty and love to me.

I pick up Lucky and kiss his little snout. "Did you protect the castle while I was busy fucking up the most important interview of my life, Lucky Charm? Of course, you did." I sing him the silly little song my grandmother always used to sing him upon greeting, figuring the poor little guy probably misses hearing Grandma singing it as much as I do.

I check to see if Lucky relieved himself on a disposable mat on the balcony, rather than waiting for me to take him out for our daily walk—he did—and when that's settled, I head into my small kitchen to make myself a sandwich.

When I've got my lunch made, I settle onto my couch with my food, laptop, and Lucky. And then, the same way I did last night, I research every side hustle and get-rich-quick scheme I can find on the internet. But after two full hours of research, I haven't found anything with a better shot at helping me than what I've already been doing to cover my living expenses. And that's not a good thing, since the chances of my current side gig panning out are slim to none.

First off, I don't know what the fuck I'm doing with my crazy side gig and never have. That much is clear, given that I've never earned more than a thousand bucks total in an entire *month* of doing it, and to keep my spot in the program, I'll need to make twenty times my best monthly total in half the time. That's what the lady in the billing department told me today—that I'll need to pay twenty grand—exactly half of the full invoice amount—by midnight on the very last day of the grace period, in order to keep my spot. If I pay that, they'll let me negotiate a payment plan for the rest, she said. It's my only hope.

I close my laptop and sigh.

"Well, Lucky. I'll see you on the flipside, buddy." I pat his fuzzy head and rise from the couch, and Lucky hops around on his couch cushion in response, thinking my body language means I'm going to take him for our daily walk. "Sorry, buddy. I'll take you for our walk after I jack off for cash."

I head to my bedroom with my laptop and close the door behind me, so Lucky won't follow me. The last thing I need while trying to get hard, stay hard, and reach orgasm in front of a bunch of online strangers, is to see Lucky's soulful brown eyes staring at me from his doggie bed in the corner.

Once I've got my bedroom door closed, I head to my closet to select today's superhero mask. Today, "Superhero Salami Slinger" will be jacking off as Spiderman for the pleasure of my online audience, whoever they are.

With my mask selected, I draw my blinds, strip off my clothes, and slide into bed next to my laptop. Before logging into my account, I pause to get myself into the right headspace. I'm not an exhibitionist by nature. I even felt shy wearing Speedos at swim meets growing up. So, doing this requires me to imagine I'm someone else.

Plus, it's been a while. Almost two months, so I'm rusty. When Mom and Max gave me the amazing news that I could move in here, rent-free, and that Max would continue paying Grandma's monthly mortgage, as he did before, until my graduation in two years, I was thrilled to stop slinging my salami online and apply for a much less lucrative tutoring position, instead, in order to cover my now much smaller monthly expenses. But now, thanks to my father, here I am, slinging my salami again. This time, not to cover rent for the small room I used to rent at a place with some buddies, but to try to keep my lifelong dreams alive.

With a long exhale, I slide the Spiderman mask over my face and log into my account. Well, I try to, anyway. I've forgotten my password, thanks to my hiatus, so I have to do the whole rigamarole to get a new one.

Okay.

Take two.

With my new password confirmed, I log into my account, click into my dashboard, and push the button to begin a livestream. First off, I make some brief opening remarks, including teasing my small audience about some "exciting, new stuff" I'll be unveiling over the next two weeks. What exciting, new stuff am I talking about? I have no fucking clue. All I know is I've got to come up with something new, exciting, different, and dazzling—and *pronto*—something that sets me apart from all the other creators on this platform who jack off for cash—some of them, as superheroes—or I can kiss my dreams of becoming a vet goodbye.

"And now, without further ado . . ." I pan the camera down to reveal my naked torso and thankfully hard dick and promptly get to work on myself, since that's what these anonymous people came here to see.

Jacking off in front of a crowd has never been my favorite thing, to put it mildly, but I've always managed to get past my initial shyness and rise to the occasion for the greater good. But this time, with everything on the line, I'm finding it more difficult than ever to keep my body on track.

Panicking, I close my eyes and try to imagine the hottest, sexiest porn I've ever watched while continuing to stroke my full length with gusto—and to my surprise, the image that pops into my head, unbidden, is the redhead's gorgeous face. *Charlotte.* The asshole who'd rather fuck my father than me. *What the fuck?*

I try to evict Charlotte from my brain and replace her with a celebrity crush. An ex-girlfriend. The pretty woman from the gym who always does deadlifts. But nope, I keep coming back to Charlotte. Not the thing I told her I'd think about when beating off—the look on her face when she saw the tow truck. Nope. I'm seeing her belly laughing with her friend. Doing those silly dance moves. Getting out of her car in that white-hot, white jumpsuit thing. Fucking hell, she was fucking gorgeous in that thing. Holy fuck. When I saw Charlotte in that white outfit, I forgot to be angry with her for a split-second there. By the time I remembered again, my tongue was practically dragging on the street. Or hell, maybe I found Charlotte so hot in that moment partly *because* of my anger toward her? I don't know. All I know was the moment felt hot as fuck and infuriating, all at once, and now, thinking about it, it's making me hard and getting me there.

I keep going. Stroking myself while imagining Charlotte. She's spread eagle in my bed. I'm eating her pussy like a madman. Making her scream my name and come against my mouth.

My balls tighten sharply.

And here we go. Suddenly, I'm gripped by waves of pleasure. Warmth spurts onto my hand. *Success.*

I open my eyes and check the tip jar on my screen, hoping I've earned some kind of personal best. But to my disappointment, I've actually underperformed this time, compared to my personal best from about six months ago. I guess being on hiatus for two months wasn't a good thing, in terms of staying relevant and keeping the algorithms working in my favor. If I keep pulling this paltry amount with each show, I'd have to whack off thirty times per day, every day for the next two weeks, to pay that twenty grand and be able to negotiate a payment plan for the rest. Not physically possible. Obviously, I need to come up with a new strategy. Something different I can do on the platform that will set me apart from all the other dudes whacking off.

I thank my audience for their generosity, tease them again with something "new and' amazing" coming to my channel soon, and log off. After ripping off my mask, I drag my naked ass into my bathroom and take a hot shower, where I wrack my brain for ideas. Something to set me apart. But I can't think of anything. Nothing I'd actually be willing to do to my body, anyway.

When I first started doing this, I naively assumed the size of my dong would give me an advantage in the market. I've been in enough locker rooms at swim practices and meets to know I'm bigger than most guys. But as it's turned out, there's more to being successful on the platform than simply having a fit body and big dick. Some guys with smaller dicks than mine do much better because they're great showmen. Way better than me at talking dirty to their audience. Others are buffer than me. Like, bodybuilder types. That's not for everyone. Some prefer a fit, leaner physique, like mine. But those swole guys fracture the market. There are even some other superheroes, I've come to find out. So,

I'm not even special on that score. And my paltry earnings reflect that.

I step out of the shower, dry myself off, and stare at my naked body in the mirror. I've got a fit, well-proportioned body and a big dick. *But what else do I have to offer?* I swear, if I knew what to do, I'd have done it by now. At this point, the only thing I know for sure is that I'd better come up with something soon, or I can kiss my spot in the vet program goodbye.

6

AUGGIE

"Good boy. Now, go get it, buddy!"

I toss Lucky's red rubber ball again across the grass for him to fetch, and he hops away gleefully to chase it down. I'm sitting on a large lawn underneath a shady tree on-campus, taking a break from my daily walk with Lucky to people-watch and think.

Usually, when I'm out with Lucky, I've got my earbuds in and a podcast going. But today, I've been brainstorming in silence, hoping the lack of aural stimulation will allow my brain to *finally* come up with The Big Idea. The magic bullet that will get my Superhero Salami Slinger account cooking with gas. If I can't figure out something soon, I'll be fucked.

Just as Lucky drops his little ball in front of me, a couple friends from the vet program stop and say hi. When one of them tries to pet Lucky, the poor little guy hides behind me, quaking in fear, so I explain his background—his year at a shelter and likely abuse before then—and the resulting anxiety he now feels around all strangers; and my friend kindly gives Lucky the space he needs.

My friends sit down for a bit, and we chat about our

upcoming exams. And then, about our mutual anxiety surrounding those all-important summer internships. When those topics have run their course, we move on to talking about our plans for the upcoming weekend. One of my friends says she's attending her niece's sixth birthday party on Saturday, and that her sister, the birthday girl's mother, has hired a "princess" to show up and make her daughter and all her little friends lose their shit. Laughing, we muse about the power of princesses and fairytales, and we all agree it'd be awesome if, as adults, we could still be that easy to thrill.

Whoa.

I suddenly feel like I've been struck by a lightning bolt.

My Big Idea.

I think I've got it!

I tell my friends I'd better get back home to study, so they get up and say their goodbyes. As they're walking away, I grab my phone and run a couple searches—and what comes up confirms I'm on to something.

"Come on, Lucky. Playtime's over, little buddy." There's no need to attach a leash to Lucky's collar to make him hop along after me. Since Grandma died, my little tripod follows me wherever I go. So, I simply shove Lucky's rubber ball in the pocket of my hoodie and take off in the direction of my building. I'll need to swing by a craft store before getting started and make a few things, as best I can. But once I do all that, it should be easy enough to execute my idea and see if it pans out.

My mind is racing now. *Fleshing* things out. Pun intended. In fact, by the time I'm turning the corner onto my street, I've already figured out my first two shows. Holy shit, I think this could work.

I stop dead in my tracks. Is that *Charlotte* walking up the pathway to my building? I resume walking, eager to get a closer look. If that's Charlotte, then she's changed out of her splattered white jumpsuit from this morning. This particular redhead's wearing jeans and a T-shirt. But, wait, the woman walking alongside her is definitely the pregnant brunette from Captain's yesterday. And that's *definitely* Charlotte's ass in profile. Not that I've memorized it or anything. It's just that it was hard *not* to notice it when she was marching away maniacally and swinging her hips.

Yep, that's definitely Charlotte. *How'd she track me down?* Must have been from my car's license plate. Did she come here to demand payment for that long list of bullshit she rattled off after the tow truck left? I bet that's it. And that makes her fucking demented.

I pick up Lucky, since he gets freaked out around strangers, and stride toward the two women. When I get within earshot, I yell, "You're stalking me now?"

The redhead turns toward me, confirming she is, indeed, the infuriating demon who made me late for the most important interview of my life this morning. And when she sees my angry glare, she hisses, "*You*. What the fuck are you doing here?"

Ignoring her question—because, come on, she knows why I'm here, or else *she* wouldn't be here—I grit out, "I'm not paying you a dime, so don't even bother asking. I didn't get my dream internship today, thanks to you and your fake knee injury, so by my calculations, you owe me as much or more than I could possibly owe you for *accidentally* spilling coffee on you."

The pregnant brunette gasps, like she's just placed my face. "The boy bander!"

"Aka my *stalker*," Charlotte says with a sniff.

I have no idea what's happening. Boy bander? All I know is this woman is unhinged to have tracked me down at my place of residence. "*I'm* not the stalker here, Charlotte, and you know it."

"How could I stalk you when I got here first?" Charlotte says, crossing her arms over her chest. "And don't use my name. I told you that this morning."

"Oh, yeah. Because I only overheard that highly confidential, super-secret piece of intel when you introduced yourself to my 'smoking hot' father."

Charlotte throws up her arms. "God, your ego is fragile. Get over it, dude." She exhales. "Look, if it would help you to let it go and therefore quit stalking me to know *why* I asked your father to be my fake boyfriend, and not you—"

"I don't care."

"—then let me explain it to you: 1) I didn't think you'd say yes to me, given that you'd already made it clear you despised me; and 2) the guy I was trying to make jealous was always going on about eating the rich, and your daddy looks like a wealthy high-roller, while you look like an aged-out boy bander whose manager stole all the band's money, so now you're forced to give group hip-hop lessons at nursing homes to survive."

As pissed as I am, I chuckle. What a mind. Also, I guess that explains the boy bander reference. The crazy thing is, she's not *that* off the mark. Closer than she knows, anyway. Damn. When Charlotte burst into Captain's and launched into those ridiculous dance moves at full-throttle, I figured she had to be an entertaining, funny person, and this diatribe has only confirmed that hunch. She's as funny as she is hot. The only problem? She's also a batshit crazy stalker. The kind who tracks down her prey at his place of residence after a simple misunderstanding. Spilling that coffee was an accident, and I can't believe she'd ever think otherwise.

"It also might help you to know," Charlotte continues, her hand on her hip and her toe tapping away, "that even if your rich daddy wasn't at Captain's with you yesterday, you and I *never* would have gotten together, despite your pretty smile. You're too young for me, for one thing, and also too squeaky clean and conventionally handsome for my taste. So, run along and stalk someone else and leave me the fuck alone."

There's a lot to unpack here. But I say the thing that elbows its way to the top of the list. "I'm too *young*? How old do you think I am? I'm thirty, and you don't look any older than that."

"She's thirty-two," the brunette interjects, much to the visible annoyance of her redhaired companion. "But thanks to those cute little freckles and that button nose, she still gets carded whenever she's not wearing makeup."

"Stop fraternizing with the enemy, Tessa!" Charlotte booms. "He's an unhinged, crazy stalker, remember?"

"A stalker with a scared little three-legged dog in tow?" the brunette says with a scoff. "I don't think so, honey. There's got to be a logical explanation why he's turned up here." She returns to me. "I'm Tessa. What's your name?"

"Hi, Tessa. Auggie."

"Nice to meet you, Auggie. Are you a student?"

I nod. "In the veterinary program."

"That's so cool. Good for you." Tessa nudges Charlotte. "See? This is Auggie's *neighborhood*. He's innocently out and about walking his cute little three-legged dog, not stalking you."

I wave Lucky's only front paw. "This is Lucky."

"Hello there, Lucky," Tessa says amiably. "He's so cute. How'd he lose his leg?"

"A car accident, back when he was a stray on the streets. My grandma rescued him from death row at a shelter, and now he's mine."

Tessa's shoulders subtly droop. Clearly, something on my face or in my voice when I mentioned my grandma—combined with the fact that I've now got custody of her beloved pooch—must have conveyed my heartache, clearly enough.

"Aw, sweet baby," Tessa says, but I'm not sure if she's talking about Lucky or me. "We've been thinking about getting a rescue pup as a buddy for our dog. We've got a husky, and he's super needy."

"As most huskies are."

Tessa chuckles. "Rudy's like Velcro. That's one of his nicknames."

"Does Rudy talk and sing?"

"*All. The. Time.*"

"God, I love huskies. Never a dull moment."

"What the fuck, Tessa!" Charlotte shrieks. "Stop fraternizing with the enemy!" When Tessa protests, Charlotte shoots back, "I don't care if he's got an *army* of cute little three-legged dogs following him around like rats following the Pied Piper! He's the dickhead who called a tow truck on me and then crashed into me, *on purpose*, thereby spilling coffee all over my white outfit, thereby sabotaging the important job interview I'd unfortunately been stupid enough to tell him about."

"I didn't run into you on purpose," I insist, my impatience gathering steam. "I swear it on Lucky."

"Interesting you didn't deny calling the tow truck." She gives me a beat to deny or admit the crime, and when I don't do either, she says, "*That's what I thought.* You're taking the Fifth, huh? As all guilty men do. Now, run along home and let's both agree we'll turn around and sprint in the other direction if we happen to see each other walking around the neighborhood again, okay?"

I roll my eyes. "I'd be happy to 'run along home,' *Charlotte,* if you'd be so kind as to step the fuck aside and let me pass through the front door of my building." I motion to the door behind her for emphasis.

Charlotte looks genuinely confused. But that can't be. If Charlotte sincerely didn't know my address before this moment, then why is she here? After everything that's happened between us, there's no scenario that could possibly make me believe her presence here now is nothing but some kind of bizarre coincidence.

I smile at Tessa. "It was nice meeting you. I've got to study now, so if you two ladies will kindly excuse me and let me pass, I promise I'll happily never see you again, Charlotte, as long as I live."

In a flash, Charlotte's expression morphs from confusion to terror. "This isn't funny," she says. "You're taking this vengeance thing too far, Auggie."

I address Tessa. *The reasonable one.* "Tessa, I'm sorry, but your friend has brought you here under false pretenses. The truth is, this is where I live, which Charlotte knows full well, or else she wouldn't have come here. She came to try to squeeze some money out of me, I'm assuming, and for some reason, she wanted you here to witness it. Or maybe she thought she needed a bodyguard." I'm being funny, and Tessa knows it, based on her delighted smirk. The woman looks like a stone-cold badass, for sure, but she's also visibly pregnant. Not a great pick for a bodyguard. I return to Charlotte. "I'm not giving you a dime, like I said. And that's final. So, if you'll step aside, please, I'll be out of your hair forever."

I take a step forward, and Charlotte thankfully steps aside with a stunned look on her pretty face. At the door, I shift Lucky in my arms to be able to punch in the door code while shielding the keypad with my shoulder. When I've successfully unlocked the door, I stride through it with a polite farewell to Tessa and a "fuck you" glare at Charlotte.

When I hear the heavy door click shut behind me, I put Lucky down and stride across the lobby toward a wall of mailboxes. Before I've opened mine, however, I hear the front door to the building open behind me. Footsteps enter the tile lobby. *Charlotte's* voice says, "Prove you live here. I don't believe you."

I whirl around, feeling confused and irritated. I'm positive the door locked behind me; also, that I shielded the code when I punched it in. How'd Charlotte get the code to the door? Did she hide in the bushes and watch whoever came in before me?

"I don't have to prove a damned thing to you. The real question is: how'd you get the code to the door?"

Charlotte motions to the bank of mailboxes. "If you truly live here, then open your mailbox." She smirks like she's just captured my queen in a game of chess.

"Only to get you off my back, once and for all. Not because I owe you a damned thing." I pull out my keys and open my box, at which point Charlotte gasps audibly behind me. To emphasize my point, I pull out a short stack of mail from my box and hold up the top piece—an envelope from the University of Washington. Surely, it contains a duplicate copy of the tuition invoice that's currently sitting in my email inbox—the same invoice that's now past due—which means I should stop wasting my time here with this unhinged woman, as entertaining as she is, and get my ass to a craft store.

"That's me," I say, pointing to the addressee's name and address on the envelope. "Augustus Vaughn." In a huff, I grab my driver's license out of my wallet, and then hand both the envelope and the license to Tessa to confirm they match up.

As Tessa looks at the documents in her hands, Charlotte leans in and peeks, too; and when she sees the two names are, indeed, one and the same, Charlotte grips her friend's arm and whimpers.

"I haven't changed the address on my license yet," I say. "I just moved in. But you can clearly see I'm Augustus Vaughn, the guy who receives mail at this building's address—*because he lives here.*"

Charlotte looks pale as she looks up and grimaces at her

friend. "308," she chokes out. She grips Tessa's arm even tighter with white knuckles. *"This man lives in unit 3-0-8."*

"Correct. So you can stop accusing me of stalking you and move along to bothering someone else."

"Thank you for showing this to us," Tessa says, handing me back the documents. As I slide my license into my wallet, she adds, "Listen, Auggie, despite what you've seen of her, I assure you Charlotte McDougal is actually the sweetest, funniest, and most loyal person you'll ever meet. The best friend anyone could ever ask for. Everyone who meets Charlotte falls instantly in love with her." Tessa flinches. "Well, under normal circumstances, anyway."

"I think you'll understand why I'm finding all that very hard to believe."

Tessa forces a smile. "What I think is you're two good people who got off on the wrong foot. But it's nothing that can't be undone if you both agree to put the past behind you and start over, right?"

Why does Tessa care if I think her best friend is a stalker-madwoman, albeit a hot one, when I'm never going to see the fiery redhead, ever again, once she walks her hot little ass back out that lobby door? *What am I missing here?* "Why are you playing peacemaker, Tessa?" I ask. "Why do you care?"

Tessa presses her lips together briefly, shifts her weight, and sighs, before finally replying, "I care because Charlotte's your new next-door neighbor, Auggie—the proud new owner of unit 307."

7
CHARLOTTE

The three of us—Tessa, my nemesis, and me—don't make a sound as our elevator ascends toward the third floor. Even the scruffy little dog in the dickhead's arms is being as quiet a mouse, even as he shakes and trembles with obvious anxiety. Poor thing. I guess he's not a fan of elevators.

When the doors open, the dickhead who most *definitely* called that tow truck on me this morning motions politely for Tessa and me to exit first. When we do, he puts down his scruffy bundle and follows along behind Tessa and me. A few steps into our journey down the hallway, Tessa glances down at Lucky and says, "He's so cute. I love the way he hops along on his three legs."

"He's surprisingly mobile. He can chase a ball like a champ."

"Oh, I'd love to see that."

I glare at Tessa, chastising her for fraternizing with the enemy again, and she rolls her eyes in reply. I don't care if my best friend thinks I'm being mean to the nice man. After twelve years of dealing with all manner of people on long flights, I'm exceptionally good at reading people; and my flight-attendant instincts tell me Augustus Vaughn one-hundred-percent called that tow truck. He might also have crashed into me on purpose, too, in order to spill the hot coffee in my hand, but I'm admittedly not positive about that part. Either way, I'm not inclined to forgive and forget, no matter what Tessa wants me to do.

I do concede, however, that my sworn enemy's three-legged rescue pup is awfully cute. Also, the fact that Auggie took on his grandma's fur baby is a *teeny-tiny* point in his favor. I also admit, begrudgingly, that Auggie has some phys-ical appeal, despite him not being my usual type. If I didn't loathe him, I *might* be inclined to say yes to a date, if he asked, simply out of curiosity. But since I do loathe the man, it's a moot point.

"If it makes you feel any better," Auggie says, jerking me from my wandering thoughts. He's addressing me. Leveling me with those stunning blue eyes of his. "I didn't get my dream internship today, thanks to our run-in. As it turns out, being twenty minutes late for an interview isn't a selling point."

I snicker. "That's karma for you, baby."

"*Karma*? I did nothing wrong."

"You called the tow truck."

He scoffs. "I didn't. But if I had, it wouldn't have been wrong of me. You *chose* to leave your car parked with its ass hanging out, *baby*. Nobody, including me, put a gun to your head."

He's not wrong. But I'd never admit that to him.

"Anyone could have called that tow truck," Tessa inter-jects, as we come to a stop in front of my door. "You were blocking traffic in front of a bunch of stores and businesses, Charlotte."

She's also not wrong. But still, I'm not willing to let the

boy bander off the hook that easily. I frown at Auggie. "Why did you stop here? You're not coming inside, for fuck's sake."

Auggie shrugs. "I just want to peek through the door. I'm curious." When I look annoyed, he adds, "I've heard some rumors from the building manager about this unit."

My stomach flip-flops. "Rumors?"

"About it being in less than stellar condition. Was the former owner your family member? If so, I'm sorry for you loss."

"No, I didn't know the guy. I bought the place in an online auction, sight unseen. The owner died without an heir."

"Huh."

After making his vague grunt of a comment, Auggie doesn't move from his spot in the hallway. Apparently, he's determined to be a looky-loo. And so, with a deep exhale, I turn to the door, position my shiny, new key, and slide it into my shiny, new lock.

Click.

"Here we go," I whisper to Tessa, as butterflies whoosh into my belly.

"It's gonna be fine," she murmurs back, patting my shoulder.

I try to open the door wide, but something blocks its movement, midway, from the inside. My brow furrowed, I poke my head through the gap and shriek when I behold the chaos on the other side of the door. There are stacks of random stuff *everywhere*. And I do mean *everywhere*. On every surface. Covering every fucking inch. Also, the place smells terrible.

"Oh, god," I blurt. "It's a hoarder's paradise in here, Tessa. Fucking hell."

I yank my head from the doorway, feeling dizzy. I figured I'd need to do some deep cleaning, of course. Also, since the unit came furnished, that I'd also need to haul away some gross, out-of-date furniture. I've foreseen needing to paint and pull up old, stained carpeting, too. *But this*? It's going to take me weeks to clear out the place before I can even begin to deep-clean and figure out what else needs to be done to spruce it up. Which means—oh, God—there's no way in hell I'll make Carlo's deadline now. No freaking way. The only question now is: should I try my best, even though I already know my best isn't going to be good enough, or flee right now and go into hiding?

"Let me see," Tessa says, nudging me to the side. When I make room in the doorframe for her, Tessa pokes her head into the gap and blurts, "*Whoa.* How did he live here? Every nook and cranny is jam-packed. Ugh. It smells awful, too."

As she's peeking, I slide my back down the hallway wall, ultimately coming to a rest on my ass on the floor. I'm vaguely aware that Auggie is now peeking through the gap in the door and repeating the gist of what Tessa said, but I'm too upset to care or reply. I'm at the end of the line. The end of my rope. I took a huge gamble in an effort to fix a massive mistake, and it didn't pay off. It's as simple as that. In fact, it's now clear my gamble has failed miserably.

All of a sudden, a warm, furry body climbs into my lap. A wet tongue licks my hand where I've just wiped away a salty tear. It's exactly what my beloved childhood mutt, Candy, used to do to comfort me when I cried, so I break down, hug Lucky to me, and let my tears flow.

"Aw, sweetie," Tessa says. She sits down next to me on the floor and pats my arm. "It's going to be okay, my love. I just texted a guy I know and asked him to bring a crew in here ASAP and get everything hauled away and cleaned in record time."

"I can't let you do that," I murmur from behind my hands.

"I already did."

"You've already done way too much for me, T."

"And you've done a million things for me. That's friendship, Charlotte. In fact, we both know you've done far more amazing things for me than I could ever repay you for. I wouldn't even be with Ryan now, if it weren't for you." She pauses to look at the phone in her hand. "My friend just replied. He says he'll bring a crew here tomorrow morning at seven and they'll handle everything. Not to worry."

With Lucky still in my lap, I lean over and rest my temple on Tessa's shoulder. "Thank you. I'll repay you after I sell or rent the place out. I promise."

"Absolutely not," she replies. "Consider this my house-warming gift."

"I love you so much."

"I love you, too. It's going to be okay."

I sit up and wipe my cheeks, and that's when I realize Auggie is now staring down at me, his mouth hanging open. "Lucky's terrified of strangers," he murmurs. "He won't even let my brother touch him."

I pat Lucky's head. "Go on, buddy. You'd better go back to your mean, heartless, petty daddy now. Big surprise, he doesn't like you comforting me."

"No, that's not what I meant. I'm thrilled Lucky's comforting you. I'm just shocked, that's all." When I don't speak because I'm feeling too beaten down to muster a reply, Auggie's features soften in sympathy. "I'm sorry your place is such a mess. You didn't know that was coming?"

I shake my head. "I knew the place would require some deep cleaning and fixing up. But, no, I didn't expect the place to be *this* bad." I push Lucky gently off me and stand up, and Lucky hops over to Auggie's feet. "I'll be okay," I say, brushing off my jeans. "Thanks for your concern."

Auggie picks up Lucky. "If you need anything, I'm just a door away."

"Don't remind me." It's a bitchy thing to say, given his kind tone, but there's no bite to my delivery. Suddenly, what happened with Auggie this morning feels like the least of my worries.

"I'll leave you alone now. Bye, ladies."

"Bye, Auggie," Tessa replies. "It was nice to meet you."

"You, too."

With that, Auggie disappears into his unit next-door with Lucky bopping happily behind him—and to my surprise, he doesn't flash me a single scowl or glare before shutting the door.

"Okay, my love," Tessa says, clapping her palms together, "my friend gave us an assignment. He told me to rent a storage facility for tomorrow for all this stuff. He said the crew will throw away any obvious trash, but everything else will be boxed up and put into storage, so you can go through it at your convenience later and see if there's anything worth keeping or selling."

The tiniest tingles of hope prickle at my soul. "That's a great idea."

"He's a pro. I'm sure there's a storage place close by, considering how close we are to campus."

"Let's do it."

Tessa taps on her phone and quickly finds a storage facility only two miles away, and just that fast, I'm no longer wallowing in self-pity. I'm a woman on a mission, thanks to Tessa.

As we head toward the elevator, Tessa says, "After we get the storage unit, do you have time to get the kids with me and take them out for ice cream cones?"

"Are you kidding? I've got nothing but time till the crew works their magic. And, yes, I'd love to eat my feelings with my three favorite people."

We reach the elevator, and Tessa presses the call button.

"Auggie's kinda cute," she says. She's playing it cool. I know her well enough to know she wanted to deliver that sentence with a whole lot more enthusiasm than that.

"Girl, don't even try to make Auggie a thing. Even if I were to somehow bury the hatchet with him, which is highly unlikely, he's way too good looking and squeaky clean for me. The sex would be mediocre, at best."

"You don't know that. Don't judge a book by its cover."

I snicker to myself. Tessa obviously thinks I'm assuming *Auggie* would be terrible in bed. Which he probably is. Hot guys don't have the same work ethic in bed as their ugly-hot counterparts. That's a scientific fact. But in this instance, I was actually referring to the little secret I've never admitted to anyone: namely, that I can't let go enough, sexually, when my partner is too hot and therefore makes me feel self-conscious.

"Auggie likes you, Charlotte," Tessa teases, as we step into the elevator.

"No, Auggie hates me."

"Nope. When Lucky started cuddling you, the look on his face was like you'd turned water into wine."

"Okay, so he was amazed his scaredy-cat of a doggie curled up on my lap. Lucky liking me isn't the same thing as *Auggie* liking me."

The elevator doors open and we step out. "No, I think the two things are related. I think Auggie saw his terrified rescue pup trusting you and suddenly felt overcome with the primal urge to put his baby inside you."

We both crack up. Leave it to Tessa to make me laugh, even through tears.

"Well, if that's the case, then, no thanks." I pause. "*Although* . . . the man's got some damned good genes."

"That's an understatement. Think how pretty the babies would be!"

"And did you see how fit he is? I didn't even notice that

yesterday when he was sitting down. How'd I miss his hunky, hot bod?"

"It's from all the break-dancing he did in the boy band."

We both burst out laughing.

"Oh, no," I say. "He was the *break-dancing* one? And here I was considering giving him a shot."

We laugh again.

"You didn't notice his hotness yesterday because you were too busy freaking out about Dumbass Brody to notice."

I snort. "*Brody*. Such a dumbass. What was I thinking?"

"I have no idea, girl. No fucking idea." It's a funny statement, regardless. But even funnier because Brody is Tessa's employee. She, better than anyone, knows the man is dumb as a box of rocks. A great bouncer, probably, but the man can't carry on an interesting conversation to save his life. The fact that I bothered with him at all proves, emphatically, just how abysmal my dating life has become over the past few years.

We're walking up the sidewalk now, heading to Tessa's car. She says, "Were you really considering giving Auggie a shot?"

I shrug. "Not really, no. Although now that I think about it, I suppose it might be convenient to have a fuck buddy right next door."

"*Fuck buddy*? Girl, aim higher. That boy's going to be a *veterinarian*. They make bank. And did you notice how gentle and sweet he is with Lucky? That man's going to make a great father one day. Auggie's definitely husband material."

"Jesus, Tessa. Slow down. You're giving me whiplash. I can't stand the guy, remember? And even if I could, he's not my type, like I keep saying. I need a little edginess to get my juices flowing."

"Oh, Charlotte. You're so frustrating." We reach Tessa's SUV and head to our respective doors. Over the car's roof, Tess says, "By the way, how's your usual type been working out for you, Nut Job? Because Brody is your *exact* type, and that didn't turn out so great."

I glare comically at her and she chuckles.

"Just saying."

"Well, don't."

Still laughing, Tessa unlocks the car and we pile inside. As we're putting our purses in the back and securing our seat-belts, I say, "Okay, *fine*, just to humor you, I'm game to weigh the pros and cons of me taking a big ol' bite of the boy bander's ass. I mean, if he'd even let me. The man's not my biggest fan."

"Girl, trust me, he'd not only let you take a bite of his ass, he'd shove a bare ass cheek at you and *beg*."

We guffaw.

"Seriously, though," Tessa says. "He gave himself away at Captain's. And then again upstairs in that hallway. I don't care what words he might say to you, he's *extremely* attracted to you."

"Maybe he was when he first saw me, but I threw ice water onto his proverbial boner when I asked his daddy to help me make Brody jealous. It also didn't help matters that I acted like a total lunatic in front of him this morning. I don't know what got into me today, T. I acted like such a jerk. I wasn't myself."

Tessa pats my arm. "You've been under a lot of stress since the layoff. Also, I wouldn't rule Auggie out just yet. Something tells me he likes himself a spitfire. When you two were spar-ring, his eyes were on *fire*, girl." As Tessa pulls her car from the curb, she adds, "You're not planning to live here for long, so why not have some fun with your next-door neighbor while you're here?"

"Why are you so intent on pushing me toward this man?"

"I'm not *pushing*. I'm guiding, ever so gently."

"No, you're actually being really pushy. *Why?*"

Tessa sighs. "I just have a good feeling about Auggie. He's

got a genuine sweetness about him. A gentleness. Which makes perfect sense, now that I know what he's planning to do for a living."

"You haven't seen him being a total dick, the way I have. He's not all unicorns and rainbows." I twist my mouth. "Although, to be fair, he was *mostly* reacting to what I was throwing down."

Tessa audibly shrugs. "It's not that I care about Auggie, specifically. It's more that I'd love to see you venture beyond your usual type for a change. I don't think your type is all that good for you, babe. *Carlo* was your type. And look what happened there."

She doesn't know the half of it.

I didn't always keep secrets from my best friend. The first time I kept one from her was two years ago—the day I found out what my then-boyfriend, Carlo, really did for a living. But since I couldn't tell Tessa about that, truthfully, I lied and said I'd broken up with Carlo because he'd cheated on me—something Carlo would never do. Not a chance. And the lies have only piled on, ever since.

"Okay, point taken," I say on a sigh. "I've got a defective picker. But even so, this conversation is pointless because I've already decided not to date while I'm here. I need to spend every spare minute getting that condo into shape, as soon as possible. That's especially true, now that I've seen it. Which means, from this moment on, I'm going to wipe Auggie Vaughn from my hard drive and pretend he doesn't even exist."

8
CHARLOTTE

Four days later

I step back from the wall I've just finished relieving of its peeling, faded, hideous wallpaper and exhale. It's taken me all day, but I've finally stripped my entire living room of its godawful wallpaper. That was my only goal for today: to complete an entire room. But now that I've done that, I want to keep going. At least, I'll start prepping the bedroom walls for stripping tomorrow. It turns out I'm a one-woman, home-improvement army, dude. Go, me.

Actually, no, that's not true. I'm a two-woman army, backed by a full, kick-ass crew. I wouldn't be here now, working so productively, if it weren't for Tessa and the amazing guys she hired to help me. Those amazing men got this place cleared out in two short days, and then spent yesterday, the third day, deep-cleaning it with me. That's the only reason I've been able to start my first improvement project on day four, instead of day fourteen, which, in turn, means it's still possible, at least in theory, for me to get this place into shape and sold in time to pay back that money. *Hallelujah.*

I pick up my bucket and lug it into the kitchen for dumping and refilling. But before I turn on the faucet, I freeze at the sound of muffled footsteps in the hallway. *Is that one of Carlo's colleagues taking matters into his own hands? Did Carlo lose control of the situation, despite his assurances?* That's the terrifying thought that's been keeping me up at night for almost a month now, on top of the generalized anxiety I also feel about my layoff.

While I'm still frozen and listening carefully at the sink, a muffled, cheerful male voice says, "Are you hungry, buddy? Yeah, me, too. Let's eat!"

Phew. It's only my annoying next-door neighbor and his three-legged pooch. What a relief. I haven't run into Auggie since that first time in front of the building, and I'm hoping the trend will continue. I don't have time to spar with him again. And flirting is out of the question. I've got work to do.

Breathing a huge sigh of relief, I turn on the faucet, refill my bucket, and head into the bedroom. Thanks to Tessa's crew, it's empty now. I've set up an air mattress in here and that's all there is, other than my big suitcase in a corner.

After setting down my bucket, tools, and a stepstool I had to go back into the living room to retrieve, I get to work, taking down all wall decorations—an amateurish oil painting, a funky, clunky oval-shaped mirror that's covered in dust, and a framed movie poster for Hitchcock's creepy thriller, *Rear Window.* After that, I grab a hammer and pull out every nail in every wall and then tape the baseboard and outlets in preparation for wiping down the walls.

Finally, I'm ready to get to the heart of my work. I drag the stepstool into position, climb up, and swipe with the sponge. But in short order, something in the wall a few inches below eye level catches my attention. Right where the *Rear Window* poster used to hang, there's a small hole in the wall that doesn't look like one of the nail holes I've just created. For one thing, it's bigger than any of those holes; but more importantly, there's a pinpoint of light flickering through it.

I toss the sponge into the bucket below me, step down a rung on the stepstool, and lean my face into the hole—and that's when I behold my annoying next-door neighbor, Augustus Vaughn, naked on his bed and jerking off in front of a laptop. To be fair, he's wearing a Deadpool mask on his head, so I can't see his face. But that fit body most definitely looks like Auggie's. And those are absolutely his large hands. Not to mention, the fit man with big hands is beating off in *Auggie's* bed, so who else could he be?

I jerk my head away from the wall, shocked by what I've seen. There's a fucking *peephole* in my wall? *And it's aimed directly at Auggie's bed?*

My breathing turns erratic. Labored. My pulse is skyrocketing. This is a truly shocking discovery. Also, damn, Auggie's got a big dick.

I realize that last thing shouldn't be a top concern at the moment, but, damn, that was quite a dick. I don't think I've ever seen a dick quite that impressive before, as a matter of fact, other than in porn. Auggie's cock is not only long, but thick and girthy, too. I bet the sensation of a dick that big, stretching you out and then filling you up, feels insanely pleasurable. My clit is suddenly pulsing, just thinking about it. Or maybe my body's simply reacting to the sight of Auggie's naked body, in general. It was absolutely stunning. Perfect. Athletic and fit, without being too bulky. Most of my lovers have had dad bods, which is great with me. But I must admit . . . *Damn.*

Stop it, Charlotte. You can't think about boning the man at a time like this! For fuck's sake, there's a fucking *peephole* in your bedroom wall. Now, pull it together!

Okay, I've gotten control of myself now. I'm focused on what matters. The peephole. What should I do about it? Go straight next door now and tell Auggie what I've discovered, or let him finish masturbating first? Based on that opened laptop and the Deadpool mask, I don't think Auggie was getting himself off, privately, all by his lonesome. I suppose he could have been watching porn on that laptop. But then why the mask? That'd be kinky. Or maybe he's over there having video-chat sex with a special someone who's got a thing for Dead-pool? No, neither of those scenarios feels right. The mask doesn't make sense if that was a private, intimate moment. I think the most logical conclusion is that my darling next-door neighbor wishes to hide his identity from whoever's watching him jerk off. Is Auggie jerking off for some kind of online audi-ence? He must be. It's the only thing that makes sense.

I bring my palm to my mouth. Oh my gosh. I think squeaky-clean, veterinarian student Augustus Vaughn has a secret life . . . as an online sex worker/porn star! If I'm right about that, did the former owner of this place catch wind of it, and then drill a hole in the wall to be able to watch Auggie's show, free of charge? Holy shit. This is a mindboggling discovery.

I can't resist. I have to take another quick peek. A teeny-tiny one. If Auggie's putting on a show for a bunch of strangers on the internet, as I strongly suspect, then it doesn't seem like such a horrible, unforgiveable crime to do that. If my eyeballs join a slew of other eyeballs, and only briefly at that, would that *really* be a mortal sin?

I climb the ladder a rung and peer through the hole again, and this time, Auggie, hard as a rock, is grabbing something off the floor next to his bed. When he returns to his prostrate position, he places a three-sided, squared-off, U-shaped metal contraption across his pelvis on either side of his hips. There's a red curtain hanging down from the top bar. As the fabric falls down and hangs, its obscures Auggie's dick from the laptop, the same way curtain contraptions like this one might hide puppets from an audience during a puppet show. Ha! Come to think of it, this entire set-up totally reminds me of a kiddie puppet show—

Oh my god.

I've no sooner had the thought than Auggie's hard cock, wrapped in tin foil, pokes out a gap in the middle of the red curtain. Holy fuck! *Is this an X-rated puppet show?*

Auggie's head is moving like he's talking under his mask, so I strain to hear. But dang it, I can't make out anything but distant, muffled sounds.

All of a sudden, Auggie picks up a stick next to him on the bed and pokes it through the curtain, alongside his foil-covered cock. It's a redhaired, paper princess that's attached to the end of the stick. Which means . . . *Auggie's foil-covered cock must be a knight in shining armor!* Yep, it's definitely a puppet show. A highly X-rated one.

From where the laptop is resting on the bed, I'm deducing the red curtains obscure Auggie's upper torso from his audience's view. But from where *I'm* standing on this stepstool, I can see *everything*. The puppet show itself. Auggie's head and some backstage maneuverings. Also, a few other sticks on the mattress, in addition to the paper princess he's now using, all of them lying in wait for their turn in the show.

All of a sudden, the princess and the knight are joined by a red paper dragon on a stick. Oh no! The dragon is breathing fire—paper flames on a stick! And now, the dragon is dragging the princess away. Whatever will the tin-foil-covered cock-prince do?

Enter a white stallion, which Auggie's cock hops on and rides across the length of the stage to hilarious effect. In fact, I'm laughing so hard, I quickly turn away from the wall for a moment to make sure Auggie can't hear me.

Surely, Auggie's making bank doing this show, because it's *fantastic*. Five big-cock stars, if you ask me. Auggie is gorgeous to look at naked, first of all. Sexy as hell. But on top of that, his show somehow manages to be silly, zany, and fun, in addition to being a sexy smoke show.

The princess is surrounded by flames now.

But never fear, Auggie's massive cock bounds onto the scene to save the day. In short order, the tin-foil-covered knight jumps off his trusty steed and quickly sheds his armor with the help of a rather large hand that breaks the fourth wall and rips the foil away. As the princess remains surrounded by paper flames, that same big hand begins stroking the knight's hard length, up and down, repeatedly, until, finally . . . *success*. White ejaculate spurts out the knight's thick head, causing the paper flames to disappear behind the curtain. Oh my god, that was pure insanity. And so much sexy fun, I can barely keep my balance on this stepstool.

There's a pause in the action. A moment when nothing is happening onstage. From what I can see of Auggie behind the curtain, it looks to me he's collecting himself. But soon, we're back. The paper princess springs to life and presses herself against Auggie's wilting cock, presumably thanking him for "coming" to her rescue. Ha. Pun intended, I'm sure. A moment later, the wilting cock and the paper princess both disappear behind the curtain, replaced by a little sign I can't read from here. Shoot.

Auggie removes the curtain contraption and sits upright. He shoves his mask-covered face into his laptop screen, gesticulating and bobbing his head. Presumably, he's talking enthusiastically. *Oh, how I wish I could hear what he's saying.*

His gesticulating done, Auggie blows kisses at the screen and waves goodbye, and a moment later, he closes his laptop and rips off his mask, confirming, as suspected, the handsome, sweaty, naked man behind the mask, the dude with the shockingly impressive cock, is indeed Augustus Vaughn.

Auggie's hair is askew, thanks to the mask. His face is flushed. He runs a palm down his face, looking a bit forlorn. And then, with a visible sigh, he slides off his bed and saunters out of view—but not before giving me a mouthwatering view of his naked ass. *Damn, boy.*

I'm probably going to hell for watching that long. It was an unthinkable, inexcusable violation of Auggie's privacy to do that, most likely. And yet, as horrible as it was for me to keep watching till the bitter end of the show, I can't honestly feel sorry I did it because that was the most entertaining, hottest, funniest thing I've seen in a long time. Maybe, ever. I didn't even know it was possible to simultaneously laugh and *lust* like that, all at once. But now I know. *Bravo, Auggie Vaughn.* My gorgeous next-door neighbor. A wholesome-looking vet student in his real life . . . and now I know: a secret, kinky penis puppeteer behind closed doors.

I pull away from the peephole, my mind racing, and pace around the room. With a dick and a shtick like that, Auggie's got to be killing it in the online penis puppetry game! Is that a thing out there? If so, I had no idea.

The real question is what "killing it" looks like in the penis puppetry game, in terms of money earned? I know very little about online sex workers and porn stars; but I've heard it's possible to make six figures and more doing kinky stuff online. Is that puppet show the reason Auggie's able to live in a condo near campus, all by himself, even though he's a student? I bet it is.

As I pace around my bedroom and gather my thoughts about this unexpected new information, I'm in danger of wearing an O-shaped loop in the already worn carpet. *What. Should. I. Do?*

I definitely have to tell Auggie about the peephole. That's

the right thing to do. Surely, the former owner used it to spy on him doing his racy shows, and also, possibly, doing who-knows-what else in private, with whatever parade of women Auggie's had in his bed. Auggie's not *my* type, granted, but he's the *world's* type. There's a reason boy bands are huge. I'm sure Auggie's had quite a few eager guests in his bed for Lloyd Graham to covertly watch. The thought makes my blood curdle and my stomach churn. Nobody deserves to have their privacy invaded like that. *Nobody.* Not even someone as annoying as Auggie Vaughn.

Out of nowhere, the devil on my shoulder pokes at me. "Okay, hear me out," she says. "What if you tell Auggie you watched his puppet show . . . and then use that information to get the money you need for Carlo?"

"What?" I mentally shout, thoroughly disgusted. *That'd be blackmail, She-Devil. A truly despicable thing to do. Not to mention, a crime.*

"Yeah, but you've already committed a crime against Mr. DiMarco, haven't you?" my inner She-Devil retorts. "So it wouldn't even be your first crime."

It's not the same thing, and you know it. Committing a crime against a criminal isn't nearly as awful as committing one against an innocent person like Auggie. Also, I'm not a career criminal, for fuck's sake. True, I made a singular mistake, once, but I don't plan to continue the trend. If I used this ill-gotten information against Auggie in any way, even if I promised to pay him back with interest later on, I'm sure I'd inflict untold distress and harm upon the poor guy and he doesn't deserve that, even if I'm right—and I know I am!—and Auggie's the bastard who called that damned tow truck on me.

I plop down onto my air mattress, mulling the situation. Maybe Auggie would be willing to teach me the ropes, so I can make some fast, easy money, like he does? Or even better, maybe he'd let me join *his* show for a while—just until I've resolved my present emergency? The idea makes my heart rate spike, even though I don't have the first clue how I'd finagle that outcome. I bet if I were to join Auggie's show, we could double whatever he's currently making, maybe even triple it, by making my naked, female, body parts part of the plot and/or scenery. I'd attract a whole new audience to his shows, I bet, and a wider audience would translate into even *more* money for both of us to split, right?

Yes. I'm suddenly seeing it all so clearly. The only question is how I should broach the topic with Auggie, since I can't tell him about the nature of my current financial crisis. I'd need to tell him about the peephole. That part is settled. But what should I tell him I witnessed when I looked through it?

I can't admit I watched Auggie's entire puppet show without revealing I was a very bad girl. A Peeping Charlotte. At least, I can't tell him that, right away, before he's learned to like and trust me. Once he knows I'm not nearly as bad a person as he's been led to believe—by me and my horrible actions, to be clear—perhaps he'll then be in the right head-space to hear me out about a joint puppet show. By then, I'm sure I'll have figured out some story to tell him about *why* I need money fast. In fact, I could simply tell him I got laid off and leave it at that.

Okay.

That's my plan.

When I knock on Auggie's door, I won't immediately tell him what I saw through the peephole. I'll tell him I peeked through it when I first discovered it, and he wasn't at home at the time. In fact, I'll knock on Auggie's door tomorrow after-noon—immediately after he comes back home from class, since that'll be a much more believable time to say I found the hole while he was gone.

From there, I'll let Auggie get over the shock for a bit, while also letting him get to know me better—the real me, not the horrible version I've been with him; and when I'm sure Auggie no longer thinks I'm the second coming of Satan, I'll tell him the truth about what I actually saw through the peephole, while taking great care to assure him I'd never, ever, *ever* use that private, confidential information to harm him in any way.

"Your secret's safe with me," I'll tell him. And Auggie will believe me by then because he'll know me better than he does now. He'll actually like me by then. And once that initial phase of my plan is a success, only then will I move on to phase two: springing my joint puppet show idea on him and convincing him it'd make fabulous business sense for us to join forces and make tons of money, together. Yup. That's my plan. *And it's freaking brilliant.*

9
AUGGIE

"A p-peephole?"

My brain feels like it's exploding.

If Charlotte saw me doing one of my puppet shows through her wall—if she knows Superhero Salami Slinger is *me*, she could ruin my life. Torpedo my future career. And why wouldn't she do that? She hates my guts, after all. *Oh, god, I feel sick.*

I knew I shouldn't have called that tow truck! I should have taken the high road, like I usually do in heated situations. But this woman gets under my skin like nobody else and turns me into a maniac. And so, I decided on an impulse to personally send karma her way. But now, it seems like karma's made a U-turn and decided to royally fuck me over, instead. Fuck!

Charlotte is looking at me sympathetically from my doorway with Lucky in her arms. The second I opened my door to her, the dog beelined straight to Charlotte and begged to be picked up. Normally, that shocking turn of events would have enthralled me. Ever since Grandma passed away and Lucky's entire world was shattered, I've wanted nothing more than to help the poor dog find some peace and comfort beyond *me*. But in this moment, as Charlotte's heart-stopping revelation sinks in, I've now got much bigger fish to fry than celebrating a breakthrough with Lucky's anxiety.

"I can only imagine how violated you must be feeling right now," Charlotte says sweetly, her features reflecting deep sympathy. "I'm so sorry to have to tell you about this, Auggie." Say what now? *Charlotte McDougal's sorry*? Well, that's weird. The Charlotte I know doesn't even know that word exists. In fact, the Charlotte I know would be relishing the chance to hit me with this earthquaking news.

I take a deep breath. "W-when, exactly, did you find this p-peephole?" If Charlotte discovered it today while I was at school, then I'll be okay. I'll have managed to dance through the raindrops. If it was yesterday, however, then there's a strong chance I'm totally fucked, because I did no less than *three* puppet shows after I got home from my classes, all in the name of making that fast-approaching deadline.

Charlotte flushes. "I found it today, while you were at school."

They're the exact words I was hoping to hear. But some-how, I'm still on edge. Something about her delivery—her flushed cheeks and tone—felt insincere. Am I being paranoid . . . or smart?

After shifting her weight, Charlotte adds, "When I heard you come home, I came right over to tell you what I'd found while you were out. I knew you'd want to know, immediately."

Something's not right here. *I can feel it.* If I'm right about that, then I can only hope and pray Charlotte saw something fairly innocuous she knows she shouldn't have glimpsed through the peephole—me undressing and putting on workout gear, for instance?—and now, she doesn't want to admit she's seen my naked dong. Did she peek at my big, swinging dick for a bit too long while I was changing clothes? Is *that* the source of the blush in her cheeks? God, I hope so. Because if it turns out Charlotte watched one of my puppet shows—or, worse, took a video of me doing one, in order to blackmail me with it, later—then I'm well and truly fucked. I don't know if the ethics code governing veterinary professionals prohibits the making of online porn, but I don't want to be the test case. Even if what I've done isn't *technically* in violation of the ethics code, I can't even fathom the career-ending embarrassment I'd suffer if this shit comes out.

I'm now on the cusp of a full-blown panic attack. Breathing hard and feeling dizzy. "Can you, uh, show me the peephole, please? I'd like to see it for myself."

"Of course."

I follow Charlotte out my door and through hers next door and discover her place looks totally different than a few days ago. It's empty, for one thing. Also, it smells of cleaning products, rather than like a truck-stop bathroom.

When we reach the bedroom in the back, there's a step-stool, bucket, air mattress, and suitcase in there, and that's it. Charlotte stops and points to the far wall. "It was hidden behind a framed poster for *Rear Window*. So gross. Did he think he was being clever?"

"I haven't seen that one."

"Trust me, it was an Easter egg. A gross one."

"Fucking hell." As I step forward to the wall, Charlotte offers me the step stool. But I don't need it. I'm a full foot taller than her.

I lean forward, and there it is. My bed. Exactly like Charlotte said. Plus, about a half-foot of space on either side of it.

My stomach revolting, I jerk away from the wall. If my gut feeling is right and Charlotte's not telling me the whole truth, then what did she really see through that hole?

"I can only imagine how upset you are," Charlotte says,

wringing her hands. "Who knows what the former owner might have watched you doing. The good news is he's dead and gone now. And along with him, whatever he might have peeped through that hole."

Oh, God.

My heart stops. Not because I'm worried about what the former owner saw *me* doing, but because I'm suddenly remembering my grandma's bed was positioned in the exact same place. From what I've been told, the former owner of Charlotte's place died only a week or so after Grandma did. Which was right *before* I moved in. Which means it's not physically possible that he saw *me* doing anything through that hole. But, unfortunately, it's sure as hell possible he peeped at my beloved *grandmother*.

"My grandma," I choke out. "She lived here before me—she moved in about four years ago."

Charlotte gasps. "The former owner lived here for a really long time, Auggie. For decades."

"*Fuck.*"

"Was your grandmother's bed in the same place as yours?"

I nod slowly, my stomach churning. "I bought a new bed when I moved in, but I put it in the exact same spot as hers."

Charlotte looks genuinely worried now. If she's faking her concern, she's the world's best actress. "Did your grandma live alone? Hopefully, Lloyd didn't see her doing anything all that exciting in there."

I run a palm down my face. "Yeah, she lived alone. She moved in after my grandfather died. I don't think she dated anyone while living here, so at least there's no chance he watched her getting busy with someone."

"Well, that's a relief."

"But even so, I'm sure she got dressed and undressed in perfect view of that peephole." My breathing hitches. "Fuck. What if the pervert took naked photos or videos of my grandma?" I palm my forehead. "Charlotte, I need to go through all the stuff that was here the other day. Right away. I need to look for photos, videos, cameras, digital files, storage devices, thumb drives. Anything that might suggest he was recording my grandmother without her knowledge or consent. And then, I've got to destroy whatever I find and maybe even track down and notify all his victims—anyone who lived here before my grandma and got recorded, too. Who knows when he made that fucking hole, and how many people he might have victimized before my grandma moved in?"

Charlotte's face is pale. Her green eyes, wild. "Tessa's crew boxed everything up and moved it to a nearby storage unit for me. While they were boxing and hauling, I was busy throwing away anything that looked like obvious trash and cleaning, so I didn't get a good look at everything that was here. For what it's worth, though, I don't remember seeing any cameras or devices."

"Yeah, but you weren't looking for that kind of stuff, either. You were busy with your own tasks, right?"

"True."

"For all we know, the pervert—what's his name again?"

"Lloyd Graham."

"For all we know, Lloyd fucking Graham uploaded images of my grandma to a porn site. I can't imagine old ladies getting undressed is at the top of the charts on porn sites, but on the other hand, the world is filled with every imaginable kind of sicko."

"Ain't that the truth."

"I'm not going to be able to sleep at night until I've gone through every box in that storage unit."

Charlotte grimaces. "I'm so sorry, Auggie."

"Why? You did nothing wrong. Thank you for telling me about this."

"I'm just sorry to be the one to break such horrible news."

"I'd much rather know about it and therefore be able to deal with it. I owe my grandmother that much. She was an incredible person. Always helping people out. Always lending a hand. The thought of someone taking advantage of her like this . . ." I shudder as rage courses through me. I've never been a violent person, but if this Lloyd Graham character were still alive, I'd fucking kill him.

"I'll take you to the storage unit now," Charlotte says. "Two pairs of hands and eyes are better than one. We'll go through everything, together, twice as fast."

A wave of relief washes over me. "You'd really do that?"

"Of course. I'll do whatever I can to help." She taps her chin and looks around the bedroom. "Hmm. The only question is where I put the damned key for the storage unit." She rifles through the suitcase on her bedroom floor, and not finding it there, she strides out of the room with Lucky and me following behind. In the kitchen, Charlotte opens every drawer, but the key is nowhere to be found. "Hmm," she says. "I could have sworn I put it in my suitcase or in a kitchen drawer."

I want to scream. But somehow, I keep my voice at a normal volume and tempo as I say, "Retrace your steps. Visualize the last time you had the key in your hand. Watch yourself holding it, and then putting it down."

Charlotte closes her eyes and remains that way for what feels like an eternity. Suddenly, she opens her eyes and shouts, "The windowsill!" She lopes into the adjacent living room and to a windowsill, and that's where she triumphantly holds up a key. "I put it there so I wouldn't forget where I put it!" she says brightly. And even though I'm flooded with anxiety and impatience and dying to get to that fucking storage unit, I can't help chuckling at her adorableness.

"It was a foolproof plan, McDougal," I deadpan.

"Yeah, I'm smart like that." She winks and taps her temple, and then bends down to pick up Lucky who's been begging to be lifted. "Of course, you can come with us, baby. We'd never leave you here by your little lonesome." She kisses his snout. "You're gonna be our lucky charm."

My heart skips a beat. That's what Grandma always called her beloved rescue pup. *Her lucky charm.*

I clear my throat. "Ready to go? I'm feeling pretty antsy over here."

"I just need my purse." Off she goes, before returning a moment later with her purse in hand. But as we walk toward her front door together, Charlotte gasps and stops short. "Whoops! I'm probably gonna need shoes, huh?" Off she goes again, in her bare feet, toward the bedroom with Lucky still in her arms.

When Charlotte doesn't immediately return, I call toward the bedroom, "What's the hold up in there?"

"Sorry! I'm changing clothes! I don't know if the storage unit will be warm and stuffy or if I'll freeze my tits off, so I decided to change into layers, so I'm good, either way!"

"For fuck's sake, McDougal!" I call back. "My poor, deceased grandma might be an unwitting porn star! Hurry the fuck up."

"Sorry! Coming!"

I look at my watch. Shift my weight. And when Charlotte *still* doesn't appear, I shout, "If you don't hurry the fuck up, I'm gonna barf all over your carpet out of sheer anxiety."

Charlotte appears with Lucky in her arms and calmly says, "Barf away, Augustus. I'm replacing this hideous carpet, anyway. Your puke would surely be a decorative improvement."

I'm not sure how or when it happened, but it suddenly feels like we're a team. United against a common enemy, rather than against each other. "Can we *please* go now?" I ask impatiently. "Or do you need to bake a cake first?"

"Oh, cake. God, I love cake. We should pick up a boxed mix on the way back, and I'll make us one."

"*Charlotte!*"

"Sorry. Let's go. Wait. We should bring a water bowl for Lucky and a couple bottles for us. Who knows how long we'll be there and we don't want to get dehydrated." She raises a finger. "Or hungry! I'll pack us some snacks, too."

She's right, of course. About all of it. But that doesn't mean the delay isn't driving me batshit crazy. I tell her so, and Charlotte laughs and apologizes. And suddenly it's abundantly clear the tension of our first interactions is long gone. Somehow, I think we've nonverbally agreed to let bygones be bygones. I can't believe I mistrusted her so deeply before. Clearly, her intentions are pure here. She wants to help me, and I'm grateful for it.

Charlotte re-enters the living room with Lucky hopping along at her feet. She hands me a bag and tells me it's packed with plenty of water and snacks for all. "You'll have to drive," she informs me. "My gas tank is on fumes and I'm broke as fuck, dude."

Three days ago, I was in the same position—low on gas and broke as fuck. But ever since I discovered the amazing allure of penis puppetry, I've got plenty of cash to fill my tank and also buy groceries, too. As long as I keep doing three shows per day, I'm on track to pay half that tuition invoice on time. Twenty grand. Fingers crossed.

I head into my place to grab my car keys, but while I'm there, I get the idea to look at the peephole on my side of the wall. When I get to the bedroom, it's clear enough why my grandmother never noticed it. If you don't know what to look for, you'd never see it because the hole is completely camouflaged in the swirling wallpaper pattern on the bedroom wall. Fuck that Lloyd guy. What an asshole.

When I come back out to the hallway, I tell Charlotte

about what I've discovered on my side of the wall, and she surprises me by linking her arm in mine for our trek to the elevator and purring, "Don't you worry, Auggie. We'll avenge your sweet grandma together. I promise, we'll do whatever it takes to make sure you can sleep at night and your darling, beloved grandma continues to rest in peace."

10

AUGGIE

Charlotte's phone rings and she connects the call.

"Hey, T. I'm good. I'm at the storage unit now, going through boxes. Thank you again for hiring that crew. You're a lifesaver."

Charlotte's standing on the other side of the cramped storage unit from me. For the past hour, she's been going through boxes and stacks of stuff on her side with Lucky at her feet, while I've been sifting through stuff on mine. When we got here, Charlotte and I drew an imaginary line down the center of the room, so we wouldn't duplicate efforts; and, thankfully, so far, neither of us has found anything to indicate the former owner of Charlotte's condo recorded a single illicit image or video through his disgusting hole in the wall.

"How's everything with you, love?" Charlotte asks on her phone call. "Oh, good. Listen, I'm gonna hang up and get back to work. I'm on a roll. But I'll call you later. Love you, too, girlie."

That had to be Tessa. I'm relieved Charlotte didn't mention I'm here with her, so she didn't then have to explain why we came here together. If we find out the former owner of

Charlotte's condo made my poor grandma the second coming of Jenna Jameson, the fewer people who know about that awful secret the better.

As Charlotte stuffs her phone back into her pocket, I finish sifting through my current box. "Nothing in this one, either."

"Awesome. No news is good news."

"Absolutely."

The thaw between Charlotte and me that started happening before we drove down here feels like it's now morphed into a downright friendly flame. When we first got here to the storage unit, Charlotte asked me some questions about my grandma, so I told her my favorite stories about the Late, Great Althea Martin, and Charlotte seemed genuinely interested. After that, Charlotte asked me about vet school, so I told her about that. But now that Tessa's call interrupted that particular topic of conversation, I realize that was a lucky thing—that it's now high time for me to ask Charlotte some questions about herself.

As we continue sifting through our boxes, I ask Charlotte a string of questions and elicit some basic information about her. She was born and raised in LA. Went to Catholic schools with Tessa, from preschool to high school graduation. She loves the weather in LA. The beaches. The sunshine.

"I'm only planning to be in Seattle temporarily," she says. "Long enough to fix up the condo and figure out how to make a profit on it. Hopefully, I'll get a job by then and be able to hire someone else to get the place in shape to sell."

I blush, suddenly remembering the job interview Charlotte didn't make it to the other day, because of me. "What do you do for work?"

"Well, nothing right now. I was a flight attendant for twelve years, but I got laid off."

I wince. "Sorry about your interview the other day."

"It's okay. That was only going to be a temporary side gig,

anyway. Something to bring in some money while I'm looking for a new flight-attendant gig. It's not like it was my dream job or anything."

I'm surprised and relieved she's letting me off the hook about all that, so completely. I ask, "You liked being a flight attendant?"

"So much. It was more than a job to me. It was my identity. I can't wait to get another job in the skies and get back to my old life."

I ask some questions, and Charlotte tells me about her old job and why she loved it so much. She tells me about her favorite perk of the job: free flights. The ability to visit friends and family and travel on a whim. She lists all the places she's been and says she's still dying to see so much more.

"Since getting laid off, I haven't felt like myself at all," she confesses softly, and my heart physically squeezes at the vulnerability she's showing me. "Unfortunately, you met me at my worst, Auggie. I'm sorry I've acted like such a nightmare toward you. I think I've taken out all my stress on you."

Charlotte's apology feels sincere, so it's easy for me to reciprocate. I look up from the box I've been sifting through. "I'm sorry, too. I should have given you the parking spot. That's what I'd normally do in a situation like that. I don't know what got into me. I'm not normally a dick like that."

"You weren't a dick. I was the dick."

"No, I was, too."

"In response to me."

I think she's right about that, so I don't contradict her. And I sure as hell don't admit I was, in fact, the one who called the tow truck. Hell no. That's a secret I'll take to my grave, baby, especially now that we're getting along. Upon reflection, however, there *is* something I'm willing to admit to her now. Something I'm not proud of.

"I think I acted like a petty dickhead to you," I say, "at

least, in part, because my delicate ego admittedly got a bit bruised at Captain's when you flirted with my father, instead of me."

"Understandably."

"That day at Captain's, my father was delivering some bad news to me." I tell her the whole story, and to her credit, Charlotte expresses nothing but compassion and sympathy for my plight, as well as regret for the way things went down between us.

When we finish talking about my father, we both work in silence for a bit. I move a big box to get to another one and discover an old piano hiding behind a stack.

"The pervert played piano," I murmur. I tinkle the keys. "Do you play?"

"Not really. I took basic lessons as a kid, but I forget most of it. My grandma played, though. Really well. I still have her keyboard in a closet. Sometimes, when I'm bored or in need of a break from studying, I'll grab it and make up a silly song to blow off steam. Lucky thinks I'm brilliant."

Charlotte laughs. "I'm impressed you're a songwriter, in addition to everything else you've got going for you."

I blush. "No, I'm not a *songwriter*. What I do is the difference between a doodle and a well-drawn piece of art. In my family, we've always concocted silly songs on the fly. It's our *thing*. My grandma started it with my mother at bedtime, and my mother continued the tradition with my brother and me."

"I'd love to hear one of your silly songs."

"I don't think so. These days, I sing to Lucky and that's about it."

Charlotte waggles her eyebrows. "I have my methods."

I smirk. "I'm sure you do."

Charlotte moves onto a new box. "I've always wished I could play a musical instrument."

"It's never too late. You own a piano now. You might as well learn to play it."

"Nah. I looked it up and I can get four or five hundred bucks for that piano. I'd rather sell it and get the cash, than keep it, just in case I want to take lessons one day."

"If you ever decide to learn, you can borrow my grandma's keyboard any time."

"Thanks."

We share a smile and return to our respective boxes.

"Nothing but documents in this one," Charlotte mutters after a while. She sighs and looks up. "Should I go through these docs and look for anything with your grandma's name on it?"

"Like what?"

Charlotte shrugs. "Maybe Lloyd made a handy-dandy list of all the sick and twisted videos he ever recorded through his dastardly peephole. Or maybe there are bank records showing he received monthly income from a porn site?"

I wince at the thought, even though I don't think it's likely. "Lloyd was a Boomer, right? So he probably wasn't all that tech savvy."

"True. Plus, his place was auctioned off because he died without heirs, so I don't think it's likely he had someone younger coming around to help him with tech stuff."

"If someone did come around, would he have asked them to help him upload illicit naked videos of the sweet old lady next door?"

"Probably not."

"I think, for now, we should probably ignore the docs and keep looking for cameras and other digital devices. In the name of being thorough, though, we can circle back to the documents later, once we're done looking through everything else."

"Good plan, boss," Charlotte says, saluting me. "I'll bring

the box of documents back with me and look through them whenever I need a break from physical labor."

"You don't have to do that. I can look through them."

"I want to do it. You're busy with classes and studying, and I'm an unemployed, nosy bitch."

I laugh. "Thank you. But only if you really don't mind."

"I don't. I'd love to do it. I'd much rather snoop through the remnants of another person's life than doom-scroll through another dating app."

I cringe. "Ugh. Dating apps. So depressing."

"For you, too? I would have thought a hunky hottie like you would get tons of matches."

A hunky hottie? My heart stops at Charlotte's compliment, even though my brain knows "hunky hotties," whatever that means, aren't Charlotte McDougal's cup of tea. She already told me so in no uncertain terms. "You've got me pegged all wrong," I say. "It doesn't matter how many people I match with. In the end, the result is always the same. Wasted time. Not enough chemistry in person to keep pursuing it. Honestly, I don't think I'm in the right headspace to invest a lot of time in getting to know someone. The vet program is intense, and I don't have a lot of free time. The little I have, I'd rather spend with family or friends or on my own, relaxing or hanging out with Lucky."

"If you met the right woman, I bet you'd be happy to make time for her," Charlotte says. She shoots me a flirtatious wink. "Either way, I don't think you're going to have any trouble finding Miss Right, once you're out of school. You're a catch now, even as a student, but once you're a veterinarian, you'll be irresistible catnip to women."

I roll my eyes. "Says the woman who's already made it clear I'm not even close to her flavor of catnip."

"Yeah, but I'm a weirdo with a defective picker. I've always had horrible taste in men. I'm a train wreck, Auggie. Ask Tessa, she'll tell you."

Who is this humble, self-deprecating woman? Whoever she is, she's downright pleasant. A stark one-eighty from the woman who accused me of spilling that coffee on purpose and then feigned a knee injury in order to sabotage my interview.

After beaming a lovely smile at me, Charlotte moves on to a new box. As she works, I watch her for a moment, trying to make sense of this newfound chemistry I'm feeling between us. I'm not completely sure if I trust this version of Charlotte; but even so, I'm nonetheless quite certain I'd fuck her, if given the chance. I can fully accept I'm not Charlotte's usual type. But she did just now say dating apps are trash for her, like they are for me, and that she's not planning to stay in Seattle, long-term. For fuck's sake, we live right next-door to each other. *Mere feet away.* And I don't think I'm imagining our physical chemistry, no matter what she says about me not having a chance with her. So maybe, all things considered, Charlotte would be down for a little no-strings fling with me while she's temporarily living mere feet away? Is that really such a crazy thought?

Charlotte abruptly looks up from the box, making me flinch.

She smiles like she's read my damned mind. "What?"

"What?" I echo.

"*You were staring at me.*"

I open and close my mouth, and finally settle on, "You were looking down."

"A fact you wouldn't know unless you were staring at me."

"Oh."

She laughs. "*Why* were you staring at me, Augustus? Hmm?"

Okay, she's *definitely* flirting with me. "I was just thinking that I appreciate you coming here to help me out. Also, I'm relieved we're getting along better. I hate conflict."

"So do I. This is much better." With a little wink, she returns to her box, so I do the same, even though I'm feeling all kinds of confused and flustered.

Thankfully, about thirty minutes later, we still haven't found a single thing to suggest the prior owner of Charlotte's condo, the pervert known as Lloyd Graham, recorded anything through his dastardly hole in the wall. There are still a few more boxes and stacks to go through, but we're in the home stretch now, and things are looking good.

I open a new box and begin digging through it. Forks. A tattered book. A pair of scissors. A plastic chicken. A bunch of socks. Ziploc bags. *A flip phone.* The old-school kind that doesn't have a camera, thank God.

"This is promising," I say, holding up the antiquated phone. "If this was Lloyd's when he died, it's a good bet he never made the leap to a smartphone."

Charlotte pulls a face. "Unless that's the old phone he tossed into a drawer after finally buying a smartphone."

I tilt my head, weighing that idea. "If we don't find a smartphone after going through everything, then I think we can safely conclude this was his final phone. Agreed?"

"Agreed."

"And if that's the case, then a guy with a flip phone probably didn't have an iPad or other digital recording devices, either."

"Agreed. Also, he's probably not a guy who uploads digital files to porn sites, either."

"Agreed."

We exchange a grin and return to our respective boxes for several minutes.

"Oh, shit, Auggie." When I look, Charlotte is holding up a clunky, metal rectangle—*an old video camera* that's about the size of a loaf of bread. The kind that records videos on a physical cassette.

I shrug. "At least, it's not digital."

Charlotte turns the camera onto its side. "There's a cassette inside it." She pushes a couple buttons, but nothing happens. "It won't open."

"It probably needs to be charged or plugged in to open. Is there a cord in the box?" As Charlotte pokes around to look, I say, "There are services that copy videos from cassette to CD and also turn them into digital files. But what are the odds our pervy Boomer got his shit together enough to make digital copies of his videos, when his place was pure chaos and the only phone we've found was a flip phone?"

Charlotte nods. "The circumstantial evidence is definitely in our favor, I'd say."

"Assuming all this stuff represents the sum total of Lloyd Graham's possessions. Maybe he had a storage unit packed with tons more stuff. Or maybe someone from the auction place looted his place before it was put up for sale."

"The auction site certified nothing had been removed. That was one of the selling points—that there could be a surprise treasure trove of valuables, waiting to be discovered."

"They could have lied, though."

"True. And Lloyd certainly could have had a storage facility, like you said."

"I doubt it, though. The building manager told me the former owner was a total hermit who never came out of his unit. When you go through the docs, do me a favor and look for any bills from a storage facility, okay? Anything to indicate there's another place we need to be searching through."

"You've got it, boss. Oh, fuck." She holds up a bunch of cassettes—the same kind as the one stuck in the camera. "There's a whole bunch of them."

"Any CDs or DVDs?"

Charlotte sifts around. "Nope. Just more cassettes. Some blank ones, too, still in plastic."

I head over to Charlotte's box and take a look around for myself, at which point we discern the used cassettes are all dated by year in scrawled handwriting.

"How can we watch these?" Charlotte asks.

I frown. "I know it needs to be done, but I'm honestly terrified to do it. If this guy recorded my grandma, or anyone else—"

"How about I watch them first and report back to you? Depending on what I find, you can decide then if you want to watch or not."

"You'd do that for me?"

"I told you, I'm a nosy bitch. Truthfully, I can't wait to watch these. I'm dying of curiosity."

"Sicko."

"Guilty as charged." She nudges my arm playfully. "Plus, you're kind of growing on me, kid. I look forward to putting your mind at ease, hopefully."

"Thanks so much, Charlotte. You're kind of growing on me, too, kid." Fuck my life. I feel chemically attracted to this woman at this point. In any other scenario, I'd lean in and kiss her now, since I feel like she's giving me all kinds of green lights. On the other hand, I can't ignore all the times she's told me I'm not her type. Also, I'm still not sure I can trust her as far as I can throw her. So, I lean back and keep my lips to themselves.

"Do you think we'll be able to watch the cassettes on the camera, once it's been plugged in or charged?" Charlotte asks.

"I think so. *If* it can still be charged. For all we know, it's dead-ass broken. It looks pretty old."

"I didn't find a charging cord."

"Damn." I sift through the box and confirm I can't find one, either.

Out of curiosity, I pick up the camera and push a few buttons, the way Charlotte did a few minutes ago. But it won't open for me, either. The cassette is stuck inside it.

"I'm sure we can order a power cord for it, easily enough," I say. I pull out my phone, quickly find the right cord, and order one for express delivery. And when I'm done with that task, I suggest we pull out all the cassettes and line them up by year to see exactly what we're dealing with here.

When we line up the cassettes, we quickly realize some of them are labeled with a female name, in addition to the year. Three different names, in fact, that all appear multiple times throughout the cassette collection: *Mabel, Jeannie, Clara.* Mostly, though, the cassettes are marked with nothing but a scrawled year.

"Looks like Lloyd was a busy guy," I say, my stomach clenching. "Some of these date back to the 80s."

"The most recent date is from over a decade ago," Charlotte says. "Fourteen years ago."

As she's speaking, I open a new box and my stomach thuds into my toes. There's *another* three cassettes in this one—the first dated four years ago—and unfortunately, all three cassettes are identified, along with a year, with the scrawled name of my grandmother.

"Althea," I gasp out, holding up the three cassettes for Charlotte, all with their handwritten labels facing out.

"Fuck," Charlotte says.

Bile is rising in my throat. "Could you watch these for me? I'm sorry to ask, but I don't want to see something I can't unsee."

"Of course. As soon as we get the cord, I'll—"

All of a sudden, Lucky lets out a ferocious little sound that cuts Charlotte off, mid-sentence—a menacing, protective growl, the likes of which I've never heard from the pipsqueak before. What's gotten into him?

Charlotte and I look toward the opened, rolled-up fourth wall of the storage unit, and immediately discover what's spooked the little guy: a big, tall, bearded dude in black who's ambling toward us. I'm not a short man at six-four, but this tattooed mountain of a man makes me feel like a middle schooler. Also, he looks mean. Kind of scary. The sort who probably gets into regular bar brawls for the fun of it or who'd get cast as a hitman in a mob movie.

"*Carlo*," Charlotte murmurs under her breath. "*What's he doing here?*" She sounds distressed to see the man, whoever he is. On an exhale, Charlotte straightens up, smooths her palms down her sweatpants, and mutters, "*Fuck.*"

11

CHARLOTTE

"Hey, sweetheart," Carlo says. "You're looking beautiful, as always."

I'm quaking with nerves. I look past Carlo's broad shoulder, praying he's not here with one of his colleagues. When the coast seems clear, I accept his bear hug with a fake smile. I'm not sure how he tracked me down. He's definitely got a knack for that. Even more importantly, though, *why* did he track me down? When he found me hiding in that hotel room in New York City, he said he'd give me two *months* to pay back all the money—and I've still got a solid five weeks to pull a rabbit out of my hat.

"You found me," I say, trying to sound relaxed and playful. But to my chagrin, my voice comes out stressed and anxious. I add quickly, "Not that I was hiding from you. How are you?"

"Fan-fucking-tastic." Carlo motions behind me in the storage unit. "Who's this?"

Shit. In my panic, I forgot Auggie was here. I turn and find Auggie holding Lucky—with both of them wearing the same wary expression. Yet again, I try to sound light and bright as I say, "Carlo, this is my next-door neighbor, Auggie. We met the other day when I moved into my new place. He's a vet student. That's his dog, Lucky. He's a rescue and who knows what he's been through, because he's terrified of strangers, so don't take it personally when he gives you the stink-eye."

Crap. I'm rambling from nerves. I do that sometimes, especially lately. I need to pull myself together and remain calm. Let Carlo explain what he's doing here. For all I know, he's in Seattle on business and didn't come here specifically to see me —but while he's here, anyway, he decided to track me down to say a simple hello. In this storage unit. Out of nowhere. Shit. Suddenly, more words spew out of me before Carlo has even replied to my prior ones. "Auggie, my new, next-door neighbor here, has been kind enough to help me sort through all of these boxes because some of them are too heavy for me to lift by myself."

Carlo waits a beat, like he's making sure I've finished speaking. Finally, he smiles and says calmly, "Hello, Auggie. Nice to meet you. I'm Carlo, Charlotte's good friend and former boyfriend."

"Hey, Carlo. Nice to meet you."

As the two men shake hands, I ask, "How are Genevieve and the baby?"

"Both great. Thanks for the baby blanket and that cute little stuffed unicorn. Genevieve really appreciated the gesture, Charlotte."

"My pleasure. I'm thrilled for you both." There was a time when I stupidly thought Carlo was husband material—the man who'd most likely father my future babies. But the minute I found out the truth about what he does for a living, that idea went right out the window, along with our relationship. Now, I can't even imagine giving birth to this man's baby and tying myself to him, and his dark world, forevermore.

"I came to give you something," Carlo says, and every cell in my body seizes in panic as he reaches into his suit pocket.

To my relief, though, Carlo pulls out nothing but a small envelope. With a grin, he says, "You're hereby invited to Bella's tenth birthday party."

A tsunami of relief slams into me. I forgot it was Bella's birthday month! Carlo's beloved niece still thinks of me as her Auntie Charlotte, even though Carlo and I broke up two years ago. Even after the breakup, I continued swinging by Bella's house in New Jersey, the one she shares with her mother, Carlo's sister, for regular visits, thanks to my free flights perk. But with that benefit gone, I haven't been back East to see Bella since my layoff. Come to think of it, though, even if I still had unlimited miles, I probably wouldn't use them to visit Bella in New Jersey right now, despite my deep love for that cutie pie. Once a girl's stolen a bag of money from a mob boss, she realizes pretty quickly she'd better not step foot in the mob boss's stomping grounds again, any time soon.

I accept the envelope from Carlo and open it, praying there's no coded message inside, and to my relief, the card inside is exactly what Carlo said: a colorful, bright invitation to his beloved niece's tenth birthday party, to be held at the end of this month at the New Jersey home the birthday girl shares with her widowed mother, Angela, Carlo's sister.

"Don't worry about your travel expenses," Carlo says, when I look up from the invitation. "When I told Mr. DiMarco about your layoff, he insisted on paying for your flights and hotel as one of Bella's birthday gifts."

Shit.

"The big guy knows Bella would be devastated if her Auntie Charlotte didn't show up to celebrate the big 1-0 with her. *Everyone* knows that."

Welp, there's the hidden message I was worried Carlo actually came to deliver. The mention of Mr. DiMarco's name was Carlo's way of reminding me what's at stake. That, combined with Carlo's comment about "everyone" knowing

I'd never miss Bella's birthday party, was obviously Carlo telling me the party is a command appearance for me. Non-negotiable. The only question is whether Carlo's mention of Mr. DiMarco was also his way of letting me know his boss is onto me? Is that the true meaning of his comment, and he's being cryptic, due to Auggie's presence—*or am I being paranoid?*

I squeak out, "Is Mr. DiMarco coming to the birthday party?"

"He wouldn't miss it." Fuck. I should have known. Carlo's sister's dead husband was Mr. DiMarco's nephew. That's how Carlo started working for Mr. DiMarco in the first place fifteen years ago—through close family connections.

"So, here's the thing, sweetheart," Carlo says, leaning his burly back against the opened doorframe. "That thing that needs fixing? You're gonna have to fix it sooner than expected —before the birthday party."

My heart stops. According to the invitation, the party is less than two weeks away.

Carlo continues, "I know that's a much quicker turn-around than we talked about initially, but my hands are tied here, sweetheart."

Why is Carlo talking about this with Auggie standing here? It's so unlike him. He's normally incredibly discreet. "Let's take a walk and talk about this," I choke out. "Auggie doesn't need to be bothered about all this."

"Actually, I'd love to hear about it," Auggie says, stepping forward. He smiles at Carlo. "Whatever's going on, I'm here to help." He turns to look at me, his blue eyes blazing. "*You know that, babe.*"

Babe?

Huh?

What?

"*I knew it!*" Carlo says. "I just wanted Charlotte to tell me herself." He wags a playful finger at me. "You don't need to keep your engagement a secret from me. I know I was a jealous motherfucker when we dated, but I'm married with a baby now. Of course, I'm nothing but thrilled you're engaged. In fact, this news is going to help me out with Genevieve, to be honest. You have no idea—that woman's got a jealous streak even bigger than mine."

"Carlo, he's my next-door neighbor," I insist. "Nothing more." I glare at Auggie. "Tell him the truth, Auggie."

"We got engaged a week ago!" Auggie booms. "Man, it feels good to finally tell somebody that."

"Congratulations!" Carlo says, rushing over to shake Auggie's hand, which prompts Lucky to growl and squirm in the crook of Auggie's arm. "Treat her right, my man, or else," Carlo says to Auggie, clapping his shoulder and glaring playfully.

Auggie chuckles. "I will. Forever and ever."

"Good man."

What the fuck is happening? "Carlo, I swear on all things holy, this man is—"

"She's helping me save face because I haven't bought her a ring yet," Auggie interjects, his palm at the side of his mouth like he's sharing a secret. "When I asked Charlotte to marry me, it was a spur of the moment kind of thing, so I still need to get the ring."

"I asked my wife the same way. Spur of the moment. Didn't make it any less real."

"Exactly. Something just comes over you and you have to seize the moment."

"Amen. Best thing I ever did. No offense, sweetheart."

"None taken. I'm thrilled you're so happy. But I'm not in the same boat as you because—"

"The larger point I'm trying to make here, Carlo," Auggie says, "is that you and Charlotte can talk about *anything* that concerns her in front of me. In fact, I'm requesting you do that, man to man. Charlotte's going to become my wife, and that means, if she's got a problem or something to fix, then I'm going to be the one to help her fix it."

"That's right. That's what any fiancé worth his salt would do."

"And I'm Charlotte's fiancé."

"So I've heard. You love her."

"I do."

"You'd take a bullet for her."

"Yep."

"I'm glad to hear that, Auggie. Good man."

"I try to be." Auggie winks at me. "I keep telling you, babe: you don't need to keep secrets from me. If you've got a problem, then *I've* got a problem. We'll figure it out *together*."

I'm going to faint.

"I couldn't have said it better myself," Carlo says. He turns to me. "Sweetheart, stop glaring at him. He didn't let the cat out of the bag. I already knew about your engagement when I got here. I just wanted to give you the chance to tell me about it, yourself."

"What do you mean you already knew?" I ask.

Carlo chuckles. "I went to your friend's bar yesterday looking for you, and the bouncer told me you'd been there the other day with your new *fiancé*." He motions to Auggie. "If this strapping young buck ain't him, then your *actual* fiancé's not gonna be too happy you're spending quality alone-time in a cramped space with this guy. I'm telling you right now, if I swung that way, I'd be all over this hunk of man like white on rice."

"Thanks, Carlo."

"Look at you! You're a catch."

"Back at you, man."

As both men laugh, I barf a little in my mouth.

"Carlo, I need to talk to you in private," I gasp out. I'm rapidly losing my mind. Devolving into a total freakout.

Auggie chuckles. "It's okay, *babe*. You know I'm not the jealous type—unlike Carlo's wife. *Am I right?*"

Carlo laughs. "As rain. You have no idea."

Auggie returns to me. "So, you don't have to downplay your history with Carlo to me. I don't feel threatened by him—other than the fact that the big guy here could clearly break me like a twig. Haha. So, let's all be friends and talk about this problem of yours that needs fixing . . . *in extreme detail.*"

Oh my god, Auggie's painfully clueless! *Why is he doing this?* Has he had a stroke? Bumped his head? Eaten a magic mushroom?

With a charming smile, Auggie says, "Carlo, in case you have any doubts at all about me being Charlotte's fiancé, let me put them to rest now. The bar you went to yesterday to look for Charlotte? It was Captain's. The downtown location. The name of Charlotte's friend who owns the bar? Tessa. The name of the bouncer you spoke to about Charlotte's fiancé? That would be Brody."

"Yep to all of it."

"Charlotte and I were there on Thursday afternoon, along with my father, to celebrate our engagement."

Carlo flashes me a snarky look. "Now, how would he know any of those details, if he wasn't the fiancé the bouncer told me about, eh?" He returns to Auggie with a lopsided grin. "Not that I ever doubted you, though."

"So, what's up?" Auggie says. "*Tell me everything.*"

Carlo leans against a wall. "Well, in a nutshell, my friend, the situation is this: I know your beautiful, cheery fiancée looks like an angel sent from heaven. And to be fair, she is. But this angel of yours did a very bad thing last month. She made a whopper of a mistake, Auggie, and I'm left trying to clean up the mess."

My heart is exploding. "Can we *please* take a walk, Carlo? *Please*. I don't want to involve Auggie in any of this."

Carlo snickers and nudges Auggie. "That one hates accepting anyone's help, especially from a man. She likes her independence."

"She sure does."

"But this time," Carlo says, "trust me on this, Charlotte needs to accept your help, Auggie. Because if we don't help her fix her mistake, some massive shit could hit the fan for *all* of us."

Auggie looks apprehensive. "What, exactly, did Charlotte do?"

"No, Carlo. *Please*."

"She took a duffel bag full of cash that belonged to my boss after a flight. Right after we'd landed. And then, she compounded that first mistake by sinking all the money into a condo in Seattle, so it was tied up and she couldn't hand it right back to me after I tracked her down."

Auggie looks wary. "How much cash?"

"Sixty grand."

Auggie whistles. "*Holy shit*."

"In my defense," I blurt, "I'd gotten a text from my good friend in HR during the flight, letting me know I was on a list of people getting the axe the next morning. When I picked up that duffel bag, I was freaking out about losing my job. And it wasn't like I planned some elaborate heist. The bag had fallen off a luggage cart between the airplane and the line of SUVs being loaded up by Mr. Di Marco's men. When I grabbed it to bring it over, I noticed what looked like a whole lot of cash through a small hole in the zipper, so, on an impulse, I threw my coat over the bag and high-tailed it out of there. Trust me, I regretted doing it the minute I got into a taxi, but then, once I'd taken it, I didn't know how to give it back without admitting what I'd done in the first place. So then, when I realized

I'd fucked myself, I decided to do what that guy in *Ozark* always does with *his* dirty cash: I bought real estate with it, in order to *launder* it."

Carlo rolls his eyes and mutters, "*Ozark.* Do you see what I'm dealing with here, Auggie? That's like saying 'I learned to fly a 757 by watching the movie, *Airplane!*'" He chuckles and shakes his head. "You really complicated things for me, sweetheart. If only you hadn't tied up the money so fucking fast, I could have said there'd been a mix-up at the airport. I could have said the bag got onto the wrong cart and got put in storage in a sea of other lost luggage."

"I know I fucked up, Carlo. I haven't slept a wink since I picked up that stupid bag. But, *please*, can we not talk about this anymore in front of Auggie? I don't want to involve him."

"It's too late now, sweetheart. He's in it."

"*I'm in it?*" Auggie murmurs.

Carlo runs a hand over his dark beard. "This is still fixable, okay? Put your heads together and figure out a way to come up with the money in time for the party. If you do that, if you bring me the money when you fly in for the party, I can still sell the lost luggage angle. Bring the money in a carry-on, and I'll pick you both up from the airport, transfer the cash into one of our standard duffel bags, and handle the rest from there."

"So, Carlo," Auggie says tightly. "Funny story."

Carlo's dark eyes harden. "Save your breath, Auggie. This is how it works when you've asked a woman to marry you. When you asked Charlotte that all-important question, and she said yes, you put yourself on the hook to love, cherish, and *protect* her, always, no matter what—under *God*. And that includes *you* being on the hook to help her clean up any messes she might have made and take any and every bullet aimed at her."

"*Bullet?*" Auggie blurts, the color draining from his handsome face. "Please, tell me you mean that word as a figure of speech."

Carlo smirks. "Sure."

"Does Mr. DiMarco know what I did?" I choke out. "Is that the reason for the change of plans?"

"He doesn't even suspect you, and we need to keep it that way. Which means you and Captain America here need to come to Bella's birthday party and act like you're both innocent as babies. We all know you'd never miss one of Bella's birthdays. And now that everyone knows you're engaged, it'd be weird if you didn't use the party as the perfect opportunity to introduce your new fiancé around. If you don't come, and bring Auggie with you, the big boss might start wondering why you've stayed away—and that wouldn't be a good thing for any of us, Charlotte."

"What do you mean 'everyone' knows about the engagement?'" I gasp out. "If we never tell anyone—"

"Too late. The cat's out of the bag. Right after the bouncer told me yesterday, I told my sister. And you know how she is."

"*Why the fuck did you tell Angela?*" I shriek.

"No shouting, sweetheart. It's not necessary. We can communicate like adults. I told my sister because she adores you and I knew she'd be as thrilled to hear the news as me. I also told Mr. DiMarco for the same reasons. And Genevieve, too, so she can stop feeling so fucking jealous of you. By now, I have to assume everyone who knows you has heard the news."

"Goddammit," I murmur. "But why does me being engaged change the timeline to pay back the money?

"The change of timeline has nothing to do with that. The change is because there's a young buck on the team—a new guy—who's been looking for a chance to impress the big boss. He keeps sticking his nose where it doesn't belong, trying to play hero. He's got his sights set on finding that money, and then making whoever ran off with it pay for their sins, even though I already told him I'm handling the situation and he should stay in his lane. I've got a hunch it's only a matter of time before he puts two and two together, sweetheart. Asks around. For all we know, someone on the ground crew saw you take that bag. Maybe another flight attendant. One way or another, if he digs deep enough, he might hit pay dirt, so we need to move faster than originally planned. Give me that money when I pick you up from the airport, and I'll handle the rest. Otherwise, this could get bad for all of us."

"For *all* of us?" Auggie echoes lamely, his face still drained of color.

Carlo shrugs. "Charlotte, for obvious reasons. Me, because I looked the other way, and that's a big no-no in my business. And you because, at the end of the day, you're gonna have to be our fall guy, if things turn to shit on us."

"Leave Auggie out of this," I say. "I'm the one who took the money, so I'm the only one who should be punished. Auggie has nothing to do with this."

"Let's not get so dramatic, talking about someone getting *punished*. That's a strong word. I'm pretty sure, if the big guy heard all the facts, including the one about you getting laid off, he'd give Auggie here nothing but the equivalent of a slap on the wrist. Me, on the other hand? I was disloyal. I picked you over my boss, and that was a cardinal sin. In my business, guys like me don't get laid off for fucking up that badly."

Auggie is breathing hard. Like he just ran a hundred-yard dash. "How sure is pretty sure?"

"Huh?"

"You said you're 'pretty sure' I'd get the 'equivalent' of a slap on the wrist."

"Oh. Yeah." Carlo shrugs. "Fifty-fifty?"

Auggie palms his forehead. "*Jesus Christ.*"

Carlo chuckles. "It's gonna be okay, my friend, as long as you both do what I'm telling you. Come to New Jersey for the birthday party and bring the money in a carry-on. Let Mr. DiMarco see Charlotte didn't stay away; let him see her happy, relaxed face, and yours, too, and Mr. DiMarco won't believe the new guy over me, if it comes to that. On a personal note, it'll also help me for Genevieve to see you two together. Like I said, my wife's got a jealous streak a mile wide, so it'll be good for her to see with her own two eyes that you've moved on, especially with a guy who looks like this."

I feel sick. "What if I can't get the money in time for the party? What will happen then?"

"Then you'll come to the party, anyway. In fact, that'd be all the more reason for you to show up—with Auggie—to keep the big guy from suspecting you."

I look around the storage unit, feeling frantic. "I can't do it, Carlo. Call your boss now. I'll confess everything and beg for mercy. I'm the one who took the money. I'm the only one who should suffer the consequences."

Carlo shakes his head. "It's too late for that, sweetheart. I'm on the hook now, and so is he." He points at Auggie. "I'd never let anyone hurt a hair on your head, so if we need a fall guy, I'm sorry to say Auggie's gonna have to be it. Sorry, my friend."

I whimper. "If anything were to happen to Auggie, that'd be worse than something happening to me. Please, leave him out of this."

"Meh. You'll get over it. Broken hearts mend. Hearts with bullet holes in 'em? Not so much."

"*Bullet holes*?" Auggie shouts. "What happened to me getting slapped on the wrist?"

"That's still a good bet," Carlo says with a wink. He laughs at Auggie's forlorn expression. "Everything's gonna be okay, guys. If we work together and follow my plan, to a T, I have full faith we're gonna be able to fix this problem and never look back."

12
AUGGIE

"You dated a fucking hitman for the mob . . . *and now you've sicked the motherfucker on me?*"

I'm saying these shocking words to Charlotte in my parked SUV, while holding up an article on my phone to emphasize my point. The second Carlo drove away from the storage facility, we piled into my car and locked the doors. But rather than turning on the ignition, I quickly searched "DiMarco mob mafia organized crime New York Jersey" on my phone. And, *voila,* one Vincent DiMarco of New Jersey popped right up in an article detailing a slew of federal charges filed against him four years ago—charges for stuff like racketeering, obstruction of justice, and tax evasion. True, those charges didn't wind up sticking; but, regardless, the obvious takeaway from the article is that Vincent DiMarco is almost certainly heavily involved in organized crime, whether the feds can currently prove it or not.

"Okay, in my defense," Charlotte says, when she sees the headline of the article I'm showing her, "I didn't know that stuff about Mr. DiMarco at first. Which means I also didn't know Carlo was a hitman for the mob. When I found out, I immediately broke up with him."

"What the fuck did you think Carlo did for a living?"

"I thought Mr. DiMarco was a wildly successful businessman and Carlo his head bodyguard. Rich people have bodyguards, right? Yes, I figured Carlo, as a bodyguard, probably roughed people up, if they caused trouble. But I had no idea Carlo actively tracked down people on Mr. DiMarco's shit list in order to do god-knows-what to them."

"To *murder* them, Charlotte. I believe that's the word you're looking for. *Murder.*"

"Not necessarily. We don't know that for a fact."

"The man works for a mob boss."

"Allegedly."

"I think it's an unavoidable conclusion, especially when Carlo himself literally said I'd have to take a *bullet* for you, if we can't come up with the money in time."

"That was a figure of speech. And don't forget, he also said you'd almost certainly get nothing but a simple slap on the wrist, even if the shit hits the fan."

"No, he said he was 'pretty sure' I'd get the *equivalent* of a slap on the wrist. Well, what's the *equivalent* in Carlo's world? One broken leg, instead of two? A bullet in my shoulder, instead of my heart? Whatever it means, Carlo also said it's only fifty-fifty a slap on the wrist will be my fate, if we can't come up with the money you stole in time."

"Steal isn't really the right word. I picked it up off the ground after it had fallen off a cart, through no fault of mine. And I don't believe for a minute Carlo would ever let you get hurt, Auggie."

"You're being naïve. He said there's a fifty-percent chance I'll be feeding the fishes."

Charlotte snorts. "You've watched too many mafia movies."

"Says the woman who took money laundering lessons from *Ozark.*"

Charlotte sighs. "I deserve that."

With a roll of my eyes, I pull my car away from the curb, and we drive in silence for a while, both of us lost in our thoughts.

Out of nowhere, Charlotte says, "I feel like I should mention I've never stolen anything in my life before taking that duffel bag. Not even a pack of gum."

"Congratulations." I scoff. "Why were you even on that flight in the first place? By then, you knew what Mr. DiMarco is, right?"

Charlotte audibly shrugs. "Mr. DiMarco always requested me for his chartered flights, even after Carlo and I broke up; so what was I supposed to do—tell the boss man *no*? I'm not stupid. I plastered a smile on my face and worked my ass off for him and his entire entourage. Keep your friends close and your enemies closer, right? Plus, the man's generous. He was always giving the crew Broadway tickets to use during our layover or telling us to grab dinner at such and such restaurant, on him. He was always really sweet like that."

"Yeah, he seems like a real sweetheart."

"To me, he always was. That's what makes what I did even worse. I can only blame it on that text I got from my friend in HR. That's my only defense. I was temporarily insane."

I think about the penis puppetry I've been doing to pay that tuition invoice—something I'd never have imagined myself doing under any circumstances, not in a million years. And the thought makes it possible to relate to what Charlotte is saying.

"How'd you finally find out the truth about Mr. DiMarco?"

"One of my co-workers, another flight attendant, came across an article about those charges against him. I went straight to Carlo with the article and asked him for the truth about his boss and his job, and to his credit, Carlo didn't deny Mr. DiMarco was involved in some shady shit. He also admitted he did some stuff for work he couldn't talk to me about."

"Weren't you afraid breaking up with Carlo would put a target on your back?"

"Nah. Carlo is a sweetheart."

"Who kills people for a living."

"Maybe, maybe not."

"Charlotte."

"Either way, Carlo's not violent in his personal life. He's got a job to do, so he does it. In his personal life, he's actually very sweet. Calm and gentle. Everybody loves Carlo."

"Well, gosh, why'd you break up with him, if he's so fucking wonderful?"

Charlotte flashes me a snarky look. "Wow. Jealous much?"

"No, *appalled* much. You dated a fucking hitman for the mob, Charlotte. And now you've put a target on *my* back. I think I'm entitled to a little outrage and panic here."

"You're the one who put the target on your own back. I tried, desperately, to get it taken *off*, remember?"

I exhale. She's right. I'm such a fucking idiot.

"Speaking of which, why the *fuck* did you tell Carlo we're engaged? What on earth got into you?"

"I was trying to protect you!" I boom. "You were obviously freaking out about Carlo showing up, so I acted on instinct and said something I thought would make him think twice about hurting you. A friend or boyfriend *might* try to protect you, but only to a point. But a *fiancé*? That's a guy who'll do *anything* to protect the woman he loves."

It's all lies, lies, lies, meant to deflect from the real reason I said that stupid, dumb, catastrophically idiotic thing. In actuality, when Charlotte tried to lure Carlo to go somewhere else to talk *outside* of my presence, my Spidey senses started zapping me. Clearly, Charlotte didn't want me hearing about whatever juicy thing needed fixing, and that, in turn, only made me want to hear it all the more.

If my hunch is right and Charlotte truly *has* witnessed my biggest secret through that peephole in her bedroom wall, if she knows my worst, most shameful secret and plans to blackmail me with it, then I figured I'd sure as shit better get some dirt on her, too, in order to protect myself. Obviously, if I'd known Carlo had sprung to life right out of fucking *Goodfellas,* I never would have said what I did. But hindsight is twenty-twenty.

"Well, that was kind of you," Charlotte says, glancing out the passenger window at passing traffic. "Thank you for trying to protect me. That was noble and brave."

My heart pangs. I don't feel good about lying to Charlotte. But on the other hand, I'm in a truly horrific situation now, thanks to her, so I think it's fair. Granted, my own flagrant jackassery threw fuel onto the fire, but Charlotte lit the match.

The bottom line is I still don't completely trust Charlotte. Did she tell me the full truth about what she saw through that peephole? If not, then what is she planning to do with whatever secret information she now knows about me?

I shift my hands on the steering wheel and exhale. "You were noble and brave, too, when it counted most. Like you said, you tried your best to keep me out of it. I'm grateful to you for that, at least."

"A lot of good it did us," she mutters.

She's right. "Yeah, if we don't somehow come up with sixty grand before that fucking birthday party, I'm gonna become fish food. When's the party?"

Charlotte tells me the date, and I practically shit myself. I'm already killing myself to come up with the tuition money I need in the same basic timeframe. How could I possibly make enough, on top of that, to help pay off Charlotte's debt, too?

"I have a confession to make," Charlotte says.

I grip the steering wheel with white knuckles to brace myself. *"There's more?"*

Charlotte takes a deep breath, like she's mustering the courage to jump off a cliff. "I saw your puppet show yesterday, Auggie. I saw the whole thing."

Fuck. This is worst-case scenario. My biggest fear, realized.

"Now, don't freak out, okay?" Charlotte adds quickly. "I thought it was brilliant—sexy, funny, hot. *Amazing.*"

"I had a feeling you lied to me. It was written all over your face."

"Yeah, I'm a terrible liar. Sorry. I didn't want to embarrass you. I told a little white lie to spare your feelings."

"Bullshit. You lied to buy yourself some time to decide what to do with the juicy information. Are you going to blackmail me? Is that your plan for paying off Carlo in time? Because if that's it, you should know, I don't have—"

"Of course, not."

"I don't believe you."

"If I were going to blackmail you, I'd have done it already. Also, I can't very well blackmail you, when you know something much, much worse about me, now can I? Don't you think me dating a hitman and stealing sixty grand from a mob boss is far worse than you doing some funny, silly, harmless online penis puppetry in order to put yourself through veterinary school? Are *you* going to blackmail *me*? Was your accusation against me what the shrinks call *projection,* Mr. Vaughn?"

I scoff. "Why would I blackmail you, when you don't even have fucking gas money?"

Charlotte chuckles. "Yeah, that'd be kind of dumb of you."

"I'm dumb, but I'm not *that* dumb. Besides, even if you had money, blackmail isn't something I'd do to anyone, not even *you*—the most annoying human in the entire universe—a woman who thought stealing money from the fucking mob was a brilliant idea."

"I didn't *think*! That's my whole point! I saw the bag and the cash inside and went into some sort of trance. It was a moment of pure insanity, plain and simple. I had a psychotic break!"

I stop the car at a red light and run my hand down my face. "Do you swear on your love for Tessa you didn't take any videos or photos of my puppet show or anything else through the peephole?"

"I swear on Tessa. It didn't even occur to me to do that. I swear it on Tessa and her children and my mother and brothers. Also, on my father, may he rest in peace."

"Thank you. I believe you." I pause. "Sorry about your father."

"Thank you. Now it's your turn to tell me the truth and swear to it. Did you, or did you not, call that tow truck on me, Augustus Vaughn?"

I can't help chuckling. "Yes, I did."

"I knew it!"

The light turns green, and we're off again. "So what? It doesn't seem like such a crime, now that I know all the crazy shit you've done, McDougal. Stealing money from the mob? Babe, that makes calling a tow truck seem like child's play."

To my surprise, Charlotte laughs with me. "Yeah, I've definitely surprised myself lately. I can't believe I did that. *What was I thinking?*"

"You weren't."

"I'm totally out of control, if you want to know the truth. I don't blame you for calling that tow truck. I deserved that and more." She flashes me a look of genuine remorse. "I'm so sorry I've gotten you involved in my mess. I promise, I'm not going to let anything happen to you, Auggie."

I flap my lips together. "You didn't do it maliciously. And

you got some major help from me. The thing is, I've got my own money crunch—a big, fat tuition invoice that's already past due. As it is, I'm only gonna be able to make enough with my puppet shows to pay half of it in time, so I can negotiate a payment plan for the rest."

"How much is full tuition, and how much do you make per show?"

I tell Charlotte the numbers, and she looks decidedly underwhelmed by my average earnings.

"Shoot," she says. "I thought you had to be making bank. At least four times that amount per show."

"That's actually really good for me. I used to make a fraction of that when all I did was jack off in a superhero mask." I explain what I used to do as Superhero Salami Slinger and that the puppet show is actually a new tactic for me—the big idea I had after my father abruptly retracted his promise to pay for all four years of my schooling.

"Sorry, but it's peanuts, Salami Slinger," Charlotte says. "At least, compared to what some really successful creators make on that site."

"Yeah, *women*. The highest earners are female."

Charlotte waggles her eyebrows. "Funny you should say that. I've done some research, and I think if *I* join your puppet shows, if we add my *female* naked body parts as characters and topography, and we make a push to grow your monthly subscribers list and maybe create a VIP club with special access and perks, we could make ten times what you're making as a solo act." In an enthusiastic ramble, Charlotte elaborates on her idea, and I can't deny she might be onto something. At least, I can't see a downside in giving it a shot, other than, possibly, wasting valuable time.

"We'd have to talk in detail about boundaries," Charlotte continues. "And also meticulously plan every show, so they'd be like a choreographed dance. You know how they have intimacy coordinators on movies?"

"No."

"Oh, well, they do." She bops in her seat. "I'd make cute little props and costumes for our puppet shows. Stuff that would be much more eye-catching and fun than paper drawings and tin foil. No offense."

"I'm deeply offended."

"We'd make it so fun to watch, people would throw money at us—and soon, we'd have enough to solve *both* our financial emergencies!"

I'm dubious, but I don't say so. I'm admittedly terrible at this stuff, and Charlotte seems enthusiastic and confident. Maybe Charlotte peeping at me through that hole in the wall will turn out to be a blessing in disguise?

While I'm still processing everything Charlotte said, we reach our building and I find a parking spot across the street. After turning off my ignition, I turn to Charlotte and say, "Okay, let's try it. Count me in."

Charlotte's pretty face lights up. "*Really?*"

I nod. "With this caveat. We can't afford to give this idea a try for too long without success, only to realize, too late, we needed to try a different strategy. If it's not going really well, after, say, four days of trying, we'll need to pivot and figure out a Plan B."

"Having a Plan B gives you an excuse to fail."

"No, having a Plan B will keep me from becoming fish food."

"Will you stop saying that, please?"

"If we're not on track to meet our end goal after four days, then you're gonna need to get a loan from someone for the full amount, I don't care who you ask—if it's family or Tessa or whoever—but you're gonna have to fix this, somehow, Charlotte, before I'm at risk of getting the 'equivalent' of a slap on the wrist or worse."

Charlotte leans back in her car seat. "That's fair. I can't ask my mom for money. With my dad gone, she's on a fixed income. But I promise I'll bite the *bullet* and ask Tessa, if it comes to that, so *you* don't have to take a *bullet* for *me*." She winks.

I don't know how it's possible, but I'm smiling like a goof at her right now. "Thank you. I appreciate that."

"It's the least I can do. But, please, give our idea at least a few days to get going before I'm forced to tell Tessa what I've done. If I tell her, she'll swoop in and save me, and I don't want to make her do that, unless it's absolutely necessary, okay? But if it is, I promise, I'll do whatever it takes to make sure you're safe. Just give me some time to prove my idea is a winner before making me involve my best friend."

I believe everything Charlotte's said to me, so I nod and say, "Deal."

We shake on it.

We're parked now. Sitting in my car. So I lean my head back and make myself comfortable, since it doesn't seem like either of us is eager to exit the car.

"FYI, I can't miss school this week," I say. "I've got important labs and classes, and then a couple exams. But after that, I'll be on spring break, so we'll have plenty of time to do multiple shows per day then, *if* this idea of yours winds up being a good one."

"Oh, that's great news. What a lucky break." Charlotte bites her lower lip. "Are you hungry? I think we should grab some food and talk about our first batch of shows. Once we have plotlines, we'll pick up supplies to make props and costumes."

"Do you like tacos?"

"Love 'em. I'm from LA, remember?"

"I know the perfect place." I start the car and pull away from the curb, and off we go to my favorite taco place.

"Hey, Auggie?" Charlotte says a few minutes into our drive. "I know this might be a tall order, but I think we should try our best to have fun together. If we're having fun, our audience will, too. As long as we're gonna be naked together, multiple times per day, we might as well enjoy it."

Holy shit. I knew, intellectually, this joint puppet show idea would require joint nudity, but hearing Charlotte say it out loud, so starkly, is sending tingles across my skin. I clear my throat. "Yeah, I think that's a good idea. Let's try to relax and have fun with it."

"Fantastic. It's a bad situation, true; but we might as well make the best of it."

"Agreed."

Charlotte looks out her side of the car. But after a moment, she returns to me. "What did that little sign at the end of your puppet show say? I saw the show where the prince saved the princess from the fire-breathing dragon by jizzing all over the flames. At least, that's how I interpreted what I was seeing, without the benefit of narration."

I laugh. "I can't believe you saw me doing that."

"It was awesome. The whole thing was impressive." She side-eyes me. "Especially the prince."

Whoa. If I wondered if Charlotte was flirting with me earlier, I'm not wondering now. The woman literally just called my dick *impressive.* "Uh, all my puppet shows end the same way. With a sign I pull out that says, 'And they lived happily ever after.'"

She whoops. "I love it! That's how we'll end all our shows, too, even when they're not technically a fairytale. It'll be our catchphrase. An inside joke with the audience."

"Sounds good to me."

Charlotte looks out the window again. She murmurs,

"This is gonna be good. Everything's gonna be okay." She sounds like she's trying to convince herself, more than me, and that kind of worries me. With a loud exhale, Charlotte returns to me and paints a smile on her beautiful face—but the tell-tale fear in her green eyes makes my heart race. "You'll see, Auggie," she says brightly. "At the end of this, everything's gonna be great. We'll pay off your debt and mine and put this behind us. I'm sure of it."

13
AUGGIE

"Get into position, please. I want to set the framing."

I'm speaking to Charlotte. She's sitting on the foot of my bed, fully clothed, watching me set up a tripod and ring light for our imminent first foray into puppetry porn. We've spent the whole afternoon plotting, planning, and prepping. Also, chatting, laughing, and swapping stories through it all.

The tension and resentments between us have vanished now. We're a team. United by our joint cause. The only things I feel around Charlotte at this point are attraction and excitement. I can't believe I'm about to get naked with this sparkling woman and smash my body parts against hers in the name of making money. I'd have preferred to get naked and smash body parts in private, of course; in the name of nothing but mutual, molten lust. But I've become increasingly horny around Charlotte, the more time we've hung out and gotten to know each other, so at this point, I'm grateful for any reason to get to see her without a stitch of clothing on.

At my request, Charlotte scoots her full length onto my bed, at which point I start fiddling with the framing on my phone's camera. Earlier, we agreed to dispense with any kind of curtain contraption for our joint puppet show, and instead let the audience see our full, naked bodies at all times throughout our shenanigans. For one thing, we'd have to make a curtain big enough to fit across both of us, which wouldn't be easy. And for another thing, a curtain would drastically limit our movements. Charlotte thinks, and I agree, that maintaining the look of an actual puppet show isn't nearly as important, in terms of maximizing our earnings, as letting people see every inch of our naked bodies at all times.

"Sex sells," Charlotte told me, when we talked about this earlier. "I loved your puppet show, but I think we should be less focused on getting the plot and technicalities right, and more focused on having fun and giving people hot bodies to look at. We'll explain it up front—that it's like the "Lion King" musical. Have you seen that one?"

"No."

"There are puppeteers dressed in black on-stage, the whole time, holding the puppets. And soon, you don't even remember the people are there. We'll tell them to focus their attention on the prince, or the hills and valleys he's valiantly traversing to save the princess; but even so, we'll fully expect them to stare at your dick and my tits the whole the time."

I was impressed with Charlotte's logic. It was one of many brilliant strategic suggestions on her part. In fact, it didn't take long into our strategy session for me to realize Charlotte's one-hundred-percent the brains behind this operation—that my job here is to shut up, get hard and stay that way, and do as I'm told.

"Okay, the framing looks great," I say, straightening up from the tripod. "Lemme spackle the hole, real quick, so I don't see it midway through the show and wilt." God help me, if I were to glance at the peephole during our show, and then remember that my poor grandma was probably spied on through it, that wouldn't be a good thing for my hard-on.

"While you do that," Charlotte says, "I'll put the props in order, so they're easy to grab off the mattress in the moment."

"Good thinking, boss." I grab the spackle jar and get to work on the wall, while Charlotte organizes the array of silly props we made together this afternoon.

"Have you noticed the hole is precisely placed in the middle of a flower?" Charlotte says behind me, referring to the pattern of the wallpaper. "I can see why your grandmother never noticed it."

"Yeah, I noticed." It's all I'm willing to say. Talking about this is making me feel sick, and that's not a good thing to be feeling when I'm moments away from whipping out my dick and rubbing it across Charlotte's tits and belly, all in the name of The Prince traversing meadows, hills, and valleys, in search of his princess.

The hole filled, I turn around, poised to say something to Charlotte—and stop short when I find her lying seductively on my bed in her bra and panties.

"*Oh.*" We've talked about shooting an enticement video first, fully clothed. A clip where we tease the amazing things to come, but only if you pay for a monthly subscription to our channel. I'm not complaining, though. Charlotte looks incredible. Sexy and curvy. Soft in all the right places. Frankly, I can't remember the last time I've had a woman on my bed I've wanted to fuck as badly as I want to fuck Charlotte McDougal. Over the last few days, this woman's pissed me off like nobody else. Made me laugh that way, too. And today, she's flat-out impressed me with her brilliant mind. If that's not a recipe for a hard dick, then I don't know what is. "You look amazing, Charlotte."

She smiles wickedly. "Thank you. I've decided we should do the enticement video in our underwear, rather than fully clothed. We'll tease them a bit and make them want to see the rest. Cool with you?"

My dick is tingling like crazy at the sight of her. "You're the boss."

Charlotte motions for me to join her state of undress, so I pull off my T-shirt and Charlotte's green eyes blaze with approval. I take a deep breath and remove my pants, revealing that I've now got a straining, aching hard-on behind my briefs. There's no way of hiding it now: *this woman turns me on like fucking crazy.*

Charlotte grins seductively. "Looks like The Prince is good to go."

"So far, so good. But the camera's not on yet. He gets stage fright, sometimes."

"No worries there. I'll help him with that."

My cock jolts. What does she mean by that? We've already talked about boundaries. Per Charlotte's, there will be no mouth kissing, intercourse, or penetration of any kind during our shows. But based on my lack of boundaries, Charlotte could certainly give me a hand job during the show, if The Prince starts to feel shy. That would be allowed and welcomed, from my perspective.

I'm in my briefs now and my dick is straining. I crawl onto the bed next to Charlotte with the remote for the video camera in my hand. As I lie down, I say, "I want you to know, in private, one on one, I've never once had a single problem with my equipment. Especially when—" I stop myself. I was about to say, "especially when I'm *this* attracted to the woman I'm lucky enough to get naked with." I can't say that to Charlotte. Not when we've expressly agreed this is a means to an end—a simple business arrangement. Yes, we've also agreed that while we're doing our shows, we might as well enjoy ourselves. But I think me admitting I'm thrilled, ecstatic, *euphoric* to be getting naked with Charlotte is out of bounds for me to admit.

We're lying nose to nose now. Mere inches apart in nothing but our underwear. The slim corridor of air between our bodies feels super-charged with electricity and arousal. At least, to me. Who knows how Charlotte is feeling toward me. I truly can't tell if she's starting to feel a genuine attraction to me, or if she's making the best of a necessary evil.

"Especially when what?" Charlotte prompts, her eyebrow raised.

"I don't remember."

Charlotte giggles. "Are you nervous, Auggie?"

"A bit. Yeah."

Charlotte runs her fingertips up my arm, making my cock jolt behind my briefs. "Just have fun and stay in the moment. Don't think too much about the plot, or the costumes or props, or getting every detail right. If we're having fun, the audience will, too, and the tips will reflect that."

I nod.

Charlotte runs her fingertip across my abs this time. I've already told her my body is hers to play with, however she wants, so I'm glad she's feeling comfortable enough to touch me. She says, "Besides my stated boundaries, my body is yours to do with as you please. If you get a fun idea in the moment, then run with it. Have fun with it, Auggie. *Go for it.*"

"Okay," I croak out. *My mind is racing. No kissing, either on the mouth or between her legs, and no intercourse or penetration of any kind.* Those were Charlotte's stated boundaries. All of a sudden, I can't think of anything else there is to do with a naked woman, besides those things.

"Are you okay?" she says.

"Yep."

"Are you sure you don't have *any* boundaries?"

"I'm sure. I'm down for anything."

"Oh, that's great." She motions to the pile of props on the bed behind me. "Because I was thinking of shoving one of those sticks up your ass during the show. Cool?"

"What the fuck?"

Charlotte bursts out laughing. "Kidding."

"Don't do that."

"I was kidding, Auggie."

"That's a stated boundary."

"I was kidding."

"Don't mess with me like that. It's hard enough for me to stay hard on-camera. I'm not an exhibitionist by nature."

Charlotte looks down at the bulge in my briefs, which is still at full mast.

"You look pretty hard to me."

"Because I'm lying here with you, practically naked, and there's nobody watching yet."

She touches my cheek. "You're so sweet. You're gonna be just fine, Auggie. I'll take the lead. I've got you."

"I'm actually really good at this sort of thing, behind closed doors," I mutter. "I'm damned good."

"I'm sure you are."

"I don't want you thinking I'm bad at this in real life."

"I don't. I'm sure you're fabulous." Charlotte bites her lip. "To be clear, you're perfectly okay with me touching your naked dick during the show?"

"Mm hmm." It's all I can muster. If I say more, I'll say too much. Sound too eager.

"Awesome. You can do the equivalent to me, too. But only on the outside, okay? I don't want any part of you penetrating any part of me, *on-camera*. I'm not ready to become a full-fledged porn star here. Baby steps, okay? *Outside only*."

We've already talked about her "no penetration" rule, which I fully respect, so I don't know why she's—

Wait.

She doesn't want me penetrating her . . . *on-camera*? Did I imagine the emphasis Charlotte put on that qualifier? Does that mean she'd be okay with parts of me penetrating parts of her . . . *off*-camera, or am I reading into her wording?

I clear my throat. "I've got no aspirations of becoming a full-fledged porn star, myself. I think penis puppetry is going to be the full extent of my porn career."

"I'm so glad we're talking about this in advance. Things could get spicy in the moment, and one thing might lead to another, and I don't want either of us to have to throw on the brakes during the actual show and ruin the sexy, fun vibe for our audience."

One thing might lead to another? How? In what way? We've got our plot. One I'm planning to follow, meticulously. If *Charlotte* chooses to do something, off-plan, I'll be more than happy to follow her lead and veer off-plan, too; but I'm not the one who's going to be leading that charge. And I'm certainly not the one who'll want to throw on any brakes, either, if things happen to get surprisingly spicy.

"Okie dokie," I choke out.

"Great. Let's do the enticement video first." Charlotte hands me one of the Lone Ranger masks we picked up today, and we both slip them on. When I do my solo shows, I wear masks that cover my entire face. But Charlotte thinks the audience will like being able to see at least parts of our facial expressions during the show, so we're giving these less intrusive Lone Ranger masks a whirl.

"Ready?" Charlotte purrs.

"Ready."

I grab my nearby laptop and log into my account, and then press the button to start a video on a timer. After the seconds wind down and the red light goes on, we welcome whoever might be watching, whether now or later, and do our best to entice them to subscribe. When that's done, I turn off the camera and give Charlotte a high-five.

We wait ten minutes to allow for new subscriptions, and then, without further ado, Charlotte says, "Showtime, baby." Without a lick of hesitation, she removes her bra and flings it across my bedroom. And, suddenly, I'm lying on my bed, mere inches from Charlotte McDougal's glorious, naked tits.

"Wow," I breathe. Shit. I didn't meant to say that out loud.

"Thank you. Underwear off on the count of three." She counts down, and we simultaneously rip our bottoms off. And that's it. I'm now lying naked and hard with Charlotte, mere inches away from her.

Charlotte looks down at my straining, naked dick. "Now, *that's* what I call a moneymaker."

I blush. "I'd say the same about you. All of you, though. You're drop-dead gorgeous, Charlotte." I'm physically quaking with adrenaline and arousal. It's insanely erotic to lie naked with a woman I'm deeply attracted to, one I'm dying to fuck, touch, and taste, while knowing I'm not, in fact, going to have sex with her. Maybe that's the very thing—the forbidden fruit aspect of it all—that's turning me on the most. Or maybe it's simply the fact that this woman is the hottest woman I've ever been lucky enough to be naked with in my life. Add to that, she knows my most shameful secret, and I know hers, so there's nothing for either of us to hide, literally or figuratively. It's freeing, honestly, to be this completely myself with someone, especially when she's this fucking hot.

"Give it your all," Charlotte whispers, as our timer ticks down again. "Really go for it."

"I'll do my best."

The red light goes on, and we start with some brief opening remarks. We explain "The Lion King" musical thing. And warn them we've never done this before, so it could totally go off the rails. Charlotte says, "But that's half the fun, right? Not knowing if Superhero Salami Slinger will make it to our planned happily ever after or lose his load prematurely because he can't hang on. I guess we're about to find out."

And off we go.

Charlotte kicks things off with a brief opening narration—a spiel about a lonely prince who lives in a kingdom far, far away. While Charlotte talks, she dresses my cock in the little purple cloak and feathered cap she made for it. But since we only talked about her doing this beforehand, and didn't actually rehearse it, the actual doing of it cracks her up. *Hard.* Her laughter is so infectious, in fact, I'm soon laughing, too.

"Sorry, guys," I say to the camera. "Like she said, this is our first time. We're obviously not pros here." When I pull myself together, I take over the narration, as planned. I talk about the lonely prince's daily walks in the nearby meadow, during which he contemplates his eternal loneliness and horniness. As I talk, I sprinkle little paper flowers onto the meadow—Charlotte's naked belly—and she giggles seductively as the flowers fall on her.

My stage set, I get onto my knees in order to drag the prince across the meadow for his daily walk. But as I bend down to drag my shaft across her, the prince's hat falls off, which makes Charlotte giggle again. Charlotte replaces the hat, and when she does it, her fingertip brushes across my tip.

I shudder at her touch, and her face noticeably lights up. Tentatively, she removes the hat and brushes her fingertip across my tip again. Only this time, her fingertip comes back slick with pre-cum.

"*Oooh,*" she purrs. "The lonely prince is searching so vigorously for his princess, he's starting to *sweat.*" She slides her fingertip into her mouth and sucks my pre-cum away. *And that's it.* I can't even remember the rest of whatever it is we've planned.

With blazing green eyes, Charlotte grips my hard shaft.

"The prince is standing tall," she purrs. "In order to peek over a fence at a fair maiden on the other side of the meadow. He's captivated by her. Mesmerized. One look, and he knows she's the one for him."

None of this is in the script. Or maybe it is, and my brain is scrambled. Either way, I'm rolling with it. "As he walks toward her," I say, as Charlotte begins giving me a legit hand job, "it starts to drizzle in the meadow. Soft little drops, all over." I guide Charlotte down onto her back and begin planting soft kisses onto her belly, and she practically mews with pleasure in response.

Holy shit.

This most definitely wasn't in the script.

Emboldened, I kiss my way up to her tits and kiss her cleavage. And when she runs her hands through my hair and lets out a little moan, I take one of her hard nipples into my mouth. Earlier, Charlotte didn't identify soft kisses to her torso as a prohibited act; and nothing in her body language now is telling me to stop. In fact, the way she's gyrating and cooing, it feels like her body is screaming, *"Go, go, go."* I pause, anyway, making sure I haven't misunderstood. And in that brief pause, Charlotte whispers, *"Yesss."*

Hot damn. I murmur something incoherent about a rainstorm hitting the mountains, and then proceed to lap and suck at her nipples voraciously, causing Charlotte to let out a moan of pleasure that sends a rocket of arousal straight into my dick.

I start kissing my way down her body, toward The Promised Land. That's what I'd normally do next, if we were doing this privately. I'd eat her pussy till she was screaming my name. But since that's not allowed, I change course and kiss her hip bone. The flesh above her pelvic bone. The inside of her thigh.

"Oh my god," Charlotte whispers hoarsely, writhing. "You

can kiss between my legs. Only on the outside." It's a change from what she said before we started. And I'm all for it.

Quaking, I run my fingertips along her slit, up and down, and she shudders with arousal. After a few more strokes, Charlotte abruptly sits up, pushes me back, and straddles me. My eyes go wide, since I'm thinking she's going to slam herself down on my cock and ride me, but, no. That's what this would mean if we were alone and this were real. In this context, however, I've got no idea what's going to happen next.

Breathing hard, Charlotte slides her arms around my neck, presses her forehead against mine, and begins grinding herself against the full length my shaft. Up and down she goes, getting herself off like I'm her own personal dildo.

"The prince is drenched in rain," she grits out in a halting, strained voice. "So he's wiping himself off with a royal towel."

A groan escapes me. Charlotte's pussy is wet as she grinds herself against the length of me. Surely, her clit is swollen and hard as she simulates fucking me, and the thought makes me jerk and jolt with the urge to let go.

I'm not allowed to kiss her mouth, so I sit up and kiss her cheek. Her jawline. Her neck. I nibble her ear. Skim my lips precariously close to hers, without actually touching them.

The effect of all this upon Charlotte is obvious. She's turned on. For real. Like crazy. Unless, of course, she's acting and I'm a total fucking idiot.

"If you stick your fingers inside me, I'll come," she whispers into my ear. "I'm right on the edge. Make me come."

It's another sharp detour from the earlier boundary she set when she was in her right mind—no penetration of any kind —so, I pause. Will she regret it later, if we don't follow the rules she set while sitting at my kitchen table?

"Do it," she grits out. "Do it."

"You're *sure*?"

"I'm sure. Do it now. I'm so close. Do it. *Please*."

Well, fuck. I slide two fingers inside her, and she cries out with pleasure. As I finger fuck her, slowly, I moan along with her. I feel drugged by the insane amounts of lust pumping through my veins. By how wet she's become. She's so fucking wet, my fingers inside her are making sloshing noises as I methodically stroke her G-spot.

As I finger-fuck her, I start kissing everything surrounding her mouth. My fingers are pulling her toward the finish line. I can *feel* her pleasure spiraling.

Suddenly, I'm treated to the best, most delicious sensation in the world: Charlotte's innermost muscles rippling fiercely around my fingers. As she comes, she throws her head back and moans and groans at the top of her lungs.

When the warping around my fingers ceases, I slide my fingers into my mouth and jolt at the sweet taste of her. I'd give anything to fuck her right now. *Anything.* Even more to spread her legs wide and eat her pussy like a starving man. But since I'm not allowed to do either, I stare up at her with hungry eyes, nonverbally begging her to let me break every fucking rule we agreed upon.

"Well, would you look at that," Charlotte says, peeling her blazing eyes off mine in order to look down at my straining cock. "The prince has been searching so long and *hard* for his princess, he's sweating again. Even more than before. Poor guy. Here, Prince, let me wipe the royal sweat off the royal brow for you, sir."

Charlotte slides off me, her green eyes locked with mine. She's clearly enjoying this, far more than I ever would have believed. I'm assuming she's going to wipe the royal brow with her fingertip, like before, but to my surprise, this time, Charlotte gets onto her hands and knees, bends down like a kitten lapping at a bowl of milk, and licks the full length of my cock, from my balls to my tip, with a wide, eager tongue.

"Oh my god," I choke out, gripping the bedspread beneath

me. I didn't see that coming. Is she *trying* to end this show prematurely, before our big finale? Because if she keeps doing that, that's exactly what's going to happen.

Charlotte licks me again. And then again. Until I'm clearly on the verge of a premature release. Suddenly, she jerks up onto her knees next to me, and says to the camera, "The prince sees smoke in the distance! It's the princess, sending him a smoke signal. The prince must traverse hills and valleys to get to her and save her!"

We never even got to the part of the show where the princess gets captured. We've completely skipped that part. But I don't think anyone in our audience cares.

I toss Charlotte roughly onto her back, squeeze some lube into her cleavage, and then run my wet, aching cock across her incredible tits. I grope her as I rub myself against her. Run my hand through her hair. Whisper that she's so fucking hot, I'm losing my goddamned mind. And finally, when I feel like I'm on the bitter edge, I push Charlotte's incredible tits together and jack off my aching cock with them, until I'm losing my load all over her chest.

We'd planned for the prince to find the princess engulfed in a forest fire before this moment. *But I can't wait.* I'm way too turned on.

After coming all over Charlotte's tits, I collapse onto the bed next to her in a sweaty, exhausted heap.

"That was so fucking hot," Charlotte says. "Oh my god." She laughs. "Sorry, guys. That wasn't much of a puppet show. But I bet you don't mind, do you? Make sure you're set up to get a notification every time we go live or post. We're going to be doing *a lot* of these shows in the near future, and you don't want to miss a single one. Say goodbye for now, Salami Slinger."

I'm gasping for breath. But I raise my arm and choke out, "Bye for now."

With a chuckle, Charlotte says, "See you again soon. Tips welcomed and highly appreciated. Bye."

She grabs the remote and shuts off the camera before snuggling up to me. "Holy shit, Auggie! That was one hell of a puppet show!"

I laugh. "That was a puppet show?"

"It was incredible. Should we peek at how much we made during the livestream?"

"Oh, yeah. *That.* Yeah, I suppose we should. Don't forget, we'll make more on the video later. This number will only reflect new monthly subscriptions and tips during the actual livestream."

"I'll keep that in mind."

I navigate to my dashboard and press a couple buttons. And then gasp in shock at dollar amount staring at me. "Holy fucking shit!" I blurt. "You're a genius."

"We did good?"

I look up from my screen, my eyes wide. "Charlotte Fucking McDougal, we just made almost two thousand bucks!"

14

CHARLOTTE

"You were right," Auggie admits. "This is a cinematic masterpiece."

"And you thought I was exaggerating."

"I stand corrected. You actually undersold it."

I'm snuggled up with Auggie and Lucky on Auggie's couch. We're both in sweats while watching the silly horror flick, *Anaconda*. When Auggie and I sat down to relax and enjoy some pizza about an hour ago after our second and final puppet show of the day, we immediately started brainstorming ideas for tomorrow's shows, since it's now clear we're on to something lucrative here. And that's when I had the bright idea to do a parody of the movie currently playing on Auggie's TV, *Anaconda*, starring Auggie's cock as the titular character. But since Auggie has never seen the film, we're watching it to come up with ideas.

As we've watched the silly movie together, our bodies have slowly drifted together and entangled on the couch. At this point, my legs are draped over Auggie's lap like it's the most natural thing in the world, and Auggie's palm is resting comfortably on my thigh. It's crazy how physically at ease we are with each other by now. I guess it speeds up the bonding process when two people get naked and fool around for an online audience, twice, including one person shooting copious amounts of splooge onto the other person's tits both times. Combine that physical stuff with the fact that we know each other's worst secrets and what you get is rapid-fire bonding like nothing I've experienced before. At this point, I feel like I've known this delightful man my whole life, rather than a few short days.

Auggie laughs and points at the craziness on his TV screen: the anaconda is currently swallowing a screaming man whole. "How the hell are we going to pull that off, McDougal?" he asks. "If it were the other way around, if the *researcher* was eating the *anaconda* whole, that'd be a whole lot easier to act out." He snickers. "Not to mention, a whole lot of fun for me."

I giggle. "Our shows don't have to be logical. The audience will go along with whatever stupid thing we do, as long as it's all in good fun. To parody this scene, all I'd have to do is grip your cock and shout: 'Plot twist! *I'm* the Queen Anaconda now, and *this* is the researcher!' and then shove your dick in my mouth and swallow the researcher whole. Easy peasy. I guarantee nobody in the audience will think, 'Hey, that's not how it went in the movie.'"

I've rendered poor Auggie speechless. He's opening and closing his mouth like a fish on a line. Obviously, he thought he was being a saucy man-minx with me—but now he knows: there's nobody who can out-sauce and/or out-minx Charlotte McDougal.

"Uh, yeah, that would definitely work," Auggie finally says stiffly, after pulling himself together.

I bat my eyelashes. "Unless, of course, you're not comfortable with me shoving your dick all the way down my throat, on-camera?" I'm pretending I don't know his answer, just for the fun of it. So far, I've licked Auggie's length during our two shows, but I haven't actually *blown* him. Not properly, anyway. But I have no doubt he'll tell me he's perfectly willing to let me deep-throat him, any ol' time. It's written all over his handsome face.

"Um . . . No, yeah, sure, I'm down for whatever. You're the boss here."

Ha. Poor Auggie. He's trying to sound cool and calm but failing miserably. In fact, the man just abruptly covered the crotch of his sweatpants with his large hands. Hmm, I wonder why Auggie suddenly feels the need to do that?

"Okay, great," I say. "Then that's the plan for our *Anaconda* grand finale. I suggest we do that show down the line a bit, though. I think we should build anticipation before then—let each show get a little bit hotter and sexier. By the time we get to a show where Queen Anaconda swallows your dick-the-researcher whole, I want us to have grown our subscriptions quite a bit from what they are now."

Auggie's face is red. He nods stiffly. "Whatever you say. I'm your lowly minion, Queen Anaconda."

"Since we're not going to be having actual intercourse during any of our shows, we need to hold something back, so we have somewhere to go, later on. We can't do too much, too soon."

Auggie shifts his position slightly on the couch, but he doesn't move his hands from his crotch area. "Sounds good. I'm at your service for whatever you decide to do. You've clearly got a knack for this."

"Thanks. I'm having a blast."

"Me, too." He opens his mouth like he wants to say more, but then closes it. He swallows hard and returns his attention to the movie, so I do the same.

"By the way," I say after a while, splitting the silence. "I was shocked I came, on-camera. I wasn't expecting to do that." I came during both our shows, as a matter of fact. And both times were *scrumptious*.

"No? I'm surprised. I figured . . ."

"It's automatic with me? No. Trust me, no matter how much money is at stake, I wouldn't have come, both times, if I wasn't *genuinely* feeling it with you. You played me like a violin, Auggie Vaughn. You hit the ball out of the park. You were masterful."

Auggie's lit up like a Christmas tree. "There's nothing hotter than watching a woman come. Nothing. And you were incredible to watch. The faces you made? The sounds? Oh my god, Charlotte. No wonder they tipped us so big."

"Well, I'm sure part of their impulse to tip arrived upon watching you splooge all over my tits."

"Yeah, but again that's all about you. They loved it because I splooged all over *your tits*. You're the star here, Charlotte. You're the big draw. *Men* are the ones watching in droves, right?"

"That's what the data tells us."

"And men can watch a dick shooting out cum literally any time they want. All they have to do is look down. What they can't do is watch cum getting sprayed on *tits*? Even better, tits as gorgeous as yours. And even better than all that, they can't watch a woman coming—for *real*—any time they want. Man, seeing that—especially the way *you* do it—is like getting a glimpse of a magical unicorn. A glimpse of heaven."

My heart is racing. It's intensely flattering to hear these compliments and superlatives spoken about me and know, for a fact, he's being perfectly sincere.

"Do you think me coming for real is important," I ask, "or do you think I could get away with faking it, sometimes? With the number of shows we're going to be doing, it could get harder and harder for me to get there, as I get more and more exhausted."

Auggie shifts again on the couch, enough for me to briefly confirm he's still hard behind his sweatpants. Apparently, talking about this stuff isn't as ho-hum for him as he's trying to pretend. He clears his throat. "Um, I mean, I think a real orgasm is always the goal. Ideally. But we could come up with a signal or something if you're not feeling it, so I know to speed things along and help you sell it."

"That sounds good."

"I'm not sure I'll be able to come as much as we need, either. At this rate, we're gonna have to do three shows a day, every day, at least."

I consider that. "Okay, if we get to the point of total physical exhaustion, we'll brainstorm things we can do to tantalize and titillate that won't require either of us to blow a fuse. But for now, we'll stay the course, because, damn, people freaking *loved* those two shows, Auggie."

"Of course, they did. You're incredible, Charlotte. Like sunshine in human form."

My hearts flutters. "Aw, I bet you say that to all the girls you finger-fuck while anonymous strangers watch online."

Auggie laughs. "You caught me. It's true. I do say it to all of them."

As I guffaw with him, I feel a sudden, undeniable desire to lean in and kiss him. Why not? We've already been naked together. Twice. He's made me come. Twice. He's come on my tits. Twice. And now, we're eating pizza, drinking beer and wine, and watching a movie. That sure sounds like a perfect date night to me. And what better way to end a perfect first date than sharing a perfect first kiss?

No, Charlotte.

Bad idea.

It would complicate an already complicated situation. Things are already confusing enough. Also, as a practical matter, we probably shouldn't waste a drop of sexual energy behind closed doors—and I know full well what usually happens when a man kisses me well. Sweep me off my feet with a pitch-perfect kiss, sir, and you're gonna get fucked.

Yeah, the smart move here is definitely for us to keep all our pent-up sexual tension bottled up and only set it free when we're on-camera. Once we've earned enough money to pay Carlo and put this entire mess behind us, then perhaps we can reward ourselves with some delightful kissing and whatever else follows—in private.

Auggie turns away from the movie, having a thought. "Hey, can you usually get yourself off, pretty reliably?"

I snap my fingers. "Like clockwork. I have a magic vibrator that gets me off in two minutes."

"Perfect. We'll keep that vibrator on standby during every show. If you're feeling like it's not going to happen for you, then you'll incorporate the toy into the plotline on the fly, and I'll roll with it."

I sigh with relief. "Great idea."

"And, of course, you should always feel free to use me, any way you want. I'm at your service. Your human dildo."

I giggle. "I'll keep that in mind. I'm not too worried, though. Usually, I can't get there with someone who's extremely good looking. But somehow, normal rules don't apply with you."

He waggles his eyebrows. "You think I'm extremely good looking?"

"You know you are."

"You said I'm not your type."

"You're not."

"But you think I'm extremely good looking."

"Objectively."

Auggie looks at me quizzically.

"Okay, to be fair, from about ages eleven to fourteen, every square inch of my bedroom walls were covered in boy-band posters that looked just like you. So, there was a time when I admit you were the epitome of my type. But over the years, I started gravitating to dating only ugly-hot men."

Auggie chuckles. "Ugly-hot?"

"Men who'd consider me out of their league."

"*I'd* consider you out of my league."

I snort. "Oh, come on."

"It's true."

"You smiled at me at Captain's. Clearly, you thought I was very much in your league."

"I told you. I thought maybe you were someone I used to know. I wouldn't have had the courage to smile at you like that, otherwise."

"You can't be serious."

Auggie shrugs. "I'm shy. It takes me a while to come out of my shell. I'm not the guy who's ever gonna hit on a woman in a bar."

My heart and clit are pounding in equal measure. He's absolutely adorable. And, man, did I have him all wrong. "Who did you think I might have been?"

"Kelly Gessler. My first big crush from summer camp at age fourteen. She starred in all my teenage wet dreams that summer. She was my first real kiss. My first handjob, too. *She was amazing.*"

I laugh. "Did Kelly have red hair and freckles?"

"She sure did. And a big, sparkling personality, just like you, too."

I bat my eyelashes. "Sounds like you've got a type, Mr. Vaughn."

"Oh, I do, Miss McDougal." He slides his big hands across my thigh, causing goosebumps to erupt across my skin. "*And you're it.*"

I glance down and discover Auggie's still sporting a

gigantic boner underneath his sweats. One he's not even trying to hide anymore.

"I really like you," I eke out, my heart hammering against my sternum.

"I really like you, too."

If this were a date, we'd kiss now. No doubt about it. But it's not a date. And I'm not going to kiss him. And then fuck him. And make things even more confusing and exhausting than they already are.

I lean back sharply. "I didn't have my first kiss until age seventeen. Before that, I had to settle for kissing the boy banders on my bedroom walls."

"The truth comes out. I'm everything you've been dreaming about since age eleven." He laughs. He's making a joke. But I must admit, the words ring true.

I swallow hard. "Listen, Auggie, I feel like things could get confusing and messy, if we don't talk about something. I think we should agree to hold off on doing anything physical together, unless we're on-camera. Boners and orgasms are a finite thing, on a daily basis. We can't afford to waste a single one of either."

Auggie covers his crotch with his hand again. But it's too late. I know he's still hard under there. Turned on. Feeling every bit as swept away in this moment as I am.

"Yeah, okay," he says. "I hope you know I wasn't assuming we'd ever—"

"No, I didn't think you were. *I'm* feeling the impulse to kiss *you,* if I'm being honest. But I think that's a bad idea. It'd be confusing. And a waste of sexual energy. Also, I really, really love kissing. When it's good, it's my kryptonite. So if our kissing went well, I don't think it'd end there. In fact, I know it wouldn't. And . . ." Fuck. I'm rambling. Saying way too much.

As I smash my lips together, Auggie leans all the way back onto the couch and spreads his thighs, thereby causing the steel rod of his hard-on to stick straight up behind his sweats toward the ceiling. "Fuck," he mutters. "I'm so fucking turned on by you, Charlotte. I'm going fucking crazy." He rubs his eyes and exhales. "Honestly, this is a special kind torture. Seeing you naked. Fooling around with you during shows. Hanging out like we do. Laughing so much. And yet, I'm not allowed to kiss or fuck or eat you."

I exhale. "I'm sorry."

"Don't be. I'm not saying I'm entitled to do any of that stuff. I'm just telling you that's *all* I want to do. I'm obsessed." He turns his head and grins. "So fucking obsessed, it physically hurts."

My heart is hammering. "I'm right there with you. But we have to be smart, Auggie. We really do."

"I know. There's a lot on the line."

We stare at each other for a long moment, both of us looking mightily disappointed that we're handling this with such maturity.

"We need to keep our eye on the prize," I say, but I'm saying it more for my own sake, than for Auggie's. "When we've got all the money we need, then we can kiss and bang till our heart's content. In fact, let's have ourselves a kiss-and-bang-a-thon for ten days straight, once we've crossed the finish line. But not until then."

He takes a long, deep breath. "Talk about incentive."

"Something to look forward to, for sure."

"Absolutely."

I bite my lower lip. "When and if we get to the bang-a-thon portion of our program, it'd have to be a no-strings-attached sort of thing. I'm still applying for jobs, every day, and my ultimate goal is to unload the condo, as soon as I can."

"Yep. No strings attached. Agreed." He winks. "Fingers crossed we make all the money we need in record speed, so we can get to the bang-a-thon portion of our program, sooner rather than later."

"Also, so we don't get killed or maimed."

"That, too. But mostly so we can get to the bang-a-thon as soon as possible."

We both laugh.

"Hey, you wanna know a secret?" Auggie says softly.

"You're secretly a penis puppeteer to pay your way through school?"

"Another one."

"You've got a massive cock?"

"Another one. You'll never guess, so I'll just tell you." He grins adorably, his blue eyes sparkling. "When you called me an aged-out boy bander that time? You were closer to the mark than you could possibly know."

I gasp and swat his broad shoulder. "*Augustus Vaughn, you were in a boy band?*"

"No, no." He laughs. "Not a real one. A fake one. In middle school."

"*Tell. Me. Everything.*"

"I was in this volunteering club at school. On weekends, we'd do all sorts of different things. Pick up trash. Play with dogs at the pound." He flashes me snarky side-eye. "*Visit old people at nursing homes and put on shows for them.*" When I cackle and squeal, Auggie laughs heartily. "Can you guess what my friends and I did for audiences at old folks homes?"

"*Tell me.*"

"We performed a lip-synching, dancing rendition of our favorite NSYNC song: 'No Strings Attached.'"

I lose it. I leap up and scream. Jump around the room and pull at my hair. But when that bit of hysteria is over, I rush to Auggie's laptop, find the song on YouTube, blare it at top volume, and demand a private performance.

Laughing, Auggie shakes his head. And no matter how

much I beg and plead, how fiercely I try to coax, cajole, and otherwise persuade and convince, Auggie Vaughn refuses to be my own personal boy bander.

"*Boooo*," I yell, flopping back onto the couch. "I had *NSYNC on my tweener walls, for fuck's sake! Don't you realize this would be a tweener dream come true for me?"

"I don't remember the choreography," he insists. "This was, like, seventeen years ago."

"So, make something up on the fly. I won't know the difference."

"I tell you what. When we reach our goal, I'll do a performance for you as a reward."

"Really?"

"Yes."

"Do you promise?"

"What will you give me in return, as *my* reward?"

"A kiss?"

"*Sold.*"

"Well, damn, that was easy."

He shrugs. "I really, *really* want to kiss you."

"Okay, *fine*. You drive a hard bargain: I'll throw in the fuck of your life, too."

He bursts out laughing. "Double-sold."

Auggie holds up his beer to me, so I hold up my wine.

"To reaching our goal in record speed," he says.

"Yes. And to kissing and fucking and making my tweener fantasies come true as our rewards, in addition to not getting killed or maimed."

"Hell yeah to all of it. *Cheers.*"

"Cheers."

We clink glasses, and while we're still sipping our respective drinks, Auggie's phone on the coffee table buzzes. He looks at his screen and tells me the charging cord for the video camera has arrived. Apparently, it downstairs in his mailbox.

"Lucky probably needs to go out, anyway," he says, rising from the couch and stretching. "I'll go get it now and take him out."

"Bring it to me when you come back up," I say. "I'm dying to see if the camera works, once it's plugged in."

"I might walk Lucky around the block. How late will you be up?"

"I'm a night owl. Come by whenever you're back."

We head out of Auggie's place with Lucky hopping at our heels, and while Auggie and Lucky head down the long hallway, I slip through my door. Once inside my condo, I close my door and exhale loudly. *Damn, damn, damn.* Did Auggie have that much big dick energy at Captain's? If he did, and I missed it, then I was blind. I have to assume this crazy situation has brought out something new in him—something unexpected that's exceedingly attractive to me. Otherwise, the fact that I didn't smile back at him at Captain's was proof positive that I'm an epic dumbshit.

I head to my bathroom and do my nighttime routine. When that's done, I grab a glass of water and sit at the folding card table in my living room and wait. When there's a knock at the door, I peek through the peephole to confirm it's him, and when I open the door, I'm shocked to feel my heart fluttering. *Jesus.* I'm fluttering like a teenager being picked up for prom!

"Long time, no see," I joke.

Auggie hands me a padded envelope—the charging cord for the video camera. We stowed the video camera, cassettes, and documents at my place after coming back from the storage facility.

"Let me know if it works," he says. "Hopefully, we got the right one."

"Why don't you come in to see?"

Auggie takes a deep breath like he's bracing himself for something, but, ultimately, he follows me inside. While he waits in the living room, I grab the video camera from my bedroom and come back and plug it in with the new cord. But nothing happens.

"Maybe it needs to charge fully to start working?" I suggest.

"Nah. Once it's plugged in, it should be fully functional." Auggie takes the device from me and monkeys around with it for a bit. But when he's done, he concludes we've got the right kind of cord, but the camera itself must be broken somehow and not able to receive the charge.

"What a bummer," I say. "How are we going to watch all those cassettes?"

"We'll find ourselves a working camera, that's how." Auggie pulls out his phone, runs a couple searches, and finds the exact same model of video camera for a cheap price. "New camera on its way," he says with a wink. "We should have it in less than a week."

"Sorry for the delay. I know you're super stressed about what might be on those cassettes."

Auggie flashes me a crooked smile. "I'm *mildly* stressed about that. I'm *super* stressed about getting the money we need."

"It's funny how a person's priorities can change, huh?"

"Life is funny that way, for sure."

Something passes between us. A nonverbal recognition, perhaps, of how much has changed between us in only a few short days.

"So, what's your schedule tomorrow?" I ask, and Auggie replies that he's got class in the morning, but he's free to do shows with me after that.

"Do you want to bring Lucky here on your way to school tomorrow? There's no reason for him to be left alone while you're gone."

"Really? He'd love that."

"Great. I'd love the company. I'll even take him for a walk."

Auggie thanks me profusely, and we talk about timing. He tells me about a little park, on-campus, where Lucky loves to play ball, and I say I'd be happy to take him there. Auggie says he always grabs coffee and an egg sandwich in the morning when he takes Lucky out first thing, so I give him my breakfast order. And through it all, sexual energy is crackling between us. It's undeniable.

"Well, goodnight, Charlotte. Sleep tight."

"Goodnight, Auggie. You, too."

He heads to my front door. But before opening it, he stops, turns around, and says, "Or, in the words of a certain boy band who lived on the walls of a young Charlotte McDougal's bedroom: *Bye, bye, bye.*"

I lose it. That's the title of a smash-hit *NSYNC song—one with an iconic music video featuring the exact same hand gesture Auggie just performed while saying the titular words —"bye, bye, bye."

"Just a little dangling carrot for you," he says, brimming with swagger.

I laugh. "Like I need *another* dangling carrot? Sir, I assure you, I'm already feeling *deeply* motivated."

Auggie's blue eyes sweep the length of my body. "Good to know the feeling is mutual." He opens my door. "Nighty night, Charlotte." With that, he saunters out of my doorframe with Lucky at his heels and shuts the door behind him, leaving me staring at my closed door in physical awe of the sexual attraction I'm feeling for him. Holy hot damn. I had it all wrong at Captain's. Auggie Vaughn is one hot motherfucker. And if I ever thought otherwise, I was hopelessly distracted, stubborn as a mule, or a goddamned fool.

15

AUGGIE

Three days later

I barrel into my place after practically sprinting the two blocks from campus, throw my backpack onto my couch, and jump into a hot shower. At school today, I could barely concentrate on the lectures and labs, because I couldn't stop daydreaming about Charlotte and the crazy, silly—and ultimately, white-hot—"puppet shows" we've been doing, multiple times per day. But every bit as much as that stuff, I've also been thinking about all the time I've spent with Charlotte, fully clothed and hanging out. Damn, I'm having a blast with that woman.

In between shows, we've settled into a routine of sorts. After our first show, we walk Lucky together—take him to that little park for a game of fetch. While there, we grab food or a smoothie and talk. Unwind. Make each other laugh. And then, head back.

After our second show, we cuddle up on my couch to

watch a show or movie, but always wind up talking again. And after the third and final show, we grab a full meal . . . and talk and cuddle and hang out some more.

Put it all together, along with all the naked fooling around we do during our shows, and all the time I've been spending with Charlotte feels like the best romantic relationship of my life. Except, of course, that's not what it is. And I know that. Somewhere in my brain, anyway.

Aw, fuck. I'm catching feelings for Charlotte and I know it. But how could I not? I've never felt *this* comfortable, this fast, with anyone. And I've also never gotten naked and fooled around this much, on a daily basis, over and over again, with a single girlfriend I've ever had. So in the end, I can't help finding the whole thing extremely confusing.

I get out of the shower, dry off, and trim my facial hair. After that, I pat on some of the new aftershave I had rush-delivered after calling my brother, Max, last night for a recommendation. Before my brother met his wife, he used to be quite the successful lady killer. So, of course, he's the one I called when I decided to try to make myself as alluring to Charlotte as humanly possible in anticipation of today's batch of shows.

Last night, Charlotte said she's planning to introduce a "new element" into today's performances, but she didn't specify *what*. I didn't ask, since she's now our fearless leader in all porny things, and I've learned it's much better for me to simply go along for the ride and not know what's coming. That's how I keep from overthinking, I've discovered. But logic would *suggest* that Charlotte's new element is almost certainly the introduction of full-throttle oral sex into our shows. At least, that's what I'm hoping. I swear, I've never wanted to eat a pussy more in my life—and that's a mighty big statement coming from a guy who's pretty much obsessed with doing it when I'm into someone.

I look at myself in the mirror. This is as good as it gets with me. I'm ready to roll. Or rather, to make some more porn palmed off as puppetry.

With a skip in my step, I head out my door to Charlotte's and knock, and a moment later, there she is—the amazing woman I had the distinct pleasure of playfully slapping across the face with my hard cock yesterday during an "interrogation" scene that quickly went off the rails in the best possible way.

"Hey there, partner," Charlotte says brightly. She widens her door and I follow her inside. Two steps in, I'm met with Lucky greeting me happily. But after only a couple of head scratches, he hops back over to Charlotte and stands at her heels.

"Excuse me?" I say, laughing. "*She's* your favorite now?"

"We've become besties," Charlotte says.

"Clearly." Obviously, Lucky's enjoyed his daily fix of Charlotte as much as I have. I can't say I blame him. She's irresistible.

"I made us turkey sandwiches today," Charlotte says. She's been doing this every day, since I first dropped Lucky off with her. She has lunch ready for us when I get home from school. While we eat, we talk the day's upcoming shows and whatever else.

"Awesome. Thank you."

"I used gouda cheese on both sandwiches," she says. "But I can take yours off, if you don't like that kind."

"No, I love gouda. In fact, to paraphrase the immortal words of the bestselling boy band, ever: 'I want my sandwich that way.'"

Charlotte snort-laughs. If there's one thing I can always count on, it's that Charlotte McDougal is gonna laugh at any and all boy band jokes. They literally never miss with her.

Still giggling, Charlotte hands me my sandwich on a paper

plate and we head to her card table in the living room. Before taking her seat, however, she says, "You smell delicious."

My heart jolts. "Must be my aftershave. I took a quick shower before coming over and put some on."

"It's yummy. Keep wearing it, please." She leans in close and takes a long, sensuous whiff of my neck. "*Yumm-o.* You smell good enough to *eat*." She raises a singular eyebrow, suggestively, and my body electrifies at her implication. Oh yeah, she's *definitely* hinting she's planning to introduce full-blown oral sex into our shows today. To be honest, I'm dying to eat *her*. But if she's thinking the other way around, that's great by me, too. Not only for my own personal enjoyment, but for the sake of the show.

We're making money hand over fist now, and people obviously love everything we do, but I feel like we've done everything there is to do with my cock, short of oral sex and actual sex, over the course of the past eleven shows. It's definitely time for us to level up in order to keep our audience's full attention and the money pouring in.

By now, Charlotte's stroked my hard cock endless times. Licked it like a popsicle too many times to count. She's played my cock like a flute during our Revolutionary-War-themed show, pretended it was a joystick while controlling the robot-version of me, and gripped it like a microphone while belting out an enthusiastic rendition of "I Want It That Way."

For my part, I've dragged my hard cock across every inch of Charlotte's naked body, other than her bullseye, unfortunately—usually, while my dick is clad in some sort of hat and/or costume. That is, until the hat or costume inevitably falls off and makes us both laugh with glee. I've titty-fucked Charlotte, many times, usually until I'm gasping and groaning and ultimately showering her tits, face, or ass with my load. I've slapped her across the face while interrogating her and across her bare ass cheek to "punish" her for being a "bad girl"; I've poked her in the ear with my cock, so it could supposedly whisper its request for the secret code to The Cave of Wonders. And on and on. So, yeah, as much fun as we've had over the past shows finding more and more creative things to do with my hard cock that won't breach Charlotte's currently stated boundaries, I do think the time has finally come—pun intended—to introduce a new sex act of some sort.

"You smell damned good yourself," I reply suggestively. "Good enough to eat, I'd even say." I raise a singular eyebrow, like she did a moment ago, and Charlotte snickers.

"*Patience*," she says, taking a seat at the card table. "The show ideas I've got for today wouldn't include that. Today is going to be all about our beloved prince *finally* getting to thoroughly explore this cave right *here*." She points to her mouth and flickers her tongue. "*The Cave of the Magic Eel*."

I laugh. "Whatever you say, boss. You're our resident porn genius." I should be thrilled Charlotte's planning to blow me today. Three times. That's what she just tacitly confirmed. But I can't help feeling a tad bit disappointed. We've already agreed not to fuck on-camera, and I'm honestly glad about that. But knowing there's my favorite thing in the world still left undone—eating her till she's screaming my name—is slowly driving me mad. I've tasted Charlotte's pussy via the juices slicked onto my fingers, many, many times, so I know she's gonna taste incredible when I finally get to eat a full meal of her. But, man, the anticipation is fucking killing me.

"Today's shows will be as follows," Charlotte says. "Drum roll, please." When I drum lightly on the card table, she says, "The Loch Ness Monster, *Anaconda*, and The Astronaut on Planet Pussy! In that order."

I stop drumming and flash her a thumbs-up. "Awesome. Whatever you think, boss." *Hot diggity damn.* When we brainstormed those particular shows, we said *those* would be the ones that would end in full-throttle fellatio for our grand finale. So now, it's doubly confirmed: I'm gonna get my dick sucked today. Deeply and repeatedly. By the hottest woman alive.

Charlotte chuckles. "What do you think of me calling my mouth 'The Cave of the Magic Eel?' Do you like that?" She sticks out her tongue again, letting me know, as before, her tongue's the aforementioned eel in the title.

"Love it. It's a great idea to have a name that differentiates it from The Cave of Wonders."

"Okay, good. I don't want our audience to misunderstand and think we're finally gonna fuck and then feel let down."

"Good call. As usual, you're a genius."

We've been calling Charlotte's pussy The Cave of Wonders since our second show, and our fans have been *extremely* vocal about their desire to watch The Prince, as he's now generically called, regardless of whatever plotline we happen to be performing, finally getting to "explore," "pillage," "plunder," and/or "pound" The Cave of Wonders.

"When we do The Loch Ness Monster show, will The Prince be wearing a kilt?" I ask. "Will he have a little set of bagpipes to play?"

Charlotte giggles. "Kilt, yes. Bagpipes, no. I could play The Prince like bagpipes, though. What do you think of that idea?"

"Love it."

She laughs. "I've been working on the funniest costumes and props all day. You're gonna die when you see them."

I crack up with her. "I think you've found your calling, McDougal."

"I think you might be right." She takes a bite of her sandwich, and her green eyes sparkle at me as she chews her food. She lays her elbow on the table. "How was your day?"

"Good. Same stuff as usual. I did land an interview for an internship, though."

"That's fantastic! Is it a good place?"

"Pretty good. They don't have a full-blown *pro bono* program, like that other place. But the vets who work there are top-notch, so I'd learn a lot by watching them and working alongside them."

Charlotte expresses excitement and asks several questions, and we talk about the topic a bit longer, before I turn the tables and ask about her day.

"It was good. I walked Lucky. Sanded the cabinets in the kitchen. Talked to Tessa. Made costumes and props."

"Sounds like a good day to me. Any news in the job search?"

Charlotte flaps her lips together. "No. The only replies I've gotten so far have been standardized emails saying thanks but no thanks. I thought with twelve years of experience and glowing recommendations, I'd at least have a few interviews by now."

"Chin up, babe."

My heart stops.

Babe?

I've never called Charlotte that before, other than when I was pretending to be her fiancé in front of Carlo. All I can hope is that it came off flirty and casual, rather than what it really was—an involuntarily slip-up that betrays my ever-growing feelings for her. My increasing confusion about this situation —about what's real and what's not. What's business and what's personal. If I'm being honest, this thing with Charlotte now feels all-too real to me. Yes, I know she's not planning on living in Seattle for long and I'm stuck here for at least the next two years of school, so even fantasizing about Charlotte becoming my actual girlfriend after all this is over is probably the height of idiocy, delusion, and naiveté. But I can't help fantasizing about it, nonetheless. *Constantly.*

I clear my throat and quickly add, "I'd bet anything your dream job is right around the corner, babe." I feel like, the more I say it, the less it will sound like a slip of the tongue and more like a casual, playful nothing-burger. "Think about it, babe. Something can be two inches away from your face, but you can't see it yet because it's right around a corner. Babe."

Charlotte practically chokes on her sandwich, as laughter bursts out of her.

"What?" My heart is exploding. Does she know what I'm feeling for her? Have I given myself away?

Charlotte flashes me a snarky look. "You don't need to tell me something can be right around a corner, honey. I'm well aware of that—also, unfortunately, that said *thing* can come barreling around said corner and smack right into me."

I crack up with her. "Oh, man. I walked right into that one."

She's still laughing. "Yes, you did. Please, promise me I won't be holding hot coffee and wearing all white when my dream job comes barreling around that corner for me."

I chuckle. "Don't worry. I'm sure your dream job will be far more careful than me and actually look around a blind corner before rounding it."

"One can only hope."

As we laugh together, I find myself marveling that I ever called that tow truck on Charlotte that day. Why wasn't my instinct to simply help her out? She was obviously frantic and frazzled. So, why did I escalate our feud, rather than lending a helping hand? It was so unlike me.

"I hope you know I didn't crash into you and spill that coffee all over you on purpose," I say. "Yeah, I called the tow truck on you, but the rest was just me being in a hurry and not looking where I was going around a blind corner."

"Of course, I know that, Auggie. Now that I know you so well, I know you don't have a mean or vengeful bone in your gorgeous body."

Gorgeous body? "Well, that's not true, since I called the tow truck."

"You had every right to do that. If I'd been in your shoes, I would have called it, too, and I wouldn't be apologizing for it now or ever."

My heart his thundering. *What's going on here?* The energy coursing between us in this moment feels intoxicating. Addictive. In any other scenario, I'd lean in and kiss Charlotte right now. No doubt about it.

A huge, beaming smile splits Charlotte's pretty face. "It's crazy how things have worked out, huh?"

I'm buzzing. Is it too much to hope that Charlotte might be catching real feelings for me, despite that thing she said several days ago about anything between us being no strings attached?

"Yeah, it's pretty crazy," I manage to say. "That's life for you. It can be unpredictable."

"Ain't that the truth." With an exhale, she lays her napkin over her empty paper plate. "So, are you ready to do a show now, partner? Is Nessie ready to explore the depths of The Cave of the Magic Eel for the first time?"

Partner. Charlotte's taken to calling me that lately, and I can't help thinking it's her way of reminding me what this is. *And what it's not.*

"Yep," I report. "Nessie the Monster is ready to rise to the occasion. Let's do it."

16

CHARLOTTE

I'm lying naked across the width of Auggie's bed, in profile to the tripod, while Auggie kneels beside me facing the camera, a vibrator in his hand and his straining cock in full view of our rabid audience.

As he slowly lowers the vibe toward my naked body, Auggie says, loud enough for our audience to hear, "As the astronaut lowers the exploratory shuttle down, down, down toward the glorious topography of Pussy Planet, his heart and cock are pounding with excitement. He can't wait to find out if the rumors are true—if there's actually a beautiful creature— a siren—inhabiting this strange, new world."

It's our third show of the day, and we're both exhausted. But after the astonishing success of our first two shows—"The Loch Ness Monster" and "Anaconda"—nothing could stop us now from putting on this third show today, not even physical exhaustion.

We suspected our ever-increasing audience of monthly subscribers would get off on watching me giving Auggie a blowjob for the first time, which I did during our first show today, "Loch Ness," and then repeated during "Anaconda," both times to roaring success. And by "roaring," I'm referring not only to the audience's enthusiastic reaction, but also to the sounds Auggie made, both times, when he finally unleashed down my throat. Damn. The man reached a state of rapture, both times. As a matter of fact, Auggie admitted to me afterwards, both times, he'd completely forgotten about the camera.

But even though we knew our audience would enjoy the introduction of fellatio to our shows, we never in a million years could have predicted the *tsunami* of tips and comments those two shows garnered, compared to everything else. Auggie said the audience loved it so much because *I* came so hard immediately after *he* did. Watching him get off so hard got me so damned wet and horny, it took no time at all for Auggie to finger me to powerful orgasms during both shows. But I told him we'd have to agree to disagree. To me, the hottest part of both shows was the way Auggie let loose like never before. He was out of his head. Totally in the moment and not performing whatsoever. I'm sure, paradoxically, our audience could feel that and they rewarded him for it.

Auggie hovers the vibrator about an inch over my clit. This is the first time we're using my vibe in a show. After the intense orgasms I've had today, I told Auggie I might be too wiped out to get there a third time, without a little help from my battery-operated boyfriend. And so, we modified the script and turned my vibe into a prop.

"Landing gear engaged," Auggie says in his clipped astronaut voice. "Thrusters set to low." He flips a switch on the vibe and a soft buzzing noise fills the bedroom. It's a sound I know well, and the nerve endings between my legs suddenly tingle in anticipation, like Pavlov's dogs hearing the dinner bell.

"Landing pad tingling," I purr. I tilt my pelvis up toward

the buzzing device in Auggie's hand, making it clear I'm excited for its landing, but Auggie lifts the vibe slightly, denying me. Teasing me. Making it clear *he's* in charge of my pleasure this time. I fucking love it when he does this, and I'm sure the audience does, too.

"After a lifetime of fantasizing about this moment," Auggie says, "the astronaut is finally going to become the first man, ever, to touch ground on the *virgin* soil of Planet Pussy."

That's my cue. *Virgin.* We improvise a lot during our shows by now. But we do still plan for certain trigger words and cues, so we don't forget to include important plot points or funny lines.

With a snarky look on my face, I turn my head toward the camera and deadpan, "I can practically hear all of your eyerolls and snickers, people. May I remind you this is *fiction?* It's called *acting,* for fuck's sake." I return to Auggie and bat my eyelashes. "Sorry about that, Mr. Astronaut. Please, continue. *Virgin* soil. First man, ever. Let's go. I'm horny as fuck."

Auggie cracks up, even though he knew that's what I was going to say in this moment. The gist of it, anyway. Apparently, my delivery was funnier than Auggie anticipated. As he chuckles, his massive hard-on bobs and sways. His stunning abs contract and clench and his smile lights up the entire room. Even from behind his Lone Ranger mask, Auggie's blue eyes are twinkling like sapphires. It's my favorite thing, watching Auggie Vaughn enjoying himself, whether he's doing it during a show or when we're walking Lucky or snuggled up on his couch.

I turn to look at the camera again, even though we didn't plan for me to do it twice. "Do you see what I have to deal with here? The man's funny bone is even bigger than his boner. *And that's saying a lot.*" I return to Auggie to find him cracking up again. Even more enthusiastically. "Seriously?" I say, even though I absolutely love it. "Pull yourself together, Salami. You've got a wet and aching Pussy Planet to explore."

God, I love Auggie's laugh. He never fakes it. Ever. Which only makes it all the more adorable and satisfying when he loses it. Frankly, the fact that Auggie can't get through a show without busting up, at least once and usually more, is one of our secret weapons. Our audience's comments make it clear they love it when Salami Slinger breaks and can't keep going, every bit as much as they love it when Salami Slinger makes me come so hard, my eyes tear up.

"Okay, back to our expedition," Auggie says, wiping his eyes. "Sorry about that, guys." He returns the vibe to its former spot, hovering above my clit. "Landing gear engaged. Thrusters set to low. Clitoris Peak locked in as my precise landing spot."

He begins lowering the device, but suddenly jerks it up a couple inches before making contact with my flesh. "Houston, we have a problem. Sensors are picking up potential radioactivity in the topography surrounding Clitoris Peak. We'll need to gather soil samples for safety check before landing the shuttle. Stand by."

Auggie places the vibrator next to my naked hip on the bed, leans over, and begins planting soft kisses and swirls of his tongue over my lower torso—my belly, hips, and pelvis. When he works his way up to my breasts, he laps his tongue over my hard nipple while brushing his fingertips teasingly across my pelvic bone. When his fingers begin stroking the folds between my legs, his mouth becomes more voracious. He's now enthusiastically kissing, licking, and nibbling on my neck and jawline, and his formerly stroking fingers are now dipping in and out of me.

Holy shit. I didn't think it was possible for me to get this aroused *again* today, given how exhausted I am and the intensity of my two prior orgasms; but Auggie's somehow figured out a way to get me ramped up to full-throttle, yet again.

As Auggie's fingers continue penetrating me, and my pleasure continues rising higher and higher, I moan and writhe and shudder. When we started this project, we didn't foresee our shows devolving into straight-up porn the way they have. But now that we're here, and making so much damned money doing it, I can't deny I thoroughly enjoy it. As it turns out, I get off on being watched. It turns me on to know there are people jacking off while we're getting off, too.

Auggie begins dragging his fingers across my G-spot, just the way I like it. When my moans intensify, he chokes out, "The planet is now confirmed habitable. Wet and warm. So fucking wet." He slides his hand out of me and two fingers into his mouth. "It's sweet, too. Fucking delicious. *Narcotic*." He's panting. "The astronaut would rather die than leave Pussy Planet without landing his craft. He's touching down now, no matter what happens next. If he dies, it was fucking worth it."

That wasn't scripted. But, fuck, it was hot.

There's pre-cum beaded on Auggie's tip by now. Clearly, he's every bit as turned on as I am. I grab his hard cock to get his full attention. I know that look of impending intoxication on his face; if I don't remind him what comes next, he's going to forget every damned thing he's supposed to do.

"Ask mission control for their help now," I gasp out, while my hand strokes his shaft up and down.

"Oh. Yeah." Auggie looks at the camera, his eyelids at half-mast. I'm losing him. He's drunk on lust. Turned on like crazy. "I-I need your help. Is it safe to land directly on Clitoris P-Peak, or should I land the craft in a nearby meadow?" He motions to my belly, the meadow. "We need your instructions *now*, Mission Control." He pushes a button on his laptop, and the poll we've pre-loaded for this precise moment pops onto the screen.

We already know our audience will instruct Auggie to land the spacecraft on my clit, and not on my belly. *Duh.* But when it costs $10 to vote in our poll, and people can vote an unlimited number of times, we try to include at least a couple "choose your own adventure" moments in all our shows. People love to have a say in their porn, it turns out; so, we're happy to oblige them, especially when the result of every poll is precisely what we've planned for, anyway.

While we supposedly await the result of our latest poll, Auggie continues doing amazing things to me, until I'm so turned on and wet, my eyes are practically rolling back into my head. When I groan loudly and arch my back, Auggie leans down, presses his mouth against my ear, and hoarsely whispers, "When we reach the finish line of all this, I'm gonna fuck you so hard and deep, you're gonna gag on my cock coming *up* your throat."

An orgasm throttles me—one that makes me scream and burst into tears of euphoria. As my innermost muscles clench and unclench fiercely around Auggie's hand, he groans so loudly, I'm sure every neighbor on the third floor of our building can hear him. His body quaking with lust, Auggie throws the vibe down, straddles me, and grits out, "Open your fucking mouth."

Whoa. He's going to fuck my face? I didn't see that coming. We didn't talk about doing it this way. *But I'm all for it.*

Without hesitation, I do as I'm told. Not for the camera. Not for the money. But because, in this moment, I want nothing more than to get fucked, the only way that's currently allowed, by Auggie's massive cock. I've actually never performed this sex act, not like this, with anyone else. So, when Auggie grips my hair and thrusts his cock in and out of my mouth, and up and down my throat, I'm shocked at how much I love it. How much it's getting me off. Good lord, this is wild. Animalistic. *And so fucking hot.*

As my pleasure ramps up along with Auggie's, I claw at his smooth, bare ass. I'm his sex toy in this moment, and he's completely in charge.

When it sounds like Auggie's getting extremely close to losing his load, I pat around the mattress, find the vibrator, and turn it on high. I bring the buzzing device to my clit and instantly feel like I'm being electrocuted with pleasure. My toes curl. My heart thunders. And all the while, Auggie Vaughn continues using my body like he doesn't give a shit about me. *Delicious.*

When my orgasm comes this time, I let out a strangled cry that's so loud, even when muffled by Auggie's cock, I'm pretty sure every floor of our building is getting an earful this time.

That's it for Auggie. He can't hang on. When he comes this time, it's so far down my throat, it feels like he's spraying my internal organs.

Wait. What's that? As I'm taking Auggie's release down my throat, I feel the sensation of warmth squirting against my inner thighs. Am I pissing myself? As Auggie pulls out of me, I touch the affected area, feeling confused and disoriented.

When my movement attracts Auggie's attention, he turns and swipes his fingers across my thigh. "You squirted," he announces. "Fuck, yeah, baby."

Breathing hard, he maneuvers until he's between my legs —and once there, the man licks my inner thighs voraciously. When he's done, he lifts his head and, his blue eyes blazing, says, "Best thing I've ever tasted in my whole fucking life."

"I've never done that before," I gasp out. "Oh my god, Au —" I stop myself, thankfully, before blurting his name. For a second there, I forgot about the show. The audience. The camera. "Awwwwww-woo," I say to cover for my near-disaster. "That felt incredible. Awww—*woo*." I turn to look at the camera. "If you don't tip the shit out of our jar to celebrate my first squirter, ever, I'll never forgive you. Especially our VIPs.

Catfish2000? JunkyInMyTrunky37? I'm talking to you and anyone else who wants to join our VIP club to see all our amazing extras. Tip us a hundred bucks now and we'll give you VIP access for a full week."

"Sign us off, baby," Auggie says.

I grin at the camera. *"And they lived happily ever after."*

With a chuckle, Auggie grabs the remote and turns off the camera, like usual. But then, he does something that's *not* usual—something he's never done before. Usually, we look at our numbers right away. This time, however, Auggie levels me with burning blue eyes and says, "If I don't lick up the rest of that cum and eat your pussy till you come again, I might literally die."

We've never fooled around off-camera before. Never even kissed. So, crossing this line now, for the first time, is a big deal. Quite possibly, a slippery slope, too. But right now, I'm not thinking with my head. I don't care about my boundaries or rules or saving all our sexual energy and chemistry for shows. It's now clear we've got *endless* sexual chemistry. It's a waterfall that will never run out or trickle off, no matter how much we mess around. We're mutually addicted. Can't get enough. And right now, there's nothing I want more than to finally feel Auggie Vaughn's mouth on my most sensitive flesh.

"Yes."

Without hesitation, Auggie spreads opens my thighs and dives in. As he licks and laps and laves, he slides his fingers inside me and strokes and finger-fucks and coaxes in a rhythm that matches the movements of his voracious mouth. It's the best oral I've ever received, by a long mile. And soon, I'm barreling toward yet another release. This one, privately, for my pleasure and Auggie's and nobody else's.

I grip Auggie's sweaty hair as he eats me hungrily. Noisily. Like he's a junkie getting his fix. Until soon, I'm on the bitter brink of the abyss. Holding on for dear life while simultaneously aching to let go and jump. Finally, I let out a long, tortured groan as my arousal shreds my nerve endings and spirals higher and higher. And a second later, my eyes roll back into my head while sheer bliss obliterates me.

I scream Auggie's name, along with several curse words, and buck and jolt on the bed like a flopping fish. When my orgasm finally ends, Auggie raises his head, panting. His chin and lips are slick with my arousal. After taking a deep breath, he shoots me a wicked, exhausted grin, and says, "Carlo can kill me now. I'm okay with that."

We both burst into laughter.

"Well, I'm *not* okay with that, so . . . *no*."

Auggie flops onto his back next to me, grinning from ear-to-ear. "That was even hotter than my hottest fantasies about me doing that to you."

I smile. "You've *fantasized* about eating me out?"

"Oh, God, Charlotte. You have no idea."

I giggle. "And here I thought I wouldn't be able to come again during our third show, let alone again afterward. I've never had this many orgasms in my life. I'm usually a one-and-done kind of girl, if I'm lucky."

"What can I say. We've got nuclear chemistry." He's right. Our chemistry is *supernatural*, I'd even say—the kind people would kill to experience, if only once.

We've never cuddled after a show before. Normally, we're too busy looking at numbers to do something like that. We usually save our cuddling for later, for when we're hanging out on Auggie's couch. But this time, without either of us saying a word, that's what happens next. I lay my cheek on Auggie's bare chest, and he pulls me to him and strokes my hair. And that's how we remain, silently, for several minutes, until Auggie speaks first.

"I can't wait to kiss you," he whispers. I can hear his heart thundering against my ear.

I'm surprised. When he started that sentence, I thought he was going to finish "I can't wait to . . ." with the words "fuck you." But the fact that he's ended it in such a wholesome way, after everything we've done together, honestly makes my heart go pitter-pat. After only a few pitter-pats, however, anxiety suddenly flickers through me. Are we both starting to feel things that could fuck up my plans and goals? We agreed anything we do off-camera would be no strings attached. And I've told him I want nothing more than to get a new job and get back to my old life. Well, the truth is my feelings on those things haven't changed, despite the fun we've been having. Even when Auggie makes my *heart* go pitter-pat, my *brain* always knows we're in a bubble together. One that's admittedly amazing and perfect while we're in it; but it's plainly situational and won't last when the situation is over.

"It's okay," Auggie says, before I've figured out how to respond to his lovely comment. "I know you've got big plans, Charlotte. I know this is no strings. Don't worry; my brain fully understands the situation."

Aw, poor Auggie. The subtext of his comment was clear enough: his *brain* fully understands, even though his heart is experiencing some measure of confusion.

I clear my throat and pat his bare chest. "Let's check the numbers. I'm dying to see them."

Without making eye contact, Auggie sits up and grabs his computer. He presses a few buttons and gasps, and then silently tilts his laptop toward me.

The number on his screen makes me scream. We've made the most ever during this show. Clearly, we're on a steep, upward climb, in terms of our earning power, and there's no peak in sight.

"At this rate, we'll have the money for Carlo with a full three days to spare," he says excitedly.

"Okay, but let's not take our foot off the gas when we get

there, okay? If we reach our goal earlier than expected, we'll keep going so we can bank some big money for you—so you can pay your full tuition, instead of only half. You don't need a payment plan hanging over you and stressing you out."

Auggie shoots me a lopsided grin. "That'd be amazing. Thanks for thinking of that, Charlotte."

I take his hand. "Of course. You've done so much for me. You're my hero—my knight in shining armor. I should be wrapping your whole body in tin foil, not only your dick."

I'm expecting him to chuckle with me, but he doesn't. In fact, he looks downright tortured. "Hey, I just, uh, remembered I've got a big test tomorrow. I'd better get some studying in."

That felt weirdly abrupt. Also, not very convincing. I mean, yes, I'm sure he's got a big test tomorrow. They test the fuck out of those poor vet students. But it feels like Auggie was thinking one thing while saying another.

"Okay, good luck," I say. "And don't worry, once we cross the finish line on all the money we need to give Carlo, all rewards shall be administered without delay. The shows we'll do after that to raise money for *you* won't affect the administration of any and all promised rewards, whatsoever."

I was hoping my clarification would wipe the pained look off Auggie's face. No such luck. With a tight smile, he stands and quickly starts throwing on his clothes, so I do the same.

When we're both dressed, I open his bedroom door and find Lucky waiting patiently behind it. I scoop our fur baby up and kiss his little snout. "Sorry we left you out here again, buddy, but Daddy was busy fucking Auntie Charlotte's face in front of a bunch of horny strangers, and we didn't want you to see that." I glance at Auggie, hoping this time I've made him smile genuinely. But it's clear I've only made matters worse with my comment. In fact, Auggie suddenly looks like I've punched him in the gut.

Oh.

Fuck.

Daddy and *Auntie Charlotte*.

I bet that's it.

Duh, Charlotte. You're such a dumbfuck sometimes. The boy just basically confessed he's catching feelings for you. Surely, hearing you refer to us that way—rather than as Mommy and Daddy—only drove the point home that you don't foresee a future for us, despite how incredible this little fling has been.

As I walk across Auggie's living room toward his front door, he says behind me, "The new video camera got delivered while I was at school today. I'll bring it to you when I drop off Lucky tomorrow morning."

"If it lets me play those cassettes, I'll watch as many as I can while you're at school."

"Thanks for doing that. There's no rush, though. I know you're busy with the condo."

"It's not a bother at all. I'm curious what's on them."

"Are you sure you want me to drop off Lucky again tomorrow? You don't have to keep—"

"Yes, I'm sure. I *love* hanging out with him. I'd be upset if you didn't bring him to me every morning." Damn it. There's definitely something Auggie's holding back. Something on his mind that's making this moment feel stilted and awkward. I reach his front door and turn around. And for a beat, he looks into my eyes with a forlorn look on his face, like he's dying to say something but stopping himself.

Finally, Auggie forces a smile and says, "You killed it today, McDougal. They can't get enough of you."

They, huh? "You killed it today, too. You were on fire. Both on- and off-camera." Poor Auggie. He doesn't have an exhibitionist bone in his body, and I know it. So, I'm sure he's got conflicting feelings about his newfound career as a porn star. Knowing that only makes it even more impressive to me that he's been willing to go to such lengths to help me get every penny needed. "Goodnight, Auggie," I say, breaking the thick silence. "Thank you again for everything. I'm sorry I got you into this."

"Don't be. I'm having the time of my life." He opens the door for me. "Goodnight, Charlotte. I hope you have the sweetest of dreams."

17
CHARLOTTE

I sit at the card table in my living room and pull Lucky onto my lap with the new video camera Auggie dropped off a few hours ago in front of me. Unlike Lloyd Graham's broken camera from the storage unit, a little red light turns on when I plug this one in. That's a good sign. Also, the empty cassette compartment on this one actually opens and closes. Will this new camera actually *play* the box of cassettes on the table in front of me? That remains to be seen. I've finished working on my kitchen cabinets for today, though; and now, I'm eager to find out.

I sift through the box of cassettes, trying to decide which one to watch first. Besides the name of Auggie's grandma, Althea, there are also three other women's names sprinkled throughout the various cassettes: Mabel, Jeannie, and Clara. My gut tells me to start my journey with one of those names first—to get myself acclimated to Lloyd Graham's pervy despicableness before diving into the depths and suffering through one of the cassettes I'm emotionally invested in.

At random, I pick a cassette marked "Jeannie" from about twenty years ago.

I press play on the video camera, and, *voila*, a pretty middle-aged woman with salt-and-peppered dark hair appears on the camera's tiny display screen. The woman is laughing gleefully while dancing around a living room with a cute little infant swaddled pink.

A piano comes into frame in the background—the piano from the storage unit!—which, thankfully, I was able to sell for four hundred bucks two days ago. Which means this happy woman is prancing around *this* very living room—the one I'm sitting in now. It was fully furnished back then with 1970s-style furniture and colors. But even if the décor wasn't to my taste, there's no denying the room is as neat as a pin. This was an ordered, bright and happy home that bore no resemblance to the pigsty it became later—the one that confronted me when I opened my new front door last week.

I look toward the empty corner of the living room where the piano sat in the video and feel a certain wistfulness wash over me. In fact, all of a sudden, I'm seeing this woman's ghost all around me.

A younger woman comes into frame and begins dancing with the older woman and the baby. After a bit, the younger woman takes the baby and nuzzles her affectionally while the older one moves to the piano in the corner. Clearly, the younger woman is the baby's mommy. That much is clear. Does that make the older woman her grandma? That's the vibe I'm getting.

I turn up the volume and the tinny tinkling of piano music fills the air, like it's being funneled through a straw. The sound is compressed, due to the small speaker on this camera; but still, I can tell the older woman, the grandma, is playing the instrument beautifully. So much so, I feel a pang of regret I sold the thing. Maybe I should have tracked down the younger woman or her baby to give the instrument to them? If only I'd seen this video in time.

A male voice from behind the camera says, "She reminds me so much of you, Clara. Mommy used to dance around like this with you when you were a baby. Turn Jeannie's face to the camera, love. I want to get her face clearly."

The younger woman, Clara, tilts her baby's face toward the camera, and the male voice coos, "Hi there, Jeannie-girl! Look at you, dancing with your mommy, just like Grandma danced with her!" Well, that answers the question of who's who.

"Come over here, Mom," the younger woman says to the woman at the piano. "You, too, Daddy. I want to get all of us in the shot."

"How?" the man asks.

"Turn the camera around."

"How do I do that? My arm's not long enough."

I laugh out loud, along with the younger woman on-screen.

"I'll do it, Daddy," the younger woman says gently. "Come here. Squeeze in tight. Mom, would you hold Jeannie for me?"

There's a shift. A shuffle, and then I'm suddenly looking at three smiling adult faces and a wide-eyed baby—the new face belonging to the man behind the camara: an older gentleman with graying hair that must be the Peeping Tom himself, Lloyd Graham. Lloyd's got a kindly face—and that's disturbing to me, considering the peephole he created. In fact, he looks like the type of person who wouldn't hurt a fly. The type who'd be a safe space. Man, can looks be deceiving.

The family portrait doesn't last long. The younger woman points the camera at her parents and says, "Let me get you two with her. You're never in any videos together because Daddy's always recording. Show Jeannie how to waltz."

The couple happily obliges, and the screen fills with the sounds of Clara's happy giggling from behind the camera as she records her parents cheerily taking her baby girl for a dancing whirl around the small living room.

The scene ends. Suddenly, we're in a church for Jeannie's christening. The baby's mother, Clara, is dressed up and standing next to her husband or partner, a short, squat man with glasses, while a pastor or priest says a blessing over the child.

The scene shifts again. We're in a restaurant. Clara and her partner are in the same clothes as the christening, so this must be the celebration afterward. At one point, Lloyd behind the camera calls to that same older woman from before, "Mabel, honey, say hello to Jeannie!"

"Hi, Jeannie! We love you!"

Okay, that means we've now got confirmation that all three names on the various cassettes, other than Althea, were members of Lloyd Graham's immediate family. Mabel, Clara, and Jeannie were Lloyd's wife, daughter, and granddaughter, respectively. Not women recorded without their knowledge through a peephole or otherwise. What a relief.

When the cassette ends, I pop in another one, this one dated from thirty-six years ago and not marked with a name at all. Lloyd's wife, Mabel, looking much younger than in the prior video, appears on-screen. She's dancing around in a field of flowers with a little girl who's clearly a younger version of Clara, the adult daughter from the video with Baby Jeannie.

A male voice from behind the camera, Lloyd's voice, chuckles as he watches his wife and daughter dancing around in the flowers. Clara picks a bloom and slides it into her mother's dark hair. "You, too, Daddy!" she calls out. "We all have to wear flowers in our hair today. It's Flower Day." Lloyd laughs, and the scene ends.

The next scene features Clara in some sort of school play. The one after that is Mabel showing Clara how to make something in the kitchen. I watch the rest of the cassette at double speed, confirming it's filled with nothing but scenes from a happy family life.

I take the cassette out and replace it with one marked "Jeannie" from almost fifteen years ago. It's Jeannie's fifth birthday party, which I know because there's a banner hanging in Lloyd and Mabel's living room—*my* living room—that reads, "Happy 5th Birthday, Jeannie!" Once again, the condo I'm now sitting in is neat as a pin. A bright and happy place. I watch on double speed until Lloyd Graham appears on-screen, at which point I return to normal speed and watch him waltzing around his living room—*my* living room—with his wife, Mabel, in the midst of their granddaughter's fifth birthday party.

Jesus Christ.

I can't reconcile the mere existence of that peephole with all these lovely scenes. When did Lloyd drill that hole? Did his wife, Mabel, ever find out about it? Who lived in Auggie's grandma's condo when he first created it? When I purchased the condo, the auction company said the former owner had died without heirs. Did Lloyd's family find out about his pervy extracurricular activities and ditch his creepy ass? Are they out there somewhere, unaware of his death—and if they found out about it, they'd come back and try to claim an ownership right in my condo?

I grab my computer and search "Lloyd Graham, Seattle," along with the address of my condo, and a report on a people-finder website immediately pops up. The fee to purchase the information is cheap, so I pay it and download the report . . . and immediately stop breathing when I scan the document. At the bottom, the list of "known relations" of Lloyd Graham states the following:

Mabel Graham, wife, deceased.

Clara Graham Rodgers, daughter, deceased.

Gary Rodgers, son-in-law, deceased.

Jeannie Rodgers, granddaughter, deceased.

"No," I whisper. I look down at Lucky in my lap through tears. "What happened to all of them?" I open a new tab on my computer and search for several minutes; and soon, I've got my answer: *they all died together in a head-on collision.* The accident happened while the family was headed to the airport—on their way to catch a weeklong Caribbean cruise in celebration of Lloyd Graham and Mabel's golden anniversary.

Lloyd, who was sitting in the far back row of the minivan, was the sole survivor of the crash. His son-in-law, Gary, Clara's husband, drove the van with his mother-in-law, Mabel, in the front passenger seat, and his wife and daughter in the middle row. Both Gary and Mabel died instantly. Clara and Jeannie died soon after arriving at the hospital. And at the time of the article, Lloyd was at the hospital in a medically induced coma in critical condition.

Tears flow down my cheeks as I try to imagine what poor Lloyd was told when he woke up from that coma and asked about his family members. He lived another fourteen years after that. Surely, he spent every minute of those years wishing he could rewind the clock to that fateful day and somehow keep his family safe. No wonder the happy, bright home he shared with Mabel devolved into utter chaos after the accident. Surely, the poor old man felt he had nothing to live for after waking up from that coma, and his physical surroundings reflected that fact.

It also makes sense to me now there's a ten-year time gap in the cassettes after the accident. Once his entire family perished, who did Lloyd have left to record?

I pick up the first of three "Althea" cassettes. It's dated with a year from four years ago, and it's the first cassette since the car accident. What's on it? It's labeled with "Althea," so Auggie's grandma must appear on it. *But doing what?* Whatever Lloyd shot of Althea, did she know about it—or am I about to see the very thing Auggie dreads the most?

I eject the current cassette with Jeannie's fifth birthday party on it and pop in the first "Althea" cassette. I don't currently know the answers to any of the questions barraging my brain, but, hopefully, I'm about to get some much-needed answers.

18

AUGGIE

I knock on Charlotte's front door, and when she opens it, she practically rips the thing off its hinges. "The peephole was your grandma's idea!" she shouts, as Lucky greets me at my feet. "Althea was Lloyd's *friend*. His guardian angel. *Not his victim*. Althea adored Lloyd, and he adored her!"

I'm too flabbergasted and confused to reply with anything except, "*What?*"

Charlotte grabs my arm and yanks me inside, shouting, "I can't wait to show you *everything*."

A few seconds later, I'm sitting at the card table in Charlotte's living room with Lucky on my lap and the video camera and cassettes in front of me, while Charlotte bounces and bops around in front of me, too amped, apparently, to sit down next to me while explaining the situation to me.

"Remember those names on the cassettes?" she says. "The names besides your grandma's—Mabel, Clara, and Jeannie? *Those weren't the victims of a gross peeping Tom*. They were Lloyd's beloved family members—his wife, daughter, and granddaughter! They all died in a horrible, terrible head-on car crash. Lloyd's son-in-law, too. Everyone died that day, except for poor Lloyd." With tears welling in her eyes, Charlotte launches into a detailed explanation about everything she discovered today about Lloyd Graham and his family. She tells me about some internet research that confirmed the crash and all its tragic details. And about Lloyd's wife playing the piano, and the way they loved to waltz around. A baby's christening. A fifth birthday party. But as sweet and tragic as it all is, after ten minutes, I can't take it anymore. Charlotte still hasn't gotten to the part about my grandmother.

"What about *Althea*," I interject. "What did you see on the cassettes about—"

"I'm getting there, honey. Please, be patient. Trust me, you need to understand what happened before Althea came along to understand her friendship with Lloyd and, therefore, why *she* suggested the peephole."

That last part blows my mind. I can't fathom it. "Why do you think *she* suggested the peephole?" I ask, despite her request for patience. Surely, Charlotte's made some bizarre leaps in logic to arrive at a conclusion that insane and far-fetched.

"Because Althea herself said the peephole was *her* idea in a video!"

My jaw drops. "*What*?"

Charlotte pats my head like I'm her doggie. "Never fear, I'll show you everything. But before we get to the peephole, I want you to watch all the Althea cassettes in order, just like I did, so you can watch Lloyd and Althea's friendship form and grow. The first time Lloyd took a video of Althea was four years ago—a full ten years after the cassette before that one."

Charlotte drags a chair right next to mine at the card table, sits down, and grabs the video camera. While she's busy inserting the first Althea cassette into it, I say, "Four years ago is when my grandma moved into the building. She wanted a change of scenery after my grandpa died."

"Press play." She hands me the video camera. "Keep in mind these are the first videos Lloyd felt inspired to record after the accident—after a ten-year hiatus, during which he probably struggled with intense grief and the deterioration of his mental health."

Charlotte's warning is ominous. But I admit I'm damned curious by now, so I press play, as instructed.

My grandmother appears on the camera's tiny screen. The video is clearly being shot from above—through a window, since I can see a faint, telltale reflection in the video. As the clip begins, Grandma is standing in front of the building, chatting with none other than my mother on the sidewalk, while a few yards away, my brother, Max, and I carry a green couch out the back of a U-Haul truck.

"I remember this. The motherfucker was recording us without our consent?" Reflexively, I glance to my right, to the very window where Lloyd must have been standing while shooting this video. "What kind of sicko does that?"

"A deeply lonely, isolated sicko who was agoraphobic. He noticed a pretty, energetic, animated ray of sunshine moving into his building, so he picked up his long-neglected video camera to capture the moment."

"You're reaching, Charlotte."

"I'm not. Keep watching. And turn up the sound. *Listen.*"

For a long moment, we watch my family's activities below —events that would seem highly mundane to me, if Grandma were still alive. But in this context, viewing never-before-seen images of my grandmother, so soon after her passing, and from a time when she was still spry, lively, and healthy, is bringing tears to my eyes.

I wipe my eyes and take a deep breath. And when I'm just about to say, "What is it I'm supposed to see and hear?", a male voice murmurs from behind the camera, "Are *you* the one moving in today, or is it one of the others?" As he says it, the camera zooms in on my grandmother's happy form, who at that precise moment is throwing her head back and laughing hysterically with my mother. The male voice murmurs, "Gosh, I sure hope it's you."

"*Skeevy*," I pronounce, even as my heart is bursting at the sight of my happy grandmother having a belly laugh with my mother.

"*Sweet*," Charlotte counters. "Keep watching and keep an open mind."

My scowl softens and then turns into a genuine smile, as Grandma bursts out laughing again, along with Mom. "Those two were always laughing like that," I say. "My mother always says her mom was the best mom, ever. And I always tell her, 'Makes sense. You obviously learned from the best.'"

"Oh, Auggie.'"

"She was a fantastic grandmother to Max and me, too. So generous and fun. A total blast to hang out with. I loved her so much." I could go on and on, which is what I did at her funeral when I gave the eulogy, in order to give my heartbroken mother a break. When forced to summarize the incomparable Althea Martin, since eulogies aren't supposed to last three hours, I told the packed audience in the church two months ago: "Althea was the kindest, silliest, most magnetic person you could ever hope to meet. The type of person who never met a stranger. Everyone who met Althea Martin instantly felt like her best friend." It was all the truth. *Everyone loved Althea Martin.* And how could they not? She was always laughing from her belly. Always telling the best stories and listening to yours like it was the best she'd ever heard. She was constantly breaking into her patented silly songs and even sillier dances, even in public. *Especially* in public. She could make any stranger in her orbit, even the grumpiest ones, break into wide smiles. She was a cartoon character come to life.

And the best part? Grandma's golden heart matched her sunny disposition. She was the one who introduced me to volunteering at animal shelters and got me hooked. She was the one who went to homeless shelters to feed total strangers on Thanksgiving and Christmas Eve after Grandpa died, rather than hanging out with Mom, Max, and me. That's the reason we started having two of both those holidays. One with Grandma, and another for the calendar. And, of course, Grandma's the one who rescued the little ball of anxious fur who's now sitting on my lap this very minute, missing his favorite person, ever so much.

In the video, Grandma does a little dance, as Max and I walk by with her beloved dining room table—the one sitting in her condo now—and behind the camera, the male voice chuckles at her exuberance.

"Well, that's not creepy," I say sarcastically.

"It's not. I mean, yes, it *would* be, without the rest. But keep an open mind and keep watching. Lloyd didn't have any friends or family left at this point. He never went outside— and inside, he was drowning in stacks and piles of useless stuff. And then he saw your pretty, vivacious grandma, moving into his building, and laughing and dancing with people she obviously adored, and I think maybe, the very sight of her, and the obvious love she had with her family, lit a teeny-tiny little fuse inside him. It made him smile and chuckle. It gave him hope. I'd bet anything watching Althea laughing and dancing around, while her hunky grandsons moved her in and her daughter cracked jokes with her, was the first time that poor man had cracked a smiled in ten fucking years. No wonder he wanted to memorialize the moment. That's what this video is about—Lloyd feeling the urge to laugh and smile for the first time in ten years. It's not meant to be something creepy about your grandma. He's a guy who always memorialized the happiest of occasions in his life, so he memorialized this one, too." Charlotte motions to the box of cassettes. "That's what's on all of these, Auggie. I've watched them all. Some on double speed. And they're all filled with memories of a happy life. The family Lloyd loved and adored. I think seeing your vivacious grandma made him smile and remember a flicker of what it felt like to love and be loved." Charlotte's crying as she speaks by now. Clearly, she's highly invested in all of this.

The cassette ends, and I put the camera down on the card table. I'm glad it's over, honestly. I'm feeling intensely emotional—missing my grandma from the depths of my soul. I swallow hard. "What's on the next Althea cassette?"

"See for yourself. Here, let me set it to double speed, because it's lots of the same stuff, over and over. When you get to the most important part, I'll put it back on normal speed." Charlotte exchanges the cassettes and sets the speed, and, suddenly, I'm watching clip after clip of my grandmother coming and going from the building, all of it shot from the same vantage point as in the first cassette. Over and over again, in double speed, Althea Martin comes and goes from her new building without looking up or realizing she's being recorded. But suddenly, about midway through, she stops on her way out of the building, looks straight up at Lloyd's camera, smiles, and waves enthusiastically.

"*Whoa*," I murmur.

"It gets better."' Charlotte slows things back down to normal speed on the camera and also hikes up the volume. Once she does that, the next clip features Grandma not only smiling and waving at Lloyd above her, like before, she beckons to him enthusiastically to join her down below while mouthing, "*Come with me!*"

"I can't, Althea," Lloyd murmurs from behind the camera.

He knows her name? Did she come to his place to introduce herself to her new neighbor? Also, was he speaking only to himself from behind the camera or did he actually look up, so that Grandma could make out his words? Either way, Grandma puts her palms together, like she's begging him to come with her. It's not clear what Lloyd does in response this time. But whatever it is, Grandma responds by putting her hands on her hips and tapping her toe comically.

"I really can't," Lloyd murmurs. "*Sorry.*"

This time, Grandma drops the "I'm waiting" routine. She pats her heart, and then blows the man above her a kiss before turning and heading off.

Tears spring to my eyes, but I stuff them down. I must admit, it's classic Althea Martin. A touching and poignant—and deeply *kind*—exchange. One that admittedly touches my heart.

After that first back and forth, it becomes a rinse and repeat situation throughout the rest of the cassette, so Charlotte speeds it up for me again. In double time, I watch Lloyd capturing Grandma coming and going from the building, time and again. Mostly going, however. Each time Grandma leaves, she stops below the window and invites Lloyd to join her. And when Lloyd communicates his refusal somehow, presumably, she smiles, touches her heart, and blows him a kiss or a wave or both.

"Did you notice he rarely gets her coming back?" Charlotte says.

"Yeah, I did notice that."

"That's what makes me think maybe she knocked on his door or something on her way out. I think maybe she let him know whenever she was leaving, so he could quickly grab his camera and shoot a new video of her."

"Why on earth would she do that?"

"Maybe she knew it made him happy? I think it's pretty

clear your grandma enjoyed their little routine. Keep watching and you'll see what I mean."

She's right. In the earliest clips of Grandma's comings and goings, her body language is kind and enthusiastic but pretty conventional. Toward the end of the second cassette, however, her movements become increasingly sillier and sillier. In those later clips, whenever Grandma stops to wave goodbye and beckon for Lloyd to join her, she does a crazy little dance that elicits hearty chuckles from Lloyd. Clearly, Grandma's having a blast mugging for Lloyd's camera. She's overtly *trying* to crack him up. No doubt about it. And Lloyd is having the time of his life. Or at least, the best time he's had in many long years.

All of a sudden, right after yet another clip of Grandma leaving the building, Charlotte pauses the video. "Did you notice?" she says.

"No. What?"

"That time, for the first time, Althea didn't beg Lloyd to come out with her before launching into her silly dance. From this point on, she never beckons and begs him to come with her again. I think, either from the passage of time, or maybe due to some conversation they might have had, she now accepts his limitations. He's not going to leave his place. *Ever.* And she's decided to accept him for who he is. Isn't that lovely?"

"She never beckons to him again?"

"Not that he captures on video, anyway."

"That's interesting."

"Isn't it? I'd bet anything they had some sort of heart to heart, and she decided to meet him where he was."

I twist my mouth. "It would make sense for her to go and talk to him, given that he was her next-door neighbor. When she first moved in, I remember coming over and she was busy baking banana bread to give out to all her new neighbors."

"Well, there you go. I bet they had a nice conversation in-person, one Lloyd didn't record because *why* would he do that? And maybe that's when Althea got a peek at Lloyd's place and easily surmised he probably had some mental health struggles. You said she was the kind of person who always wanted to help people and animals in need, right?"

"Very much so. It was a core value for her."

"Well, there you go. She plainly made it her mission to help her next-door neighbor in need."

"That makes a lot of sense, actually. But how do we get from all these comings and goings to the peephole? For my own mental health, I need to fast-forward to that part now, Charlotte."

"We'll watch the third cassette soon, I promise. But there's one thing you need to see on this second cassette first." She presses play in normal speed, and we watch Grandma doing her usual silly dancing and waving and kiss-blowing several times. But then, suddenly, Grandma is standing in a whole new place—one we've never seen in any of the other video clips: the hallway right outside Lloyd's condo. The same exact spot I stood a moment ago, while knocking on Charlotte's front door. *And she's got Lucky in her arms.*

"Is it recording?" Grandma asks.

"Yep. Go ahead."

"Hello world!" Grandma says brightly in a silly voice—the one she always used when giving voice to her beloved dog. She waves Lucky's sole front paw at the camera. "My name is Lucky Martin, and I've finally found my forever home with a weird old lady who won't stop talking and singing to me about I-don't-know-what." Lloyd chuckles, at the same time Charlotte and I do the same. "I hope I don't bark a lot, once I get comfortable in my new home, or else my new neighbor, Mr. Graham Cracker, might get mad at me!"

"Never. Never, Lucky. Bark away. Be happy, little buddy."

Grandma drops her voice. "At the shelter, they said he never made a peep. Literally. They also said he's scared to death of men, but he seems to be doing okay with you." She scratches Lucky's head. "Do you like my friend, Graham Cracker, honey? Isn't he nice?" She smiles at the camera. "Thank you for recording this happy day for posterity. As far as I'm concerned, today is Lucky's birthday."

"Happy birthday, Lucky," Lloyd's voice behind the camera says.

"I think I'll make a birthday cake to celebrate," Grandma says excitedly. "A bacon one for Lucky, and a chocolate one for us. I'll bring you a slice later."

"Thank you."

"You bet. Or you can come over to eat it. When it's done, I'll knock on the wall. Knock back twice for 'I'll come over' and once for 'bring the cake to me.'"

"I'm sorry, Althea. But I can't—"

He lowers the camera, so we're suddenly looking at Lloyd's shoes, while the audio continues.

"Oh, I know that, love," Grandma says. "I was just being playful. Giving it a shot. But don't feel any pressure. I'm happy to bring the cake to you."

The camera shuffles and the video clip ends. And the next several clips are of Grandma coming and going again, except in this new batch, Lucky's almost always following at her heels. Also, there are a few guest appearances in the clips in this batch, as well. In one, Mom walks alongside Grandma and Lucky, and Grandma turns to look up and wave and dance in a slightly different spot than usual. Apparently, she felt the need to wait for Mom to be looking away. In another clip, *I'm* the one walking with Grandma. But there's no Lucky in tow.

"If there's no Lucky, then I must have been taking her to a doctor's appointment or the grocery store," I say. "Everywhere else, she brought Lucky." As she did with my mother in that prior clip, Grandma waits for me to be opening the car door for her before turning around to wave and dance for Lloyd.

Three clips later, I'm with Grandma again. This time, we're walking *into* the building, and she's hanging on my arm, chattering away, while Lucky hops along behind us. And this time, when Grandma gets to her usual spot below Graham's window, she stops and points energetically toward the street behind us, causing me to turn and look. While I do that, Grandma looks straight into Lloyd's camera above, waves, and does a ridiculously enthusiastic shimmy that prompts Lloyd to crack up behind his camera.

"What the fuck, Grandma?" I say, laughing. "I had *no* idea."

"Clearly, that was by design."

"Why didn't she tell me about him? We were super close. I wouldn't have judged her."

"Would you have told her about your penis puppeteering, if she were still alive?"

I pull a face that says, "Good point." But what I say is, "The two things aren't equivalent, though. Her friendship with Lloyd wasn't something to be ashamed about. She was being kind to someone in need. It was totally on-brand for her."

"I think maybe she enjoyed having a special, secret friendship. Everybody's got secrets, Auggie. Maybe she didn't feel the urge to tell her grandson about her budding friendship—and maybe even her budding *romance*—with the widower hoarder agoraphobe next-door."

I wince. "*Romance*? Is that what the peephole was for?" I run my hand through my hair. "Okay, I've seen enough. Let's skip ahead to the peephole now. Please, Charlotte."

"Okay. Just so you know, you're missing out on a few cute scenes of their growing friendship. She came over and played Mabel's piano a couple times and sang to him. But you can watch those videos later, if you want. I'll fast-forward to the peephole scene now."

"Bless you."

Charlotte inserts the third and final Althea cassette and fast-forwards to a specific part. As she's doing that, she says, "This is the very last cassette Lloyd ever recorded on, unless the one that's stuck in his camera came after this one." Charlotte stops fast-forwarding and lets the video play at normal speed. And there's my grandmother again on the tiny screen—this time, indoors and with a wall behind her. She's standing mere feet away from Lloyd's camera and facing him.

"Okay, it's on," Lloyd's voice says from behind the camera.

"*Why*, exactly, do you want to record me explaining this?" Grandma asks. "I'd honestly prefer for it to be our little secret, Lloyd."

Lloyd replies, "And it will be, as long as we're both still alive. But God help me, if you go first, and one of your grandsons finds that hole on *your* side of the wall, they're gonna come over here and beat down my door and soundly kick my saggy ass. And rightly so."

Grandma laughs. "I wouldn't worry about that too much. The wallpaper in my bedroom will make the hole practically invisible on my side. Also, you'll be relieved to know the grandson who'd probably kick your ass *first* and ask questions *second* just moved to California with his family, so he won't be coming around much anymore. Luckily, the grandson who still lives nearby and is always coming around has the mind of a scientist—he's in his first year of vet school here—so, I can assure you he'd ask questions *first* before ever hauling off and kicking an old man's saggy ass."

"Is that one Max?"

"No, Auggie. Max is the patent lawyer in California."

"Well, even if Auggie paused to hear me out, he'd never believe what I'm telling him. But either way, *someone's* gonna find this hole on *my* side of the wall after I've finally kicked the bucket, and I don't want that person thinking I was a dirty old man. Maybe people I used to work with at the University would hear about it. Everyone always loves a good scandal about a dead guy, right? So, please, Althea, humor me and make this video, or I'm sorry, I'm gonna have to spackle the hole right up."

Grandma rolls her eyes and gestures to the wall next to her like she's a model on a gameshow introducing the grand prize. "Hello there to my family—Gigi, Max, and Auggie, and to whomever else might wind up living in either of our units one day. My name is Althea Martin, and I'm the owner of Unit 308. Well, part owner. The bank owns half. But I digress. For the record, it was my idea, and mine alone, for my dear friend here, Lloyd Graham, to drill this hole in his bedroom in Unit 307. Lloyd suffers from agoraphobia, and he gets really lonely all holed-up in here sometimes." She glares at the camera playfully. "Unfortunately, he's too *stubborn* to get a smart-phone like I keep telling him to do, so we can FaceTime and—"

"It's not that I'm stubborn. I can't understand all that techy stuff. It stresses me out and I can't—"

"It's okay, honey. I was teasing you. I shouldn't have. It's okay, Graham Cracker. Like I said, this hole will be our version of FaceTime." Grandma winks at the camera and blows a kiss. "So, anyway, yes, *I* suggested this hole, so that, whenever sweet Lloyd is feeling lonely or blue, he can look through it, any ol' time, and see me on the other side. In fact, he can knock on the wall, any old time, and I'll even do a little dance for him, if I'm there and actually *hear* the knocking." With a chuckle, she touches her hearing aid. "Good luck with that, huh?"

"Well, to be clear, I'm never going to look through the hole without knocking on the wall first and getting a knock or holler in reply that the coast is clear for me to look."

"The coast is clear?"

"So I don't unwittingly catch you *indisposed.*"

Grandma snickers and waves at the air. "If you happen to catch a glimpse of my saggy boobs or wrinkled butt, then good for you." She waggles her eyebrows. "Good for me, too, because Lord knows, thinking a handsome man *might* be peeking at me at any given moment of the day or night would definitely add some cha-cha-cha to my boring, old life."

"*Althea,*" Lloyd says, as my grandmother whoops with laughter, and I can practically hear the deep blush on the man's face in his voice.

"Jesus Christ, Grandma," I mumble.

"I love her so much," Charlotte says. "I hope I'm half as sassy and fun at her age."

"Explain the poster, too," Lloyd says. "It's her idea, too, world. She's the one with the wicked sense of humor, not me."

Grandma hoots with laughter and points to the unhung, framed *Rear Window* movie poster on the floor nearby that's leaning against the wall. "Isn't that hilarious? It's my gift to Lloyd. A secret nod to our fun little secret." Grandma puts her hands on her hips. "Is that good? Anything else you'd like me to clear up?"

"I think that'll do it. Thank you very much."

The clip ends, and a new one begins, but I press pause on the camera. "Is there anything else that's an immediate must-see?"

"Nope. You've seen the most important stuff." Charlotte scoots her chair even loser to mine, and then pivots, so that our knees are now touching. She takes both my hands in hers and says softly, "I hope this is a relief for you."

"It is. Thank you." I pause, my Adam's apple bobbing. "I miss her so fucking much, Charlotte."

"I can see why. She was a beautiful soul."

"She lit up every room. Made even the most mundane

activities or errands a grand adventure. She was sunshine in human form." Saying those words out loud suddenly makes me realize why I'm so fucking attracted to Charlotte—because all those descriptors perfectly describe her, as well.

"The rest of this last cassette is footage of your grandma playing little songs for Lloyd on his piano or bringing him birthday cake on his birthday. Stuff like that. You can watch it later, if you want. There's absolutely no footage shot through the peephole, and it's never mentioned again." Her face falls. "Fair warning, though. Toward the very end of the cassette, it's pretty clear your grandma's health was failing. She started to look pretty frail, so be prepared for that, if you watch."

I swallow hard and nod. "It was hard to watch in real time. In the end, she had a caregiver living with her. But I used to come over and hang out with her a ton, whenever my mother couldn't make it, or to give her a break. So, I watched her rapid decline as it happened."

"I'm so sorry, Auggie. So, so sorry."

I don't know for sure who leans in first, or if we both do it together, but the end result is that our lips are suddenly pressed together in a tender, heartfelt kiss—one neither of us pulls away from. In fact, it doesn't take long before we're both actively deepening the kiss. And then, kissing passionately. As our tongues swirl and our lips devour, I feel electrocuted by arousal and yearning. I'm flooded with the feelings that have been growing inside me, steadily, for this incredible woman. *I want her.* Body, soul, heart, mind. *I want her to be mine. All mine.* But in this moment, I'll settle for claiming every inch of her body, from the inside out.

We've talked about waiting for sex until our financial emergency is over. But I'm not thinking clearly right now. I'm feeling swept away by desire, need, and affection—and especially, a kind of white-hot attraction I've never experienced before.

"I want you inside me," Charlotte murmurs into my hungry lips, reading my mind. And so, without hesitation, I stand from my folding chair, lift Charlotte from hers—prompting her to wrap her thighs around my waist and slide her arms around my neck—and with Charlotte clinging to me like a baby monkey, I stride into her bedroom, my rock-hard dick and pounding heart leading the way.

19
CHARLOTTE

Auggie's quaking and breathing hard as he lays me down on the air mattress in my bedroom. He immediately begins stripping off his shoes and clothes with enthusiasm, so I do the same, dying to finally feel his thick, girthy cock plowing me. Intellectually, I know we should probably channel all this delicious sexual energy into yet another show. We haven't done one today yet, so this is going to set us back. But my body doesn't care what my mind thinks in this moment because my body *needs* this—more than it needs air in its lungs.

"I've been fantasizing about this moment, obsessively," Auggie whispers, looking down at me with blazing blue eyes. He's naked now, and so am I. The air between us is crackling with sexual energy. Heat. Lust. Yearning. *Need.*

"So have I," I admit. "I'm on the pill."

With a shudder of arousal, he crawls over me and ravenously licks and sucks on my nipples and breasts, and then works his way down my torso to the pulsing bundle of nerves between my legs. As he licks my bullseye, he slides his fingers inside me and strokes me in a rhythm that matches the movements of his tongue and lips, until soon, I'm moaning and groaning and writhing in ecstasy. Wet and ready to be filled to the brim and then pounded to ecstasy.

I grip his hair and ears and the back of his neck, as my pleasure intensifies and spirals. Until finally, a seismic quake of pleasure crashes into me—one that makes my toes curl and my vision explode with fireworks. As my release comes, I growl so loudly, I'm sure Lucky is terrified for me on the other side of the door. But in this moment, I don't care about our beloved dog or anything else, because Auggie's thick cock is suddenly stretching my entrance deliciously.

Auggie's length burrows inside me, causing zings of pleasure as it goes. It's always a relief and pleasure, that first moment of full penetration. The sensation of my body being claimed. But I've never felt anything even close to the deliciousness of this moment. Auggie's filling me bigger and better than anyone ever has, by far. Add to that the anticipation and yearning I've been feeling, thanks to all the foreplay we've been doing and the comfort level and trust we've developed, and I feel on the cusp of coming from sheer penetration alone.

As Auggie begins rocking in and out of me, I clutch his bare ass, dig my fingernails into his flesh, and hang on for dear life. I'm reveling in every sublime zing and zap of my nerve endings as he fucks me. Relishing the unparalleled, unexpected bliss that comes from getting railed by a man with a huge dick and an even bigger heart, when I'm *this* wet and aching for it, and also *this* uninhibited and trusting of my partner. This gorgeous man has seen me at my worst. He knows my biggest secret. By all rights, he should hate me; or at least, feel wary of me. And yet, It's clear from his thrusts and moans and his generalized fervor Auggie's all-in and letting loose— experiencing his own version of bliss, right along with me.

I can't stop touching him as he thrusts. Caressing him.

Goading him on. I caress his balls and taint, run my fingers down his ass crack, and gently slide a fingertip inside his anus. And soon, the man turns into the Chupacabra on me. A wild beast, in the most delicious way humanly possible.

Just when I think Auggie going to lose it, he pulls out of me, panting and groaning. He barks at me to sit on his face, so I do as I'm told. And what follows is a tongue-fucking so wild and greedy, it makes me squirt into his mouth when I come. By now, I'm sure every occupant in our building knows I'm getting fucked and getting fucked well. But I don't care. I'm delirious now. Under Auggie's spell. When I saw this man at Captain's, I never in a million years imagined he could be this hot in bed. This skilled and commanding and confident. I feel drugged by pleasure. Out of my head. It's the best sex I've ever had. Goddammit, I was a fucking idiot at Captain's.

When my squirting orgasm subsides, and Auggie's slurped every drop off my pussy and thighs, he looks every bit as intoxicated as I feel. He's drunk on lust, the same as me.

He guides me onto my hands and knees and then grips my hips while slamming into me from behind. When his cock is burrowed deep inside me, all the fucking way, I cry out in shock at the new angle of penetration. In this position, his huge cock feels like it's splitting me in two.

Auggie pauses behind me and gasps out, "Are you okay?"

"Never better. Don't stop. If you touch me while you fuck me, I think I'll come again."

I don't need to ask him twice. Auggie reaches around and fondles my clit while resuming his prior thrusting. *And it's delicious.* The dual sensation of his hard shaft filling me, fucking me, obliterating me, while his fingers work my clit with masterful precision, sends me to a place I've never been before—to a sexual Nirvana I didn't know existed. It's the aspiration, of course, to feel this thoroughly untethered. To be delivered to a state of sexual delirium. But it's never actually happened to me. Until now.

When my orgasm comes this time, I feel myself releasing fluid along with it, *again,* all around Auggie's cock and onto my thighs.

It's too much for Auggie to withstand. I feel his cock jolt and jerk, violently, inside me, and Auggie lets out the loudest growl I've ever heard from him, which is saying a lot. He's so fucking loud as he comes this time, I think it's likely we've now reached the occupants of neighboring buildings, and maybe even some buildings on-campus, with the sounds of our pleasure.

As Auggie collapses into me from behind, I collapse onto my stomach on the air mattress. And that's how we remain for a long moment, catching our breath.

When our limbs are functional again, we flop onto the floor on our backs, since the air mattress isn't big enough for the two of us.

Auggie mutters, "I've wanted to do that to you, since the minute I saw you bursting into Captain's. But that blew every fantasy and sex dream I've ever had about you out of the water. *Holy shit.*"

I stare at him, not knowing what to say. It was incredible for me, too. The best sex I've ever had in my life. But I certainly haven't been fantasizing about doing that with him since laying eyes on him at Captain's. My attraction to him has been a slow burn/slow build sort of thing. A flame that grew and grew, until it became a forest fire inside me.

"You're *surprised* I wanted to fuck you the minute I saw you?" he says, reacting to my facial expression. "Charlotte, I flirted with you the second I saw you."

I smirk. "You said you only smiled at me because you thought I might be your teenage crush."

Auggie snickers. "I lied. I was flirting with you. *Of course.*

And I *also* thought you might be my teenage crush. But that thought occurred to me only *after* I'd already thought, '*Wow, she's incredible.*'"

Oh, Auggie. I can't return the sentiment, unfortunately, since we both know I had my head too far up my ass that day to be able to see him clearly. So, instead, I simply pull his face to mine and kiss him tenderly. I didn't plan to kiss him before reaching our finish line on the money thing. But now that I've kissed him, and found out how electrifying it feels, how sweet his lips taste, there's no turning back. I'm addicted.

When our kiss ends, Auggie nuzzles my nose and says, "I'll get you a tissue." He gets up and heads to the attached bathroom. And when he returns, and he hands me a wad of toilet paper, which I use to clean up the massive load he left inside me that's now dripping onto my thighs.

When that task is done, I sit up, matching the position Auggie took on the floor next to me when he sat back down. "We just paid to have sex, you know. Basically. We could have used that same amount of sexual energy and time to put on a show and make money, but we gave it all up to jump each other's bones, off-camera."

"No regrets here. You?"

"None. It was well worth it, if you ask me."

He sighs with relief. "One hundred percent."

"But we can't make a habit of it. We shouldn't do it again until we've got every penny for Carlo."

Auggie's shoulders droop, but he doesn't push back.

"We need to put that whole mess behind us, as soon as possible," I say. "And then, we'll do what we just did, at our leisure, as much as we want, as our reward."

Auggie nods. "I hate to admit it, but I agree that's the right call." He brushes his fingertips across my bare thigh. "I think we should try a new approach in the next few shows. Now that we've actually had sex, I'm even more confident I don't want to do that, on-camera. Ever. So, I feel like we've now gone as far as we can in terms of the sex acts we're willing to perform, on-camera."

"I agree. I feel like sex is our hard line in the sand."

"Agreed. If I'm being honest, I feel like I crossed a line for myself when I fucked your face. When it was over and I came to my senses, I felt like that was a bridge too far for me, in terms of what I want to be doing on-camera."

I blush. "I'm sorry, Auggie. I never meant to—"

"You didn't. I wanted to do it in the moment. I was totally into it. But afterward, I realized that's gonna have to be a one-time thing for me. I'm just not cut out to be a full-on porn star, babe. It's just not me."

I take his hand. "I only want you to do what you're comfortable with. I know we've strayed pretty far from the original concept of your puppet shows. I never meant for things to get quite as porny and raunchy as they've become."

"I've had a blast. Truly. Time of my life. But I'm thinking maybe we could crowdsource some new show ideas, in addition to the usual stuff. We could ask people what they'd want to see you do, naked. And then make them pay extra for the pleasure. There's a woman who makes millions on the site, simply by showing her bare feet in different scenarios. In Jell-o. In baked beans. In mud."

"You're kidding."

"No, for real. So, let's see what our superfans might pay to see you do, in addition to the usual shows. It might free us up a bit, in terms of the time and sexual energy we'll need to muster, multiple times a day."

I snicker. "I can see right through you, Auggie Vaughn. You're hoping, if we can find a successful, profitable alternative to our usual shows, we'll be able to have sex, off-camera, every night."

Auggie laughs. "You got me. That's partly true. But I'm also hoping to shift the focus onto you. You're a natural at this, and I'm not."

I shrug. "Okay, we'll give it a try. Who knows, it might turn out to be a stroke of genius. No pun intended. It sounds like *stroking* your cock won't be as big a plot point in these new kinds of videos."

"That'd be my goal, anyway. I'll keep doing whatever it takes to reach our goal. Don't worry about that. But I can't deny I'd much rather be your sidekick and lean into *you* being the star. Let me be your hype man—your prop, if you need one—and leave the rest to you."

"I'm game. But if it becomes clear we're not on pace to make our deadline after we pivot—"

"Then we'll scrap it. In the end, I promise, Charlotte, I'll do whatever it takes to have every dime needed by the time we board our flight to New Jersey."

20

CHARLOTTE

"Atta boy!" I call out to Lucky. "Now, bring it back, buddy! That's it!"

I'm playing fetch with Lucky on our usual patch of grass, while Auggie fetches smoothies for us from our usual place. Today is a variation from our normal routine, however, in that, usually, we come to this little park on-campus *after* our first show of the day to relax and recharge before round two. Today, we came here *before* our first show, due the videos I showed Auggie when he got home from class and the unexpected—but yummy—sexcapade that followed.

No regrets about the sex. I feel nothing but purring satisfaction about what happened between Auggie and me about forty-five minutes ago. So much so, I've scrapped plans to tell Auggie about the job interview I had this morning while he was at school. It was only an interview, after all. Not a confirmed job. So, why put a damper on the incredible afterglow we're both feeling by telling Auggie about a job interview that might not lead to anything?

I know Auggie would be happy for me to land a new flight-attendant gig. Especially one *this* good. He knows that's all I've wanted since my layoff—to get back to my old life. But I also know this crazy situationship we've found ourselves in has been as confusing as it's been fun—a wild ride neither of us saw coming. Just this fast, Auggie feels like my best friend, next to Tessa. A bestie who's amazingly fun to kiss and fool around with. So, I think it'd be naive of me not to realize Auggie might react to the news of my job interview this morning with some conflicting emotions.

As I'm tossing the rubber ball for Lucky across the grass again, my phone rings with a call from Tessa.

"Hello, Crazy Girl!" I bellow in greeting.

"Maddy had her baby girl today!" Tessa blurts. Maddy is Tessa's sister-in-law—the wife of one of Ryan's three brothers.

"Aw, how wonderful. Is everyone healthy? Did they go with Billie as her name?"

"Yup. Both mommy and Baby Billie are doing great. The entire Seattle Branch of the Morgan family is flying down to LA tomorrow morning, first thing. Are you still game to stay here with Ru-Ru? We'll be in LA for a week, probably."

Shoot. I forgot I volunteered to house- and dog-sit for Tessa and Ryan when the time came. Usually, one of Ryan's local family members watches their husky, Rudy, when they travel. But this time, all their usual dog-sitters will be traveling to LA to meet Billie. Back when I volunteered, I thought I still had five more weeks to pay Carlo back. I also hadn't yet dragged poor Auggie into my mess, so we didn't need to be productive and put on multiple shows per day, every day, to meet our new, shortened deadline back then. "Yes, of course, I'm still game to stay at your place," I say, my mind racing.

"Awesome. Thanks. Why don't you come tonight, since we've got an early flight tomorrow. We'll have dinner and catch up a bit. What's kept you so busy lately? You hardly ever text or call me back."

"Sorry. I've been busy doing projects around the condo." I

pause, trying to decide if I should let the confession that's on the tip of my tongue free, and finally decide to go for it. "Also, having sex with Auggie."

"You've been fucking the boy bander next door and you didn't tell me?" Tessa shrieks. *"Tell me everything!"*

Chuckling at Tessa's exuberance, I glance across the large lawn and notice Auggie walking toward me with two smoothies. "I'll tell you everything tonight. He's heading toward me right now. Can he stay with me at your place this week? He'll be on spring break all next week, so the timing would be perfect."

"Of course, he can stay!" Tessa snickers. "Auggie can come and make *you* come, all week long. Have yourself a sexy little vacay at our place, girlie."

Before I've replied, Auggie reaches me. As he hands me a smoothie, he says, "I asked for extra strawberries, exactly the way you like it."

"Thank you." I point to my phone. "Tessa. Hang on, girlie. Let me get Auggie up to speed." I put Tessa on mute and explain the situation, and Auggie expresses excitement.

"I'll need to bring Lucky," Auggie says. "I don't want to leave him with a friend, even a future vet. He's scared of everyone besides you and me."

I unmute the call, advise Tessa she's now on speaker phone, and then deal with the Lucky situation. Not surprisingly, Tessa says she'd be thrilled for Lucky to come along. In fact, she says her dog, Rudy, will be thrilled to have a new friend to hang out with.

"Lucky might not feel quite as thrilled," Auggie cautions with a chuckle. "The poor little guy is scared of any new creature, whether human or animal. I'm sure this week will be good for him, though."

We talk a few logistics, at which point Auggie and I say we'll head back to our building to pack a bag and then head over to Tessa's place immediately after that. After disconnecting the call, Auggie scoops up Lucky's rubber ball while I throw away our empty smoothie cups. Just as I'm turning away from the trashcan, however, I notice a stoic face across the large lawn that sends a chill racing down my spine.

"*Auggie*," I whisper-shout. My heart thrashing, I bound to him and grab his arm. "Don't look, but I think I see one of Mr. DiMarco's bodyguards over there."

"Where?"

"Don't make it obvious when you look. He's sitting on a bench, way on the other side of the lawn. Eating an ice cream cone. Black shirt."

"I'll throw Lucky the ball so I can look casually." Auggie turns and tosses the ball, prompting Lucky to race after it. When Auggie turns back around to me, he looks dubious. "Are you sure that's him? He doesn't seem to be watching us."

"I'm pretty sure."

"How sure? What percentage?"

"Sixty percent?"

"That's not that high."

"I only flew once with the guy I'm thinking of, and we didn't speak during the entire flight. He slept through most of it. It was my last flight before I got laid off—the one where I got that text from my friend in HR—so I wasn't all that focused on my passengers. I was totally freaking out."

"He was on the flight that ended with you doing the stupid thing?"

I look around, feeling paranoid, and then nod.

Auggie peeks over at the guy again. "He's awfully far away to be deciding he's some guy you only saw once and didn't speak to. Up close, maybe you'd realize that's not him. Actually, I think he's here with that little girl there."

"No, I think the girl is here with that woman in blue." I

point my chin about ten yards from where the man is sitting on the bench.

Auggie throws the ball and peeks again. "Would a paid killer get himself an ice cream cone before doing his job? That seems like a weird thing for a professional to do."

"Unless he's trying to blend in. And maybe he's not here to kill us. Maybe he's here to beat the crap out of us, as a warning."

"A warning about what? We know our deadline, and we're working hard to meet it. What's there to warn us about?"

"Maybe he's that nosy guy Carlo warned us about. Maybe he's got a hunch, so he came here to watch us and see what we're up to."

"Or maybe he's just some guy who reminds you of the sleeping guy on the plane. Maybe you're just . . ."

"*Paranoid?* Yes, I am. I've been insanely, intensely paranoid, since the minute I got to my hotel room in New York and counted that money and realized what I'd just done. But just because I'm paranoid doesn't mean that's not the nosy guy." I shake out my hands to ease the sudden torrent of anxiety flooding me. "What if Mr. DiMarco found out it was me? What if he knows Carlo looked the other way, rather than immediately reporting me, and now he's sent that guy—"

"Let's not jump to conclusions here," Auggie whispers hoarsely. "And let's not panic. At least, not visibly. If that's one of the bad guys, which isn't for sure, then we don't want him knowing we've seen him. It'll be easier to ditch him on our way to Tessa's house, if he thinks we're totally clueless."

"I'm scared, Auggie."

"It might not even be him. In fact, I'd bet anything it's not." He hugs me and kisses my cheek, while I try to get my breathing under control in his arms. I feel Auggie's lips press against my ear. His sweet, soothing voice says, "Pretend to laugh. I'm telling you a joke."

I follow instructions, and I'll be damned, the simple act of faking laughter relieves a bit of my stress. Or maybe it's simply Auggie's strong arms around me that's calming me down. Whether that's one of Mr. DiMarco's goons or not—and at this point, I truly don't know—having Auggie here with me makes all the difference. I'm deeply sorry I've dragged him into this mess; but now that he's in it and I can't undo it, his presence at my side is a balm for my ragged, tortured soul.

Auggie takes my face in his hands. "I've got you. I'm going to peck your lips now, like we're having a great ol' time. And then, you're going to smile and laugh again."

He kisses my lips, exactly like he said he would, and I do my part. Actually, I do more than my part: I smile broadly at him in return. *Genuinely*. Simply because looking into Auggie's ocean-blue eyes makes me feel genuinely safe and grounded again.

Auggie takes my hand and we start walking back to our building with Lucky hopping along happily behind us. "He's not following us," Auggie murmurs after a few minutes of walking. He stops in the middle of the sidewalk, so I stop, too, since he's holding my hand. "Whether that was him or not," Auggie says, "I want you to know I won't let anyone hurt a single hair on your beautiful head, Charlotte McDougal. That's a promise."

"Thank you. I won't let anyone hurt you, either." We're not bulletproof, so I'm not sure how either of us could possibly make good on these promises, if push came to shove. But if Auggie can make promises that can't be kept but feel amazing to hear, then so can I.

To seal our pact, apparently, Auggie leans down and kisses me tenderly, causing my heart to flutter in my chest and butterflies to ripple inside my belly. I slide my arms around his neck and deepen our kiss, feeling swept away by the energy coursing between us. When we pull apart, my legs feel wobbly. My heart is pounding.

"I'm so sorry I dragged you into all this, Auggie."

Auggie slides his fingertip underneath my chin. "Don't apologize to me anymore. I wouldn't change a thing, Charlotte. I've never felt more alive, or had more fun, in my whole fucking life."

21
AUGGIE

"Do you have any photos of Billie?" Charlotte asks, referring to Ryan and Tessa's brand-new niece who arrived today. We're at Ryan and Tessa's dinner table, having just finished a great meal, and Ryan's making everyone laugh with the story of Billie's birth, as it was relayed to him earlier today via FaceTime by his younger brother, Keane, Billie's smitten new daddy.

"I've got a bunch," Tessa says excitedly. She swipes at her phone. "Here's a cute one of all three of them, right after Billie was born. Look at Keane's face. He looks equal parts elated and terrified."

"Sounds about right," Ryan says, and we all chuckle.

Tessa hands Charlotte her phone, and Charlotte gasps and coos at the photo. "What a gorgeous family. Oh my gosh. Billie's beautiful." To Claire in her lap—Ryan and Tessa's adorable two-year-old—Charlotte says, "Are you excited to meet your new cousin tomorrow, Claire Bear?"

The little girl nods enthusiastically. "I'm going to teach her how to draw."

"Well, she's not big enough to draw just yet," Tessa says.

"But you can certainly give her a gentle hug and tell her about how you're going to do that with her when she's older."

"You're coming, too, right, Auntie Charlotte?" the little boy, Zachary, asks Charlotte. He's seated next to her at the table, at his request.

"No, not this time, buddy," Charlotte says. "Auggie and I came over because we're going to watch Rudy while you're all in LA visiting Billie."

"*Oooooooh*," Zach says. "I thought *Auggie* was here to watch Rudy, and *you* were coming with us to meet Billie. Can you come?"

"I wish," Charlotte says. "Don't worry, I'm sure I'll meet Billie one of these days. Maybe her parents will bring her to Claire's next birthday party."

The little boy replies to that, and I'm struck by how enmeshed Charlotte is in his and his sister's lives. Zachary assumed Charlotte would come on a family vacation, and now, it's also clear it's a perfectly natural thing to expect Charlotte to attend his sister's next birthday, too. Plainly, Charlotte's a full-fledged member of the family, as far as these kids are concerned, and that fact only makes Charlotte even more attractive to me.

Kids can't be bribed into loving you, in my experience. They only feel genuine love for an adult, the way these two obviously feel for Charlotte, when that adult invests *time* in them. I know this, due to my close relationship with my own niece and nephew, Ripley and Marcus; so I'm positive Charlotte has made a real effort with these kids. It's yet another reason to feel things for Charlotte I probably shouldn't.

"Isn't Billie adorable?" Charlotte says to me, offering me Tessa's phone. Lucky's on my lap, so I shift him slightly to take the device from her, and the second I look down at the photo, I'm shocked to instantly recognize Ryan's brother.

"Is your brother an actor?" I ask Ryan.

Ryan confirms my hunch and confirms the name of the show his brother's most known for—one I recently binge-watched.

"I've watched every season!" I say. "Your brother was my favorite on the show—the best part of the whole thing."

Ryan laughs. "I'll tell him you said so when I see him tomorrow. He'll be thrilled."

I pepper Ryan with questions, and he fills me in on his brother's journey in Hollywood, including the fact that the part I've seen Keane in has been a breakthrough role for him, one that's opened lots of new doors.

"Good for him," I say. "Is it weird having a famous person in your family?"

Tessa interjects, "Keane's not the only famous Morgan sibling. Ryan's other brother, Dax, is the lead singer of 22 Goats. Have you heard of them?"

My jaw clanks open. "I saw them the last time they came through Seattle! I love those guys!" I nudge Zach next to me. He's sitting between Charlotte and me. "Is your mommy pulling a joke on me? Do you really have an uncle in 22 Goats?"

Zach shrugs like it's no big deal. "I have *three* uncles in Uncle Daxy's band. Uncle Daxy, Uncle Fish, and Uncle Colin."

I palm my forehead. "That's so cool." I can't imagine being a kid who gets to grow up considering all three members of 22 Goats as family, on top of one day getting to watch his Uncle Keane killing it in a popular show.

"Dax and his two bandmates grew up together," Ryan says. "Most of my siblings and their spouses have lots of close, longtime friends, so every little one in our family has lots of honorary uncles and aunties, just like their Auntie Charlotte here."

"I'm only *honorary*?" Charlotte jokes. "How dare you." Laughing, she kisses the top of Claire's head. "I'm your favorite of all the honoraries, though, right, Claire Bear?"

Claire looks confused. "Awno-berries?"

We all laugh, and try to help Claire with the pronunciation.

"Uncle Fish is *my* favorite awno-berry," Zach says. Apparently, the word's going to stick that way. He continues, "Uncle Fish and Auntie Ally came to my birthday party and dey brought me a guitar and Uncle Fish showed me how to play it and den dey played a song for everybody."

"Shoot. I can't compete with that," Charlotte quips. "Darn it."

Everyone but me laughs. I'm too stunned by what I'm hearing to engage like a normal person. Fish is the bass player of 22 Goats, and he also produces music for his girlfriend or wife or whoever she is. There's a song they did together, a duet, a few years back that was a smash hit. The kind that's on the radio every time you turn it on. In every grocery store and every bank. Was *that* the song they performed at Zach's birthday party? *Did this lucky kid get a personal concert people would pay good money to see?*

I probably shouldn't ask the question I'm wondering, so I don't look like a total fanboy loser, but I can't help myself. "Did Fish and Ally play 'Smitten' at your birthday party, Zach?"

"No. Dey played a song about dinosaurs because my party was a dinosaur party."

"Oh, cool."

"You know Fish and Ally's music?" Tessa asks.

"I know 'Smitten.'"

Tessa chuckles. "You're so sweet, Auggie. You're practically bursting right now." She winks at Charlotte. "The next time we have a family party, the kind where even the LA Branch of the family makes the trek, you'll have to come and bring Auggie along so he can meet everyone."

My heart explodes with excitement. Not only because I'd

love to meet Ryan's famous family members, both honorary and actual, but even more importantly because this suggestion would mean I'd get to hang out with Charlotte again in the future, even after our present emergency is over and she's moved back to LA or wherever.

"I'd love to come," I say, a goofy grin on my face. I look at Charlotte, expecting her to be smiling the same way I am, and my heart sinks. If I'm not mistaken, Charlotte's flashing a look at Tessa meant to convey something along the lines of "What the fuck are you doing?"

From Tessa, Charlotte looks at me and smiles thinly. "Yeah, if that works out, that'd be great. The future is kind of blurry for me right now, though, so we'll have to see how it goes."

Fuck. My cheeks feel hot. "Oh, yeah, no worries. If it works out, great; if not, all good." *Fucking hell.* I need to calm down and stop envisioning myself dating Charlotte in the future. Clearly, dating me, long-term or otherwise, isn't on Charlotte's To Do List, so I need to scratch it off mine, too. That's easier said than done, though. At this point, I feel like my heart is going rogue.

"Can I pet Lucky now?" the little girl in Charlotte's lap, Claire, asks me.

"Yeah, let's give it a try. He's stopped shaking, so maybe he's finally ready to meet you."

"Me, too?" Zach asks.

"Sure thing. Actually, let's try this on the floor, okay? That might be less scary for him, if we're all down low, at his level."

We're done eating now, so I can't imagine Tessa or Ryan would object. But when I look at them, they're both smiling and nodding, so I take Lucky to the corner of the dining room and plop onto the floor with him. With a little help from Charlotte, both kids scramble from the table and sit, cross-legged, next to me—and the minute little Claire starts cooing to

Lucky, my furry buddy shocks me by leaving my lap and going straight to her.

"Look, Mommy!" Claire shouts excitedly. "Lucky's not scared of me!"

"He likes you," I say. "Thank you for being so gentle with him. Zach, do you want to pet him, too? Be gentle, and I think he'll be okay."

The little boy joins in petting Lucky, and to my thrill, Lucky seems absolutely thrilled by the attention he's getting.

"Can Rudy meet Lucky now?" Zach asks, referring to Ryan and Tessa's blue-eyed husky. Throughout our meal, the big, white dog has been obediently sitting at Ryan's feet on a leash to allow Lucky time to acclimate to his new surroundings before adding another dog to the mix.

"I tell you what," I say. "Why don't we let the dogs say hello to each other, off leash, in the back yard? I think that'd be the best place for that."

Ryan and Tessa both say that sounds like a fabulous idea, and the whole group heads outside.

When Ryan brings Rudy over to Lucky, still on his leash, the big dog is friendly and gentle. So, we decide to let him off leash next and see what happens. When freed, Rudy immediately strikes "play pose"—front paws splayed, bottom raised high, happy, goofy expression on his face, and tail wagging— and Lucky immediately returns the gesture. It's something I've never seen him do before, and I'm blown away. I was certain Lucky would cower or run to safety behind my feet and only interact with Rudy after some gentle coaxing, but for whatever reason, Lucky's totally comfortable with this big dog. In fact, just this fast, the two dogs are now running off to frolic all over the spacious yard.

"I've never seen Lucky playing with another dog like this," I marvel. "Wow! This is incredible!"

While my eyes are still trained on Lucky's frolicking, happy form, Charlotte slides her hand in mine and leans her cheek against my shoulder. "It makes my heart soar to see him having so much fun," she says. A certain tenderness in Charlotte's voice makes me bend down and twist to glimpse her face, and when I see the glimmer in her green eyes, I can't resist leaning in and kissing her.

"Can I run around with dem?" Zach asks.

"Me, too!" Claire shouts.

"It's up to Auggie," Ryan says.

I break from my tender kiss with Charlotte, blushing. "Yeah, go for it, kids. Lucky's obviously not scared of any of you."

When the kids sprint off to play with the dogs, Ryan looks between Charlotte and me, briefly, a grin on his face. "Why don't I get the fire pit going and make some cocktails?" When we all agree that sounds like a plan, Ryan says, "Make yourselves comfortable. I'll be right back."

———

This is my idea of heaven. Hanging out with good people. Sitting around a fire pit, chatting and sipping a damned good cocktail while happy kids and dogs run around like maniacs on a nearby lawn. The icing on the cake? I've got my arm around Charlotte, and she's snuggled into me the same way Tessa's snuggled into her husband.

I look at Charlotte next to me and admire the way her beautiful face looks when illuminated by flames from the fire pit. She's stunning. Truly, the most magnetic woman I've ever been with.

Shit.

A deep-seated yearning envelops me. A sense of dread. I'm gonna be so fucked at the end of this, and I know it. But what's there to do about it? Shut myself off from all the fun I'm having now to protect my future self from getting hurt? That seems like cutting off my nose to spite my face.

My phone buzzes with an incoming FaceTime call that pulls me from my thoughts. It's my mother.

"Okay if I take this here?" I ask the group, holding up my phone. "It's my mom. She's been trying to reach me all week."

Everyone encourages me to answer the call here, rather than going somewhere else, and when I connect the call, and then show Mom my surroundings—the three people sitting around the fire pit with me and the kids and dogs running around the nearby lawn—my mother "oohs" and "aahs" with delight.

I turn the camera back to me. "What's up with you?"

"I'm having fun and wanted to say hello to you. You haven't been texting back or returning calls."

"Sorry, I've been super busy."

"There's a certain tiny redhead here who's been *dying* to say hello to her Uncle Auggie all week." Mom chuckles at something off screen. "Yes, love. Okay, he's all yours."

My bespectacled, five-year-old niece, Ripley, grabs the phone and overtakes my screen. "Hi, Uncle Auggie!"

"Hey, there, cutie pie! What's new?"

It's all Ripley needs. Without further prompting, she tells me *everything* going on in her happy life. *Everything* about the amazing time she's been having with Grandma Gigi and Grampy during their visit.

"Wow, that's so cool," I say.

"Who's *dat*?" Ripley asks, her little eyebrows raised behind her glasses. She points at Charlotte sitting next to me, half visible on my screen.

"That's my friend, Charlotte."

"She's pretty. She has hair like Mommy and me."

"Yes, she does. Charlotte." I nudge her leg. "Say hi to my niece, Ripley."

Charlotte says hello, and what follows is a much lengthier chat with Ripley, and then my mother, and then my whole family, than I'd ever intended or foreseen.

"How did you two meet?" Mom asks Charlotte. She's the one holding the phone now. The group is doing exactly what we are—they're sitting around an outdoor fire feature in Max and Marnie's stunning back yard with a bottle of wine.

"We're neighbors, actually," Charlotte says. "I just moved into the building."

"Oh, how *wonderful*," Mom says, her face aglow.

Uh oh. Time for me to change the subject. Mom is clearly pumped to see me sitting at a gathering with a pretty woman and another couple. And since she's got a glass of wine in her hand, there's no telling what she might say next.

"Okay, we have to go, Mom," I interject. "Have a great time, everyone."

"Before you go," Mom says, "did you get a summer internship yet?"

"No, but I interviewed for a pretty good one today during on-campus interviews. I'll keep you posted."

"Text me all about it!" Mom says, when it's clear I'm going to dip.

"I will. Bye now."

"Wait! Can you come down and visit for a few days during spring break?" Mom says. "We all miss you."

"I'll see if I can swing it. I'll text you, Mom. Love to everyone."

"Pweeeease come!" little Ripley's voice begs nearby.

"I'll do my best."

"Bye, *Charlotte*!" Mom calls out. "It was lovely to meet you, honey!"

"It was lovely to meet you, too, Gigi!" Charlotte calls back. "Auggie says the nicest things about you!"

"We'll have you over for dinner when we get back to Seattle!"

"Sounds fun."

Jesus Christ.

After another round of goodbyes, I finally hang up. "Sorry about that. She's dying to have another set of grandkids."

Everyone chuckles.

"My mother's the same way," Charlotte says. She pokes my leg playfully. "You didn't tell me about your interview today. Tell me all about it."

"There's nothing to tell. I don't have the position yet."

"Is it a place you're excited about?"

"Yes and no. The vets there are really experienced, so I'd learn a lot, but it's not the kind of place I'd prefer to wind up, long-term."

Remorse washes over Charlotte's face, and I know she's blaming herself for my blown interview at the place that was my top pick.

I take her hand and whisper, "That's water under the bridge, McDougal."

Tessa asks, "What kind of place do you want to wind up, Auggie?"

I briefly explain my professional goals to the group, and my ultimate long-term dream of owning my own veterinary practice that mostly services nonprofits, rescues, and animal shelters, and everyone—Ryan, Tessa, and Charlotte—expresses admiration for my goals.

"If you don't get the internship you interviewed for today," Ryan says, "hit me up. The wife of a buddy is a vet. Maybe she can hook you up."

"Thanks. I appreciate that."

Ryan addresses Tessa. "I should probably put the kids to bed, huh? We've got an early flight tomorrow."

"Yeah, good idea. I can do it, if you want."

"Nah." He touches his wife's baby bump and winks. "Relax. Catch up with your bestie who's been MIA lately." He playfully glares at Charlotte before getting up from the fire pit. In short order, Ryan's on the lawn wrangling his kids for bed, at which point Zach asks *me* to come upstairs to help put him to bed.

"I want to show you my cars," Zach explains.

"You're not gonna play cars right now, bubba," Tessa calls out to her son. "You need to get lots of sleep for our big day tomorrow."

"I just wanna *show* him," Zach says.

After getting nonverbal permission from Tessa, I say to Zach, "I'd love to see them." I'm still holding Charlotte's hand, so I kiss the top of it before releasing it and whispering to Tessa, "If I wind up being lured into playing cars for a few minutes, please forgive me."

"I'm thoroughly expecting it," Tessa says with a chuckle.

I wink at Charlotte. "I'll be back soon."

"I'm looking forward to it."

Butterflies. I'm feeling them, big-time. Even though I know I shouldn't.

I jog to catch up to Ryan and the kids, and try, try, try, not to let myself imagine what it'd be like to put *my* two kids to bed upstairs while my wife, Charlotte, remained behind, pregnant and glowing with *my* baby in her belly, with her bestie in *our* back yard—the sprawling, perfect backyard of the dream home, and dream *life*, we're building together.

22

CHARLOTTE

The minute our men and Tessa's two cuties have disappeared through a sliding glass door leading into the house, Tessa leans forward, arches a dark eyebrow, and coos, "You and Auggie seem awfully cozy. Quite the one-eighty from the last time I saw you two together, when you wanted to wring the man's neck."

I try to play it cool. "It turns out, it's hard to resist The Hottie Who Lives Next Door. Who knew?"

"Especially when he's as sweet and adorable as Auggie. What a cutie pie."

"I must admit, when I got to know him, I didn't mind him looking like 'The Dreamboat' in a boy band nearly as much."

Tessa snickers. "How big of you to make that concession."

We crack up.

"I was a lunatic the day of that job interview," I admit. "I was stressed out, and I took it out on him."

Tessa tilts her head. "Speaking of job interviews, why didn't you tell Auggie about yours today, especially after he mentioned *his*? Did you already tell him about it before coming over?"

"No, I haven't told him. I figure the interview might not lead to anything, so why mention it?"

"You told *me* about it."

I sure did. I texted Tessa excitedly the other day after receiving the email inviting me to interview, and then again today right after the interview ended to let Tessa know I thought I'd crushed it. "Telling you is different from telling Auggie," I insist. "I always tell you everything." Except that I don't. Not anymore. Not since I found out what Carlo does for a living. Not since I picked up that fucking duffel bag full of cash. And certainly not since I've been doing all sorts of crazy things online with Auggie. I wish I could tell Tessa about all of it. But I'm too ashamed. Plus, I'm scared telling Tessa about Carlo's world might put her and her family in danger, and I couldn't live with myself if ever I did that.

"Do you think maybe you didn't tell Auggie about today's interview," Tessa says tentatively, "because you're starting to develop feelings for him, and you're scared those feelings might make you reconsider the parameters and goals of your job search?"

Fucking Tessa. She's just articulated my biggest fear—that I've been having so much fun with Auggie, a man I've known mere days, I might feel tempted to forego my professional goals for him. He's still in school and will be for the next two years, for fuck's sake. I can't let myself get swept away like that —like a schoolgirl with a crush—no matter how much I might adore my hunky next-door neighbor.

I sip my wine calmly. "Auggie and I have already discussed it, maturely, and agreed we're going to keep our fling fun and casual while I'm in Seattle." I waggle my eyebrows. "You know, we're gonna make like JT and the boys and keep things 'No Strings Attached.'"

Tessa looks disappointed, despite my attempt at levity; but before she says anything in reply, the faint sounds of uproarious kiddie-giggling wafts from the open window above—the one leading into Zach's second-floor bedroom. It's the perfect distraction—an easy escape hatch out of this uncomfortable topic of conversation.

"Sounds like the kiddos are having a blast with Ryan and Auggie," I say, popping up from the patio couch. "Come on, T. Let's go spy on the kids and find out what's making them laugh like little hyenas."

———

At the top of the stairs, Tessa and I peek into Claire's bedroom first, since it's the first in the hallway, but it's empty. From there, we creep to the next opened door—Zach's bedroom—and discover the source of all that giggling. Both kids are sitting on the floor in their jammies while Auggie and Ryan, sitting shoulder to shoulder on Zach's small bed, give them a puppet show with socks on their hands.

Not surprisingly, given that Augustus Vaughn is undoubtedly the mastermind of this puppet show, the plot turns out to be a silly affair that's not really a plot at all—just a whole lot of puppet prat falls that elicit guffaws and unbridled joy from both kids.

Tessa whispers, "I'm swooning."

Shoot. I wish so badly I could make a snarky comment in this moment about this being the most G-rated puppet show Superhero Salami Slinger has ever performed; but obviously, the identity of Auggie's X-rated alter ego is a secret I'll take to my grave. And so, what I whisper back to Tessa, instead, is, "My ovaries are exploding."

"Mine, too. If I weren't already preggo, I'd be getting knocked up tonight."

I snort. "Girl, I'm on the pill, and I might still get knocked up tonight."

We cover our mouths to stifle our giggles, but it's too late. Our laughter has attracted Ryan's blue gaze.

When he sees us peeking through the doorframe, Ryan tells us to come in and watch the rest of the show, so we amble into the room and sit behind the kids on the floor. After several minutes of haphazard puppetry, however, the thin plot, such as it is, winds to a close. With a secret little wink to me, Auggie booms, *"And they lived happily ever after!"* And all four of us on the floor giggle and clap; except, of course, as I'm laughing and clapping, I'm also exchanging knowing, secret glances with Auggie about his coded reference to our own, illicit puppet shows.

Ryan and Auggie make their sock-covered hands take a bow, and Tessa and I get up from the floor. But when the men begin removing the socks from their hands, both kids protest and beg for another show.

"Nope," Ryan says. "No more delays. We've got an early morning, remember?"

Claire bats her eyelashes. "Daddy read me a story?" The kid knows full well Ryan won't refuse her. It's now a well-documented fact: Claire Morgan's got her smitten daddy wrapped firmly around her little finger.

"Just *one*," Ryan says, prompting Tessa to chuckle at how easily he retracted his supposedly firm, "no more delays" proclamation.

Well, now Zach wants a book read to him, too. But it's *Auggie* he wants reading to him, not his mother or me. And so, while Tessa and Ryan head off next-door with Claire Bear, I sit next to Auggie on Zacky's little bed and watch him read the kid a story about the best way to lure a gorilla out of a bathtub.

As Auggie reads, I lean against his back and enjoy the slight rumble of his body as he speaks. The soothing tones of his voice. The kindness that wafts off him. But soon, it's too much for my poor ovaries to take, so I sit up straight to save myself, just in time for the "big reveal" of the book: the punch-line to all prior suggestions about how to get that dang gorilla out of the tub.

When Auggie reads the punchline, Zach and I laugh with him.

"That's a good book," Auggie says, closing it.

"It's my favorite," Zach says.

"You've got good taste." Auggie pats Zach's little chest and pulls up his covers. "Goodnight, buddy. Sleep tight. Thanks for showing me your cars."

When Auggie gets up from the bed, I scooch closer and kiss Zach's cheek. "Goodnight, cutie pie. I love you."

"I love you, too."

"Door opened or closed?" Auggie asks, standing in the doorframe.

"Open, with da hall light on and also will you turn on my nightlight, so I won't get a nightmare?"

As Auggie gets everything in place according to Zach's specifications, I say, "I'm sorry you've had a nightmare. That's no fun."

"I get lots of dem," Zach says. "Mommy, too."

"Your mommy gets nightmares?" I ask, surprised by the revelation. It's the first I'm hearing of it.

Zach nods solemnly. "Lots and lots, I've heard Mommy screaming really, really loud in her bedroom. One time, I went to see if she was okay, but da door was locked. So I knocked really hard and I yelled, 'Are you okay in dere, Mommy?' And den Daddy opened da door and he was really sweaty and he said, "Go back to bed.' And I said, 'Is Mommy okay? Did she have a nightmare, like me?' And Daddy said, 'Yes, she was just having a nightmare, buddy, but she's okay now. Go back to bed.' But den I heard her screaming *again* another time, so I came back and knocked again, and *dat* time, Daddy opened da door and—"

Auggie and I can't take it anymore. We explode with laughter, interrupting Zach's rambling, clueless, adorable story. Unfortunately, Auggie and I made the mistake of locking eyes, and that's when we both couldn't hold back our laughter. If Ryan makes Tessa scream half as loudly as Auggie makes *me* scream in the throes of passion, it's no wonder poor little Zacky was worried sick about his beloved mommy. I'm positive I want to be a mommy one day, but one thing I'm not looking forward to when that happens is being in the middle of amazing sex and having to stop and open the door to my worried kindergartner.

"Why are you laughing?" Zach asks, scrunching his cute little nose.

"Because you're very cute and brave, and I'm so, so proud of you for wanting to take care of your mommy," I reply, forcing myself to pull it together.

"But why were you *laughing*?" Zach says. The kid's not stupid. I didn't provide an answer that makes a lick of sense.

"Hey, do you want to know a cool trick to keep nightmares away?" Auggie says, plainly changing the subject. "If you do this trick at bedtime, it makes it almost impossible to have a nightmare."

"Really?"

"It's not perfect, but only because nothing's perfect, but it works almost every time. Do you want to know how to do it?"

Zach nods excitedly.

"Okay, so after you get snuggly into bed, and the lights have been turned off, you pull the covers up and sing yourself a silly song. You can also get someone else to sing one to you. Either way, it'll work like a charm. But singing one to yourself works the very best."

Zach crinkles his little brow. "Like 'Wheels on da Bus,' you mean?"

"That one would definitely work. But the trick works even

better if it's a made-up silly song. One you make up on the spot about your day, maybe."

Zach's little shoulders droop. "I don't know how to make up a song."

"Sure, you do. We're all born knowing how to do that."

"We *are?*"

"Yep. All you have to do is let your mind wander and kind of float around. Think about something fun or funny, and let your mind go, and the words will tumble out."

Zach looks thoroughly confused.

"I'll show you," Auggie says. "Did something silly ever happen to you?"

Zach considers the question. "Once, I spilled apple juice on da floor in da kitchen. And den Rudy licked it all up, so you couldn't even tell, and Mommy said, 'Thanks to Rudy, we don't even need a mop!'" Zachary giggles at the memory.

"That's perfect," Auggie says. "A core memory. Let's sing about that." He pauses to choose his words. And then, he sings in a lilting, gentle voice, "I spilled some juice, cuz my arms got loose. But that's okay, no need for a mop, not even a bucket, cuz Rudy came along to save the day and *lick it.*"

Zach and I applaud.

"That was amazing," I say, and it's the truth. Auggie wasn't singing in a serious voice; he was simply joking around and having fun. But just that snippet made it clear the man can definitely carry a tune.

"Anudder one!" Zach says, his little face lit up.

"How about you try it now," Auggie prompts.

"Can you do one more?" Zach begs. And just like Ryan before him with Claire, Auggie can't refuse a tiny, pleading face.

"Okay, one more," Auggie says.

"Do one about something silly *you* did this time, Uncle Auggie."

Uncle Auggie. Auggie and I exchange a brief look—one that acknowledges his upgrade to uncle status.

"Okay." After pausing, Auggie sings, "I've got a salami sandwich and it's yummy and fun to eat. It's fun having a salami sandwich, even though I'd make more bread with some really pretty feet."

I burst out laughing at Auggie's coded song with its secret subtext, as Zach naively guffaws about Auggie's actual, kid-friendly words.

"Bravo," I say, clapping. "A masterpiece."

Auggie winks at me. "You liked that one, Auntie Charlotte?"

"I did. I'm in awe of you. You've actually got quite the knack for this silly songwriting thing."

"I had the best teacher, ever." He explains to Zach, "My grandmother loved singing silly songs. She did it all the time."

I rub Auggie's back, comforting him about the loss of his beloved grandma. "You have a really nice singing voice. With that face and that voice, you truly could have been in a boy band. The world missed out."

Auggie laughs. "Unfortunately, I don't have the dance moves, so I never would have made the cut. Plus, I get stage fright." He winks. "Well, I used to, anyway."

I feel myself blush. "I can't wait to judge your dance skills for myself when you perform your middle school *NSYNC routine for me."

Auggie scowls. "I was hoping you'd forgotten about that."

"Not a chance, baby. I'd sooner forget my own name."

Auggie rolls his eyes before returning to Zach. "Okay, it's your turn now. You can sing about anything and it doesn't have to rhyme. Let your mind wander and the words will tumble out.

Zach gives it a whirl, and the disjointed, rambling song he produces is truly the cutest thing, ever. When he's done,

Auggie and I applaud and praise him, and Zach expresses excitement.

"I think it's already working!" he says. "I can feel tonight's nightmare going away!"

"See? I'm telling you. It works like magic."

"Will you tell Mommy and Daddy the trick, so Mommy doesn't have another nightmare?"

"We sure will," Auggie says, patting Zach's little arm.

"It's so sweet of you to want to take care of your mommy," I say, just as Ryan and Tessa enter the room.

Zach excitedly tells his parents the fabulous trick "Uncle Auggie" taught him, so he won't have nightmares, and, of course, he also tells Tessa, "You can do da trick, too, Mommy, so you won't have any more nightmares!"

Tessa looks confused, so Ryan leans in and whispers into her ear—something that makes it hard for Tessa to keep a straight face. As Tessa reacts comically, the other three adults in the room chuckle and swap amused, knowing glances.

"I'll definitely give it a try, buddy," Tessa says. She leans down and kisses her son. "Thank you for always looking out for me. Goodnight, love."

Hugs, goodnights, and "I love you's" are administered across the board, and a minute later, we four adults are standing together in the hallway. We talk briefly about logistics for tomorrow, since I've volunteered to drive Tessa and the family to the airport. When that conversation is over, Ryan and Tessa head to their bedroom for the night, while Auggie and I head downstairs to check on Lucky.

When we find our beloved dog, he's snuggled up with Rudy on the couch and doesn't look the least bit interested in following us back up the stairs. Our fur baby settled, we head to our guest bedroom, holding hands as we go, our mutual body language making it clear we're both planning to finish off an amazing day with another round of amazing sex.

When we get to the guest bedroom, Auggie shuts the door behind us and turns to me with molten lust in his gorgeous blue eyes. "Hey, beautiful lady," he says flirtatiously. "Can you guess my mission for tonight?" The question is rhetorical, I think; also, my clit is pulsing like crazy, so I'd rather get down to business than pepper him with guesses.

"Tell me and then fuck me, please."

With sparkling blue eyes, Auggie takes two steps to me, slides his palms on my cheeks, and smiles wickedly. "My mission for tonight is to make you scream so fucking loud when you come, little Zachary Morgan comes knocking on our door to check on his beloved Auntie Charlotte."

23
AUGGIE

All it takes is one deep kiss, and we're both instantly ravenous, even before making it to the bed. The way we're going at each other, you'd think we've both been celibate and horny for a decade, while awaiting this precise moment. How is it possible we're both *this* hungry for each other, yet again? For my part, my desire for Charlotte is endless. Infinite. Off the charts. Mind-blowingly all-consuming. I can't get enough of this addictive woman. And by the way Charlotte's currently clawing at my shirt to get it the fuck off, I think it's pretty clear she's feeling a similar addiction.

My shirt off and hurled across the bedroom, Charlotte progresses to the metal buttons on my jeans. I help her out and get myself completely naked in lightning speed, while Charlotte quickly does the same. When we're both freed of our pesky clothes, I push Charlotte's back against the nearby wall with a thud that's probably got Zach's ears ringing down the hallway and kiss the hell out of her there, while the tip of my hard dick nudges into her belly. When we arrived earlier, we put our bags on the bed, and I'm unwilling to delay our horny crazy-train for a split-second—not even long enough to clear off the bed.

We're making out like wild animals now. Moaning, groaning, and groping while smashing our bodies together like our lives depend on it—and it's fucking amazing. This entire day with Charlotte has been incredible, from the moment I got home from school and Charlotte showed me those videos to this moment right here. To top it all off, *today* is the first day since all this craziness started that Charlotte and I didn't do a single show. That wasn't our plan; the day just got away from us. The end result, however, is that now, more than ever, Charlotte feels like *mine*. Like my real-life, actual girlfriend, rather than my fuck buddy or porny business partner. At this point, my relationship with Charlotte, whatever it is, feels better and more natural than any official romantic relationship I've ever had. In fact, it's better than any relationship in my wildest dreams.

Groaning with excitement, I pin Charlotte's arms above her head against the wall with one hand while stroking between her legs with the other. After a few strokes, when I sink my fingers deep inside her, she moans and begs me to fuck her. But I'm not going to do that, despite how wet she is for me. How urgently she's asking for it and how badly I want it. *Not yet.* I use the wetness from her pussy to make her clit slick, and then massage that hard nub around and around with my fingertips, until Charlotte's legs wobble and her breathing turns labored and erratic. As her pleasure spirals higher and higher, Charlotte begins whimpering and gyrating her pelvis, like her body is *aching* to be penetrated.

I release her hands, so I can properly finger fuck her while also continuing my assault on her clit. And that does it. After only a few seconds into my dual attack, Charlotte stiffens and groans, and then comes so hard, and with such a loud groan, I quickly cover her mouth with my palm to keep Zach firmly in his bed.

My cock hard and straining and my heart racing, I pick up Charlotte by her bare ass and sit down with her on the edge of the bed. She doesn't hesitate. With animalistic passion, Charlotte slams herself down onto my cock, all the damned way, and begins riding me like she's a cowgirl riding a mechanical bull at a honkytonk.

As Charlotte gyrates rhythmically on top of me, I devour her lips and grope her ass. And it doesn't take long before we're both absolutely frenzied. The energy between us is so explosive, in fact, so intense and all-consuming, I feel perilously close to blacking out with pleasure.

When Charlotte begins making telltale sounds—the ones that signal she's close—I slide a fingertip into her ass crack and apply gentle pressure to her anus. At this latest stimulation, she moans and groans and moves on top of me, even more feverishly, but she doesn't come. *She needs more.*

I nibble at her neck and jawline. I press my lips against her ear and tell her she's a drug and I'm an addict. That sex has never felt this fucking incredible. I tell her she's hot. Sexy. Beautiful. *Perfect.* The hottest woman alive. And after only a few minutes, she's positively *feral.*

While I'm balls-deep inside her, Charlotte throws her head back, groans loudly, and unleashes a kind of bliss on both of us that's got to be leagues better than any drug the "Just Say No" folks warned us about as kids. As Charlotte's innermost muscles ripple forcefully against my cock inside her, I'm catapulted to another dimension. Hurtling through space. She's coming. I'm coming. And the result is a euphoria, the likes of which I've never experienced—a moment of white-hot, sublime pleasure that's unrivaled by anything I've felt before. Forevermore, every time I have sex with any subsequent partner, this feeling right here will be the "white whale" I'll be chasing across proverbial oceans. Sadly, however, I already know nobody and nothing will ever compare to this, because nobody will ever compare to Charlotte McDougal. She's the best I'll ever have. The hottest woman alive. *And I'm in love with her.*

Fuck.

The realization makes me shudder again, one last time, even as my orgasm winds down.

Fuck, fuck, fuck.

I'm in love with her.

I'm not falling for Charlotte.

I'm not *en route.*

I've arrived.

I'm at my destination.

I love her.

With all my fucking heart.

As I ponder that inconvenient truth—that predicament, since I know Charlotte doesn't feel the same way about me— she wraps her thighs around me and bursts into tears. Worried, I lean my head back and take her face in my palms.

"Are you hurt?" I'm awfully deep inside her, and I'm well aware my dick is much bigger than average. A lot for anyone to take, but especially someone of Charlotte's size, and especially when the sex was *that* energetic and unleashed.

The second I see Charlotte's face, however, even before she speaks, I exhale in relief. She's not crying tears of pain. She's not even crying, really. She's euphoric, and her body has released in more ways than one.

"That was . . . *incredible,*" she gasps out. "You know when you see people flopping around on the floor at a Baptist Revival? It was like that, only the sexual version of it. Oh my god, Auggie."

Maybe Charlotte simply meant to allude to the *physical* flopping that overtakes a person who's feeling enraptured; but

I feel like that comment hits the nail on the head for me regarding how *spiritual* that felt. How *supernatural.* If I speak, it's fifty-fifty I'll confess, "I love you, Charlotte. I'm in love with you." So, rather than speaking, I kiss Charlotte's swollen mouth passionately in reply, and she returns my kiss with equal fervor.

When I finally feel capable of speaking without blurting something I'll surely regret, I pull back from Charlotte's lips and say, "I'll never forget this day with you, as long as I live." I leave it at that. We're about to spend the week together in this beautiful house, with nothing to do but fuck and make shows and hang out with Rudy and Lucky. So, I'm sure there will be several more unforgettable days and nights to add to this one. But for now, this day has to be logged as literally the best of my life.

Charlotte swipes her fingertips through my sweaty hair. "Logically, it was pretty stupid of us to take the entire day off from shows, huh? We probably shouldn't have done that, in the name of getting to our goal as quickly as possible."

"We had time to burn. And don't worry, now that I'm on spring break, we'll make up the time, if needed."

She snickers. "I don't know about you, but I'm not sure I can have six orgasms per day, every day, for the next five days."

"You won't need to, and neither will I. We'll do the stuff we talked about and crowdsource ideas, too. Do your super-fans want to see you mowing the lawn, naked? Do they want to see you hanging from that chandelier in Ryan and Tessa's dining room, naked, while I eat you out from below? The possibilities are endless, really. The weirder we get, the less they'll expect either of us to actually come. It'll be about the journey, not the destination—putting you into weirder and weirder naked scenarios."

She giggles. "That's actually a great idea."

"You're surprised by that?" I snicker. "Even a broken clock is right twice a day, baby."

Charlotte laughs and nuzzles her nose into mine. "This week is gonna be so much fun. I'm so glad you're here with me."

"Me, too." It's the understatement of the century. I'm elated. Counting my lucky stars. Feeling like I've won the lottery. True, this woman unintentionally slapped a target on my back with a hitman. Not ideal. But at this point, regardless of that one, pesky little thing, I feel like Charlotte is the best thing that's ever happened to me. *My lucky charm.* If only she'd feel the same way about me, my entire future would be set.

Charlotte pecks my lips. "I'd better shower and get some sleep. Tessa's flight is butt-crack early tomorrow."

"I'll come with you to the airport, if you want."

"Nah, get some sleep. I don't think there's enough room in the car for another adult, anyway, because of all the luggage they're bringing. I'll pick up coffee and breakfast on my way back to repay you for all the times you've done that for me."

"I do that because I'm already getting it for myself and you're watching Lucky for me, remember? There's nothing to repay. But thank you."

She drags her teeth across her lower lip. "Wanna come shower with me?"

"More than I want to breathe."

Charlotte slides off me and we head to the attached bathroom together, where we make out and explore each other's slick, wet bodies. When that bit of fun is over, we slide into bed, facing each other, and smile like goofs at each other.

"Goodnight, Charlotte," I whisper.

She pulls a playful face. "I'm scared I'm gonna have a nightmare, Uncle Auggie. Will you sing me a silly song?" She pokes my abs underneath the covers. "Pretty please with sugar on top?"

I chuckle. "What do you want me to sing about?"

"Anything. Just like you told Zacky, let your mind wander and the words tumble out."

It's a dangerous game for me to play—a huge risk to take—considering the fact that the only word coming to mind, as I lie here, naked, with Charlotte in the moonlight is the word *love. Love, love, love. I love you, Charlotte McDougal.*

I smile. "Sorry, I think I'm done singing silly songs for the night. My mind is drawing a blank. Why don't you give it a try?"

Charlotte makes a funny, pouty face, but ultimately, she huffs out, "*Fine.*" After giving it a moment of thought, she says, "This is a lot tougher than I thought."

"It can be anything. Let your mind wander."

"You've got a real talent."

"Nah. Anyone can do it. Relax your mind."

Charlotte closes her eyes and remains still for a long moment. When she opens them, she smiles and sings, "Hello there, Auggie Vaughn. Let's have a talkie, son. You're a stone-cold hottie. With a three-legged doggie. Thanks for letting me join you for Lucky's walkies and for getting off my rockies. I'm having so much fun with you, Auggie Vaughn. Can't wait for the rest of this week together, and beyond."

And beyond?

Wait, what?

Did Charlotte sing that heart-stopping part, simply because it rhymed, or was she telling me she's thinking about exploring this relationship after our mutual emergency is resolved?

"That was f-fantastic," I choke out.

Charlotte looks anxious. Does she realize what she just said? Does she want to take it back? "I've got another one," she says quickly. She sings, "My life is in flux right now, Auggie dear. I'm pretty fucked right now, as you know, don't know what my future holds. But no matter what happens next, Auggie dear, I promise you this . . . I won't wind up in *Milwaukee, dear*. Cuz in a *cit*-y like *that*, this LA girl would freeze her titties off and turn into a polar *bear*." Charlotte giggles, so I join her in laughing, even though the lyrics felt like a bit of a gut punch. *Okay, message received, Charlotte. The word "beyond" in your first song meant nothing.*

I'm tempted to roll over onto my other side, so I don't have to fake a smile. But the allure of Charlotte's smiling face is too great. I pull her to me and hold her close and tell myself to savor the here and now and not let my stupid brain think about the future or anything else.

"This is the safest I've felt in a really long time," Charlotte whispers into my chest.

I kiss the top of her head. "Good. Sleep well, beautiful. I've got you."

"I know you do. I've got you, too, beautiful."

I kiss her hair again. And a few minutes later, her body goes slack in my arms.

I lie awake listening to Charlotte's rhythmic breathing for a ridiculously long time, despite how exhausted I am. Until eventually, I finally reach a place, mentally, where I can make a firm deal with myself: from this moment forward, I'm going to live in the present moment and be happy with Charlotte, for however long this amazingness lasts. It's far better to appreciate and enjoy happiness, as it's happening, after all, than to waste that same precious amount of time feeling heartbroken it won't last forever.

24
AUGGIE

One week later

We did it.

Fuck yeah.

It's just after four o'clock in the afternoon on Friday—exactly one week since we arrived at Tessa and Ryan's gorgeous house—and we've now made every penny needed to bring with us on our flight to New Jersey tomorrow. At the moment, Charlotte and I are driving in my car to our building to pick up some stuff for our trip tomorrow, and from there, we'll head to the bank to withdraw all our cold, hard cash. We crossed our sixty-thousand-dollar finish line today around noon, which means we still have some time before picking up Tessa and her family at the airport this evening to put on a couple more shows and bank some extra cash for me.

We could have reached our finish line for Carlo's money well before today—maybe as much as three days ago—if we'd abstained from all the off-camera sex we enjoyed this week and instead used every available moment and every possible boner and drop of sexual energy for shows, shows, shows. But fuck it. We both knew we'd get the money in time, even if it was on the last possible day, because I've been carefully tracking our trajectory the whole time. So, we decided to make the most of our time together in paradise, both on-camera and off. I'm so glad we did. It was the best week, ever.

I turn onto our street and easily find an open stretch of curb across the street from our building. As I pull into the open spot, I quip, "It's our lucky day in more ways than one."

Charlotte giggles. "It's a glorious day."

We exit my car and begin trekking up the pathway toward the front door of our building, hand in hand. We're practically floating. So relieved we've met our goal, our feet are barely touching the ground.

"Coming back here to live, after spending a week at Tessa and Ryan's snazzy house, is going to be a tough pill to swallow," Charlotte jokes.

"This place is a hovel, by comparison."

She chuckles. "Their house would be my dream house, I think, if only it had an ocean view."

There it is again. Charlotte frequently lets me know, if only subtly, that she still plans to return to LA, the same as she ever did. Or maybe I'm just overly sensitive and reading into her comment.

I press the code to the front door and open it for Charlotte. As we enter the lobby, I say, "Staying at Ryan and Tessa's place has made me rethink my career goals, somewhat."

Charlotte looks puzzled. "In what way?"

We stop at the mailboxes and open our respective boxes.

"Just, you know . . . I'm wondering if maybe I shouldn't be quite as selfish as I've always been in terms of planning my ideal career."

Charlotte closes her mailbox and squints at me. "Selfish in what way?"

I shrug and look down at the short stack of mail in my hands. It's all junk, as usual.

"Auggie, how are your professional goals selfish?" Charlotte prompts.

We head to the elevator and press the call button.

"I've always been singularly focused on what I thought the *perfect* kind of veterinary practice would be for *me*, personally. As an *individual*. But that kind of practice wouldn't put me at the high end of the income scale for veterinarians, so maybe I should compromise a bit, in order to make more money, so I can afford a house like Tessa and Ryan's one day." The thing I'm not saying, of course, is that, if Charlotte dreams of winding up in a house like Tessa and Ryan's, I'd be willing to shift my professional dreams and goals a bit, if it'd mean she'd wind up in a house like that with *me*.

We step into the elevator. As the doors close, Charlotte says, "I think your dreams are the most *unselfish* I've ever heard. Since middle school, you've always wanted to help the most helpless of creatures. Knowing you, I don't think you'd be completely fulfilled in your life, if you did something else, so please don't."

I look down at my shoes, feeling too vulnerable to look Charlotte in the eyes when I say the next part. "Well, yeah, that might be true of me *now*. But down the line, what would be more important to me? Being able to take care of neglected and abandoned animals, or being able to take care of my family in the best possible way?" I muster the courage to look up. "Pets owned by wealthy people need medical care, too. And they're still animals in need. So, really, helping them would still make me feel like I'm serving an important purpose, at the end of the day. If Rudy got cancer, for instance, or broke a bone, I'd be proud to be the vet to help him get better. There'd be no shame in that."

The elevator opens and Charlotte and I step out silently. But midway down the hallway, she says, "I agree there'd be no *shame* in that. Of course, not. It's an honorable profession, any way you do it. But we're talking about *you*. Auggie Vaughn. And *you* can't change who you are, at your very core, for the sake of taking care of some hypothetical family who doesn't even exist yet. Be true to yourself, and the rest will follow, exactly the way it's meant to. If circumstances change, and you want to shift your professional course down the line, then you will."

Jesus. She's missed my meaning. *Again.* Why doesn't Charlotte understand I'm talking about *her*? Imagining *Charlotte* as my future wife—the mother of my future babies—the heart of the family I'm dreaming of building and housing in comfort and style, the way Ryan and Tessa, and my brother and his wife, have done for *their* families?

Only a month ago, I wouldn't have thought it possible of me, but I'd give up a whole lot, even my current professional goals, to make it work with Charlotte. Hell, I could apply to transfer to a vet school in LA, if that would mean we could stay together. But I can't do any of it if Charlotte doesn't see a future with me the way I see one with her. The problem is, every time I try to suss out if Charlotte's feelings for me might have changed and deepened beyond our original "no strings attached" arrangement, she doesn't take the hint and give me any clarity. And, unfortunately, I'm not willing to go out on a limb by saying "I love you" to a woman who hasn't given me *any* indication she'd say it back to me.

We've reached Charlotte's front door now. She slides her key in the lock, and we step inside the unit. Quickly, Charlotte grabs the birthday girl's wrapped present from her big suitcase, and we head next door to my place to gather our next required item: my carry-on suitcase.

When we step inside my place, Charlotte plops onto my couch while I head into my bedroom to grab the bag. But when I come back out to the living room, Charlotte's holding up her phone with a snarky, mischievous smirk on her pretty face.

"What?"

She waggles her eyebrows. "It's time to pay your debt, Augustus Vaughn. You promised me a boy band performance as my reward when we had all the money, remember?"

"Shit."

Charlotte laughs. "You promised, and you're a man of your word."

"Yes, I am. *Unfortunately*." I exhale. "Okay, McDougal. Cue up the song. One horrendously terrible boy-band-lip-synch-attempted-dance fiasco coming right up."

"It's already cued up. 'No Strings Attached.' Let me know when you're ready."

It's the song my friends and I lip-synched in middle school, so she couldn't possibly be sending me yet another coded message. And yet, even though my brain knows that, my heart irrationally feels like she's selected the song to remind me of our agreed-upon arrangement.

I stand before her with my head bowed. "Ready."

Charlotte cues the song, and to my surprise, every word comes back to me. In fact, I actually think I'm doing a pretty good job of lip-synching here. Surprisingly good. My dance moves aren't as successful, unfortunately. In fact, I'm at such a loss for choreography, I wind up turning the whole perfor-mance into a striptease, basically—one that leaves me standing before Charlotte, naked and hard, as the song winds down.

As the blaring song ends, Charlotte pops up from the

couch, throws her arms around my neck, and kisses me passionately, which, predictably, leads to me ripping off her clothes and laying her down onto my couch.

After eating her out and making her come, I sink myself inside her—all the fucking way—and rock my pelvis in and out, with gusto, as Charlotte matches my every movement. As we move together, I look into her green eyes and whisper, "You're safe now. *We did it.*"

"We did it," she whispers back. "I'm so happy, Auggie."

I touch Charlotte's cheek as I kiss her, fuck her, *claim* her, wordlessly confessing my love for her with each thrust and kiss and touch. As our passion escalates, she draws her legs around my waist, and I grind myself into her with increasing desperation.

"You're so fucking gorgeous," I murmur, as my body breaches hers. "You're perfect." *I love you, I love you, I love you.* I'll never feel this kind of passion with anyone else, ever again, and I know it. So, I'm trying desperately to forget that and simply savor the moment.

With a loud moan, Charlotte grips my neck, stiffens, and proceeds to have an orgasm beneath me that hurtles me into a veritable seizure of pleasure. I growl through my powerful, quaking release, as Charlotte grips my ass and moans loudly.

When the world finally stops spinning, and my heart rate lowers to a pace that allows me to function, I press my lips against Charlotte's ear and softly whisper, "You're a unicorn."

She hugs me to her. "So are you."

We lie like that for a long moment. And finally, head into my shower together.

As the hot water rains down on us, we're both feeling so relieved and carefree, so unburdened, we start singing each other silly songs. Charlotte goes first, singing a silly song about us having our *dirty* money a day *early* and taking it to *Jersey* on a Saturday, not a *Thursday*.

And when it's my turn, I sing a parody of a boy-band song on the fly, one inspired by the *NSYNC song I just performed for her. Charlotte loves it. In fact, she's positively guffawing.

"Yes!" she says, laughing. I pull her to me, and we enjoy a long, euphoric kiss as hot water pelts us. All good things must come to an end, however. And after a few minutes of kissing, Charlotte breaks away and says, "We'd better get to the bank. I don't want to risk getting there anywhere near closing time."

"Agreed."

We hop out of the shower and quickly get dressed and grab the stuff we came for. As we head into the hallway, we hold hands, and walk to the elevator, once again like we're floating on air. But as we're heading out the front door together downstairs, Charlotte abruptly stops and grips my forearm.

"What?" I follow the trajectory of Charlotte's gaze, and that's when I see what's spooked her: a dark-haired guy leaning against the hood of my SUV across the street. He looks kind of like the guy who sat on the bench with an ice cream cone a week ago, but I'm honestly not sure.

"I'm positive I've seen him before," Charlotte croaks out, her voice tight and filled with dread. "*I served him a rum and Coke on a flight with Mr. DiMarco.*"

25
CHARLOTTE

uggie and I look at each other with wide eyes. *Why is that man leaning against Auggie's SUV?*

The guy waves, like he's our friendly Uber driver at the airport. And when we don't move, he saunters over to us, holding up his palms. "Carlo sent me. He has something important he's got to do all day today and tomorrow morning before Bella's birthday party, so he asked me to come out here and get the bag from you ahead of time today, so I can get back and set everything up before the party, just like Carlo talked about with you." He waits a beat. And when Auggie and I look at each other silently and in mutual panic, he says, "Carlo told me everything, okay? Actually, I figured it out and went to him about it, and we made ourselves a side deal. But you don't need to concern yourselves with that. All you need to know is that I now owe Carlo a big favor, and this is the way I'm gonna even the score with him—by helping you out. I've got no beef with either of you, okay? Carlo has an emergency, so I came to get the money, since he won't have time to do what he was planning to do tomorrow before the party."

Auggie nods at me, letting me know he thinks this is legit,

and I'm inclined to agree. This guy wouldn't know all the details of our arrangement with Carlo, if he hadn't heard them from Carlo himself, exactly as he's said.

"We don't have the money in cash yet," Auggie says. "We're going to get it now from the bank."

"I'll come with you."

Man, he's one scary-looking dude. I know Carlo is in the same field of work, but, somehow, Carlo has never lost his humanity. His easy warmth. I'm sure Carlo's good at his job, or else Mr. DiMarco wouldn't have kept him on for so long. But Carlo must be better at compartmentalizing the bad stuff than this dude, because this guy looks fucking deadly, even when he's smiling, as he is now.

To our dismay, he strides to Auggie's car and walks around to the passenger side, telegraphing he's intending to drive to the bank with us . . . *in the same car.*

"Can we maybe call Carlo and confirm this is what he wants us to do?" I ask, suddenly feeling unsure. Talking to a paid killer while standing on a public street feels less iffy than voluntarily getting into a car with one.

"He's got an emergency. No calls." He raps on the passenger-side window. "Door's locked."

Auggie shifts his weight. "We're gonna be heading somewhere after the bank, so you should probably drive separately."

"That's not possible. Once we have the money, I'll be out of your hair—off to the airport to catch a flight to JFK, so I can 'find' the money there. But until then, I can't take any chances with you two. For all I know, you're gonna get skittish and do something stupid like try to lose me on your way to the bank —and I can't let that happen. I'm in this thing up to my eyeballs now, too, thanks to my side deal with Carlo. So, I'm gonna make sure this transfer goes off without a hitch." He shoves his shirt aside, revealing a gun in his waistband. "I have no intention of using this on either of you, okay? I'm here to help you. But I also want to make it clear I don't have time to negotiate or fuck around. I've got my orders from Carlo and a plane to catch. So, let's move it."

On wobbly legs, Auggie and I get into his car, with me in the backseat, Auggie driving, and our new friend in the passenger seat.

The short drive to the bank is silent and tense. But ten minutes later, we arrive without incident—with our limbs and organs pristine and intact.

All three of us pile out of the car, but as Auggie and I head toward the bank, our new friend stays behind, leans his ass against Auggie's SUV, and says, "I'll wait out here."

About twenty minutes later, Auggie and I come out of the bank with the cash in a bag, our hearts thundering. When the guy sees us walking toward him, he straightens up. And when we reach him, he says, "You got it all?"

"Yep," Auggie says on an exhale. "Sixty big ones. All cash. It's all there."

"*Sixty?*" the guy says, his eyebrows jerking up. "What about the interest?"

"*Interest?*" Auggie shouts, as I simultaneously shriek, "Carlo never said anything about interest."

The guy looks at me. "Sure, he did."

"No, he didn't," I insist, and Auggie backs me up. "Carlo said we had to repay the sixty grand and that's it."

"No, Carlo told you about the interest," the guy grits out, his voice turning steely. "If not, then we've got a problem, because that's standard procedure. *Anyone* who steals from the big guy, no matter who they are or who they might have fucked, owes interest on money they took, if we're so kind as to look the other way and let it slide. *No fucking exceptions—for anyone.*"

"Okay, but . . ." Auggie says. "This isn't really a standard deal, right? Carlo explained that to you, right? So—"

"No exceptions," he barks. "If you're telling me that Carlo brokered a special deal with you—one that nobody else ever gets because you're his ex-girlfriend, then I'm not sure I can trust him to keep his side deal with *me*, to be honest. If that's the case, then I think I'd better take this information straight to the big boss and let him know—"

"No! Don't do that!" I shout, as Auggie says something similar. "We must have forgotten about the interest. It slipped our minds because we're not used to this sort of thing. We're amateurs, you know?" I feel like I'm on the cusp of hyperventilating or passing out, but somehow, I manage to add, "*Of course,* Carlo didn't give me a special deal. But can we maybe pay the interest in a week or two because we don't currently have anything more than that, so we'll need some time to get more."

"I can't do that."

"Can I ask what's probably a stupid question?" Auggie asks. "If the money is going to be 'found' at JFK, then how could it possibly earn interest?"

The man's dark eyes harden to steel. "It's two different things. We've got a separate slush fund. That's where the interest will go. One thing doesn't have anything to do with the other. The simple fact is *nobody* is allowed to take money from our boss without paying interest on it. *Ever.* No exceptions. But hey, if you don't have the money, that's fine. I'll call the big guy now and let him know he should ask Carlo about this."

"Don't do that," I blurt, my throat tight. "Please. I don't have Carlo's current number, but if you'll call him and loop him into this discussion, I'm sure we can—"

The guy steps forward menacingly. "*No, we can't.* Either you've got the interest now, or the deal is off. It's as simple as that. I said I'd help Carlo in exchange for a big favor, but I'm not gonna go out on a limb this big for him or anyone else. Fuck that." He's getting increasingly agitated and angry, that much is clear—and that's making *me* feel increasingly panicked.

Auggie steps in front of me, putting his body squarely between me and the scary dude. "I'll pay you the interest right now. I just need to go back into the bank to get it."

Oh, God, no. Auggie could only be talking about his tuition money. As far as I know, that's literally the only money he's got squirreled away—the twenty grand he managed to save before I came along to fuck up his life—the fifty-percent down Auggie needs to pay by midnight *tonight* in order to reserve his spot in the program and negotiate a payment plan for the rest.

"No, Auggie," I whisper, tugging on his shirt.

"You were holding out on me, huh?" the guy says. "I figured."

Auggie puffs out his chest. "What's the interest rate? Tell me what we owe you, and I'll go into the bank and get it.

"Our standard interest rate is twenty-five percent."

Auggie jolts at this horrific news, as a whimper simultaneously escapes from my throat. I'm no math wizard, plus, my brain is freezing from panic, so I pull out the calculator on my phone with a shaking hand—and then gasp at the resulting number. Holy shit. This scary motherfucker is saying we owe him an additional *fifteen grand* on top of the sixty we just handed him!

"We can't pay that much," I say. "Auggie needs that money for school. His tuition deadline is tonight at midnight."

The scary man leans forward. "I guess you should have thought of that before stealing money from my boss, huh?" He straightens up and swats Auggie's shoulder. "Now, get back in there and get the interest payment. I need to catch a flight."

Fuck, fuck, fuck. I look at Auggie, on the verge of bursting into tears, and he grabs my hand and squeezes it. "It's okay."

"No, wait. Sir, please."

"You'd better go," he says to Auggie. He grabs my arm. "She'll stay out here with me while you get it. Consider her collateral." He motions to the bulging gun in his waistband to emphasize his point.

"I'll be right back," Auggie says stiffly.

I cry silent tears as I watch Auggie walking into the bank. I've been a wrecking ball crashing into that poor man's life—a disastrous force of total ruination.

Several minutes later, when Auggie exits the bank, he's holding a large manila envelope.

"It's all here," he says when he reaches the guy, handing it over. "Fifteen grand."

The guy opens the envelope and thumbs through its contents, counting to himself softly. "Looks good." He tips an imaginary cap to Auggie and me. "See you two at the birthday party tomorrow. Pretend you don't know me when you see me." He stuffs the envelope into the bag of money from earlier and marches away. A moment later, he turns a corner and disappears.

When the guy is gone, I fall into Auggie's arms and sob. But he doesn't hug me for long, out in the open. Pretty quickly, he shuttles me into his car and locks the doors.

"I'm so sorry, Auggie," I say, as tears stream down my cheeks.

"I'm just glad he's gone and you're safe."

"But you need twenty grand by midnight to keep your spot. How much do you have left in your account?"

"About five grand."

"Shit. Do you think they'll give you an extension for that amount?"

Auggie smiles thinly. "Today is the last day of my extension. I'm out of time."

My heart sinks. "Can you give them the five grand you have and beg them to—"

"Charlotte, it's over. Trust me. I've called in every extension and negotiated every which way. I need to transfer twenty grand on my student dashboard at midnight tonight to reserve my spot. That's the deal. But don't worry. I'm pretty sure if I apply for a deferment, they'll let me back in after a year off."

I palm my forehead. "I can't believe I dragged you into my mess. I'm so, so sorry, Auggie."

"It's not your fault."

I'm crying. Sniffling. Trembling. "Yes, it is. It's *all* my fault. I've ruined your life."

Auggie takes my hands. "I wouldn't change a fucking thing, Charlotte. I mean, yes, I wish I had the twenty grand. But I've had the time of my life with you. If the price of that is taking a year off from school and figuring out some student loans, then so be it. The most important thing is you're safe and sound. That's literally all I care about." He chuckles. "Damn. It's a good thing I didn't pay the invoice early, huh? I almost did, but then I thought we might do some more shows today before picking up Tessa and her family at the airport, so I figured I should hold off until—"

I gasp. "That's what we'll do now! We'll do as many shows as we can before 11:59 tonight and get you the rest of the money you need!"

Auggie sighs. "You're sweet to want to help, but—"

"No *buts* allowed. We can do this, Auggie. You have five grand, so all we need is fifteen grand more in, what, . . . eight hours? We can do that if we put our minds to it and tell our fans we're in a pinch and need their generous help *today*. We'll tell Tessa, sorry, you need to take an Uber home, and then we'll go back to your place and get to work."

"What about the dogs?"

"Shit. Okay, we'll go back to Tessa's and feed them now and leave them there. I'll text Tessa and let her know we were there recently but we need them to watch both dogs for us tonight and all next week. She won't mind." My adrenaline is pumping now. "We'll make it like a telethon for our audience —with a countdown clock and a graphic showing us getting closer and closer to our goal. We'll say we need to make twenty grand by midnight tonight, or—"

"Fifteen. I've got five."

"No, we'll say twenty, and hope we get fifteen. If we get twenty, even better. Then you'll have some money for expenses, while you try to figure out the rest." I grab his hand. "This is going to work, Auggie. Our fans will come through for us."

"Your optimism is infectious, I admit; but the fact remains we've never made that much in a single day, let alone eight hours."

"No negativity allowed!" I shriek. "Yes, it'll be a steep climb. But I think our fans will come through for us. They'll pay to watch us doing all sorts of zany things, one after another, to help us reach a specific goal. We can ask for pledges for this and that thing, and once each thing reaches a grand in pledges, we'll do it!"

"Love it."

"We'll ask our superfans to lead the charge on pledges— you know, Lucille1990, Catfish2000, and all the other high rollers in the VIP club. God as my witness, Auggie Vaughn, we'll get the money you need in time."

Auggie's face is lit up. "Well, first off, I truly hope God isn't witnessing any of this. And second off, fuck yeah, baby, count me in."

"Woohoo!" I grab Auggie's face and kiss him fervently, and then release him with equal enthusiasm and pull out my phone. I log into our account and start scrolling through past videos and comments to see what we might have missed. "Aha! Here's something to get us started! Four days ago, Lucille1990 said she'd pay *five hundred bucks* to watch you get your dick pierced!"

Auggie's jaw drops. "I'm not going get my dick pierced! Fuck no. Especially not for five hundred measly bucks."

"Would you do it for a *thousand* bucks . . . *per piercing?*"

"*What?*" Auggie shouts, looking distressed.

I chuckle. "I'm sure people will add to Lucille's initial five hundred bucks to get us to a thousand a pop. We'll message her to see if she'll pay five hundred bucks *per* piercing and help us get our telethon rocking and rolling."

"Back up, Charlotte. *Per piercing?* How many piercings are you expecting me to get in my dick?"

I laugh. "You wouldn't get *all* of them yourself, silly. I'd get some, too. Why not? We wouldn't have to keep them in, if we don't like them. We'd make it clear they're paying to watch us get *pierced*, repeatedly, not to ensure we stay that way forever."

Auggie looks incredulous.

"It's really not as big a deal as you're thinking." I smirk. "This is confidential, but Ryan's got a dick piercing, and he seems perfectly fine and functional."

"*Ryan's* dick is pierced?"

"Both nipples, too." I giggle at Auggie's flabbergasted reaction. "Tessa *loves* Ryan's piercings, especially on his dick. She told me its sole purpose is to get her off, and she said it's *extremely* effective. It gives her orgasms during intercourse, repeatedly, like clockwork.

"What. The. Fuck?" Auggie looks shell-shocked. "Are you bullshitting me? You're telling me this stuff to convince me to—"

"No, it's the God's truth. I swear it on Lucky. On Zach and Claire, too."

He winces. "It feels very wrong to bring the kids into this, babe."

"Whoops. You're right. Scratch that. The point is I'll swear on whatever or whomever you want, because it's all the truth. I think you must be imagining something way scarier than what I'm talking about. It's not Ryan's *tip* that's pierced. There's no little scaffolding that goes up his shaft. He's got a piercing at the *base* of his dick. Like, you know, where his dick meets his torso?"

"*You've seen Ryan's piercing?*"

"No, no, not on Ryan. I saw it on the internet. In a photo Tessa showed me. Hang on." There's a famous rockstar who split his pants onstage several years ago, at which time the entire world found out he's got the exact same kind of piercing as Ryan "Captain" Morgan. Tessa showed me the photo of the rockstar when she told me about her then-fiancé's sexy secret over a bottle of wine during her bachelorette weekend.

I quickly find the photo and hand it to Auggie. "See? Now, that doesn't look nearly as scary as you were imagining, does it?"

Auggie doesn't reply; he stares at the photo silently. Apparently, even that kind of piercing looks scary as shit to him.

"You could take it out, immediately," I say quickly. "That's certainly what I'm planning to do with whatever piercings I wind up with."

Auggie hands me the phone back. But still, he doesn't say anything.

"If piercings are a non-starter for you," I say, "then I guess we could finally have intercourse on-camera for the first time. I bet if we—"

"Absolutely not." He shakes his head defiantly. "That's the

one thing we've got left that's only for us. I'm not going to share that with anyone. I'd rather take a year off from school than fuck you, on-camera."

My heart flutters. I don't actually *want* to have intercourse on-camera. I totally agree, it's our one private thing, along with kissing. We haven't done either on camera, and I've been glad about that. But I would have done both, gladly, if it meant Auggie wouldn't lose his hard-earned spot in the vet program.

"Okay, I'll pierce my dick," Auggie says on an exhale. "Man, that's a sentence I never thought I'd say in my lifetime." When I laugh, he shrugs. "If this doesn't work, then at least we'll know we tried everything possible."

"Agreed." I take his hand. "Are you sure about the piercing? If not, I'll—"

"Yeah, I'm sure. Let's do it. I'm in."

Oh, my heart. It's fluttering again. He's so fucking hot and adorable. "Okay, here's the plan. We'll head back to Tessa's now and feed the dogs. While we're there, we'll send private messages to the high rollers and also do a video announcing the 'old-school telethon' and set a countdown clock with a finish line of 11:55 tonight. We need to give you time to actually make the transfer, right? And after that, we'll put up a long list of zany, silly things we're willing to do, for various threshold amounts, including the piercings—which we'll make our grand finale, the last adventure of the telethon—with a minimum threshold of a thousand bucks a piercing. While we're waiting for the pledges to roll in, I'll call a piercing place and rent it out for an hour at, say, ten. Just to be on the safe side. To kick things off, we should squeeze in a few quick shenanigans 'for free'—for tips only—to get the algorithm working in our favor." I take a deep breath and exhale. "Does all that sound good?"

Auggie's eyes are wide with astonishment. "Holy fuck,

Charlotte. You're incredible at this. You're a porn-queen genius-phenom."

I laugh. "I'm feeling motivated to help you, that's all. I'm not gonna let your dreams crash and burn, Auggie Vaughn. Not on my watch. Not after everything you've done for me and the mess I've made of your life." I take his hand and kiss the top of it, feeling physically electrified by excitement. "In the immortal words of a band that probably wasn't a boy band, but could have been, I really don't know for sure, since they only had one hit, thanks to a TV show: *I'll be there for you.*" As Auggie cracks up, I turn and secure my seatbelt with gusto, and then point forward enthusiastically through his front windshield. "Onward to Tessa's house, baby! We've got tuition to pay by midnight and a whole lot to accomplish before then."

26

AUGGIE

10:14 pm

"*Titty-fucking motherfucker!*"

That's the string of syllables that involuntarily explodes out of my mouth when the needle punctures the base of my dick, and everyone watching my impalement guffaws in reaction. They cackled and hooted pretty raucously when I got both nipple piercings done a few minutes ago, too; but my reaction this time to the needle slicing my tender flesh is bigger, so, naturally, their reaction is bigger, too.

The tattoo/piercing place is devoid of patrons for this livestream, thankfully, due to Charlotte's smart planning for our grand finale event. The only two people here, in person, other than Charlotte and me, are 1) The dude who's piercing my sensitive flesh, and 2) a tattoo artist with some time to kill who kindly agreed, for a fat tip, to be our cameraman for these shenanigans. But of course, we're also joined for this livestream by a surprisingly large online audience—our biggest one yet.

"All done, my friend," the piercing dude declares, patting my bare shoulder. My shirt is off, thanks to the nipple piercings. My sweatpants are pulled down and my flaccid cock is out. "You can open your eyes now, Salami."

I open one eye and squint down at my dong with trepidation to find it glaring back at me like, *"What the fuck did you just do to me, motherfucker?"* At the base of my cock, there it is: a shiny, metal hoop that's every bit as shiny as the two metal rods newly rammed through each of my nipples. *Who am I? How is this my life?*

If someone had told me ten years ago that one of the Vaughn brothers would get his nipples and dick pierced on this exact date in time, and if they then asked me to bet on which Vaughn brother it'd be in order to save my life and the life of every person I love in this world, I wouldn't have hesitated to bet on Max to become the future pin cushion. *Of course.*

My big brother is the one who fucked his way through his twenties and partied like a rockstar after water polo games in both high school and college, whereas I was the shy, nerdy athlete who came home after swim meets to rest up and get all my schoolwork done, usually because I was excited to volunteer at the animal shelter early the next morning. Max is the one who swaggered his way through a bit of a bad-boy phase in his late teens, while *I* was the late blooming science nerd with a stutter to overcome—an embarrassment that kept me feeling shy and unsure around girls, long after the actual stammering had been dealt with and eradicated. And yet, here I am, the Vaughn brother who just got *three* pieces of hardware inserted into his intimate body parts for the entertainment of an online audience who paid to watch? *What. The. Fuck.*

As usual, I'm wearing a Lone-Ranger-style mask for this

livestream. But for the first time ever, my mask is sparkling with purple sequins—a little flair Charlotte thought would emphasize the specialness of today's marathon of craziness. After sitting up from my final piercing, I turn my masked face to the camera and deadpan, "I hope you're happy, you fucking sickos."

All four of us in the room laugh, including me.

"I'm sure they're very, *very* happy," Charlotte says, still chuckling. Her mask is sparkling today, too. But no amount of sequins could ever sparkle as brightly as her sparkling personality. She kisses my cheek, "You didn't disappoint, Salami. That was gold." She looks at the camera. "Wasn't that *amazing*? Thank you all for your generosity. We can't thank you enough. Special shout outs to our VIP sickos—Lucille1990, Catfish2000, YankeePants74, and DarlingPsycho123—for leading the charge today with major per-piercing contributions. We're so grateful to you."

Man, Charlotte nailed it today. Thanks to her brilliant strategy—asking for a certain amount to be raised *per* piercing today, and *per* shenanigan before this—we're going to reach our goal by midnight, and then some. The only downside of our strategy? Poor Charlotte is now about to get *seven* piercings—one in each nipple and *five* between her legs: two in each lip of her pussy and one in her clitoral hood.

When I pulled her aside earlier and told her, sincerely, that she could back out at any time, she smiled broadly and said, "Not on your life, Salami. I'd get a hundred piercings to pay your tuition, if only I had a hundred interesting places on my body people would pay to watch getting pierced." Good lord. If I didn't love this woman before that comment, I would have fallen in love with her, right then and there.

"Okay, next victim," the piercing guy says, motioning to Charlotte. I'm up and standing now, and he's already gotten his table covered with fresh wax paper for Charlotte.

After making a truly adorable face at the camera, Charlotte sits down and grabs my offered hand. She looks nervous.

"You don't need to do this, baby," I whisper. "We can give all their money back."

Charlotte shakes her head defiantly and squeezes my hand like a vise. "Nope. I'm doing this." She smiles at the camera and shouts, "Let's turn me into a pin cushion, baby!"

After waddling down the sidewalk from the piercing place, hand in hand, Charlotte and I slide into our respective seats of my car, ever so gingerly, at exactly 11:18 pm—which means there's still plenty of time for me to pay the tuition invoice, due at midnight, on my phone while sitting here.

"Check the final numbers," Charlotte says excitedly. We knew how much we'd amassed when walking into the tattoo/piercing place just before ten tonight, but we couldn't see the tips pouring in throughout our piercing adventure, and we're dying to find out how much we've added to our pre-piercing totals.

As Charlotte holds her breath, I log into our account and then gasp in astonishment when I behold the final number on the dashboard. "Holy shit. Our final haul for today is over twenty-eight thousand bucks!"

Charlotte whoops and cheers, until I take her face in my palms and kiss the living hell out of her. For several minutes, we kiss and laugh and then babble excitedly about our crazy day. Other than the piercings, which were a tag-team affair, Charlotte did the lion's share of crazy shit today, because *she's* the one our audience was most excited to watch doing weird stuff. One superfan, Lucille1990, paid a full grand to watch Charlotte being driven, naked and standing up, in a convertible with the top down, fast enough to make her tits and hair flap in the wind. To fulfill that particular request, we borrowed Tessa's convertible Mercedes, covered the license plates, and drove it to a nearby rained-out, deserted construction area only a few minutes away. Mission accomplished. After that, we made another superfan, Catfish2000, happy as a clam by doing a livestream of Charlotte, naked, mowing Ryan and Tessa's back lawn. Right after that, Charlotte climbed a ladder, nude, and pretended to hang Christmas lights in April, while I shot her from below. And on and on it went, culminating in the piercings we just completed.

Charlotte pulls away from our kiss and presses her forehead to mine. "You should pay the invoice now, honey, to make double-damn sure it's time-stamped before midnight."

"Right you are." With a huge smile on my face, I log into our account again, intending to transfer the money from there to my bank account . . . and suddenly realize a truly horrible thing. "Oh, no," I gasp out. "*Yesterday* was the end of the payment cycle. We won't be able to access the money we made today for another two weeks!"

Charlotte's face turns pale. "*No.*"

"*Fuck.*"

We stare at each other, both of us trying not to hyperventilate.

"Okay, don't panic," Charlotte finally says. "We can still make this work."

"*How?*"

"I've got five or six thousand bucks of available credit across several cards. How about you?"

"I-I . . ." I take a deep breath. "I don't know. F-four thousand, m-maybe?"

"Okay, that's good. We'll withdraw cash from all our credit cards and transfer everything into your bank account now. As long as we pay off our cards before thirty days, which we will, we won't even have to pay interest on the withdrawals. Plus, you've got that five grand that's already sitting in your account, right?"

I nod. "But even if we do all this, I'll still need to get my hands on another six or seven grand within . . ." I look at the clock on my car's dashboard and finish my sentence with "the next nineteen minutes."

Charlotte runs her hand through her red hair. "Could you ask your brother or mother for a temporary loan? Whoever you ask, you'd be able to pay them back in two weeks. I'd call Tessa, but if I tell her I've got some sort of emergency that requires she Venmo me seven grand in the next fifteen minutes, she's going to get in her car and physically track me down to make sure I'm not being held hostage by a madman. You, on the other hand, can believably tell your brother or mother that some money you made doing whatever side hustle they think you do to make ends meet is glitching, and you need a quick bridge loan to cover your tuition before midnight, and you'll call your employer in the morning to find out what's going on. You could say that, and your family won't freak out and think you've been abducted, the way Tessa would think about me. Welcome to male privilege."

I lean my forehead against my steering wheel for a beat, trying desperately to think of another solution. Some way to do this without involving my mother or brother. But Charlotte's right. This is our only hope.

"I'll call my brother first," I say. "He'll still be up to answer my call. My mother is probably fast asleep by now." I push the button, and, thankfully, my brother, Max, answers immediately.

"Hey, Augs," he says. "What's up?'

"I've got a bit of an emergency, Maxy-pad. I need your help."

I tell him the thing Charlotte suggested, and he doesn't hesitate to offer his assistance.

"Do you need more than seven grand?" he asks.

"No, seven will do it. Like I said, I'll pay you back in two weeks."

My phone buzzes with a Venmo notification—seven thousand bucks, sent from one Maximillian Vaughn.

"Don't bother paying me back," Max says. "If you need this for school, consider it my early Christmas present to you."

I protest. Tell him I can't accept that, and he insists he's having a phenomenal year, thanks to his new, high-paying job, and the success of the company he and his wife, Marnie, recently founded together.

"Okay, we'll talk about this more later," I say. "When I'm not watching the clock tick down and having a heart attack. For now, just know I'm beyond grateful to you, brother. Thank you so much."

"Whatever you need. Always. I hope you know that."

My heart squeezes. That's my brother for you. People can think what they want about some of his harder exterior edges, but this right here is the Max I know: a softie with a heart of gold, through and through.

"Hey, come on down for a couple days, if you can," Max says. "We're having a blast with Mom and Henry. It'd be awesome if you could join us for a bit. You're on spring break, right?"

"Yeah, I'll have to let you know about that. Gotta go, brother. I've got a tuition invoice to pay. Thank you again for saving me from catastrophe."

After ending the call, I launch furiously into withdrawing all available funds from my credit cards, while Charlotte does the same on her end. Soon, however, with about ten minutes to spare before midnight, I've got a grand total of $21,816 sitting in my bank account. Enough to pay twenty grand to the school now, and still have a cushion for taxis and dinners in New Jersey and groceries and gas whenever we get home.

With shaking hands, I log into my school's payment dashboard and submit the funds—and a moment later, at 11:54 pm, I get a confirmation email. *Funds received.*

"We did it," I whisper hoarsely. I look at Charlotte, slack-jawed and trembling. "*You* did it, you fucking genius."

"No, you got it right the first time. It was a team effort."

I kiss her deeply, feeling like I'm bursting out of my skin. Like my heart is exploding with love for this incredible woman. "Thank you, Charlotte. *Thank you.*" Now more than ever, I want to hold her face in my hands and say, "I love you, Charlotte McDougal." In fact, I want to get out of my SUV right now, climb onto the roof, and shout about my love for Charlotte to the entire world. But since I know that's probably going to lead me straight to Heartbreak, USA, population Auggie Vaughn, I bite my tongue and smash my lips together and physically force the words to remain lodged in my throat.

"Let's do some shows from our hotel room in New Jersey," Charlotte says. "Whatever it takes, so you can pay the rest of that tuition invoice, as soon as possible. I don't want that hanging over your head during the summer, when you're working hard at an internship."

I can't help feeling like the subtext of that statement was "I don't want you worrying about the rest of that money this summer, when I'm long gone."

I smile ruefully. "Don't worry about that. I'll figure out the rest later. Right now, I only want to celebrate our accomplishment. *We did it.* We got the money to Carlo, and now we've paid enough of my tuition to secure my spot in the program." I'm not saying it, but on top of all that, we're also taking off for a week that's going to be lots of fun, once we get through the birthday party tomorrow. After one night in New Jersey, we've decided to head to New York to do some sightseeing together, and I couldn't be more excited about it. "Let's focus on celebrating right now," I say, "and not even think about doing any more shows for a while, okay? This whole week, we'll be Auggie and Charlotte, and try to forget Superhero Salami Slinger and The Unicorn ever existed."

27
CHARLOTTE

When the plane touches down in Newark, New Jersey, I turn on my phone, just like everyone around me. I've got a new text from Tessa. She's attached a short video of Rudy and Lucky playing with the kids in her backyard. I heart the video and send her a text that we've landed safely.

"Auggie, look at this." I nudge his shoulder next to me and show him the clip Tessa sent, and, predictably, he's over the moon to see his furry buddy having the time of his life.

After Tessa's text, I click into the next one from an unknown number. It's from Carlo. He says he's waiting for us in the baggage claim area and that he'll drive us directly to Bella's party. Due to weather, our flight was delayed this morning by quite a bit, so there's no longer any time for Auggie and me to head to our hotel to relax and shower before the birthday party. Looks like our delay allowed Carlo to finish up whatever emergency kept him busy this morning—the one Carlo's colleague referred to when he picked up the cash from us yesterday.

I'm not skeptical about Carlo having a new number. He

changes his number frequently. Always has. When we dated, I thought that was because bodyguards for wealthy people can be targets of disgruntled crazies. Now that I know the true nature of Carlo's profession, I have to assume he changes it frequently to keep one step ahead of the law and Mr. DiMarco's enemies. Either way, I don't doubt this text is actually from Carlo, so I quickly reply to thank him for coming to get us and confirm we'll see him at baggage claim.

Our plane reaches the gate, and the captain says all obligatory things over the overhead speaker. I'm in a window seat, so I stay put and pull my scattered stuff together, while aisle seaters like Auggie pop up and retrieve luggage from overhead compartments.

As I'm grabbing my purse to stuff my phone into it, a new email notification pops onto my screen. *It's from the airline I interviewed with the other day.* With bated breath, I swipe into my inbox and read the message . . . and then practically faint. *They want me.* They're offering me a job. An incredible one that's even better than the one I got laid off from—a guaranteed assignment to first or business class on a regular route between JFK and Heathrow. All the standard perks and some new ones I've never had before. Holy shit. *I've hit the jackpot.*

Aw, fuck.

When I keep reading, I see the one bad thing.

New York.

That's where I'll need to be based.

Well, that's a bummer. I'm a West Coast girlie, through and through. A native Angeleno.

Auggie.

He's standing in the aisle, grabbing our rolling carry-ons from the overhead compartment. As he lifts his arms, his T-shirt rides up and I catch a glimpse of his toned abs. The faint treasure trail of light brown hair I've followed many times to the Promised Land beneath his waistband.

I look away, my heart thumping. *What will happen with Auggie and me when I accept this job?* LA to Seattle is about a three-hour flight, but New York to Seattle takes over *six hours.* And that's only if I can get a free *direct* flight from New York to Seattle with my flight credits, which isn't always the case. It could be a much longer travel day than that, if the stars don't align. How often could I reasonably expect to make that trip, while based in New York and working full-time? Auggie certainly couldn't visit me with any regularity with *his* schedule. I've seen how busy school is for him. For the next two years, he's going to be in Seattle, working hard to make his dreams come true. Realistically, could he *ever* come visit me, other than on spring break? Surely, the onus would be on me to make it work between us, long-distance, and I'm not sure I'm ready to take that on.

I dare to look at Auggie again, and this time, his blue eyes are on me. When our gazes meet, he grins. And just like that, I'm thinking stupid thoughts. Stuff like, "Maybe I should turn down this job and look for one based on the West Coast." But I'd be foolish to turn down this golden opportunity, especially for a man I've only just met, basically. True, it feels like I've known Auggie forever, but we've only just met in reality. And jobs like this don't come around very often. In fact, a job like this is literally a once-in-a-lifetime thing.

The line in the aisle begins moving in front of Auggie, and he motions for me to slide in front of him. I hobble into place and motion for him to hand me my rolling bag, but, true to form, Auggie says he's got it.

"How are you feeling?" he asks. We both slept on the flight, so this is the first time we're chatting since takeoff. He juts his chin toward my crotch area, making it clear he's asking how I'm feeling in relation to all my piercings.

"Sore," I admit. "I'll be relieved when I can finally remove everything after the birthday party."

Auggie shifts his weight like he's got ants in his pants. "Same here. *Yeesh.*"

We both laugh.

We would have taken out our piercings by now, but we didn't get the disinfecting solution the guy recommended after leaving the piercing place last night, and then we had to speed to the airport at the crack of dawn this morning to catch our flight. Which, as it turned out, was delayed for hours. And now, thanks to that delay, there's no time to swing by a drugstore before heading to the birthday party. I'm sure we'll remove our piercings at our hotel tonight, once we get our hands on that solution. Either way, though, we won't be having sex for at least a week, per the instructions of the piercing dude, so in that sense, it doesn't really matter if we get everything out tonight or tomorrow, since our fun little vacation in New York will be PG-rated, regardless. I definitely foresee *lots* of kissing and making out in our near future, though.

The ripple of movement at the front of the plane reaches us, so I waddle up the aisle, gingerly, toward the exit, taking great care not to rub my intimate bits together as I go, while Auggie follows behind, presumably doing basically the same thing. When we exit the tunnel contraption and enter the wider gate area, I say to Auggie, "C texted he'll be picking us up at baggage claim. Thanks to our delay, he's able to pick us up and drive us to the party, after all."

Auggie's blue eyes widen. "I'd rather take a cab."

"He's already here. And it's for the best, Auggie. Everyone at the party would expect C to come get me. He's a very chivalrous person, and everyone knows that. They also know our split was amicable, and that C still considers me his good friend."

Auggie looks stressed, but he says nothing.

A sign directs us to an escalator for the baggage claim area, so we board it together and ride down silently. When we reach the bottom, I say, "There's nothing to worry about. We've paid the money. Our only job now is to confirm our innocence by showing up with happy, smiling, innocent faces. *We can do this.*"

Auggie exhales. "There he is."

I look, and, yep, Carlo is standing a short distance away near a crowded baggage carousel.

"Smile," I whisper to Auggie. "From this moment on, we don't have a care in the world. We're a happy couple on vacation."

"Happy, happy," he deadpans.

"Carloooooo!" I say brightly, my arms outstretched, as we close the gap between us. "So great to see you!"

"Hey there, sweetheart," Carlo says, before pulling me into a bear hug and pecking my cheek. "You're looking beautiful, as always. How was the flight?"

"Delayed quite a bit, as you know, which was annoying. But once we got in the air, we both crashed after takeoff and only woke up at landing."

"Good for you. That's always the best way to fly." He extends his hand to Auggie. "Hey there, big guy. Good to see you again."

"You, too. Thanks for the lift."

"You bet. Were you walking kind of funny, just now? Everything okay?"

"Yeah, I'm just a bit stiff from the long flight."

"Gotcha. Happens to the best of us." Carlo points to the two rolling carry-on bags on either side of Auggie. "Which one contains the you-know-what?"

My heart stops. "Don't play like that, Carlo."

His face drops. "I'm not playing. If *you* are, then don't."

I look at Auggie, suddenly too stressed to form words, and he comes to my rescue.

"We gave it to your colleague yesterday in Seattle. He came to get it from us, per *your* instructions."

Carlo's face drains of color. "Did he give his name?"

Auggie and I look at each other. Did the guy ever say his name?

"I-I don't think so," Auggie stammers out.

"No, he never said it," I confirm.

Carlo asks what the guy looked like, and Auggie and I furiously describe him.

"Paolo," Carlo mutters, running a large palm across his dark beard. "Fucking *Paolo*."

Auggie is panting, same as me. He sucks in a huge inhale, probably trying to calm himself down, and blurts, "You seriously didn't send him? If you're pranking us, then tell us now. *Please*."

"I didn't send him."

"Fuck," I choke out, as the full horrendousness of the situation dawns on me. "We gave him everything, Carlo. Every dime we owed. *Plus interest*."

"*Interest?*" Carlo booms. "*What?*" A vein pulses in his neck. "Charlotte, we had a plan! You know I'd never change a plan without telling you myself. *Never*."

"Fuck," Auggie murmurs under his breath. He's pacing, gingerly, in little circles, like a duck with a broken wing. "*Fuck, fuck, fuck*."

Carlo grabs my arm. Not roughly. He's just feeling a surge of adrenaline, I think, and he wants my full attention. But Auggie leaps to my defense and grits out, "*Let go of her*."

I'm impressed and flattered. But he's misread the situation. Carlo wouldn't hurt a fly. Well, I mean, I'm sure he's killed people. But he wouldn't hurt me.

To his credit, Carlo lets go of me and raises both palms, letting Auggie know he meant no harm or threat. When the moment is diffused, Carlo inhales deeply, like he's searching for any drop of Zen he can muster, and says, "Tell me every fucking thing Paolo said and did, without leaving anything out. I want every detail, no matter how small it might seem."

Our threesome heads into a corner of the bustling baggage claim area, so we can talk away from the all the crowds and hustle-bustle. As my heart crashes and my stomach churns and tears stream down my face, I ramble the whole story to Carlo, with occasional assists from Auggie. Throughout our telling, I keep hoping against hope Carlo will break into a crooked smile and say, "Gotcha! Haha! You should have seen your faces!" But no such luck. The more we talk, the more it's clear Carlo is deeply distressed by our fuck-up. We've been hoodwinked. Conned. Bamboozled. Paolo somehow caught wind of Carlo's plan—and our three-way *guilt*—and he then used the juicy information to con himself into a cool and easy seventy-five grand.

"He said we'd see him at the party," I gasp out hopefully. "So, maybe we've got this all wrong."

"He won't be there," Carlo says flatly. "He's gone rogue. I'm sure he said that so you wouldn't be suspicious of him."

Auggie's chest heaves. "Unless . . . Could it be Paolo was sent to get the money from us at someone's *else's* direction?"

Carlo runs a rough hand through his dark hair. Auggie's meaning is clear enough. He's wondering if maybe Mr. DiMarco himself caught wind of my thievery somehow—and Carlo's simultaneous betrayal of him, too—so, the big boss sent Paolo to Seattle to see if the information he'd obtained was correct. If that's the case, then, surely, we confirmed everything well enough, by handing the money over.

"What should we do?" I whisper-shout, wringing my hands. "We're all out of money, Carlo. Maxed out on all our credit cards, so we can't even offer a goodwill peace offering to the big boss to convince him to give us more time."

"The big boss didn't send Paolo to you," Carlo says. "I'd bet anything on it. If my boss found out about me looking the other way when you took that money, I'd already be at the bottom of the Hudson. Trust me on that. Paolo was acting alone. Getting an easy payday. I'm sure of it."

"Can you give us a short-term loan?" I beg. "We can get you the money in two weeks. We just need—"

"I can't do that, sweetheart. I've got a wife now. A baby. My wife wouldn't understand me doing that. She pays all the bills. Plus, I never lie to her."

I look at Auggie. "Don't panic, okay? I'll call Tessa now and beg her to—"

"There's no time for that," Carlo interrupts. "We're already late for the party and it's after banking hours. Even if she agrees to send you the full amount, you wouldn't get it till tomorrow at the earliest. Probably several days later than that, given the amount we're talking about. And even then, I'd have to convert to cash, stuff it into a black duffel bag, and 'find' it at the airport. There's no time."

"So, what now?" Auggie says.

Carlo shrugs. "Our only choice is go to Bella's birthday party and convince my boss you're the same happy, carefree, fun-loving flight attendant he's always known and adored, except for the fact that you're now even happier because you're engaged to the best guy, ever. You have to convince him you're light as a feather and not feeling guilty or scared about a damned thing. Make him believe that, and we'll be okay."

"I don't know if I can pull that off," I choke out. "I feel like I could barf at any moment. My knees are wobbly. I can hardly breathe."

"You don't have a choice." Carlo glares at Auggie. "And neither do you, Captain America, so wipe that terrified expression off your face and try to look like you're living the dream." To my shock, Carlo's scowl suddenly morphs into a wicked smile. "You know what? Come to think of it, I think maybe this thing with Paolo could be a blessing in disguise." His smile broadens. "I think maybe Paolo could be our fall guy now. Maybe this is our lucky break."

"What do you mean?" Auggie asks, taking the words right out of my mouth.

"Now that I know that motherfucker is a greedy traitor, I can blame *him* for swiping the money in the first place. As long as you both do a good job today at the party, my boss won't doubt me for a second when I tell him I've discovered Paolo's the thief." Carlo's jaw sets and that vein in his neck bulges again. "Convince the big guy you're as carefree as ever today, and I give you my word Paolo will take the fall for everything." His dark eyes glint with homicidal rage—which, in Carlo's case, isn't a figure of speech. "I can't wait to put that bastard in the big man's crosshairs." His nostrils flare. "Trust me, my friends, that traitorous motherfucker's gonna deserve every fucking thing that's coming to him."

28

AUGGIE

"*Charlotte!*" a dark-haired woman calls out gleefully. "You made it!"

"I wouldn't have missed it for the world," Charlotte replies.

The brunette kisses Charlotte on both cheeks, and when she's done doing that, she moves along to greeting Carlo—her big brother, from what I was told during the drive over here.

"Thank you for bringing Charlotte to us," the brunette says in the midst of her embrace.

Carlo chuckles. "You would have kicked my ass if I didn't."

When the siblings disengage, the brunette smiles warmly at me. "And who's this handsome hunk of a man?"

Charlotte clears her throat. "Angela, this is my fiancé, Auggie."

"I was hoping this was him! I've heard so much about you from Carlo, Auggie. You're gonna be an animal doctor?"

"That's right. Nice to meet you, Angela. Thank you for having me."

"Welcome to the family." She hugs me enthusiastically, and when that's done, she says to Charlotte, "Bella's gonna be so happy her beloved Auntie Charlotte made it. She got so spoiled when you could come by once a month. She's missed you so much lately."

"I've missed her, too. No more free flights, unfortunately."

"I heard you lost your job from Carlo. Sorry to hear that, sweetie. I know you'll find something soon. Something even better. Mr. DiMarco always says you're the best stewardess he's ever had." She snorts at the sexual innuendo and then swats my broad shoulder. "That's served him on a *flight*, I mean. If there are other stewardesses he's *had* who've maybe impressed him in other ways, I don't wanna know about it."

Pretending to laugh, Charlotte holds up the brightly wrapped gift she's brought for Bella. "Is there a gift table, or?"

"There is, but Bella will want to open *your* gift in front of you." She grabs Charlotte's free hand. "Come with me, Charlotte Mickey-D."

I follow the two women into the crowded party, marveling at the swarm of bustling partygoers. It's nice all these adults have shown up to celebrate a kid's tenth birthday, but it feels more like an adult's milestone birthday to me, like a 40th, than a kid's tenth. I'm sure Bella would much prefer to celebrate her big day with a handful of her besties, maybe at a trampoline park or an ice-skating rink, than with all these adults crammed into her mother's house. Where are all the kids?

As we make our way through groups of people standing around with cups and paper plates of food, I notice Carlo greeting a beautiful woman and a baby across the party. He kisses the woman on the lips and takes the baby into his arms and proceeds to gleefully pepper the baby's fat little face with kisses. Damn. It's bizarre to feel my heart touched by Carlo's obvious affection for his family, when my brain knows full well he inflicts pain or worse for a living. It's awfully hard to reconcile the two diametrically opposed things in my head.

"Look who's here, Bella!" Angela, our hostess, bellows,

causing me to jerk my attention toward our apparent destination: a thin little girl in a motorized wheelchair—the kind with a headrest that keeps its occupant's head firmly in place. This little girl is frail and visibly disabled. Also, absolutely beautiful.

"Happy birthday, my love!" Charlotte says brightly, and the little girl's dark eyes light up.

Charlotte bends down to hug the girl and kiss her cheek. She strokes her hair and whispers to her softly. And by the time Charlotte straightens up again, the two women and Bella are all crying happy tears. I'm sure I'd be tearing up, as well, or at least fighting tears, if I weren't so fucking afraid I'm about to get blindsided and turned into hamburger meat and/or fish food.

Charlotte introduces me to Bella, and the little girl greets me in a strained, soft voice.

Charlotte and I pull up chairs next to Bella's wheelchair, and with Angela looking on, Charlotte holds up the brightly wrapped birthday gift.

"I wonder who this could be for?" Charlotte teases. "Your mother? Carlo? Auggie? *Me*?" Charlotte giggles at Bella's excited reaction. "Of course, it's for you, my love! Should we find out what's inside?"

Charlotte begins carefully unwrapping the gift, and as she does that, I glance around the party, nervously, hoping I won't see Paolo's face anywhere. If that dude shows his face here today, that'd be a very bad sign. For Carlo, certainly, and probably for Charlotte and me, too. Maybe I've seen *Goodfellas* too many times, but if Paolo feels safe coming here today after taking that money, when he *knows* Carlo and Mr. DiMarco will both be here, I'd have to think that would indicate he's being protected by someone higher up in the organization than Carlo.

Did Mr. DiMarco himself send Paolo to get that money

from us in Seattle? Perhaps he didn't trust Carlo anymore. Perhaps he wanted to see what we'd confirm about Carlo's role in Charlotte's crime. If so, did we give Paolo everything he needed to prove Carlo's disloyalty and ultimately put Charlotte and me in grave danger? I'm practically jumping out of my skin at all the hair-raising possibilities.

Suddenly, there's a palpable shift in the crowd—a collective tittering aimed toward the front of the house. I turn to look toward the source of the commotion, and there he is. *Vincent DiMarco.* The silver-haired "businessman" I've researched endlessly since this whole fiasco began. He's accompanied by a well-dressed, elegant woman of around his age whose entire vibe screams *WIFE.* Two large men in dark suits are trailing immediately behind the couple, and, thankfully, neither of them is Paolo.

"Excuse me," Angela mutters, before beelining across the room to greet her most honored guests. I can't hear what Angela is saying from this distance, but her body language makes it clear she's fawning all over the couple.

While Angela is kissing ass, Carlo appears at his boss's side and whispers into his ear.

"Charlotte," I murmur, nudging her leg. When she looks across the party toward Mr. DiMarco, it's just in time to see his dark eyes hardening in reaction to whatever Carlo's whispering to him. The change in his demeanor was subtle. The man is probably an expert at maintaining a poker face by now. But it was definitely there, ever so briefly. *He's fucking pissed.*

Mr. DiMarco mutters something to Carlo. Four or five words, at most. And in response to that, Carlo nods and marches off toward the front of the house. About five seconds after Carlo disappears, Charlotte abruptly pulls out her phone like it's just buzzed in her pocket. After swiping her screen, she nudges my leg and tilts the phone toward me. She's just now

received a text from that same unknown number as before—
the one Carlo used earlier today:

> All's well. No time to say goodbye. There's something pressing I need to handle. Travel safe back home and sleep tight. Best to you and A.

Can we reasonably rely on this "all clear" message from Carlo? I don't think he'd *intentionally* deceive us at this point—he's in this mess, every bit as deep as we are; but what if *Mr. DiMarco* is deceiving *Carlo*? What if the big boss sent Carlo to "handle" something just now, but in reality Carlo is walking into a trap at the hands of Paolo? Jesus Christ. This whole situation is turning my brain into a pretzel and my stomach inside-out. If I survive this party, I'm never going to watch a mafia movie again.

"*Charlotte*," a soft female voice says. "I'm so glad you made it." It's Carlo's wife, holding her baby in her arms.

Charlotte pops up from her chair and greets the woman warmly.

"Thank you for the lovely baby gifts," Carlo's wife says. "You really didn't have to do that."

"It was my pleasure. I'm thrilled for you and Carlo. What a beautiful family."

"Thank you." The woman smiles in a way that feels genuine and warm. "You've gone out of your way to make sure I know you're happy for us." She looks down at Bella in her wheelchair. "Happy birthday, sweetheart."

Charlotte touches my arm. "Genevieve, this is my fiancé, Auggie. Honey, this is Carlo's wife, Genevieve, and their daughter, Sofia."

We make polite small talk with the woman about the party and the gift Charlotte brought for Bella, but after a couple minutes, when the two women start talking about the baby's sleep schedule, it feels safe to sneak another peek at the mob boss across the room. He's not there. A quick scan reveals he's now in the midst of making his rounds. Saying his hellos with his wife at his side.

Shit.

We just locked eyes. He knows I've been staring at him. Double shit. He's heading over here, while his wife remains behind to chat with a woman who looks 100 years old. Fuck!

"Well, if it isn't my favorite redhead," Mr. DiMarco booms when he reaches me. Which means he's talking to Charlotte, obviously. "Long time, no see, sweetheart," he adds while hugging Charlotte. "Great to see you again."

"You, too."

When their embrace is over, Charlotte introduces me to the man, and I stammer my way through a brief hello. Is he being this friendly because he doesn't know what Charlotte did, like Carlo said, and now blames Paolo for the missing bag of money . . . *or* did Paolo tell Mr. DiMarco everything, and Mr. DiMarco believed him, and now this clever man is simply lulling us into a false sense of security before Paolo sneaks up on us from behind and throws us into a woodchipper? Who's fucked here: Paolo or Carlo, Charlotte, and me?

"I heard you got laid off, sweetheart," Mr. DiMarco says, holding both of Charlotte's hands. "That's a tough break, kid."

Charlotte shrugs. "It happens."

"I know lots of people in the airline industry. As my engagement gift to you, let me make a call."

Charlotte's chest heaves. "Oh gosh. Thank you so much for the offer, but there's no need to do that."

I sigh with relief. If he's offering to help Charlotte, he must not know she took his money. Unless he's doing an artful job of lulling, I guess. Either way, I'm glad Charlotte shot him down because the last thing we need is to be indebted to this man, again. For any reason.

"I *insist*," the man says. "You're wonderful at your job. The best. Any airline would be lucky to have you, and that's what I'll tell my buddy when I call."

"No, please, don't," Charlotte blurts. She forces a smile, pretty convincingly. "There's no need. I actually got a job offer today, mere hours ago. The email was waiting for me when our plane landed."

Damn, she's good. Charlotte would have mentioned an email like that to me, if she'd really received one. Talking about our respective job and internship searches has been a staple of our conversations. But I definitely agree with her strategy to say whatever it takes to keep this guy at arm's length in a way that keeps him from feeling snubbed.

The big guy asks Charlotte about her new, supposed job, and Charlotte rambles some impressive fake details about it—stuff that smartly makes it sound like her dream job, so he won't feel tempted to pick up the phone for her to secure something better.

"Well, that sounds perfect," Mr. DiMarco says. "Good for you. You deserve it."

"Thank you so much." She flashes me an anxious look, and I wink at her, letting her know she did good. Her lies were believable, and he's clearly bought them, hook, line, and sinker.

I feel like maybe I should join in and say something supportive like, "They knew the best candidate when they saw her!" But before I've decided if that's a good idea or not, a guy approaches Mr. DiMarco and whispers into his ear, so Charlotte and I step back to give the pair some privacy.

Angela appears and asks Charlotte to help her with something in the kitchen. And off the women go, but not before Charlotte pecks my cheek as a parting gift.

Someone else is talking to Bella now, the birthday girl, so I can't return to her. I fidget. Try different positions with my hands and arms. But I'm not sure what to do with myself. Go to the food table? Stay here and wait for Mr. DiMarco to finish his conversation? I think maybe we're still technically in the middle of a conversation, one that guy interrupted. When he walks away, will Mr. DiMarco expect to turn around and see me still standing here?

I've no sooner had the thought than the guy who interrupted walks away and Mr. DiMarco turns around to face me again. When he sees me still standing here, his face lights up. "Oh, good. You didn't wander off." He beckons to me. "Come with me, Auggie. Let's have a chat."

Oh, fuck.

On wobbly legs, I follow the mob boss and one of his stoic bodyguards to the back of the house, through a sliding glass door, and into a large backyard. The big boss takes a seat at a corner patio table, so I follow suit, while the dude in the dark suit stands nearby at full attention. Everything about this feels like a movie, except for the part that it's all-too real, and I don't see any cameras anywhere, and the woman I love—the woman I'd literally die for, if it came down to it—stole money from this powerful, scary man and his dark eyes are now boring holes into my fucking face.

"So, Auggie," Mr. DiMarco says. "It warms my heart to see Charlotte so in love and happy."

"Thank you, sir. I love Charlotte with all my heart."

"I can see that. I have zero doubts you'll love, honor, and protect her, exactly the way she deserves."

Did he emphasize the word protect or did I imagine that? "Yes, sir. I will."

Shit. I can't live like this—in a constant state of fear. What

I need to do for my own sanity and Charlotte's safety is make sure this powerful, scary man knows if there's ever *any* shit that's going to hit *any* fan in relation to Charlotte McDougal, *I* want to be the one who gets splattered with it, instead of Charlotte. *Every last drop of it.*

I swallow hard. "I'm glad you've mentioned me protecting Charlotte, sir. I hope you know, as her fiancé and future husband, I'll do *anything* to protect her. Literally, anything."

"As you should. You love the woman. She's gonna be the mother to your babies. It's your job to protect her."

"And I take that job, seriously."

He nods. "If ever Charlotte was in harm's way, for any reason—for instance, if ever she did a stupid thing and brought a shit storm upon herself, let's say—you wouldn't hesitate to step in to protect her from whatever consequences might come her way because of what she did."

I nod slowly. *He knows.*

Mr. DiMarco lays his clasped knuckles onto the table. "For instance, if Charlotte did something stupid, like, I don't know, steal sixty grand from *me*, I bet you'd want to protect her from whatever consequences might naturally flow from her doing such a stupid thing like that, right?"

Every drop of blood has drained from my brain. I'm incapable of speech. I glance at the nearby bodyguard. Is that guy going to wrap his thick hands around my throat and end me, any second now?

"Eyes here, Auggie."

I shift my eyes to Mr. DiMarco, and he chuckles at whatever he's seeing on my face. "You got something to tell me, son?"

"*I* took the money," I blurt. "It was all me and only me. Charlotte had nothing to do with it. I'm very, very sorry for taking it, sir. It was a huge mistake. I tried to pay it back, but things got fucked up."

He smiles. "That was quite the trick, *you* taking the money, since a) Carlo saw Charlotte pick up that duffel bag off the tarmac, which he then told me about, immediately, right then and there; and b) in corroboration of what Carlo told me, you're nowhere to be found on the CCTV footage I asked Carlo to get for me, which he did. On the contrary, the one picking up that bag was Charlotte, and Charlotte alone."

I feel like I'm going to puke. My mind is scrambling. Useless. Hurtling through space. "Charlotte wasn't in her right mind, sir. Please, have mercy on her. During the flight, she found out she was getting laid off the next morning, and she freaked out. The bag was on the ground. You saw that, right? And yes while it was very wrong for her to pick it up and walk away, it wasn't a heist or a planned theft. She did something stupid, spur of the moment, when she was in the midst of a panic attack about her imminent layoff, and . . . Please, sir. Please, hurt me, not her." Breathing hard, I wait for the man's reply, and when one doesn't come, I add, "We tried very, very hard to pay you back. We had the full amount—sixty grand—for you yesterday, but then, we got duped and gave it all to—"

"*Paolo.* Yes, I know." He leans back and smirks. "If you think there's a goddamned thing that happens in my organization that I don't know about, think again."

My chest heaves. "Paolo told us he was working with Carlo."

Mr. DiMarco shakes his head. "Because that's what we let him think. And now, the dumbfuck thinks he got away with double-crossing Carlo."

I process that for a beat. "Wait. So, you and Carlo set a *trap* for Paolo?"

He nods. "And letting him know Charlotte took that money was the bait. I told Carlo to let Paolo overhear some of his supposed phone calls—times when he supposedly confirmed plans with you two. I wanted to see what he'd do with that information. Well, now we know. He went to Carlo with that information first, in order to blackmail him. *Not to me.* He said to Carlo, 'What's in it for me to keep quiet about what you did?' And after making that supposed side deal, he then flew to Seattle and got himself an easy chunk of change for himself." His dark eyes flash with rage. "In the CCTV footage, Paolo was watching Charlotte like a hawk the whole time she picked up that bag. *The whole fucking time.* But was it *Paolo* who came to me to report what he'd seen, so I could decide how to deal with it? No. It was Carlo, who by all rights shouldn't have even seen her do it, because he was busy talking to me at the time. But that's Carlo for you. Best in the biz. I swear, the man's got eyes in the back of his head. Thankfully, he's also as loyal as the day is long. He told me, without hesitation, even though, under any other circumstance, he'd take a bullet for Charlotte. And because he did that, when he asked me, as a personal favor to him, to go easy on Charlotte, I granted his request. 'Let her stew and shit her pants and lose some sleep,' I said. And then, after you entered the picture, Auggie, we let Charlotte worry about *you* being made to pay for her sins, on top of everything else." He chuckles. "That was Carlo's genius idea. He knew Charlotte is a caregiver type— which means worrying about *you* getting hurt would be even worse for her than worrying about herself. So, Carlo added that little bonus element into her punishment when he paid Charlotte a visit and happened to meet you." He leans back. "Have you been shitting a brick, son?"

"Very much, sir. Night and day, basically. And so has Charlotte."

"Good. I think the punishment fit the crime, then. Don't you? I mean, the money itself isn't the issue. I blow more than sixty grand on shopping sprees for my girlfriend or on a night at the strip club. And like you said, the money fell into Charlotte's lap when she was out of her head about losing her job."

He shrugs. "The kid seized an opportunity. Can't say I blame her for that. She's a single girl, making her way in the world. Honestly, I kind of admire her moxie for going through with it. It was a ballsy thing to do. Stupid, but ballsy."

I take a deep breath. "Do I have your solemn word you're not going to hurt her?" He's wearing a gold chain with a cross around his neck, so I add, "Do you swear to God?"

He chuckles. "I just told you we're all good, Auggie. I never say anything I don't mean." He winks. "Okay, yes. I'll swear to God, just for you." He pats my arm. "Don't worry, okay? I like Charlotte. She's a good kid. So fucking funny. That girl made me laugh harder than anyone on every flight she worked for me. Plus, I've got Bella to consider. That kid's got enough to worry about without also worrying about her Auntie Charlotte." He leans back. "You can tell your fiancée all is forgiven. We'll consider it my engagement present to you both."

I exhale with relief. Maybe I'm naïve, but I actually believe this man. "Thank you, sir. Thank you so, so much."

He frowns. "Speaking of your engagement, though, we need to talk about that embarrassing excuse for an engagement ring you've put on Charlotte's finger. For fuck's sake, Auggie, please tell me that's a placeholder and you're gonna get the girl a big, fat diamond, as soon as humanly possible."

I can't believe he noticed my grandmother's ring. Charlotte's wearing it today, because we knew we needed *something*, and it's pretty and better than nothing. We figured nobody would even notice it, but if they did, we figured, they wouldn't think twice about the smallness of the diamond because I'm a student and therefore understandably on a limited budget. Apparently, we figured dead-wrong, though, because the look on this man's face tells me he's deeply displeased with me.

"Yes, it's a placeholder. It's a family heirloom with lots of sentimental value, so that's what I gave her for now, while I'm a student and money is tight; but, yes, I'll get Charlotte something much better as soon as I can afford it."

Mr. DiMarco furrows his brow. "Now see, I'd accept that load of horseshit explanation, considering your student situation, if I didn't happen to know you've got a surefire way to make some big money, so you can afford a much bigger diamond for Charlotte right fucking now."

My heart sinks into my stomach. An easy way? What does he mean by that?

Before I've mustered the courage to ask, he leans forward, smiles wickedly, and says, "Put on your mask and put on some more puppet shows, Salami. Or, hell, get some more piercings, and you'll have enough for a big, fat diamond in no time flat."

Holy shit.

My jaw nearly clanks onto the patio table.

When I don't speak because he's rendered me speechless, Mr. DiMarco chuckles and says, "Who do you think is Lucille1990?" He winks and points to his own chest. "And how about *Catfish2000*?"

"*Carlo*?"

He touches his nose. "I gotta hand it to you, Auggie, you and Charlotte are damned entertaining. You made it fun to pay myself back. I didn't foresee doing that, to be honest. It's a first. But once Carlo found out what you two were up to, I couldn't resist helping you out a bit. Call me a softie, I don't know. In the beginning, I never thought Charlotte would be able to raise the money in time for the birthday party. That was part of the psychological torture, see. Making her come here, empty-handed, and look me in the eyes. But then, when Carlo found you two online and showed me, I said, 'Now *that's* what I call doing whatever it takes. If some of those deadbeat dumbfucks *really* wanted to repay me, they'd find a way, like these two. Look at 'em go!' So, I started paying you, here and there, to help *you* pay *me*. Yeah, I knew I was paying myself back, but I was having too damned good a time doing it to help myself. Especially as the shows went on, I must admit I became a genuine superfan. 'Titty-fucking motherfucker!'" He bursts out laughing. "That was pure gold, Salami. Funniest thing I've ever seen. I laughed so hard, I cried. My wife came in and thought I was having a heart attack." He motions vaguely to my lap. "How are you healing down there, by the way? Based on the way you've been hobbling around the party, I'm guessing you're not feeling too good, huh?"

I can barely speak. But I manage to say, "Yeah, I'm pretty sore."

"I can only imagine." He belly laughs again and wipes his eyes. "Now, that's a man in love who'll do *anything* to protect his woman. Good for you. You've got my full respect."

I don't know what to say. But thankfully, I don't need to figure something out because, suddenly, the party inside begins collectively singing "The Birthday Song."

Mr. DiMarco claps his palms together and rises from the table. "If I don't get in there, my wife's gonna be mad at me for missing the cake. Tell your fiancée—The Unicorn—we're all good. Her debt is hereby released. Happy engagement to you both." With that, the mob boss sends a clipped hand gesture to his bodyguard and marches into the house, leaving me to hobble after him, slowly, feeling equal parts dizzy, disoriented, incredulous and relieved . . . and also wincing with every step I take.

29
CHARLOTTE

My hand is clasped firmly in Auggie's as we ride in the taxi to our hotel. We're both feeling relieved and euphoric. When we get to our hotel, we won't be able to celebrate our good fortune with some hot sex, unfortunately, due to the piercing guy's strict instructions. But I'm sure we'll order a bottle of champagne and make out like teenagers. I can't wait.

After Auggie came back inside from his private conversation with Mr. DiMarco, I was shitting a brick. A truckload of bricks. But he whispered to me that it was all great news. "We're free," he whispered. "The debt is forgiven. I'll tell you everything he said after we leave." I couldn't believe my ears, but I trust Auggie completely, so I felt hopeful.

As quickly as we could, we said our goodbyes and extricated ourselves from the party. And then, with our rolling bags in tow, we practically sprinted several blocks to a nearby Starbucks. And that's where we bought iced coffees, took them to a quiet, outdoor corner table, and sat and talked for over an hour.

When Auggie told me everything Mr. DiMarco had said, I

felt a mixture of emotions, and still do. Euphoria. Relief. Shock. Mortification to find out Mr. DiMarco and Carlo had watched Auggie and me doing all those crazy, sexual things. *Mr. DiMarco is Lucille1990 and Carlo is Catfish2000?* I could puke, every time I think about it. But, mostly, I'm thrilled and relieved to finally put all the stress, fear, and paranoia behind me, and behind Auggie, too, forevermore.

I look over at Auggie next to me in the cab and grin at his handsome profile as he gazes out the front windshield. He's so damned cute. And *brave*. Despite being scared, Auggie went outside with a freaking mob boss and had a private conversation with him and then walked away to tell the tale. Even better, he walked away *triumphant*. With Mr. DiMarco singing his praises and wishing us well. Honestly, I swoon every time I think about what Auggie has done for me. I'm deeply sorry for dragging him into my mess, but if that part was an unavoidable, canon event, then I'm awfully glad it was Auggie Vaughn who was by my side for all of this.

Auggie turns his head and looks at me. Apparently, he's sensed my gaze on him. "I still can't believe it," he says. "My mind is blown."

"Mine, too. Talk about a rollercoaster ride of emotions."

"Why is Bella in a wheelchair? I didn't want to ask while we were there."

"Cerebral palsy. A severe case of it. When Bella was little, the doctors said there's only a forty percent chance she'll make it to twenty, so Angela, and everyone connected to her or Carlo, treats every one of Bella's birthdays like a national holiday, just in case it's her last."

Auggie looks pained. He processes that for a beat before saying, "No wonder you'd never miss her birthday. It all makes sense now."

"Well, I'd also never miss one of Zach's or Claire's birthdays, either. With kids, the most important thing is spending time with them. Being present. Sure, they love presents and all that. But nothing beats spending quality time with a kid to let them know you genuinely care."

As Auggie smiles at me, the passing streetlights flicker across his gorgeous features, making him look even more beautiful than usual. "You're an amazing person," he says softly. "I already knew that, but today took my admiration for you to a whole new level."

My heart flutters. "Yeah, I'm an amazing person who stupidly took you-know-what from you-know-who." I'm being vague, due to the taxi driver sitting in front of me. But Auggie's smile tells me he understands my meaning.

"Yeah, and I'm the guy who called the tow truck on you. Nobody's perfect."

We both laugh. Clearly, the two things aren't the same.

Auggie's smile broadens. "The day I found you and Tessa in front of my building, and Tessa said you're the best, most amazing friend a person could ever hope to have, I thought she was delusional or full of shit. But now, I can plainly see her description was spot-on."

My fluttering heart is pounding in my ears now. "I feel the same way about you."

Auggie squeezes my hand. "You're so damned smart, Charlotte. Like when you told you-know-who about that so-called dream job." He chuckles. "You handled that perfectly. The last thing we need is for you to owe him *again*, only this time for doing you a huge favor."

My pounding heart suddenly thuds into my toes. *Shit.* I forgot about the job offer I've failed to mention to Auggie. I take a deep breath and speak on my exhale. "I was telling the truth to Mr. DiMarco. I really did get a job offer today, right when we landed. All the details I mentioned at the party were real."

Auggie looks shell-shocked. "Oh. Wow. C-congratulations. W-when do you start?"

"I haven't accepted the offer yet. They gave me forty-eight hours. If I take the job, I'll need to be in Dallas for training on Monday." He looks like I've punched him in the stomach. We've got big plans to paint New York City red together, starting tomorrow. If I take this job, we'd have to scrap those plans. But even more disappointing for Auggie, I'm sure, is the thought that this job, if I take it, would almost certainly be the death knell of our situationship. I mentioned all the most pertinent details to Mr. DiMarco while Auggie looked on. First class. Regular route servicing JFK to Heathrow and back. *Based in New York.* So, Auggie has to be cataloging all those details in his head now and realizing this job would likely mean the end of us.

"Why haven't you accepted the offer yet?" he asks. "It seems like your dream job, from everything you've said you're looking for. Do you want to negotiate more money?"

Yeah, it's my dream job—except for the part about it being based in New York. Doesn't Auggie realize *that's* the sticking point for me—the reason I didn't immediately reply *fuck yes*— because the thought of not seeing him every fucking day of my life, the same way we've been doing, breaks my heart?

"It's not about the money," I reply evenly. "The salary and benefits are better than I made at my last job. It's more that I want to take some time to think about being based in New York. It's been a crazy couple of weeks. I want to sleep on it and think about everything tomorrow with a clear head." Could I rationally forego the job of a lifetime, literally, to give a *two-week* relationship a chance to continue to grow and flourish into something lasting? That'd be far more than a leap of faith. It'd be a nosedive into the Grand Canyon.

Auggie looks anxious before looking out his side of the car, so I look down at my hands in my lap and try to corral my own anxieties. I notice the ring on my hand—Althea's beautiful ring—and feel a surge of emotion overtaking me. Through those cassettes, I've come to love and adore Auggie's grandma, even though I've never actually met her. Knowing she wore this ring, and adored it, made me feel proud to wear it today. Also, as dumb as this sounds, I liked wearing Auggie's engagement ring today, *period*. It felt nice on my finger. It felt right. I liked introducing him around as my fiancé. No, I *loved* it. Frankly, I'll be sad to take this ring off at the hotel. Sad to be single and un-engaged and back to reality again.

Auggie looks away from the window to level me with blazing eyes. "Charlotte, listen to me. I think you'd wind up regretting it if you passed up this job. If the time you're taking to think about it has anything to do with me, then take me out of the equation. Put yourself first. You don't do that very often. That's clear to me now. You take care of everyone else. This time, I want you to take care of yourself and nobody else."

My spirit sinks into my toes.

I know he's trying to be supportive and encouraging. I know he's looking out for me. I also know, two weeks ago, before I'd ever laid eyes on Auggie Vaughn, I would have accepted that job offer in two seconds flat. But the thing is, I *have* met Auggie Vaughn, and I've now felt things with him I've never felt with anyone else. Even in the midst of turmoil, I've had the time of my life with this sweet, sexy, adorable man.

The woman I am today understands what he's trying to do. He's putting me first, above all else—even his own heart. His own desires. But the little girl in me, the one who was raised on fairytales and rom coms and boy bands, can't help feeling disappointed he's not fighting tooth and nail to keep me by his side, the same way the tin-foil-covered prince always slayed every fire-breathing dragon to keep the princess by *his* side during our earliest puppet shows.

I hold Auggie's blue gaze, feeling conflicted. Rejected. Confused. *Grateful*. Hell, I don't know what I feel, to be honest. I do think he's right about one thing, though: if I don't take this job, I'll probably wind up regretting it. Wondering "what if?" Objectively, it really is the opportunity of a lifetime. The best job I could possibly hope for in my line of work. Accepting it should be a no-brainer—and, logically, the no-strings-fun I've had with Auggie shouldn't change that. "Thank you," I say. "I think you're right. I'll reply when we get to the hotel to accept the position."

Auggie subtly recoils, like I've slapped him across the face, even though *he's* the one who just told me to take the fucking job. If that's not what he really wants, then he'd better say so. *And right fucking now.*

I stare at him, nonverbally telling him to beg me not to go, and Auggie gnaws on his lower lip like he's considering saying something. But in the end, he forces a smile and says, "Congratulations, Charlotte. You deserve this."

Fight for me, Auggie. That's what my eyes are trying to convey. I can't promise it would make any difference in the end. There are no guarantees in matters of the heart, and the odds are stacked against us. But what if it *would?* There's only one way to find out. *Fight for me. Fight for us.*

"Looks like our trip to New York is off, huh?"

I exhale. "Yeah, I guess so. I'll need to head back to Seattle tomorrow, so I can pack up all my stuff and clear out the condo, get a real estate agent to help me figure out next steps, and then fly out to Dallas on Sunday to be there in time for training on Monday."

Auggie's Adam's apple bobs. "That money I owe you—the extra you took out on your credit cards."

"We'll get paid in two weeks."

"But if you run into any issue at all with interest before then, I can go back to doing solo shows to—"

"Don't do that. The new job comes with a signing bonus of ten grand, so I'll be able to pay off all my cards with that. And don't you dare go back to doing solo shows, Auggie. You hate doing them. You need to figure out another way, going forward. If I'm going to put myself first, then you need to promise to do the same." Why are we talking about money, when I want to know what he's truly thinking and feeling?

I stare at him again, nonverbally begging him to speak his truth, but he doesn't say a word. Instead, Auggie exhales a long, tortured breath, looks out his side window, and remains mute. So fuck it. I do the same. I'm irritated we're talking about money, rather than our feelings. And I'm annoyed he's not covering himself in tin-foil and doing whatever it takes to be able to say, "And they lived happily ever after." This time, not in a stupid show, but for fucking real.

We reach our hotel, and the driver pulls up in front of it. Auggie pays the tab with cash, and we exit the car and head to the trunk to retrieve our rolling bags.

"Thanks," I say, grabbing my bag from the driver.

"You bet," the driver replies. But as he's heading back to his driver's side door, Auggie calls out, "Hey, can you wait a minute? I think I'm gonna need a ride to the airport."

What?

"I'll run the meter while I wait," the driver says.

"That's fine. Thanks."

My voice tight, I choke out, "You're going to the airport?"

Auggie exhales and runs his hand through his light brown hair. "Now that our trip to NYC is off, I think I should catch the last flight out to San Francisco. My whole family wants me to visit while my mom and her fiancé are still out there, and late-night flights are always the cheapest. If I'm gonna go, I should just go now and let you focus on everything you need to do before going to Dallas."

I can't help feeling like he's literally *fleeing* the scene. Saving himself. Doing the emotional equivalent of running out of a burning building with his arms flailing. And, honestly, maybe he's right to do that. Smart. I've always been a "yank the Band-Aid clean off" kind of girl. Make a clean break. But this one time, the thought of saying goodbye to Auggie that way breaks my heart. I need more time with him. *I'm not ready to say goodbye.*

We didn't book a return flight to Seattle yet because we didn't know, for sure, what would happen out here. So, in that sense, Auggie doesn't have any firm plans he's cancelling in order to do this. In fact, the only one who's cancelled anything as of this moment is me. Which I'm sure is a huge disappointment for him. But doesn't he want to share one last night with me? We can't have sex, true, due to our piercings, but we could cuddle and talk and make out—all the things we did together last night, when we also couldn't have sex, and it was wonderful. Doesn't he want to spend what's surely going to be our last night together for who-knows-how-long, naked and in each other's arms?

"Yeah, all that makes sense," I say flatly. "Have a great time with your family."

"Thanks. Text me when you land safely in Seattle."

Oh, so he's expecting us to continue texting after this sad and unexpected goodbye? After we walk away from each other now, will we text as friends or fuck buddies or what? And for how long? What's the plan? Whatever it is, how long before one or both of us loses interest in texting, or meets someone else, and the amazing spark between us becomes a distant memory?

"Text me when you land safely, too."

"I will." He smiles ruefully. "I've had the time of my life with you, Charlotte McDougal."

I'm too emotional to speak. I've had the time of my life

with him, too. But I can't say it. If he's gonna go, then I need him to go now. What's the point of prolonging our goodbye?

Auggie shifts his grip on his rolling bag's handle. "Do you think Tessa will be okay watching Lucky for the full week?"

Seriously? I love Lucky, too, but I don't want to talk about the fucking dog right now. I want Auggie to kiss me goodbye and then realize, the second our lips meet, he can't do it. He can't take the high road and walk away from me. His heart won't let him.

"Tessa thinks we're staying in New York for the whole week, remember? I can't imagine she'd feel differently about watching Lucky, simply because we're no longer going to be together on our travels."

"Yeah. That makes sense." He looks physically pained. After shifting his weight, he suddenly exhales, steps forward, and takes my face in his hands. I'm expecting him to kiss me, but he stares into my eyes for a long moment, like he's memorizing every inch of my face; and then, finally, thank God, the man leans in and gives me the kiss of a lifetime. A tender, heartfelt fusion of our lips and souls that makes my heart stampede and every hair on my body stand on end.

"Auggie," I choke out against his lips.

"Keep in touch, okay?" he murmurs into my lips, his voice breaking. "Be happy. That's all I care about. I want you to be safe and happy."

"I want that for you, too."

"Bye, Charlotte McDougal."

"Bye, Auggie Vaughn." I wipe my eyes. "Travel safe."

And that's it. He slips into the waiting taxi with his carry-on. But before he closes the door, I remember the ring on my finger. I take off running toward the car, yelling his name. And luckily, he pops his head out the window, a concerned look on his face.

"Your grandma's ring!" I call out, breathing hard. "The ring, Auggie!"

His chin wobbles. "Keep it. It's yours now." With that, he slides his head back into the car, and a moment later, I'm staring at the taxi's retreating taillights.

He's gone.

Tears spring to my eyes and roll down my cheeks as I watch the taxi turn a corner and disappear. My brain knows he's being smart to go. This thing between us was never built to last, so it's better to cut the cord now, cleanly, than to drag it out. That's what my brain keeps reassuring me, anyway; but my heart isn't buying it. In fact, my heart aches like it's ceramic that's been physically shattered.

With a deep sigh, I slog into the hotel, straight to a perky woman behind a desk.

"Hello there," she says. "Checking in?"

"Yes. McDougal. Charlotte."

"I've got your reservation right here, Miss. Non-smoking with a king and a view. At your request, we've had champagne chilling in the room for quite some time. It's probably warm by now, so we can certainly send a new, chilled bottle—"

"No, that won't be necessary. It's just me in the room now. No champagne celebration to be had, as it turns out."

The woman's face falls. She juts her lower lip in sympathy, ever so slightly, while maintaining a generally professional demeanor. "Whatever you wish, Miss McDougal. How many keys?"

"Just the one."

"You're still checking out tomorrow?"

"Yes."

"Do you need a late checkout?"

I pause. "Actually, you know what? On second thought, I think I'm going to head to the airport and catch a flight back home now. I'll sleep on my flight."

"I'm sorry, it's too late for a refund."

"That's all right. I expected that." Suddenly, the thought of going up to that hotel room alone, when I thought I'd be spending the night there with Auggie, is too much to take. If I'm going to feel lonely and heartbroken, I'd rather feel that way on a flight headed home than in an empty, lonely hotel room in New Jersey that greets me with a warm bucket of sad, celebratory champagne.

Outside in the cold night air, I order an Uber to the airport. And while I'm waiting for the car, I swipe into my emails and tap out a reply to the job offer:

I'm thrilled to accept your offer. I'll plan to be in Dallas for training on Monday. I'll await further instructions and details regarding my travel, but for now, please let this email serve as my official acceptance. I can't wait to join the team. Thank you.

I stare at my reply for a long moment without pressing send. I should be thrilled to send this. *Ecstatic.* But the truth is I feel sick. Lost. Detached. *Rejected.*

I stare up the street, hoping the headlights of Auggie's taxi will magically appear.

I check my texts, hoping he's sent me one that says, "I've changed my mind! I'm coming back! Don't go anywhere!" But, alas, no such luck.

When my Uber appears in the near distance with no word from or sign of Auggie, I take it as my sign to stop being an idiot and to start acting like a responsible, mature adult. One who knows life isn't actually a fucking fairytale. There are tradeoffs in life. Compromises. Prices to pay. And this time, the price of my dream job is living in New York and foregoing the chance to see what might have happened with Auggie and me. What we might have become.

And who knows? After graduation, he might decide to move to New York, if I'm still there. Or I might be able to get myself reassigned to a shift based on the West Coast by then, if that's what I want to do. Life is fluid. You never know. The only thing I know right now is that this is my dream job and I'd be felony stupid to turn it down, exactly like Auggie said.

I press send on the email, just as the Uber is stopping in front of me. I stuff my phone into my coat and head to the car with my bag and open the back door.

"Charlotte?" the driver says, as is protocol.

"Yes. Your name, please?"

"Eduardo."

"That's it." I slide into the backseat. "To the airport, please. I'm starting my dream job." It's a weird thing to say, but I need to say it out loud to someone, and this guy happens to be here.

"Good for you. Congrats."

"Thanks. I'm excited about it." It's not the truth, and I know it the second the words come out. But I have to believe, after the pain of this sad farewell has faded, the words will become true. Excitement will be mine. In fact, with a little time and distance from the sadness of tonight, I'm sure I'll hardly ever think of Auggie, and his beautiful smile, and even more beautiful heart, ever again.

30
CHARLOTTE

Seattle

Two days later

I'm hungry.

Eagerly looking forward to chowing down on the two chicken tacos I'm carrying in a small paper sack. But even more than that, I'm excited to finally get to see what's on Lloyd's final cassette—the one that was stuck in his old video camera until about fifteen minutes ago. At least, that's what I think it is, since it's the only one not labeled. My hunch is Lloyd used to label his cassettes after filling them up and taking them out of his camera. Hence, my assumption he never got the chance to do that with this one, since its label is blank.

After finishing up all my packing and cleaning at the condo today, I decided to head out to my favorite taco place nearby, one last time—the one Auggie introduced to me; and on my way out my front door, I got the bright idea to grab Lloyd's nonfunctional video camera and take it with me. There's an electronics store a few doors down from the taco place, and I figured I could ask someone there to take a look.

Lo and behold, it took all of two minutes for the guy behind the counter to extract that stuck cassette, unscathed. And now, here I am, mere moments away from finally getting to watch it.

I reach my front door, fumble with my keys briefly, and head inside—and when I step foot into the empty space, my shoulders droop. There's no Lucky greeting me. He's still at Tessa's for the week while Auggie's in California. And worse, there's no *Auggie*. No Auggie coming home any minute from school. No Auggie lighting up every room he enters with his bright smile and sparkling blue eyes. No Auggie making my heart go pitter-pat and setting my lady parts on fire.

I place the tacos onto my card table, along with the unstuck cassette, and run off to grab the functional video camera. The guy at the electronics store bought Lloyd's broken camera from me earlier and said he'd buy the working one from me, too, so I'm planning to bring it to him tomorrow before leaving for the airport. Probably right after the building manager comes for this card table and chairs and my air mattress. As far as the stuff in the storage unit goes, I sold all of it yesterday to a scavenger dude—a guy who buys storage units, sight unseen, picks through them, and then sells whatever he can at flea markets. More power to him.

And that's that. I'm all done with my chores and planning, other than the appointment I've got later today with a real estate agent recommended by Tessa. So, with nothing else to do before my meeting, why not spend some time watching the final cassette? Maybe even the whole cassette collection again, if the mood strikes me. With Auggie in California and Tessa busy being a mommy and wife and running her empire, I've got nothing but time on my hands until my meeting. What better way to help me feel less lonely and blue on my last day in Seattle than watching Althea making *Lloyd* feel less lonely and blue?

I quickly wolf down my tacos while scrolling mindlessly on my phone, and then wash my greasy fingers in the kitchen sink before returning to the card table. Without further ado, I pop in the newly unstuck cassette into the working camera, and eagerly press the play button.

A clip of Althea playing Lloyd's piano and singing to him pops up. Nothing new there, although it's a pleasure to watch. I always love hearing Althea sing and play.

Abruptly, the scene cuts out and a new one begins. As I watch the next clip, a feeling of panic crashes into me.

No.

This can't be happening.

No, no, no.

The clip is only a couple minutes long. But it rocks my world. When it's over, the screen turns blue. And when I fast-forward on visual mode to the end of the cassette, there's nothing else to see. The rest of the cassette is blank.

Panting, I rewind to the beginning of the second clip and watch it again. And after my second viewing, I feel even more panicky and anxious. No wonder Lloyd insisted on Althea making that video about the peephole! *Because he foresaw doing this very thing, even back then.*

"Oh, god," I blurt, suddenly remembering the current location of that box of Lloyd's documents we brought back from the storage facility. This very morning during my cleaning binge, I tossed that box into the large recycling dumpster downstairs. I scanned its contents a few days after bringing the box home and easily surmised it was filled with a bunch of random, pointless stuff—bills, old letters, receipts, hand-written lists, blank forms, medical records. And then, when we got the new camera and confirmed Lloyd wasn't a pervy creep like we initially thought, I never looked at the documents again. Is that box still downstairs? God, I hope so, because now that I've seen this last video of Lloyd's, I need retrieve it, *pronto.*

I race downstairs, panting like I've just finished a cycle class. And thank God, the box is still in the recycle bin and within fairly easy reach, in theory. *If* I'm willing to dumpster dive to get it. *Which I am.* In fact, without a second thought, I do what should be an unthinkable thing: I climb into the dumpster to retrieve the damned box.

Luckily, the dumpster is filled with mostly recyclables, which aren't too messy or slimy; at least, when compared to the contents of the adjacent, smelly trash dumpster. Which means, by the time I'm dropping the box onto the ground below me and then inelegantly hurling myself over the edge to follow it out, I'm not covered in anything too vomit-inducing, goopy, or skeevy. Obviously, I'll take a shower, immediately, when I get back upstairs to my place. But right now, I'm too eager to find that needle in a haystack not to crouch down, right here and now, and immediately sift through the box's contents.

It takes me about twenty minutes to find the specific sheet of paper I'm looking for, but find it, I do. And when I hold it in my trembling hand and read it, over and over again, there's no denying its meaning. I run a search on my phone—and the answer I'm seeking is clear-cut. Undeniable. I run another search, this one slightly different than the first; and again, the result is the same. The answer is clear-cut. Which means, whatever happens next, is entirely up to me.

Still sitting on the ground next to the recycle bin, I stare into space for a long moment, trying to figure out what to do. But I need more time to think. More time to reflect.

Breathing hard, I grab my phone again, and this time, push the button to call to Tessa's recommended real estate agent.

"Hi, Charlotte," the woman says in greeting. "Are we still on for two?"

"No, sorry. Something's come up and I'm going to have to cancel."

"These things happen. Would you like to reschedule?"

"No, I'm leaving tomorrow for a week in Dallas, and then going to New York to start a new job after that. I'll get settled and be in touch. At this point, I think we're going to have to play it by ear."

31
AUGGIE

That's the message I just now posted in my family group chat—the group populated by my mother, her fiancé, Henry, my brother, Max, and his wife, Marnie. We had a great time this past week together at Max and Marnie's house overlooking the San Francisco Bay. Spending time with family, and especially those two kids, was the perfect way to try keep my mind off Charlotte. To try to stop missing her desperately. To yearn for her painfully. It didn't work, of course. Not at all. But it was worth a try.

As it turned out, even five days with family in a beautiful location, time spent playing princesses with my niece and making my nephew belly laugh, time spent sitting around a firepit at nights with the best people in the world, didn't do a damned thing to make my mind and heart forget about the woman I love but can't have.

I know I did the right thing, though. Standing on that

sidewalk with Charlotte in front of our hotel, I knew, if I went upstairs with her and slid into bed with her, if I touched and kissed her and smelled her hair, I'd wind up begging her not to take that amazing job. At the very least, I'd beg her to try a long-distance relationship with me. And I didn't want to do that to her. Not when she had her dream job, literally, in the palm of her hand. I love her too much not to insist on her putting her dreams first. And so, that's what I did, as painful as it was. My mother always says, "If you love someone, set them free." So, that's exactly what I did.

Knowing I did the right thing doesn't mean I'm not fucking miserable about it, though. Especially when I *don't always* know I did the right thing. In fact, more than half the time, I'm finding myself wondering if maybe I fucked up. What would have happened if I told Charlotte I loved her in front of that hotel? So what if she didn't say it back to me, like I was so fearful of in that moment. *So what?* As it stands now, I'd prefer to have been definitively rejected to this state of torturous limbo, one in which I can't stop wondering "What if?"

My Uber stops in front of Ryan and Tessa's gorgeous home —the paradise where I got to have the best week of my life with Charlotte. I thank the driver and get out of the car, feeling excited to pick up my Lucky Charm. As lonely as I've been, that little furball is going to be a balm for my aching soul.

I knock on Tessa and Ryan's front door, and Tessa appears in the doorway. She hugs me in greeting and welcomes me inside, and we catch up in the entryway for several minutes.

"Have you heard from Charlotte lately?" I ask, trying to sound casual. Like I'm not physically aching to hear the tiniest shred of news about her. Charlotte and I have exchanged some texts this past week, but it was superficial stuff. Not even in the same stratosphere as kinds of conversations we had while living next-door to each other.

"She's putting in long days of training," Charlotte says. "Learning the ropes at the new airline. She said it's all the same stuff she already knows; she just needs to learn how *they* like things done."

"Gotcha. Cool." It's actually what Charlotte told me, in a nutshell, when I texted to ask how it's going in Dallas. I was hoping Tessa would have something more exciting to tell me. For instance, that Charlotte mentioned she's been missing me. I doubt Charlotte has been feeling like I have this week—like all the sunshine has drained from the atmosphere. Like all the birds in the sky have stopped chirping. Even ice cream seems like a pointless exercise. I clear my throat. "Thanks so much for letting Lucky stay here this week."

"We had a blast with him. He's a member of the family now. He's been sleeping with Claire in her bed all week. I hope that's okay."

"It's awesome."

"They're joined at the hip. He's in the family room with the kids. They're watching a cartoon before dinnertime."

I follow Tessa into the heart of the house. I'm surprised Lucky didn't greet me in the entryway after hearing my voice. I've never once come home to my condo and not been *immediately* greeted by an excited Lucky. To be fair, though, this house is much bigger than my place. Plus, if he's with the kids, it's possible one or both are literally holding him hostage.

Welp, so much for the hostage theory. When we arrive in the family room, Rudy the husky hops off the couch to greet me, while Lucky stays put on Claire's lap—but the little girl isn't holding Lucky down or otherwise keeping him in place. Clearly, Lucky is free to go and *choosing* to remain in Claire's lap, even after seeing me walk in.

"Hey, Lucky," I say, striding toward him. He wags his tail

and bobs his head happily, but he doesn't get up to greet me. On the contrary, the way Lucky's staying put in Claire's lap feels intentional. Like he's saying, "Don't you *dare* try to take me away from here, motherfucker."

"Hi, Uncle Auggie," Zach says. He's sitting on the couch next to Claire.

"Hey, buddy. Good to see you." I address Tessa. "Hey, is Lucky feeling okay?"

"Yes, as far as I know. The kids just played with both dogs out in the back yard, and Lucky was zooming around the yard like a champ. Maybe he's tired."

"Yeah, that's probably it. Has he been eating and drinking normally?"

"Yep. No issues."

"Good. That's great." I drop it, not wanting to admit I've just realized my own dog doesn't give enough of a shit about me, after only one week away, to leave the comfort of his new favorite person's lap to welcome me back.

I sit next to Claire and stroke Lucky's head, and my dog gives me every indication he's delighted by my presence and touch. Thrilled, even. But, still, he doesn't move from Claire's lap and into mine, as I'd normally expect him to do. I don't think that's by chance. I think Lucky is letting me know I'm going to have to drag him out of this Nirvana he's found with Tessa's family, kicking and barking. As far as he's concerned, I was nothing but a beloved foster parent till he found his forever home.

The thought of me leaving here without Lucky breaks my already broken heart. Not to mention, even if Lucky wants to remain here, it's not up to him. Surely, Tessa's already got more than enough on her plate with her family, career, Rudy, and a third baby on the way.

"Sorry, buddy," I say, patting Lucky's head. "All good

things must come to an end, little dude. It's time for us to go home."

Claire suddenly realizes what's happening. Up until now, she was too absorbed in her cartoon to grasp the situation. But now, in a flash, she wraps her little arms around the dog and calls out to Tessa, "*Mommy, no.* Please! Let him stay!"

Tessa looks deeply sympathetic to her daughter's plight, but she shakes her head and says, "Honey, I know how much you love Lucky. We all love him. But I've reminded you all week long: he's not going to stay with us forever. We were only dog-sitting for Auggie, remember? Auggie loves Lucky the same way you love Rudy, remember?"

The little girl bursts into tears and nuzzles her tiny nose against the top of Lucky's furry head. "I love you, Lucky," she chokes out. "I love you so, so much."

"Oh, honey," Tessa says. "This isn't goodbye forever. I'm sure Auggie will let you visit him sometimes. Right, Auggie?" Tessa looks at me hopefully, her eyebrows raised. And suddenly, I know what I need to do, assuming Tessa would be open to it. Like Mom always says, "If you love someone, set them free." Well, I love Lucky. And clearly, he's decided he's home. A week ago, I set free someone I love with all my heart. The woman of my dreams. The woman I'd pledge myself to, forever, in a heartbeat, if I could rewind the clock and redo that conversation in front of the hotel. Well, if I managed to do that, if I managed to muster the strength to set Charlotte free to follow her dreams, then, surely, I can do the same for Lucky.

I clear my throat. "Can we talk in another room, Tessa?"

Tessa looks dubious. "Sure thing."

We head into the nearby sprawling kitchen, where Tessa leans her backside against the island and waits with raised eyebrows to hear whatever I'm going to say.

"You don't have to decide right now," I begin. "Take whatever time you need to think about it. But I think Lucky would be much happier living here with Rudy and your family, than with me at my place. If you want to make him a permanent part of your family, I'm willing to let him go . . ." I choke up and stop. But after taking a deep breath, I'm able to continue: "In order to give him the best possible life."

Tears are welled in Tessa's dark eyes. "Oh my gosh, Auggie. We would *love* to have him. He's already become a full-fledged member of our family. But are you sure you can part with him? It's clear he's your baby."

"He is, but, yes, I'm sure. Although . . . Come to think of it, I should probably call my mother first to get her blessing. Lucky was her mother's dog, my grandma's dog, and I feel like I should ask her permission before we finalize anything."

"Of course. We'd only want to do this if everyone is sure."

"If she says yes, I can take him back with me, until you talk it over with Ryan when he gets home."

Tessa shakes her head. "I don't need to talk to Ryan. We've been talking about getting a second dog for a while now, and more than a few times this week, Ryan said, 'I've never liked small dogs, but Lucky's changed my mind about that. Maybe we should pull the trigger and get ourselves a second dog. A little one just like Lucky, so they can sleep with Claire every night, the same way Lucky does.'"

A surge of emotion rises up inside me. I already felt in my bones this was a great idea. But hearing that Ryan thinks so, too, only confirms it.

I head into the adjacent dining room and call my mother. Not surprisingly, it takes all of twenty seconds before she's enthusiastically and unequivocally expressing elation at the idea of Lucky Martin Vaughn becoming Lucky Martin Vaughn Morgan. In fact, before I've even finished explaining the full situation, Mom's already burst into tears of joy for our beloved Lucky.

"Your grandmother would have been so happy for him,"

Mom says. "It's Lucky's luckiest break yet. Aw, sweetie. *Are you crying?* Honey, I know it's hard to say goodbye. But you can always visit him." She clucks her tongue in sympathy. "My love, you know what I always say: 'If you love someone, set them free.'"

I pull myself together well enough to respond. "Yeah, I know. I've been thinking about that a lot lately."

"Speaking of which, have you spoken to Charlotte yet?" I broke down during my visit one night and drunkenly poured my heart out to my family over a shared bottle of wine. Mom knows I'm in love with Charlotte. My whole family does. Also, that I'm regretting what I didn't tell Charlotte that night on the sidewalk in front of our hotel.

"No. We've texted a bit, but not much."

"Like I said when you were here, I think you should call her and tell her how you feel. Charlotte can do with that information what she chooses. But that way, you'll have no regrets if you need to move on with your life. And heck, it might turn out you should start applying to vet schools in New York."

My heart throbs. "So, which is it, Mom? Should I set Charlotte free out of love, or follow her across the fucking country like a stalker? Because I can't do both, consistently."

"*Auggie.*"

I exhale. "Sorry. I'm not well."

"Tell Charlotte how you feel and *also* set her free. The rest will take care of itself, my darling."

I'm aching to follow Mom's advice. But picking up the phone to say "I love you" feels like a consolation prize, when six days ago, I could have done it in person, while looking into Charlotte's eyes, and then sealed it with a kiss.

I fucked up. That's all there is to it. And now, I'm not sure how to fix it. Or if I should even try. For all I know, Charlotte's *relieved* we parted so cleanly. Grateful to be set free from even thinking about trying to embark on a long-distance relationship with me.

"Okay, I'll think about it," I say. "Thanks, Mom. I love you."

"I love you, too. Send me photos of Lucky with his new family."

"I will."

We say our goodbyes, and I head back into the kitchen to give Tessa the good news. When I tell Tessa it's a go, that Lucky is now, officially, a Morgan, she lurches to me and hugs me warmly.

"Thank you so much, Auggie. I promise we'll give him such a great life."

"I know you will."

"And you can come see him, any time you like. We'll give you the code for the front door, and you can come, any time."

I wipe my eyes and chuckle. "We don't need to go that far, but thanks for offering. It'll be enough for me to know my grandmother's looking down from heaven, crying tears of joy to see Lucky so happy and loved."

"Aw, Auggie. You're such a sweetheart. And not only in relation to Lucky." She twists her mouth. "Do you want to be the one to tell Charlotte this amazing news? If you want to call her to tell her about it, I'm pretty sure she's available to talk right now, as a matter of fact. I was just texting with her and mentioned you were here to pick up Lucky. She said she's sitting in her hotel room, home for the night." That's all Tessa says, verbally, but I feel like her facial expression is saying a whole lot more. *What's she trying to tell me?*

"We could FaceTime Charlotte together, right now, so she can see Lucky in his new home with all of you."

I'm thinking my suggestion is a no-brainer. But to my surprise, Tessa scrunches her nose and says, "Actually, I think maybe she'd prefer to talk to you, privately, about it. Just you and her. It might be a good reason for you two to chat and catch up."

My heart is thundering. *What does she know that I don't?* "Yeah, okay. Good idea. I'll call her outside while waiting for my Uber home."

"Perfect."

We head into family room and tell the kids the news, and they both, predictably, lose their shit. Even Rudy the Husky seems elated: when the kids start screaming in joy, he dances around the family room and sings as only a husky can do.

We take a bunch of photos to memorialize the occasion, and Tessa and I swap numbers and send each other all of them. But finally, dinnertime arrives, and it feels like time for me to go, even though they've invited me to stay and eat with them.

I give Lucky one last hug and kiss, and then head outside to wait for my Uber and call Charlotte.

"*Auggie*," Charlotte says enthusiastically. "Hi."

The sound of her voice makes my heart simultaneously soar and ache. "Hi. How are you?"

"Tired. I'm in my hotel room, relaxing. Are you back home yet? I left your spare keys in your mailbox when I left. Make sure you get them."

"I'm in Seattle, but not home yet. I came straight from the airport to Tessa's to pick up Lucky."

"Give him a big hug and a kiss for me."

"Lucky's the reason I'm calling. I've got some great news about him." I begin to tell Charlotte the story, but as I do, emotion surges inside me and my voice breaks. "Sorry," I choke out. "I've got no doubts this is the right call. But that doesn't make it any easier to say goodbye to someone I love so damned much."

My words hang in the air.

I didn't mean to make Lucky a Trojan Horse, a means of

explaining why I did what I did in New Jersey. But now that those words have come out, I realize that's exactly what I've done.

"This is you in a nutshell, Auggie," Charlotte says. "You always put everyone else's happiness before your own."

"No, not *everyone's*." I pause to muster my courage. And when I've harnessed it, I say, "I only do that with someone . . . I love." *There*. I said it. I did it.

"I'm positive Lucky knows you love him. He loves you, too."

Seriously? She truly didn't understand the subtext of my comment?

My Uber arrives and stops in front of me.

"I-I have t-to go," I say, cringing as my old stammer threatens to sabotage me. I take a deep breath. "My Uber is here." It's a patently ridiculous excuse. I could easily talk to her during the drive. But I can't hear Charlotte's voice and not want to do the exact opposite of setting her free. I hear her voice, and I want to claim her. Make her mine. Put my ring on her finger and give her my name and fill her belly with my babies.

"Okay, don't be a stranger, Auggie," Charlotte says. "I got used to talking to you, every day of my life. This past week of not talking to you has felt like a year."

"For me, too. I promise we'll talk more, now that I'm back from my trip."

"I'm gonna hold you to that." I can practically hear her smile through the phone line. "Bye, Auggie. Congrats about Lucky. You did a good thing for him."

"I know I did. Bye, Charlotte. Have a blast in the new job. Keep me posted."

32
AUGGIE

I drag my sad ass through the front door of my condo from Tessa and Ryan's, ditch my suitcase inside my door, and head straight into the shower. Usually, showers do wonders to lift my dark mood. Not this time.

From my shower, I head to my kitchen to see if there's anything to eat. There's not. Between my stay at Ryan and Tessa's house and then my various trips, I've been gone almost two weeks. I open a can of tuna, eat that right out of the can, brush my teeth, and collapse into my bed.

When I wake up, I've slept for over twelve hours. I'm not surprised. I didn't set an alarm and my brain felt no need to get going. Why would it? I've got no studying to do; this is the last weekend of spring break. I've got no Lucky to walk or feed or play with. Or cuddle. Or talk to. Or look at and think of all the times my grandma snuggled with him and sang to him, "Lucky, you're my lucky charm!"

And most tragic of all, there's no Charlotte McDougal living next door. No Charlotte McDougal bursting through my front door with a zany new idea for a show. No Charlotte McDougal making me laugh, or turning me on, or just hanging out with me and making me feel *seen* like never before. No Charlotte McDougal to light up my life with her sparkling smile and make me give a fucking shit about a goddamned thing.

What have I done? I want Charlotte to be happy and safe, even if it's without me. That's what I want most. But what if me telling her I love her wouldn't have held her back? What if me telling her that would have made her change course, yes, but because she would have been *thrilled* to do it? I can't imagine it, honestly. Every indication has been that *I* caught feelings, and Charlotte didn't. Not as much as me, anyway. *But what if I'm wrong about that?*

I head to the kitchen and mix up a pre-packaged protein shake with ice that almost makes me hurl, and then head out to the campus pool for a long swim. I'm hoping I'll be able to sweat Charlotte out of me. Shake these blues away with some exercise-induced endorphins. No such luck.

As I pass Charlotte's closed door on my way back from campus, I can barely look at it. It hurts too much to know she's not in there and never will be again. They always say you don't know you're in the happiest time of your life, while you're in it. You can only figure that out in retrospect, looking back. But in this case, that's not true. I knew it then. I know it now.

After another shower, I head back downstairs to grab some essential groceries and a sandwich. And on my way back into the building, I notice the wall of mailboxes and remember I've got a week's worth of mail in mine. It's no big deal. I never get anything important through snail mail, anyway. All my bills come to me electronically these days. But I guess I should clear out the box of mailers and crap for the next round that's bound to arrive.

When I open my small mailbox, I'm shocked to discover it's chock full of stuff that's not mail: the video camera Charlotte and I bought online after Lloyd Graham's failed to function; also, its power cord; a cassette in a hard plastic case; a large manila envelope; and, last but not least, a small, white envelope with my name handwritten on its front in Charlotte's pretty, swirling hand. Predictably, there are also some mailers and other inconsequential stuff in my mailbox, but I'm far too intrigued by the other stuff to pay that any mind.

Without even bothering to close my mailbox door, I eagerly open the small, white envelope. Not surprisingly, given my name is in Charlotte's handwriting on its front, it's a handwritten notecard from Charlotte:

My Dearest Auggie,

The condo is all yours. Sell it and use the proceeds to pay for the rest of your schooling and beyond. Make all your dreams come true. Open that clinic you're dreaming about and become exactly the kind of vet you've always wanted to be. Don't compromise your dreams, or who you are, for anybody. You're a perfect, precious, beautiful soul, exactly as you are. The best human I've ever met. Lloyd got it right: there's nobody more deserving than you.

With love,
Charlotte

I'm baffled. Stupefied. Flabbergasted. What does any of this mean? *What* condo is all mine? *Charlotte's?* And what does she mean Lloyd got it right? *Got what right?* None of it makes a lick of sense to me, except for one thing. The heat thing. The thing hijacking my brain and making my heart explode with hope and excitement: Charlotte closed her note "with love." *With love, Charlotte.* The woman I love actively, consciously, purposefully wrote the word *love* with her own hand in a note to *me*.

When Charlotte wrote "with love" to me, was she referring to the generalized, societal concept of love—the *platonic* form that binds all human souls, including hers and mine, in a vague, spiritual sense? Or did Charlotte use that all-powerful word to let me know, to confess or at least hint, that she's feeling a personal, intimate, *romantic* kind of *love* for me, *specifically*? At the very least, was this phrase Charlotte's way of inviting *me* to say those three little words to her? It's suddenly so clear to me. Without question, I should have told Charlotte I love her on that sidewalk in New Jersey. *I fucked up.*

Breathing hard, I open the large manila envelope and pull out its contents with shaking hands: two letter-sized documents. The first is a typed legal form with a title at the top that reads, "Transfer of Deed." *What?* A quick scan reveals the shocking truth: Charlotte transferred full ownership of her condo to me. *Why the fuck did she do that?*

I swap the two papers in my hand and discover the second is a handwritten note, but this time the jagged script isn't Charlotte's:

To whom it may concern,
I, Lloyd Graham, leave my apartment to the younger grandson of Althea Martin. I don't know his full name, but she always called him Auggie. August Martin? I've just called an ambulance and don't know if I'll be coming back here, so I'll leave this note on my desk for whoever to find. Please find Auggie and carry out my wishes. He deserves it, more than anyone. I'll make a quick video to explain further and also so that whoever finds this can verify it was me who wrote it. Thank you, Auggie.

Lloyd

My brain is melting. My heart thundering. My face and neck both feel like they're engulfed in scorching flames. *What's going on?*

I slam my mailbox door shut and jog-walk to the elevator with everything from the box, and then press the call button maniacally at least ten times.

By the time I get upstairs and into my place, I'm out of breath. Feeling sick. I plug in the video camera near my couch, insert the cassette, and sit down—and, suddenly, there's my grandmother playing piano and singing in Lloyd Graham's cluttered, chaotic apartment. I watch in abject confusion as my heart does jumping jacks inside my chest. Normally, I'd be thrilled to watch a brand-new clip of Grandma singing, one I've never seen before. But this time, the video only serves to baffle and irritate me. *Why did Charlotte want me to see this?*

All of a sudden, Lloyd's ashen face appears on the camera's tiny screen. He looks sickly and pained. "I'm Lloyd Graham," the old man says. "I'm not feeling so good right now. I've got blood coming out of places it shouldn't be. I've called an ambulance. It'll be here any minute. If I don't come back, I want to be sure Althea Martin's grandson, Auggie, gets my apartment. You know, like an inheritance." He holds up a handwritten paper—the same one that's now sitting in front of me on my coffee table, right next to the Transfer of Deed form. "I just now wrote this out. It was me. I'll leave it on my desk for someone to find, along with the camera, so whoever finds it will know to track down Auggie and make sure he gets my place." He winces in pain. "I always thought I'd go before my best friend, Althea. She was so full of life—always being goofy and dancing around. I always told her I wanted *her* to have my place when I was gone." He fights tears. "But Althea passed last week, and now I'm all alone, so I'm leaving my place to her favorite person, Auggie Martin, or whatever his last name is. I should have asked Althea about his full name, but it's too late now. I can't imagine anyone who's more deserving than Auggie." His eyes water. "Auggie, if you see this, thank you for taking such good care of my Althea, your grandmother. *My best friend.*" His tears flow. "She was the best friend I've ever had. My lifeline. An angel sent straight from heaven. And, boy, did Althea love you, son. She loved your mom and brother, too, with all her heart. But she had a special place in her heart for you. Also, it sounds like your mom and brother are good with money. But you're the one who might need a helping hand, so I'm going to give my place to you, exactly like Althea would have wanted. Thank you for always taking such good care of her. Especially at the end, when you'd sit by her bedside and hold her hand. I watched you reading to her. Singing her all those silly songs she loved so much." He winces in pain and makes a guttural sound. Wipes the tears from his eyes. "Auggie, you did everything for Althea I wish I could have done for her myself. I wanted to go to her, so many times, but something inside my noggin is broken now, and I just couldn't do it. Not even for Althea. I'm ashamed of that. I'm sorry, Althea. I let you down. Oh, and Auggie, if you find a hole in my bedroom wall, and you peek through it and see your grandma's bedroom, I want you to know, I swear to God, it was Althea's crazy idea to drill that hole. She said so in one of the cassettes. Find it, please. I'd look for it now, but they're knocking on my door. The ambulance is here, I think. I—" He winces sharply, and the video on the small screen suddenly spirals like the camera is falling. There's a thudding sound. And that's it. Everything turns to static, briefly, before turning a solid blue. Lloyd must have dropped the camera. I bet that's why it was broken with this cassette lodged inside it.

When and how did Charlotte get this final cassette out of Lloyd's broken camera? How long did she know about its contents and Lloyd's handwritten will? But most importantly of all, why the fuck did she even carry out Lloyd's final wishes at all, when she could have easily destroyed all this stuff, once she found it, and nobody, including me, would ever have known?

I grab my phone with a trembling hand and place a call to the only attorney I know—the guy who also happens to be the smartest person I know. My big brother, Max. He's a patent and business lawyer, so he doesn't handle wills and stuff in his practice, but he's got to know a whole lot more about this sort of thing than me.

"Yo," Max says in greeting.

"I need some help. Some advice." I ramble the whole story, and Max sounds as shocked as I feel. I told him about my feelings for Charlotte during my visit at Max's house, but nothing I told him then could have prepared Max or anyone else, including me, for what I've found in my mailbox today.

After hearing me out, Max says, "Okay, let's take things one at a time. First of all, you can't transfer real property to someone without their consent. That's settled law in every state. The recipient needs to sign the transfer paperwork and accept the property. Period. So, as nice a gesture as it was for Charlotte to fill out that form and try to transfer the place to you, Charlotte still owns her place. There's no doubt about that."

I sigh with relief. "Thank God."

"If you tried to enforce the transfer deed in court, you'd lose."

"Max, you know I'd never do that. I'm not trying to figure out how to enforce any of this. I'm trying to understand *why* Charlotte gave this shit to me, rather than burning it all the second she found it."

"The handwritten will. Did the dead guy sign and date it?"

"No. He didn't date it, and he only signed his first name at the bottom. There's no doubt he wrote it, though, thanks to the video he left. It's definitely not a fake."

"I've got no doubt he wrote it, but that's not the legal standard for it to be enforceable. Without a full signature and date, it's not a legally enforceable will. Period. Does it state his wishes? Seems like it. But under the law, wishes don't make something enforceable."

"Even if it's in his handwriting? I didn't realize it at first, but it's the same writing as on a bunch of his other video cassettes."

"Doesn't matter. A simple google search would have told you all of this, Auggie. Any will, whether handwritten or typed, isn't legally enforceable unless it's fully signed and dated. You didn't bother to google before calling me?"

"No. I panicked."

Max chuckles. "I'm sure Charlotte googled. There's nothing ambiguous about the law on this stuff. It's black and white."

A chill races down my back. My brother is right: there's no way Charlotte didn't google the fuck out of all this stuff before stuffing it into my mailbox. She had to know she didn't *need* to do this for me, not in a legal sense. *So, why'd she do it?*

After telling my brother to hang on for a minute, I google the requirements of a handwritten will, just for good measure, and, yup, there it is. Everything Max said. Next, I google the requirements of a video will, and the result is the same: they're not enforceable. I tell Max what I've found, and he says he's found the same thing.

"It makes sense video wills aren't valid," Max says. "There'd be too many issues with deepfakes and manipulation. Also, questions about timing of the video in relation to any written wills. I'm sure Charlotte knows the video will isn't enforceable, either, assuming she's got access to the internet."

That last part was Max's way of chastising me again for

calling him before running a simple internet search. "To summarize," I say, "any way we slice it, Charlotte is under zero legal obligation to give me Lloyd's condo, and it's unfathomable to think she didn't realize that."

"Correct. And the transfer of deed didn't do a damned thing. You should probably call her right away to let her know she's still the owner of the property, so she knows she's still on the hook for property taxes." I can practically hear Max's wicked smirk across the phone line. "And while you've got her on the phone, maybe you should also tell her anything *else* you might be thinking about. *Obsessively*. You know, anything you might be wishing you'd said to her, in person, when you had the chance."

I feel like I've been struck by lightning.

I have to go to her.

Right now.

And tell her I love her.

A phone call won't do!

I have to look Charlotte McDougal in the eyes, hold her hands in mine, and tell her "I love you, Charlotte, and I'll do whatever it takes to be with you, if only you love me, too." Even if Charlotte breaks my heart and tells me she doesn't feel the same way, at least I'll know the truth and won't have to spend the rest of my life wondering.

"Are you still there?" Max says. "I'm in the middle of something here, Auggie."

"Oh, yeah. Sorry. I'll let you go. I've got a plane to catch."

"A plane?"

"To Dallas. Or New York? Shit. I'm not sure if she's left Dallas yet. Either way, I'm going to fly to her and tell her I love her in person."

"Atta boy. Keep me posted."

"Thanks a million, Maximillian. You're the best big brother, ever."

"And you're a dumbass, Augustus."

We both laugh. In this instance, he's not wrong.

"Good luck, Auggie. Love you."

"Love you, too."

I hang up and press the button to call Tessa. Charlotte said she'd be training in Dallas for a week, and it's been about that long now. Is she spending one more night in Dallas or has she already arrived in New York, her new hometown?

"Lucky's doing *great*," Tessa says in greeting. Thank God, we swapped numbers when we traded photos yesterday, or else I'd be having even more of a coronary right now.

"Glad to hear it. Listen, do you know if Charlotte will be in Dallas or New York tonight? I want to surprise her by flying to her, but I don't know where to go."

Tessa squeals and shrieks, "Please, tell me you're *finally* going to get your girl!"

My heart leaps. "You think she'll be receptive?"

"Oh, god, Auggie. Charlotte made me promise not to tell you this, but I don't care anymore. She's been miserable this whole week without you. She misses you *so* much and totally regrets taking the job."

"*She does?*"

"When we talk at night, she's always stuffing down tears. She keeps saying the job isn't what she thought it'd be. That life isn't fun anymore, if she's not with you. And I keep saying, 'Okay, well, call him and tell him that.' But she won't say it first. She said she's already told you, well enough, in her own way, and now the ball is in your court. Does that make any sense to you?"

"It sure does." I clutch my heart. "I love her, Tessa. She's *the one*. My reason to breathe. My future wife."

Tessa squeals again. "Please, please tell her all that."

"I will. Assuming I fly to the correct city. Is she in Dallas or New York?"

"I'll look. I have access to her location. Hang on." There's a pause, during which I feel like my heart is going to explode and splatter all over the walls of my small living room. After what feels like an eternity, Tessa blurts, "*New York*! She's at JFK airport right now. She must have literally just arrived."

It's a slight bummer. Dallas would have been a shorter flight. "Off to New York, I go! Keep track of her for me, okay? Whenever she arrives at a hotel, shoot me her pinpoint location, so I have it when I land."

"You've got it. Go, Auggie, go!"

"Give Lucky a big hug for me, okay? Tell him not to worry, Daddy *finally* pulled his head out of his ass and is on his way to tell Mommy he loves her more than life itself."

Tessa whoops. "I'll let Lucky know. Ryan, too. He'll be *thrilled*. Keep us posted!"

"Roger!"

"*Rabbit*."

I laugh.

"Sorry," Tessa says. "Ryan's whole family always does that. The weirdos have rubbed off on me. Now, go!"

"Be sure to send me that hotel location."

"I promise. Now, go, go, go—go get your girl!"

33
CHARLOTTE

I put my book down. I'm in bed in my hotel room in New York. Trying to distract myself, so I won't think about Auggie. But it's not working. Did he see the stuff I left for him yet?

I check my phone.

Still nothing.

He got home yesterday, and I told him I'd left his spare keys in his mailbox. So, he should have checked by now. Auggie's not the type to let mail stack up forever, especially not after a week away. Did he check his mailbox last night and see what I left there, and now he's feeling overwhelmed and stressed out and needs times to gather his thoughts? But what's there to think about? The condo is his now, no strings attached. *Unlike me.* I want *all* my strings tied up with Auggie's now because there's no better man in this world than Auggie Vaughn—as a general proposition, but also, specifically, for *me.*

Could it be Auggie's not sure of his feelings for me? Perhaps for Auggie it's the difference between signing a letter "with love," like I stupidly did versus signing it with only "love." That little "with" makes all the difference, doesn't it? *Shit.*

I must have spent at least forty minutes trying to decide how to close out my handwritten note to Auggie. Sincerely? Warmly? Thanks for the amazing memories? I tried them all on a piece of scratch paper to see how each one would look before permanently marking up my pretty notecard, but nothing looked right to me besides the word *love* on its own.

Love, Charlotte.

I was *this* close to writing that. But then, I chickened out. And now, I'm regretting those four extra letters so much. W-I-T-H. Why'd I chicken out and include those, rather than taking a full leap of faith?

I check my phone again. Still nothing. Should I call him? I look at the clock.

No. I told myself I'd let *Auggie* call *me* after finding that stuff in his mailbox.

The hotel phone on the nightstand next to me suddenly rings loudly, making me jump an inch off the mattress.

"Hello?"

"Hello, Miss McDougal. There's a delivery for you here, and the delivery person is asking for your room number, so he can bring it to you, personally. Apparently, you need to sign for it. I told him I'm not allowed to divulge a guest's room number without permission. Do you authorize me to give him that information, or would you prefer for *me* to sign for the delivery and keep the package at the front desk for you?" She speaks to someone on her end of the call. "Yes, sir. I understand that."

I'm not expecting a package. Perhaps my new employer sent me a welcome fruit basket or something. Whatever it is, I'm sure it can wait until morning. I'm not in the mood to get out of bed for any reason, but especially not to open my door to some random delivery dude. "Will you sign for it and keep it at the front desk for me, please? I'll get it in the morning."

"Charlotte!" a male voice shouts. *Auggie?* Was that Auggie's voice? I've no sooner had the thought than Auggie's voice sounds directly in my ear this time. "It's me, Charlotte. Auggie. I'm here in the lobby of the hotel."

"*What?*"

"I was trying to be sneaky and surprise you at your door, but they won't give me your room number. So much for that idea."

I can't believe it. I'm overjoyed. I sit up in bed, quaking with adrenaline. "What are you doing here? Why didn't you just text to ask my room number when you got here?"

"*Because I was trying to surprise you.*"

I laugh. That's so Auggie. I quickly give him my room number and sprint to my door and then stand in the doorframe, trembling with anticipation. A few minutes later, there he is. Augustus Vaughn. Sprinting down the hallway toward my room.

"I can't believe you're here!" I shout, as he draws closer to me.

When he reaches me, he wastes no time. He takes me in his arms and presses his lips to mine. My heart soars as Auggie kisses me. It's only been a week since I've tasted his sweet kiss and smelled his glorious aftershave, but it's felt like a lifetime. A gray, drab, lonely, sad, pointless lifetime.

"We have a lot to talk about," he says breathlessly. He leads me into my hotel room and the heavy door clanks behind us. "But first off, I need to tell you something. Something *urgent.*" He holds my face and looks deeply into my eyes. "I love you, Charlotte McDougal. With all my heart and soul. Forever and always. There's nobody else for me."

Tears prick my eyes. "I love you, too. Forever and always, too."

He looks shocked. "*You do?*"

I laugh. "You flew all the way across the country, not knowing if I'd say I love you back?"

"Well, I was hoping. But you signed that note '*with* love.' It felt like you were reserving plausible deniability."

I crack up. "I've been regretting my word choice, ever since. Let me set the record straight now. *Love, Charlotte.* Please. Because *I* love you. So much, it hurts."

"I love you so much, it feels like my heart is going to physically burst."

"I want *all* my strings attached to you, Auggie. I want to be a team again. But for real. In life."

"That's all I want, too. I'll apply to vet schools in New York. There are several to try. And if I'm not successful at first—"

"No, you don't have to do that." I grab his hand. "Thank you for offering, but I don't want to start my new job tomorrow. I thought I did. I thought this job was everything I could ever want. But when I got to Dallas, my world felt gray and drab and pointless without you. I realized *you're* the most important ingredient to my happiness. I'll figure out the rest. The only thing that matters now is that I'm with you."

Auggie looks deeply touched. Like he's working hard to stem the tide of emotion rising inside him. He chokes out, "Are you saying you'll come back to Seattle with me? The condo is still yours, by the way. We can pick up right where we left off."

"No, the condo is yours. But I'd love to live with you at your place while you sell it or rent it out, if you'll have me."

He exhales. "I want nothing more than to live with you. I can't stand being apart from you. But I don't want you coming to live with me because you think you don't have anywhere else to go. The condo is yours, Charlotte. None of that paperwork is legally enforceable. And even if it were, I'd undo the transfer and give the place right back to you."

I already knew Lloyd's wishes weren't legally enforceable,

thanks to a couple google searches. But legal standards didn't matter to me, in the end. Pretty quickly, I realized what I was going to do. Not because I was required to do it, but because I *wanted* to. "The issue isn't the legality of Lloyd's will," I say. "Lloyd expressed his dying wish—and it was a wish I happened to agree wholeheartedly with. Like he said, there's nobody more deserving than you."

"Charlotte—"

"No, listen to me. It's not only what Lloyd wanted as his dying wish. It's what *I* want now. In the present. I want you to have it, Auggie. It's all yours."

Auggie shakes his head. "Thankfully, it's not up to you because I have to sign the transfer paperwork to make it effective. And I'm not going to do that. Ever. The condo is still yours. The transfer never happened. So, that's that."

I'm genuinely confused. I knew Lloyd's will and video weren't legally enforceable, thanks to the internet, but it never occurred to me to google anything about the transfer document after I filled it out. I figured Auggie would need to file it somewhere, and I assumed that's what he'd do. "What do you mean you have to sign it, or I can't give you the condo? That can't be the way it works."

"Google it, if you want. It's the law in all fifty states."

My shoulders slump. "Damn."

He laughs. "Sorry to disappoint you."

I twist my mouth. "Can I still live with you?"

"Of course, if that's what you want to do."

"I do. That's all I want."

Auggie's face lights up. "That's all I want, too. Well, other than . . ." He abruptly stops himself.

I cock my head. My heart is suddenly thrumming. "*Other than what?*"

Auggie grabs my hand and points his chin at his grandmother's ring on my finger. "You're still wearing it."

"I love it. It's pretty and it reminds me of you. Of *us*."

His Adam's apple bobs. His chest heaves. "I liked being introduced to everyone at the birthday party as your fiancé. No, honestly, I *loved* it. It was the best feeling in the world . . . even though I knew it wasn't real."

My heart lodges in my throat. Is Auggie thinking what I *think* he's thinking? I can barely breathe, but I manage to choke out, "I loved introducing you as my fiancé. It felt totally natural and right to me."

"To me, too."

"I'd even go so far as to say it felt *real* to me, at the time." I take a deep breath. "That was an amazing feeling for me. The best feeling. Not scary at all."

There.

I did it.

I've let him know I'd say yes, and now the ball is soundly in his court.

"I felt all of that, too," he croaks out. "Exactly."

We stare at each other. In this moment, Auggie looks like a kid standing at the bitter end of the tallest high dive at the community pool. The kid who peeks over his shaking toes and gazes down at the blue water below and tries to muster his courage to take the necessary leap.

I squeeze his hands. "Whatever you're thinking," I whisper, "whatever's on your mind, say it. Do it. You can't make a mistake here, Auggie. I love you. I want you. I don't want anyone else but you and I'm positive I never will."

Auggie's visibly quaking now. But he takes a deep breath and slowly kneels before me, prompting me to whimper and squeal as he descends.

When Auggie's knee touches the carpet, he looks up at me with blazing blue eyes and says, "I love you, Charlotte McDougal. You make me feel like I can do and be anything. You're kind, generous, feisty, fearless, smart, and a little bit crazy in the best possible way . . . And I'd be luckiest man in the world if you'd keep on wearing that ring, but as my fiancée—for real. *Charlotte, will you marry me?*"

"Yes," I blurt without hesitation.

Auggie springs up, takes me into his arms, and kisses me. "I'll get you a better ring," he murmurs into my lips. "That one's a placeholder."

"No, I love this ring. *And I love you.*"

He kisses me again, and soon, we're passionately devouring each other.

Auggie lays me down on the bed and pulls off my pajama pants and panties, and in short order, he's having himself a voracious meal between my legs. A metal-free one, I might add. I took out all the piercings between my legs in Seattle, and everything's all healed up now—which means Auggie's voracious tongue, mouth, and fingers feel nothing but glorious and delicious and pleasurable. Even more so than usual after spending a week away from him—my *fiancé.*

When I come, Auggie groans loudly and rips off my tank top—which is when he discovers my nipple piercings are gone, too.

He pulls off his own shirt, revealing, not surprisingly, he's also removed both his nipple piercings. But when he removes his pants and briefs, I get a shocking surprise.

Auggie didn't remove his dick piercing.

It's still there, shiny and pretty and raring to go at the base of his straining hard-on.

"You kept it," I breathe.

Auggie winks. "I'm not blind or stupid, babe. I saw the hungry look in your eyes when you told me about Ryan's piercing and showed me that photo from the internet. I could tell this is a fantasy of yours."

"It is," I admit, blushing like crazy. "A huge one."

He laughs. "Well, let's find out if it works, huh? I can always take it out, if you don't like it."

I nod vigorously and pull on his arm. "*Come to momma.*"

With a chuckle, Auggie kisses me again. He fondles my clit for a bit, and then fingers me, too, to get me extra wet and ready for him. And when I'm writhing and begging him to let me test drive his sexy new hardware, he folds me in half beneath him, rests my calves against his broad shoulders, and nudges his beefy, wet tip against my entrance. He rocks his hips forward and stretches me out, making me moan, and soon, his full, girthy length is all the way in.

I groan when he begins thrusting, even louder when I feel the unmistakable sensation of metal teasing my clit, over and over again, with each deep thrust. He's turned himself into a human sex toy for me—a spectacular one with eyeroll-inducing efficiency.

"Oh, god," I choke out, as my eyes roll back into my head. "Holy shit."

"You like it?"

"Oh, god, Auggie. Don't stop. I'm almost there."

"*Already?*"

He's emboldened. Before now, I think he was being a touch careful with me—making sure the metal didn't hurt me. But now that he knows that little piece of hardware is driving me absolutely wild, he's unleashed. A man possessed. He fucks me hard, with a little snap of his pelvis each time his body is flush with mine—each time that metal hits its target—and the end result is that I feel like I'm being physically catapulted into sheer bliss.

As my pleasure spirals higher and higher, Auggie grits out a string of hoarse comments. He tells me I feel fucking incredible. *Perfect.* That he's missed me. That he *loves* me. And best of all, that he can't wait to make me his wife and to fuck me like this every day for the rest of our lives. Soon, the combination of Auggie's husky voice, his perfect words, his delicious scent, plus, all the amazingness going on between my legs, conspires to rocket me to heaven.

I teeter on the edge of the abyss for a brief flash before my body releases and I'm slammed with an orgasm that's so intense, it makes me squirt, cry, laugh, scream, howl and whimper, and then weep, all in rapid succession.

As waves of pleasure throttle me, and all those weird, conflicting sounds and tears and female ejaculate hurtle out of me, Auggie shoves himself inside me as deeply as he can go, so that my innermost muscles massage every inch of his full length. Not surprisingly, it's too much pleasure for the man to withstand—even as my body is still warping, Auggie comes along with me with a loud and primal roar.

When he's spent, Auggie collapses on top of me, thereby folding me even more beneath him, since my legs are still propped onto his shoulders. For a long, delicious moment, we both remain entangled and still, sweaty and panting, trying to regain equilibrium.

"Never, ever take that piercing out," I deadpan, eventually splitting the silence. "Or the engagement is off."

Auggie laughs and leans back, allowing me to extricate myself from our pretzel.

We lie on the bed together, my cheek on Auggie's bare chest and his arms around me.

"But are you *sure* you like the piercing?" he jokes.

"Pretty freaking sure. If I hadn't said yes to marrying you before we had sex, I'd be saying yes now. Hell, I'd be proposing to *you*."

Auggie kisses the top of my head. "So, it wasn't a dream? You really said yes to marrying me?"

"I sure did. Are you freaking out now that it's settling in?"

"Not at all. You?"

"Not at all."

"My family is gonna be so thrilled for me. I talked their ears off about you in California."

"I haven't told mine you exist."

We both guffaw.

"Will your family freak out when you tell them you're engaged?"

"Oh, definitely. But then, they'll meet you and understand. But even if they don't, so what? Nobody else will ever understand what we've been through together. How quickly and completely we got to know and love each other. Nobody could ever understand our love but us."

"Ain't that the truth."

"They're going to love you when they meet you. I have no doubt about that. To know you is to love you, Auggie."

"My family already loves you. Just from what I've told them about you and that one FaceTime call."

"That's so sweet. I can already tell I'm going to love all of them, too." I shift in Auggie's arms to be able to look him in the eyes. "I do think we should enjoy our engagement for a while. Let's not try to plan a wedding while you're still in school. We'll do it after you've graduated and passed all your licensing exams."

"Sound great to me. I'm in no rush to get the piece of paper, really. As far as I'm concerned, I'm already committed to you, right here and now."

"Me, too. I feel the same way."

"Are you sure? If you're freaking out, please tell me and we'll make that a promise ring."

I swat his chest playfully. "Don't you dare take back my proposal. It was perfect. It's not a promise ring. It's my *engagement* ring. And that's that."

As Auggie kisses me, I press my naked body against his and practically mew with pleasure and joy. I can't believe he's here. *He did it. He fought for me. He's my knight in shining armor.*

"Can I tell my family?" he whispers. "I told my brother I was coming here and he told me to keep him posted. I'm sure he's told the whole family by now and it's taking every ounce of strength for my mother not to call and ask for an update."

I laugh. "Hell yes. Let's tell the whole world."

We get dressed, since calling our peeps on FaceTime while naked, even if we're both covered by a sheet, would be awkward. And when we're both fully clothed, and I've brushed the just-got-immaculately-fucked-by-a-dude-with-a-dick-piercing look out of my hair, we make a round of calls, first to Auggie's family, and then to mine—both to my blood family and also to Tessa and her family, too. Predictably, Tessa and her family are elated, while my blood family—my mother and the one of my two brothers who picked up—are visibly stunned by my happy news. But even so, they're kind to Auggie, and congratulatory, despite their obvious shock, and the call ends with promises to get together in LA soon.

When our calls are done, we're both elated but exhausted. Especially Auggie, after his cross-country flight. We strip off our clothes and head into the shower and wind up making out languidly in there under the stream of hot water. We're in no rush. We're relishing our new status as an engaged couple.

After our shower, we order food and champagne from room service, and then crash on the couch in our soft night clothes to await our order.

"If I fall asleep, wake me up when the food comes," I say with a yawn.

"If you fall asleep, I'll let you sleep."

"No, don't. I really want to toast our engagement." I smile. "Maybe you could sing me a silly song to keep me awake?"

He returns my grin. "Okay, as my engagement present to you."

"Seriously?"

"I'll even *dance* while I'm singing to you."

I sit up straight on the couch. *"Like a boy bander, you mean?"*

"Exactly. It'll be my once-in-a-lifetime, engagement gift to you."

"And just like that, I'm wide awake."

Auggie laughs. "Don't get too excited. I've told you before: my dancing isn't all that great. But I'll give it my best shot, as my gift to you."

Auggie slides off his chair and stands before me, grinning from ear to ear. After taking a moment to think about it, Auggie sings, shaking his ass and doing classic boy-band hand gestures and movements; and the end result is that this little performance is perfect—the best, most perfect gift I've ever received. Especially because I know it's being delivered by a man who's *not* a natural extrovert or exhibitionist, like me. Knowing that about Auggie, I'm even more touched and impressed by his adorable performance.

When Auggie strikes a picture-perfect boy-band pose and stops singing, signaling his little show is done, I hop up and cheer and applaud wildly before throwing my arms around his neck and kissing him passionately.

"That was so good! I loved it!"

He laughs. "Good. Because I love you."

"Solid gold, baby. I'm telling you, it belongs at the top of the charts. What's the name of your boy band?"

"Auggie Loves Charlotte."

"Awww." I kiss him, just as there's a knock at the door. Room service has arrived.

We get the food and champagne. Open the bottle. Pour. And next thing you know, we're holding up sparkling champagne for a toast.

"To us," Auggie says. "To the happy life we're going to have together."

I know exactly what to add to Auggie's toast. I've said it many times, after all, in response to Auggie—albeit under totally different circumstances. But never has the phrase been so apt or meaningful, as in this moment. With a huge smile and a wink, I clink my glass against Auggie's and add, *"And they lived happily ever after."*

EPILOGUE
AUGGIE

It's my gorgeous wife's 40th birthday party, and Tessa and I have conspired to throw her quite the bash. It's the first party thrown at the new house—the bulk of the party is happening in our spacious backyard—and I'm thrilled to see all our family and closest friends have made it. Some of our new neighbors, too—the ones we've already hung out with a bit, thanks to a welcome barbeque thrown for us by Ryan and Tessa at their place down the street.

This is our dream house, baby. Great layout. Huge backyard. Lots of space for our growing family. And best of all, with our place being right down the street from Tessa and Ryan's house, we now hang out with those two and their four kids, and Rudy and Lucky, all the damn time.

It's all courtesy of The Unicorn, since we never could have afforded a house like this on my salary alone. That's how my high-earning wife is known by her rabid online following these days. *The Unicorn.* And she definitely lives up to her billing.

Thankfully, Superhero Salami Slinger is dead as a doornail. He never appears in The Unicorn's videos or anywhere else.

Charlotte doesn't need me, and I don't want to do it, so it's a win-win. Occasionally, I serve as Charlotte's trusty cameraman—the guy laughing and whooping behind the camera—when she's doing something funny. I also help her when she's doing something that can't easily be captured with the camera on a tripod. But otherwise, The Unicorn is a one-woman, well-oiled machine.

As a matter of fact, all traces of my old Superhero Salami Slinger account, and every raunchy video I've ever appeared in, whether solo or with Charlotte, have been wiped from the internet. When we told Ryan and Tessa the truth about Charlotte's highly lucrative profession during my fourth year of vet school, we also told them about the shows Charlotte and I used to do together. As much as we could, anyway, without divulging all the Mr. DiMarco stuff. To Ryan and Tessa, we made it sound like we did all that crazy stuff to raise money for my tuition.

But anyway, when we told Ryan and Tessa about all that stuff several years ago, and I expressed concern that all those old videos might come back to haunt and/or embarrass me during my future career as a vet, Ryan said he had a close friend who's a gifted hacker and that the guy might be willing to scrub everything from existence for me, free of charge, as a favor to Ryan.

In reply, I told Ryan I didn't think that was remotely possible. "But if it is," I added, "then I'd insist on paying your hacker friend for his trouble." The next thing I knew—about two weeks later—everything was gone. Not only that, Ryan told me his hacker buddy, whoever he was, refused to take my money.

I'm bummed I'll never be able to thank the hacker guy for what he did for me. Hopefully, Ryan expressed my thanks effusively enough to him. Because whoever he is, he's a fucking genius and a generous soul and I'm forever in his debt. I'm thrilled to be a vet now and to let Charlotte be the only online star in our family these days—and not to have to worry that one of those videos might pop up to bite me in the ass.

Speaking of ass-biting, the Unicorn doesn't do overtly sexual things for her fans, although she is always naked. The stuff Charlotte does runs the gamut from silly to mundane: doing chores around the house, dancing, cooking, baking, spinning cartwheels across the lawn, doing yoga in our home gym. It doesn't matter. As long as it's Charlotte—The Unicorn—and she's doing it buck naked and in her signature purple, sparkling mask, her fans always eat it up.

Despite her niche online fame, Charlotte still hasn't bumped into anyone in real life who says, "Wait, aren't you The Unicorn?" But maybe that's because people are too embarrassed to admit, in the real world, they're fans of that sort of thing.

As far as I'm concerned, I see no reason to feel embarrassed about what my wife does for a living. My brilliant wife works *maybe* ten hours a week, at most, and she earns a *monthly* income that's more than the highest *yearly* flight-attendant's salary. Plus, she loves what she does. So, what's there to be ashamed of, when you look at it like that?

Admittedly, even though we've told Ryan and Tessa and my family the truth, we still do keep secrets from lots of people. Our new neighbors, for instance. Also, the parents of kids at Althea's preschool we're friendly with. And, of course, Charlotte's Irish-Catholic mother doesn't have a clue what her talented daughter actually does for a living. My mother-in-law thinks her vivacious daughter is a full-time mom to Althea, while *I'm* the breadwinner of our family—the reason we recently moved into this amazing house.

I suppose, given how successful veterinarians can be in wealthy neighborhoods, it's not a crazy thing for her to believe. She knows I own my own animal hospital with three veterinarians and an army of vet techs working for me, after all, and I don't even think she realizes half my practice caters to rescue organizations. So, we let her think I'm the reason for our recent move.

Personally, I don't like Momma McDougal not knowing what a kickass businesswoman Charlotte really is. I wish she knew about Charlotte's success, and I wish she'd be accepting, if she did know. But in the end, it was Charlotte's call to make, whether to keep or tell her secret to her mother, and Charlotte unequivocally said, "Nope. My mother can *never* know."

Speaking of secrets, the one that initially brought Charlotte and me together is long dead now. We never heard from Mr. DiMarco or Carlo again after Bella's birthday party. Are those guys out there with new usernames, regularly keeping up with The Unicorn? God only knows. Charlotte and I try not to think about it.

Tessa pokes my arm, jerking me from my thoughts. "I'm gonna get the birthday cake now," she whispers.

"Okay, good. Right after she blows out the candles, look at me and be ready to push the button on the song."

"Roger."

"Rabbit."

Tessa giggles. Anyone who hangs out with any member of the Morgan family for any length of time eventually picks up the habit.

Tessa says, "I'll tell Ryan to find the birthday girl, so she's not in the bathroom or whatever when the cake comes out."

"Perfect. I'll get the guys wrangled, too."

As Tessa heads off into the house to get the cake, I head in the other direction to find my big brother, somewhere in the crowded party. When I find Max, he's hanging out with his wife, our mother, Mom's husband, Henry, and several other partygoers. I pull Max aside and ask him to marshal the troops for my big birthday surprise for Charlotte, and he says he's on it. Granted, Max rolls his eyes when he says it, making sure I know he's doing this crazy thing for me against his will. But, still, he dutifully heads off to get everyone gathered and in place.

From Max, I head onto the lawn to find my silly, happy, chatty two-year-old, Thea, full name, Althea. I know she'll want to be there when we sing happy birthday to her beloved mommy—and even more importantly, to help Mommy blow out the candles. Thea's got flaming red hair, so she shouldn't be hard to find. Plus, she's surely following around her cousins, Ripley and Marcus. Or if not them, Ryan and Tessa's daughter, Claire, who's basically a celebrity, as far as Thea's concerned. So, at least, I've got a good idea of the various faces I'm looking for to lead me to my spitfire of a daughter. We knew there'd be so many kids at this birthday party, many of them under five, we hired a slew of roaming babysitters to play with them and watch over them. So, at least, I know Thea's safe and sound, wherever she is.

Ah. There she is. Thea's with Claire and Ripley, with all of them playing with Old Man Lucky and one of our two dogs. Lucky's facial fur has turned all-white by now. He's probably not long for this world. But the good news is whenever he reaches the Rainbow Bridge, I'm positive he'll turn around and say, "I've had the best life, ever. *Thank you.*"

I lean down to the girls on the lawn and tell them we're going to sing and cut the birthday cake now, and they excitedly follow me back to the patio area. When we reach the patio, Ryan appears with Charlotte. My wife greets me and starts to say something about how much fun she's having, but she's interrupted by Tessa emerging from the house with a large, blazing cake. When Tessa and I lock eyes, she nods to signal me, so I start dutifully singing the ritualistic birthday song at the top of my lungs, and, in short order, the entire party follows suit and begins converging on the patio.

Tessa carefully places the cake onto a table and everyone, including Charlotte, Thea, and me, crowds around it. When Charlotte sees the top of the cake, and the elaborate unicorn painted in icing on it, she hoots with laughter.

As Charlotte listens to the birthday song, she's got her tiny doppelganger at her side, a huge smile on her face, and a palm resting on her growing baby bump. And for the millionth time since my beautiful wife showed me that positive pregnancy test six months ago, I feel my heart surge with excitement and love for her and our family. *We did it.* Everything we've ever dreamed about, individually and together, we've made it happen. We're living the dream, Charlotte and me. A real-life happily ever after.

Charlotte's fans have *loved* seeing her pregnant, by the way. Both times. In fact, when Charlotte announced this second pregnancy to her fans, she had her best month, ever, thanks to all the congratulatory tips that poured in. Charlotte made so much money that month, as a matter of fact, she bought me a cherry-red Ferrari as a birthday gift. Paid in full.

It was an outrageously extravagant gift, and I told her so. But, secretly, I was beyond thrilled she did it. Years ago, I told Charlotte the story of my brother, Max, and *his* Ferrari. Sorry, his *Portofino M.* Max always used to correct anyone who referred to it as a paltry *Ferrari.* But when I told Charlotte the story back then, I was making fun of my brother and his obsession with his stupid sports car. I never in a million years thought she'd file that nugget of information away and one day buy *me* the same wildly expensive car. Apparently, my face while telling the story gave me away. Charlotte could tell it was my dream car. And now, it's sitting in our garage, courtesy of my amazing wife and her online band of loyal sickos.

When the birthday song ends, Charlotte and Thea blow out the birthday candles and everyone claps.

"Thank you so much for being here to celebrate with me!"

Charlotte shouts above the cheers and applause. "This is the best birthday, ever!"

Tessa hugs Charlotte, so I head over there and hug Charlotte, too.

"Happy birthday, baby," I say, after kissing her soft cheek. "I've got one more present for you. The best one yet."

"*Another one*? Oh my gosh, Auggie." I showered her with gifts this morning. Jewelry. Flowers. A pair of highly specific sneakers she wanted for some reason. But this is her 40th, baby. A big one. So, as nice as all those gifts were, I had to go *big* with this final one. "I'm sure it's amazing, love," Charlotte says. "But best one yet?" She holds up her hand to reveal the sparkling diamond ring I gave her this morning. "I don't think anything is going to beat this."

"*Just you wait.*" I find my brother in the crowd, and thankfully, he performed his duties and marshalled the troops. Or rather, our makeshift boy band. Max, Ryan, Fish, and Henn are all standing together in a clump, awaiting my signal to take the stage.

I give the group a thumbs up and they collectively flash me one in return. I lock eyes with Tessa nearby and give her a signal, since she's going to be our emcee and song-button-pusher, and she winks and climbs onto a nearby chair.

"Can I have everyone's attention, please?" Tessa bellows. "Hello? Attention, please."

It takes a minute, but eventually everyone is quiet and looking at Tessa.

"Happy birthday, Charlotte! Let's hear it for the birthday girl!"

Everyone applauds and cheers.

"Charlotte, you're a very lucky birthday girl, because tonight, just for you, for the first and only time, the world-famous boy band, Auggie Loves Charlotte, is here to perform their global smash hit, 'All Strings Attached!'" As the crowd titters in confusion, Tessa flings her arm toward me and the rest of my boy band on the other side of the patio, where we're already standing in formation with me in the front. She bellows, "Enjoy the show, Charlotte! This one's for you!" She pushes a button, and two second later, the song begins blaring through overhead speakers.

"*What?*" Charlotte gasps out, her green eyes wide.

The intro to the song is blasting, but my vocals—the ones I'm going to lip-synch while muddling through the choreography—haven't started yet, so it's understandable Charlotte's feeling deeply confused about this ridiculousness. Thanks to Fish—the bass player of 22 Goats who's now a good friend of mine, thanks to Ryan—the song blasting the party sounds like an actual hit song—one you'd hear on the radio in the 90s. It sounds totally professional. Familiar somehow, too, simply because it's such a great parody. But as Charlotte and the rest of the party is about to find out, this song was created especially and only for one incredible boy-band fan: the one and only Charlotte McDougal.

At a small get-together at Ryan's about four months ago, I wound up chatting with Fish and eventually drunkenly telling him my big idea to give my wife a personalized boy-band song as her 40th birthday gift. I only told Fish about my big idea to ask him if he knew anyone I could hire to help me bring the idea to life. But to my surprise, Fish immediately said he'd do it. For free. For the fun of it. When I protested, Fish insisted. He handed me his phone, right then and there, and ordered me to sing all my song ideas into it. I didn't have the whole song fleshed out at that point, but I had lots of ideas and snippets. Stuff I'd been singing to Charlotte for years, here and there. So, I sang them into Fish's phone and handed it back to him.

Two months later, while Fish was here in Seattle for his mom's birthday, he called me and told me to come over to her house, *pronto*. When I got there, I was blown away. He had a full-on music studio set up in her garage, and from those silly little snippets of vocals I'd made for him months before, he'd created an entire song, except for vocals—one with music that sounded as good as any real song you'd hear on the radio.

We fleshed out the lyrics together. And when that was done, Fish set up a microphone for me, and patiently led me through the process of laying down vocals on the track. Seriously, it was one of the best days of my life. I felt like a Make-A-Wish kid.

After that task was done, Fish got to work. He bathed my amateurish vocals in autotune and other production magic until they sounded legit professional. He added his own vocals to mine to fill them out and make them pop and he also added some background harmonies for good measure. Seriously, by the time Fish was finished producing the track, I almost believed "Auggie Loves Charlotte" was an actual boy band from the 90s.

Originally, my big idea was to awaken Charlotte on her 40th birthday by pressing play on whatever boy band song I managed to come up with. But once I heard the finished song, I scrapped that boring plan and came up with a bigger, better one: wrangling my very own boy band to *perform* the song at Charlotte's birthday party. And now, here we are. Auggie Loves Charlotte, comprised of me, Max, Ryan, Fish, and a friend of Ryan's named Henn.

I became friendly with Henn last year during Ryan's birthday boy's trip, so I knew he'd be a great addition to the boy band. He's the kind of guy who's always up for anything, especially if it would involve him making a fool of himself on a dance floor. So, that was that. I asked each of the guys to help me, and they all enthusiastically said yes. Well, okay, Max had to be cajoled a bit. But in the end, his wife, Marnie, convinced him for me. And just like that, about six weeks ago, all five members of my boy band were finally in place.

Finding the right choreography for our boy band to perform, and then figuring out a way for everyone to learn the dance in time for the party was a bit of a challenge. For one thing, the band is physically scattered. Only Ryan and I live in Seattle. For another thing, none of us are professional dancers, so we had to find something simple and easy to do that *also* fit the song and *also* could be learned by a bunch of amateurs from watching a video.

Luckily, Ryan's friend, Henn, is pretty good with computers. He's in IT. So, once I found a YouTube dance tutorial that looked like a pretty easy routine that was also at the right tempo, Henn kindly overlayed "All Strings Attached" with the dance video and sent it around to the group. From that point forward, I'd done all I could do, other than my part in privately rehearsing. I had to let go of my stress about us probably crashing and burning at the party, and just accept the performance would be what it would be.

The first dance cue comes up in the song. There are still no vocals on the track, but some hard-hitting, staccato chords require some herky-jerky, over-the-top hand motions and poses. I perform them all, on cue—I think?—and the entire crowd, including Charlotte, goes apeshit—which suggests the boy banders just behind me and on either side of me have *also* hit their cues.

The beat just dropped. Time for those step-together-steps and finger snaps. So far, so good. *Phew.*

Okay, the vocals are starting now. As the lead singer of Auggie Loves Charlotte, it's now time for me to start lip-synching, with dramatic flair, while launching into the heart of the dance moves. Here we go.

In a world where hearts get tangled up,
Mine has stayed untangled, pristine;
But when you're not near me, my heart feels mangled,
Now suddenly, you're pulling all my strings.

As I sing, I do my damnedest to perform the moves I've practiced endlessly. And I think, based on the crowd's reaction, the guys just behind me and on either side of me must be doing their thing, too. I could be wrong about that, though. I think I'm in a fugue state. On the cusp of passing out.

Either way, whatever's happening, good, bad, or ugly, it's enough to make Charlotte, and everyone else, lose their everloving minds, especially the wives of every man up here. Charlotte and Tessa are leading the charge: they're clutching each other and jumping up and down screaming while Claire and Thea jump around next to them.

I can't help noticing half the party is clapping with a "what's going on?" smile on their faces. Which could mean we're sucking horribly up here *or* that they don't realize this song isn't real. You know how a song parody can be so damned good, half the people who hear it don't even realize it was meant to be funny? I think that's the case with "All Strings Attached." I truly think there are people here who think I've picked out an existing song from Spotify to lip-synch and dance to at my wife's 40th birthday party. Well, let them think it. Honestly, I'm complimented. We're giving it our all up here, after all. And the song is dope.

Even if this is the worst boy banding the world has ever seen, my wife is now crying happy tears, as the song barrels toward its big whiz-bang ending, and that's all that matters to me. I swear, Charlotte's never looked more beautiful than she does right now. I'll remember this moment as long as I live.

We're almost at the finish line of the song now. It's time for me to lip-synch my favorite part—the outro:

This one's for you, Charlotte McDougal
I love you, girl, you're my better half
Gotta love me some Charlotte McDougal
Happy birthday, babe, hope you're having a blast!

That's it. We did it. The song is over. On the word "blast," we strike our group pose—the clustered, all-too-serious, last-minute one we quickly came up with earlier during the party —a pose that includes a whole lot of squinting, smoldering, lip pursing, and hands positioned on chins. Well, *three* of us strike the ending pose, anyway. Max and Fish forget and have to skitter over and take their places after the song ends, in total silence, their footfalls echoing hilariously across the patio like scratches on a record player. It's funny as hell, honestly. Way better than what we'd planned to do, based on the hysterical, raucous guffawing their hilarious mistake elicits from our audience.

After holding the group pose for a long beat, the five members of Auggie Loves Charlotte finally break free of our frozen tableau, at which point the crowd descends upon us like hungry lions attacking gazelles. Wives tackle husbands. Kids are picked up and twirled around. Hearty laughter abounds. And best of all, Charlotte flings herself into my arms and thanks me effusively for "the best gift" she's ever received in her life.

I hug her to me as she bursts into happy tears. I don't know if it's pregnancy hormones, or if Charlotte would be crying like this, regardless, but the woman cries for a solid two minutes in my arms before she's finally able to carry on a coherent conversation with me.

"How on earth did you make this happen?" she asks, wiping her eyes.

I pick up Thea, who's tugging on my leg, and proceed to tell Charlotte the whole story.

"I can't believe Fish did all that," Charlotte says. "I'm blown away."

"Yeah, I hope you don't mind, but I kind of promised him we'd name our son Fish as payment for all his hard work. Hope that's okay with you, babe."

Charlotte cracks up. "Sorry, no. I'm cool with Guppy, though. Does that work for you, babe?"

"*Finally*. It's perfect."

We both laugh. We haven't settled on a name for our son-to-be yet. For some reason, Thea was easy for us. We both love Althea and felt good about keeping her name alive in our family. But settling on a boy's name has been much harder. There's a tradition in my family to name boys after rulers in history—the Vaughn boys are Maximillian and Augustus, and now, Max's son is Marcus—but Charlotte and I can't decide if we care about following that tradition. I guess we'll figure it out, at the very latest when the baby comes in three months.

My mother comes over to hug Charlotte and me, with Lucky in her arms. When she arrives, Thea reaches out for her, so Mom puts Lucky down and takes her beloved grand-daughter into her arms. We chat for a bit as a threesome, until Charlotte and Mom wind up chatting, separately, at which point, I glance around the party.

When I see everyone around me having so much fun—all our friends and family and so many kiddos and dogs—I can't help it. I get emotional. I can't believe my kids get to grow up in this house, surrounded by so many friends and family. They'll have birthday parties here. The kids can pitch a tent out here in this amazing backyard and "go camping" with our dogs. And best of all, Charlotte will be their mother, so they'll always know they're loved beyond measure. The thought makes me choke up.

"Aw, honey," Mom says, when she notices my tears.

"Aw, love," Charlotte echoes.

"Sorry, I'm just happy," I say, wiping my eyes.

Mom looks between Charlotte and me for a moment, before smiling and saying, "I'll give you two a minute."

When Mom leaves, Charlotte embraces me and nuzzles her nose with mine. "Thank you. For the party. The gifts. The song. For our family and our whole life together. Thank you, thank you, thank you. It's all because of you. You're my knight in shining armor."

"You're my princess. My queen. My unicorn." I smile and softly sing the last lines of "All Strings Attached": "Gotta love me some Charlotte McDougal. Happy birthday, babe. Hope you're having a blast."

Charlotte laughs through tears. "I am. Not just today. *Every* day." She sniffles. "I love you, Auggie."

"I love you, too. I always will. Forever and ever." I slide my fingertip underneath Charlotte's chin. "*And they lived happily ever after.*"

Do you want to hear Auggie's song, "All Strings Attached"? No, really. The actual song Auggie made for Charlotte? If so, visit:
www.laurenrowebooks.com/all-strings-attached

The End

Want to read about Tessa and Ryan? Their insta-love-to-

enemies-to-lovers romance will make you laugh, swoon, and fan yourself.
Check out Captain
Note: *Captain* is listed as number two in the standalone *Morgan Brothers* series of books, but it's a great place to start. In fact, that book is listed as the first standalone book in other languages.

Want to know what happened with Auggie's brother Max and Marnie? It's a spicy, funny, shocking doozy of a love story! Check out *Who's Your Daddy?*

Or, if you prefer, feel free to check out any of the romance titles in Lauren's catalogue, described below. **All books by Lauren Rowe are available in ebook, paperback, and audiobook formats.**

BOOKS BY LAUREN ROWE

Meet Me At Captain's Series of Standalone Romantic comedies

Who's Your Daddy?

When thirty-year-old patent attorney, Maximillian Vaughn, meets a sassy, charismatic older woman in a bar, he invites her back to his place for one night of no-strings fun. It's all Max can offer, given his busy career; but, luckily, it's all Marnie wants, too. But when Max's chemistry with Marnie is so combustible, it threatens to burn down his bedroom, he does the unthinkable the next morning: he asks Marnie out on a dinner date.

Mere minutes after saying yes, however, Marnie bolts like her hair is on fire with no explanation. What happened? Max doesn't know, but he's determined to find out and convince Marnie to pick up where they left off.

Textual Relations

When Grayson McKnight unknowingly gets a fake number from a woman in a bar, he winds up embroiled in a sexy text exchange with the actual owner of the number—a confident, sensual older woman who knows exactly who she is . . . and what she wants.

No strings attached.

But as sparks fly and real feelings develop, will Grayson get his way and tempt her to give him more than their original bargain?

My Neighbor's Secret

When Charlotte gets into her new dilapidated condo to start fixing it up for resale, she finds out the infuriating stranger who's thoroughly messed up her life is her new next-door neighbor.

Also, that he's got a big secret.

She confronts him and proposes they work together to get

themselves out of their respective jams, even though they both admittedly can't stand each other. Yes, he's let it slip he thinks she's pretty. And, okay, she begrudgingly thinks he's kind of cute. But whatever. They hate each other and this is nothing but a business partnership. What could go wrong?

The Secret Note: A Spicy Standalone Novella with HEA

He's a hot Aussie. I'm a girl who isn't shy about getting what she wants. The problem? Ben is my little brother's best friend. An exchange student who's heading back Down Under any day now. But I can't help myself. He's too hot to resist.

The Morgan Brothers

Read these standalones in any order. Chronological reading order is below, but they are all complete stories. Note: you do not need to read any other books or series before jumping straight into reading about the Morgan boys.

Hero

The story of heroic firefighter, Colby Morgan. When catastrophe strikes Colby Morgan, will physical therapist Lydia save him . . . or will he save her?

Captain

The insta-love-to-enemies-to-lovers story of tattooed sex god, Ryan Morgan, and the woman he'd move heaven and earth to claim.

Ball Peen Hammer

A steamy, hilarious, friends-to-lovers romantic comedy about cocky-as-hell male stripper, Keane Morgan, and the sassy, smart young woman who brings him to his knees during a road trip.

Mister Bodyguard

The Morgans' beloved honorary brother, Zander Shaw, meets his match in the feisty pop star he's assigned to protect on tour.

ROCKSTAR

When the youngest Morgan brother, Dax Morgan, meets a mysterious woman who rocks his world, he must decide if pursuing her is worth risking it all. Be sure to check out four of Dax's original songs from ROCKSTAR, written and produced by Lauren, along with full music videos for the songs, on her website (www.laurenrowebooks.com) under the tab MUSIC FROM ROCKSTAR.

Dive into Lauren's universe of interconnected trilogies and duets, all books available individually and as a bundle, in any order.

A full suggested reading order can be found here!

The Josh & Kat Trilogy

It's a war of wills between stubborn and sexy Josh Faraday and Kat Morgan. A fight to the bed. Arrogant, wealthy playboy Josh is used to getting what he wants. And what he wants is Kat Morgan. The books are to be read in order:

Infatuation

Revelation

Consummation

The Club Trilogy

When wealthy playboy Jonas Faraday receives an anonymous note from Sarah Cruz, a law student working part-time processing online applications for an exclusive club, he becomes obsessed with hunting her down and giving her the satisfaction she claims has always eluded her. Thus begins a sweeping tale of obsession, passion, desperation, and ultimately, everlasting love and individual redemption. Find out why scores of readers all over the world, in multiple languages, call The Club Trilogy "my favorite trilogy ever" and "the greatest love story I've ever read." As Jonas Faraday says to Sarah Cruz: "There's never been a love like ours and there never will be again… Our love is so pure and true, we're the amazement of the gods."

The Club: Obsession

The Club: Reclamation

The Club: Redemption

The fourth book for Jonas and Sarah is a full-length epilogue with incredible heart-stopping twists and turns and feels. Read The Club: Culmination (A Full-Length Epilogue Novel) after finishing The Club Trilogy or, if you prefer, after reading The Josh and Kat Trilogy.

The Reed Rivers Trilogy

Reed Rivers has met his match in the most unlikely of women—aspiring journalist and spitfire, Georgina Ricci. She's much younger than the women Reed normally pursues, but he can't resist her fiery personality and drop-dead gorgeous looks. But in this game of cat and mouse, who's chasing whom? With each passing day of this wild ride, Reed's not so sure. The books of this trilogy are to be read in order:

Bad Liar

Beautiful Liar

Beloved Liar

The Hate Love Duet

An addicting, enemies-to-lovers romance with humor, heat, angst, and banter. Music artists Savage of Fugitive Summer and Laila Fitzgerald are stuck together on tour. And convinced they can't stand each other. What they don't know is that they're absolutely made for each other, whether they realize it or not. The books of this duet are to be read in order:

Falling Out of Hate with You

Falling Into Love with You

Interconnected Standalones within the same universe as above

Hacker in Love

When world-class hacker Peter "Henn" Hennessey meets Hannah Milliken, he moves heaven and earth, including doing some questionable things, to win his dream girl over. But when catastrophe strikes, will Henn lose Hannah forever, or is there still a chance for him to chase their happily ever after? *Hacker in Love* is a steamy, funny, heart-pounding, **standalone** contemporary romance with a whole lot of feels, laughs, spice, and swoons.

Smitten

When aspiring singer-songwriter, Alessandra, meets Fish, the funny, adorable bass player of 22 Goats, sparks fly between the awkward pair. Fish tells Alessandra he's a "Goat called Fish who's hung like a bull. But not really. I'm actually really average." And Alessandra tells Fish, "There's nothing like a girl's first love." Alessandra thinks she's talking about a song when she makes her comment to Fish—the first song she'd ever heard by 22 Goats, in fact. As she'll later find out, though, her "first love" was actually Fish. The Goat called Fish who, after that night, vowed to do anything to win her heart. SMITTEN is a true standalone romance.

Swoon

When Colin Beretta, the drummer of 22 Goats, is a groomsman at the wedding of his childhood best friend, Logan, he discovers Logan's kid sister, Amy, is all grown up. Colin tries to resist his attraction to Amy, but after a drunken kiss at the wedding reception, that's easier said than done. Swoon is a true standalone romance.

Misadventures Standalones (unrelated standalones not within the above universe):

- ***Misadventures on the Night Shift*** –A hotel night shift clerk encounters her teenage fantasy: rock star Lucas Ford. And combustion ensues.

- ***Misadventures of a College Girl***—A spunky, virginal theater major meets a cocky football player at her first college party . . . and absolutely nothing goes according to plan for either of them.

- ***Misadventures on the Rebound***—A spunky woman on the rebound meets a hot, mysterious stranger in a bar on her way to her five-year high school reunion in Las Vegas and what follows is a misadventure neither of them ever imagined.

Lauren's Dark Comedy/Psych Thriller Standalone

Countdown to Killing Kurtis

A young woman with big dreams and skeletons in her closet decides her porno-king husband must die in exactly a year. This is not a traditional romance, but it will most definitely keep you turning the pages and saying "WTF?" If you're looking for something a bit outside the box, with twists and turns, suspense, and dark humor, this is the book for you: a standalone psychological thriller/dark comedy with romantic elements.

AUTHOR BIOGRAPHY

Once you enter interconnected standalone romances of USA Today and internationally bestselling author Lauren Rowe's beloved and page-turning "Rowe-verse," you'll never want to leave. Find out why readers around the globe have fallen in love with all the characters in this world, including the Faradays, the Morgans and their besties, alpha mogul Reed Rivers and the artists signed to his record label, River Records.

Be sure to explore all the incredible spoiler-free bonus materials, including original music from the books, music videos, magazine covers and interviews, plus exclusive bonus scenes, all featured on Lauren's website at www.laurenrowe-books.com

To find out about Lauren's upcoming releases and giveaways, sign up for Lauren's emails here!

Lauren loves to hear from readers! Send Lauren an email from her website, say hi on Twitter, Instagram, or Facebook.